WISHES AND TEARS

When a naïve encounter at a lively Coronation party leaves sixteen-year-old Janet Slater pregnant there's no question in her scandalised parents' mind of her keeping the baby. Bundled off to a home for unmarried mothers in faraway South London, Janet is about to face the hardest moment of her sheltered life alone. Forced to give her tiny daughter up for adoption, Janet promises her that one day, come what may, she'll find her . . . In the years that follow it seems that, however hard Janet tries, it is a promise that will be impossible to keep. Nonetheless, she builds her life around her secret and Paula, her lost daughter, is never far from her thoughts. And one day, her diligent searching pays off—the road to their longed-for reunion seems clear. But then a shocking new shadow falls across the fragile happiness of both their lives . . .

WISHES AND TEARS

Dee Williams

CHIVERS PRESS
BATH

First published 1999
by
Headline Book Publishing
This Large Print edition published by
Chivers Press
by arrangement with
Headline Book Publishing
2000

ISBN 0 7540 1444 4

British Library Cataloguing in Publication Data available

Printed and bound in Great Britain by
REDWOOD BOOKS, Trowbridge, Wiltshire

This is a completely fictitious story.

I would like to thank Pat Holland of the Blue Anchor Library in Southwark Park for putting me in touch with Stephen Humphrey, whom I also wish to thank for his help and the information he kindly gave me. And John Louder for help with my research.

I would like to share ten per cent of my royalties from this book between Breakthrough and Breast Cancer Care, to help them in a small way with their care and dedication in finding a cure for this dreadful disease.

Donations for Breakthrough and Breast Cancer Care will always be gratefully received.

Breast Cancer Care
Kiln House
210 King's Road
London SW6 4NZ
Telephone: 0171 384 2984 (administration and donations)
Fax: 0171 384 3387
E-mail: bcc@breastcancercare.org.uk
Breast Cancer Care helpline: 0500 245345
(10am–5pm Monday to Friday)

I would like to dedicate this book to the many women who have come through breast cancer. This gives so many others hope.

I would also like to remember the forty women who died yesterday, the forty women who will die today and the forty women who will die tomorrow from breast cancer.

This is to remember a good friend, Ruby Jagger, and her daughter, Jean Bentley.

And the many others over the years, especially my dear daughter, Julie. Every day we love and miss you.

PART ONE
1953

PART ONE

1935

CHAPTER ONE

Janet fell to her knees and, bending her head slightly, squeezed her brown eyes tightly shut. She sighed silently as her father, the Reverend Peter Slater's, loud commanding voice echoed round the village church. What was she going to do? She was only sixteen. Her father was telling his congregation about good and evil but it was going over her head. She prayed, but knew that in his eyes she had sinned. The usual sound of shuffling when the congregation stood to sing brought her back. It was her favourite hymn, but the last thing she felt at the moment was 'bright and beautiful'.

She could feel her mother's presence beside her, smell the sweet scent of her lavender water. She always wore lavender water on a Sunday, but today the heady smell induced a wave of nausea in Janet. She knew her mother was smiling. Irene Slater was always smiling. She was a pillar of strength in this village, attending to everyone's needs from births to funerals. Stowford was a small village in Sussex where everybody knew everybody else's business. Generations of local families had grown up here. All Janet's grandparents were buried in this churchyard.

At the end of the service everyone made their way out of the church and into the warm autumn sunshine. They stood in small groups for the habitual Sunday morning chat. Janet could only nod politely to the ladies. She was frightened to open her mouth in case she was sick, as she had been when she'd got up that morning. She wanted to go home. She had to tell her parents soon. She couldn't keep this secret to herself much longer. She brushed a strand of her dark hair from her face and pushed it under her hat. The cream straw framing her pretty face complemented her pink silk duster coat perfectly.

Mrs Scott, the local WI chairwoman, came up to Janet and her mother. 'Lovely day,' she said.

Mrs Slater nodded. 'Yes, it is. How is Mr Scott these days? We don't see him at church.'

'He's keeping well enough, but he does feel a little embarrassed when he keeps coughing and disturbing people.'

'I understand. And how is Mark?'

'Not very happy. I don't think he likes taking orders.'

Janet wanted to smile. Mark Scott certainly wouldn't like taking orders. He had been a real mummy's boy when they were at school together. Perhaps being conscripted into the army might do him some good. But she felt sorry for his father, who had been injured in the war.

'Will Mark get leave soon?' asked Janet's mother.

'I hope so. We do miss him about the house.' Mrs Scott glanced at Janet. 'You're very quiet today, dear.'

The Reverend's wife smiled. 'I think she's coming down with something; been poorly all week, haven't you, dear?' She smiled gently at her daughter.

'Could be this warm weather. All young girls have funny moments. I expect it will soon pass.' Mrs Scott progressed along the line to shake the Reverend's hand.

Janet flinched. She knew that what was wrong with her wasn't going to soon pass.

Slowly everyone moved on and the Slater family made their way home to the vicarage.

'I thought that was a good service this morning, my dear. Did it come over well?' asked the Reverend as they sat at the dining-room table.

Every Sunday Janet had to listen to the same conversation. If only she had a brother or sister she could talk to, someone to confide in. Even her friends in the village didn't like to come here; they always seemed on edge and had to mind their Ps and Qs.

How would her parents react to her news? She knew her father would be angry. He had always been aloof and unapproachable even though he was a Christian and should, she thought, be forgiving. In many ways Janet and her mother had always been distant too, never confiding and talking together. She had envied other children when their mothers had laughed and played silly games with them, and as a child she was rarely cuddled. She knew they loved her in their own way, but felt perhaps, somehow they couldn't let their barriers down and show their feelings. Irene Slater was seen by all in the village as a kind and well-meaning vicar's wife. Maybe she would be kind and well-meaning to her daughter? After all, till now Janet had been happy enough at home—there was bound to be a storm, but surely in the end they'd stand by her. They couldn't throw her out, could they? She had to tell them soon.

Janet sat wishing the ground would swallow her up as she watched Mrs Price, who helped her mother, bringing in their lunch.

'I'll be off now,' she said, placing the last dish on the table.

'Thank you, Mrs Price,' said the Reverend.

Suddenly Janet could stand it no longer and the smell of the food sent her rushing to the bathroom.

When she had stopped being sick she sat on the floor reflecting on how she had got herself into this mess.

*　　　　*　　　　*

Aunt Rose, Janet's mother's sister, had written and asked her if she would like to go to London to see the Coronation. Princess Elizabeth was going to be crowned Queen of England; it was going to be the start of a new Elizabethan age. After all the austerity of the war years the whole country intended to celebrate. Janet was so excited. She loved London but knew only her aunt there, and she didn't get to visit her very often. Last time Janet had seen Aunt Rose was at Uncle Alf's funeral. Now poor Rose had only Derek at home, Janet's cousin, four years older than she.

June 2 was a day Janet would never forget. She and Aunt Rose had spent the day standing in the Mall, part of the crowd that had shouted and sung as the procession of royal carriages moved past. Everyone was in a happy mood despite the rain, so that even the street cleaners got a cheer.

That evening there were parties all over Britain. The rain had stopped and pianos were brought out into the streets. Even though things were still hard to get, tables groaned under the food and drink. Earlier, barrels of beer had been set upon trestles to allow the beer to settle until everyone was ready to start celebrating in their own way.

Derek and Janet went to a street party round the corner from Aunt Rose's house. There was a piano in the road being played by a young man whose name Janet found out was Sam. She was hypnotized by his good looks. As his fingers ran over the keys she felt dizzy just looking at him. She leant on the piano like she'd see women in films do. If only she smoked she could have looked at him through an atmospheric grey haze. She was pleased she wasn't wearing her ankle socks. Sam was everything a girl could wish for; tall, dark and the most handsome man Janet had ever seen. She thought her heart would leap from her body when he winked at her. She was immediately in love with him. When someone offered her a port and lemon, she almost said she didn't drink but she wanted to look grown up and sophisticated in Sam's eyes, and it did taste rather nice.

As evening slipped into the night she knew she wouldn't leave Sam's side. She was intoxicated with Sam as well as the drink. When Derek came and told her he was going on to another party and did she want to go with him, she shook her head. She was in love and it was just like in the pictures—a tall, dark-haired, good-looking man was sweeping her off her feet. She had even imagined herself married to him, waiting at their front door for him to come home from work every evening . . .

*   *   *

'Janet? Janet, are you all right?' Her mother was knocking on the bathroom door.

'Just coming.' She quickly wiped her mouth and

7

glanced at herself in the mirror. She looked terrible. She had to tell them today.

'Janet, at last,' said her father when she walked into the dining room. 'I'm waiting to say grace, and our lunch is getting cold.'

'I'm sorry.' She sat down and stared at her plate.

After the prayers her mother offered her the tureen of potatoes. Janet shook her head.

'I don't know what's the matter with you lately. You seem to be in another world.'

Janet took a deep breath. 'I'm having a baby.'

The tureen fell to the ground with a loud crash. The roast potatoes scattered and rolled all over the floor.

Her father spluttered and choked.

Her mother's face turned deathly white. 'What did you just say?'

Janet almost wanted to laugh. It had been so easy. Just four words. Four little words that were going to turn all their lives upside down.

Her father was still coughing and choking.

'Janet, I hope this isn't some kind of a joke.'

'No, Mother. It isn't a joke.'

'But how do you know? When did this happen?'

Janet blushed.

'Oh my God. How can you be sure? Have you seen a doctor?'

Janet nodded.

Her mother stood up. 'You haven't been to see Doctor Lake, have you? It will be all over the village in no time if his receptionist gets to hear of this.'

'I went to a doctor in Horsham last week.' That part had been easy, as she worked there.

'And who's the father?' asked her mother.

'Sam.'

'Who's Sam? Is he local?'

'No. He's a young man I met when I went to see the Coronation.'

'But you're only sixteen.'

Her father wiped his face. 'I can't believe this.' He stood up and threw his napkin on to the table. 'I can't believe I am hearing this. Is this . . . ?' He waved his arms with frustration. 'You, my dear girl, are a disgrace.'

Janet felt the tears stinging her eyes.

'Is this person going to do the right thing and marry you?'

Janet shrugged.

'Does he know?' asked her mother.

She shook her head.

'Where does he live?' asked her father.

'I don't know.'

'You don't know? My daughter! You're no better than a street woman. A whore.'

Irene Slater walked to the window. 'Peter, please, your language.' She turned to Janet. 'Young lady, we had better go into the drawing room. We have a lot to discuss.'

Janet swallowed hard and followed her mother, amazed at her calmness.

'Sit down.'

Janet quickly did as her mother bid.

'Now, how did this happen?'

Janet glanced at her father, who was standing in the doorway. 'I was at a party and Sam was playing the piano, and I had a few drinks.'

'Where was Rose while all this was going on?' asked the Reverend.

'She was there.'

9

'But she didn't stop you drinking and behaving like an alley cat.'

'She didn't see me.'

'I expect she was drunk as well,' he snorted.

'Please, Peter.'

'I would have thought your sister would have behaved more responsibly when she had our daughter under her roof.'

Irene Slater gave her husband a withering look, then asked Janet, 'Does Derek know this young man?'

Janet shook her head.

'You asked him?'

'Yes. You see, I liked him and at the time I thought I wanted to see him again.'

Her father began pacing. 'So you knew what you were doing with this ... this person then? What will my parishioners think? What are we going to do? We have been in this village for generations and this is the first time anyone has brought disgrace to our name.'

Janet hung her head in shame.

'We have to talk about this,' said Irene Slater.

'Talk? Is that all you've got to say about this ... this affair?'

'I must have time to think. Janet, how could you? You have let me and your father down. We trusted you. Didn't you stop to consider the consequence of your selfish actions?'

Tears began to fill Janet's eyes. 'I didn't think I could get pregnant.'

'You have been very foolish. Of course you will have to go away,' said her mother. 'You do understand, don't you? We can't have this kind of scandal in the family.'

'What will you tell people?' Suddenly the awful repercussions of the situation began to hit Janet.

'I don't know at the moment. I'll have to think. Perhaps we can tell them you have gone away to look after a relation who has been taken ill.'

'Should send her to a leper colony,' said her father.

That brought forth a flood of tears from Janet. All these weeks of wondering and waiting for something to happen, and now it was all out in the open and her parents weren't behaving as she had hoped they would. Perhaps they were in shock.

'Peter, that wasn't very Christian. Try to be a little understanding.'

'I don't feel very Christian. Is this all the thanks we get for all we've done for you? You have been brought up well and in a Christian family and you go and flout the laws of common decency. I wash my hands of you.' Her father left the room.

Janet silently sobbed. Why were they rejecting her when she needed them most? Had she been so very naïve to hope that at least her mother would stand by her?

'Where will I go?'

'Leave it to me,' said her mother. 'I'll find out, discreetly, of course. Now I'd better clear the lunch away. Janet, are you capable of taking the Sunday school this afternoon?'

She shook her head.

'In that case I'd better do it.'

Janet was hurt at her mother's coolness. She knew what she had done was wrong and knew it wasn't going to be easy for her parents to accept the situation, but she really hadn't thought her mother would be so matter-of-fact.

11

When her mother had left the room Janet sat and looked out of the window. What was going to happen to her? Her thoughts turned to Sam. She knew he wouldn't be concerned about her, and marriage would be out of the question. He had told her of how he wanted to go to America and be in films. When she'd shown interest at that he'd made it clear he wanted to go alone. A baby and a wife wouldn't fit into any of his plans, she realized. She had loved him at the time but as they'd talked after she'd given herself to him, which she now bitterly regretted, it had been clear to her he was only interested in himself and how talented he thought he was. She'd known then he was selfish.

She touched her stomach. What was going to happen to her baby? Well, six months from now she would have all the answers.

*   *   *

Fortunately, for the rest of the day her parents were busy and when they left for evening service, she went to her bedroom.

Before going to bed she wrote in her diary. Today had been another important day, but it hadn't turned out as she had expected. She wanted to be happy; she wanted her parents to share her baby, not the hurt and pain she felt. She knew what she'd done was wrong and now she had to face the consequences. She flicked through the pages of her diary. Most were empty: she only recorded important events and there hadn't been that many in her life.

She lay thinking about all that had been said. Her mind was churning over and over. Sleep wasn't

12

going to come easily tonight. She heard her parents returning, then, a while later, her mother's footfall on the stairs.

'Janet?' she was calling softly as she pushed open the bedroom door.

Janet pulled herself up to a sitting position and switched on the bedside light. She knew her eyes were red from crying.

Her mother came and sat on the bed. 'You must forgive your father, but this has come as a great shock to us both. I'm sure when he's had time to think about it things won't be quite so bad.'

Janet knew her father was strict. Although she loved him they had never been that close. She rubbed the tears away from her cheeks. 'Does that mean I might be able to stay here?'

'No, I don't think that would be very wise.'

'What about my baby?'

Irene Slater winced visibly. 'You will have to have it adopted.'

'But, but—'

'Janet, you are only sixteen.'

'I'll be seventeen by the time it's born,' sniffed Janet.

'So how on earth do you think you could look after . . . it?'

'I hoped you'd be on my side.'

'I am very sorry and angry at what has happened but I am the vicar's wife. I too have a duty to our parishioners and we can't have a scandal on our own doorstep when your father is preaching about sin.'

'But what about me?'

Mrs Slater stood up. 'You have been a very foolish girl, but the damage has been done now so we must make the best of it. This is a small village

13

and people look up to us to set an example.'

'But what about you, Mother? Do you want to send me away?'

She turned from her daughter's gaze and straightened a lace doily on the dressing table. 'It isn't what I want that counts.' She came back to the bed. 'Good night, dear.' She kissed Janet's forehead, then left.

Janet wanted her mother to hold her and tell her she had forgiven her, but it wasn't to be.

After her mother left she sat and stared at the door. What was going to happen to her? She hugged her knees and desperately wished with all her heart that she could turn the clock back. She wanted to win once more her mother's love and trust. Janet had been happy at home even if her father always appeared to be distant. Although her life had been humdrum, she hadn't known anything different, though in the past few months she had longed for excitement. She'd wanted to be loved like the women she had seen at the pictures, and mistakenly thought Sam could give her that. She would have gone to America with him if had asked her. And now she was going to have his baby. She could give it plenty of love, she knew that. It was hers and she didn't want to give her baby away, but at sixteen what option did she have?

CHAPTER TWO

'At last.' Irene Slater looked up from the letter she was reading. 'It's from the home for unmarried mothers,' she said to her daughter.

14

Janet was pleased her father was at church conducting a funeral service.

'The nuns will have a place for you,' continued her mother, smiling.

Janet didn't speak, she was so unhappy. For these past four weeks she had been miserable. Her father hadn't spoken to her and her mother had been very organizing in a detached way. Nobody had enquired as to how she felt, or asked her opinion. She wished she could turn the clock back. When Janet had tried to talk to her mother she'd seemed embarrassed. Janet wanted to share this baby with her, ask her advice, but her mother had made it very clear she didn't want to be involved.

'I'm sorry, Janet, if I seem to be hard but we do have a standard to maintain,' she had said. 'When this is all over you can pick up your life back here again and people will be none the wiser. So the less said about this matter the better.'

Now her mother's voice interrupted her thoughts.

'Janet, did you hear what I said?'

She nodded. Did she want to pick up her life back here again? 'Where is it—this home?' she asked.

'In London.'

Janet felt happier at that. 'Near Aunt Rose?' she asked eagerly.

'No. And I must ask you not to write and tell her what has happened. I'll do that. The home is in South London, a place called Southwark.'

Aunt Rose lived north of the Thames.

'When have I got to go?'

'You said it was due in March, so you will have to go quite soon.'

'Before Christmas?' asked Janet in alarm.

'I'm afraid so.'

'But I want to be here for Christmas.'

'I'm very sorry, dear, but we can't have you waddling about the village. You are beginning to show a little now, and we don't want anyone suspecting.'

Janet felt unclean.

'Have you told anyone at the office?'

Janet worked in an accounts department.

She shook her head.

'That's good. You'll have to hand your notice in very soon—you can tell them you are looking after an aunt—and perhaps when this is all over you can apply to return.'

Janet was angry. Her mother didn't mind her telling lies if it served her purpose. She didn't want to go back to Blakes, she was the only junior in accounts and seemed to spend her life making tea and running errands. The grey-haired ladies and old men only smiled at her and conversed amongst themselves.

'You can go at the end of the month. I'll help you pack. You'll travel by train.'

It was all so matter-of-fact. Her mother hadn't shown any feelings about her or her baby. This was going to be her grandchild.

'Will you come to see me?'

'We will try. But when you get there, there will be plenty of other girls in the same predicament as you and you should all get on very well together.'

So that was it. They were pushing her out of sight till it was all over. Would she be welcomed back like a prodigal daughter afterwards? She very much doubted it.

16

At the end of October Mrs Slater kissed her daughter goodbye as she boarded the bus to the station. Janet's father did not see her off.

On the train she sat looking out of the window. The last time she had gone to London was such a happy occasion, now this journey was the result of that moment in which she had thrown all her principles away. Why had she done it? She gave a slight smile. She knew why, it was because she wanted to feel grown up. When they went to the park and Sam kissed her long and hard she felt she was in heaven. He had been her Mr Wonderful. When he began to unbutton her blouse she became a little apprehensive. Sam told her not to worry. As he struggled to get her knickers off she had feebly said no.

'Ain't you ever done it before?'

She remembered shaking her head and telling him she was worried about having a baby and he had just laughed.

'It's me lucky night then, ain't it?' he'd whispered as he kissed and caressed her breasts. 'You can trust me, darling. All the modern girls do it. 'Sides, you can't get up the duff the first time.'

How wrong he had been. She hadn't really enjoyed him pushing inside her; it had hurt and it wasn't as if it had been as thrilling as she had been led to believe in some of the magazines she'd secretly read. Now she felt he had used her.

Janet got off the bus and looked at the paper to confirm she was at the right address. The red-brick building with tiny windows looked old and run-down, almost prison-like. The house was set back from the road behind tall trees. Her mother had told her it was run by nuns. Janet sighed. So that meant more sermons and prayers. She would have liked to have been able to run far away, but she didn't have much money and where would she go? Aunt Rose wouldn't want her, not if that meant a confrontation with Janet's father. They had never seen eye to eye, as Rose wasn't religious. Janet picked up her suitcase, walked along the gravel path and up the six stone steps, then rang the bell.

'Miss Slater,' repeated the sister who opened the door and asked who she was. 'Yes, we are expecting you. Follow me.' She glided, in the way that nuns seemed to have, along the dark passage. In contrast Janet's shoes were echoing on the tiled floor.

They stopped at the second brown-painted door.

'I'm Sister Verity and this is my office, and if at any time you wish to talk to me you must feel free to do so. Now take off your hat and coat and take a seat. We have to fill in a few forms. Just routine, you understand.'

Janet did as she was told. She was asked all the usual questions: name, date of birth, her father's occupation.

Sister Verity, a tall thin-faced woman, with pointed features and piercing brown eyes, looked up quickly when Janet told her. 'This must have come as a great shock to your parents?'

Janet only bowed her head.

Sister Verity continued writing. 'Now I must have the child's father's full name.'

18

'Why?'

'So that it can be on the birth certificate.'

Janet sat and stared at her blankly. How could she say she didn't know it? It made her sound as if she was . . . 'Mark Samuel,' she said quickly.

'Does he know?'

Janet shook her head.

'I see.' When the sister had finished writing she sat back and closed the file. 'The evening meal will be in a short while, then after prayers you will be examined by our doctor. I will get Miss Long to show you to the room you will be sharing with her. She is in the day room at the moment.'

Janet noted the emphasis was on the Miss.

They moved out of the office and back along the passage. Sister Verity pushed open a door to reveal about ten girls in various stages of pregnancy, sitting in armchairs. Many were knitting, but some were talking or reading.

'Miss Long, will you take care of Miss Slater? She will be sharing your room.'

A thin short girl, who didn't look as if she had a baby hiding under her voluminous smock, stood up. She appeared to be about the same age as Janet, and had short dark hair and dancing brown eyes. She came over and a broad smile lit up her face. 'Sure. Come on, follow me.'

The sister moved away as they left the room and climbed the stairs.

'We're in here.' She pushed open the door. 'It ain't bad, a bloody sight better than the one I had at home.'

Janet stood in the doorway of the sparsely furnished room. The narrow window was open and the thin beige-coloured curtains moved gently.

There were just two single beds, a dressing table, and a cupboard built in the fire recess; the fireplace had been boarded up.

'It's a bit cold in here.' Miss Long hugged herself and moved to pull the sash window down. 'The nuns always open the windows, reckon we need the fresh air. I like my air warm and full of smoke. Thank goodness we only sleep here so it ain't that bad. What's your name?'

'Janet.'

'Mine's Freda. When's it due?'

'March.'

'Blimey, your family got rid of you quick enough, didn't they?'

Janet didn't answer, but instead asked, 'When's your baby due?'

'January. I ain't that big.' Freda patted her stomach affectionately. 'Can't say I wanner have him adopted, though, but I ain't got a lot of choice. Me stepdad threw me out.'

Janet was warming to this girl. 'How do you know it's a boy?'

Freda laughed. 'Did the test with a wedding ring—well, it was a brass one really. You hold it over your belly and if it goes this way it's a boy.' She moved her hands round clockwise. 'And if it goes the other way it's a girl. Well, I think that's the right way.'

Janet liked Freda. She seemed honest and happy.

'We'll have to do you. What d'you want?'

'It doesn't really matter, does it? We can't keep them.'

'No, that's true. Right, tea's in about half an hour so let me give you a hand with your

20

unpacking.' Despite all the apprehension she had had about coming here, Janet felt that she had found a friend.

'This is nice,' said Freda as she hung Janet's skirt on a hanger. 'Looks like you've got some nice things.'

'They won't fit me for very long.'

'Don't worry about that. The sisters will soon have you knitting and sewing so you can make yourself a new skirt. Can you knit?'

Janet nodded. 'But I'm not very good at sewing.' She put her nightdress under the pillow and hung her dressing gown on the hook behind the door. 'What's it like here?'

'It ain't bad, I suppose—bit like a prison really, not that I've been inside, but we can't do what we like and they're forever telling us we should be grateful that they're looking after us after what we done. And we do have a lot of prayers, mostly about him up there forgiving us for what we did.' She raised her eyes to the ceiling. 'Fallen women, that's what we are.' She laughed.

'Who was here?' asked Janet as she sat on the bed to test the springs.

'Maisie. Nice kid. Think she had a boy. We don't come back after we leave the hospital and so if you ain't got your mate's address you can't keep in touch.'

The dinner gong reverberated round the room.

'Come on, follow me.' Freda was out of the door.

The meal of beans on toast wasn't very exciting but it was adequate.

After tea and prayers Janet was shown into the doctor's room.

The doctor was a short, round, balding man with

21

bright blue eyes. 'Right, take your knickers off and get up on the bed.' He had cold stubby fingers that prodded and probed at Janet's very private parts. She felt humiliated and dirty. The doctor she had seen at Horsham had been kinder and apologized if he thought he was hurting her, but Dr Winter appeared to take a fiendish delight in making her jump.

'Get dressed, young lady. Everything seems to be in order,' he said, moving towards the sink and washing his hands. 'I will examine you every week, take your blood pressure and generally keep my eye on you. If at any time you feel unwell or have a show of blood you must report it at once.' He dried his hands and sat at his desk and began writing. 'That's all, you can go now.'

Janet stood outside the door for a few moments. If only Sam knew what he was putting her through would he have stood by her? She didn't think he would. Besides, how many other little Sams were there? One evening, just a few minutes, that's all it took and she hadn't even enjoyed it that much. Now this was the result. She moved towards the day room. She didn't think he would be concerned at her plight, and after all she could have made it clearer she meant it when she said no.

'So you've met our Dr Winter then,' said Freda later that evening as they were getting undressed ready for bed. 'He's got bloody cold hands, ain't he? I'm sure he runs 'em under the cold tap just to make us squirm. Winter be name and Winter be nature.' Freda laughed.

Janet took her diary from her handbag and began writing.

'What you doing?'

'Just writing in my diary.'

'Do you do it every day?'

'No, only when I've got something important to write about.'

'Oh, I see.'

When they were in bed Freda told Janet lights out was at nine thirty, and woe betide any one who was caught with their light on after that.

'It's the bloody great gap under the door that gives the game away,' said Freda. 'And those nuns creep about like the Lord Jesus Christ himself. Sometimes they frighten the life out of you when they speak and you don't know they're there.'

'What do they do to you if you get caught?' asked Janet anxiously.

'Well, you spend most of the day on your knees praying and after that it's in the kitchen cleaning the pots and pans.'

Janet grinned. It was worse than school. She settled down under the blankets and felt strange knowing, after all her apprehension since the day her mother had received the letter, that she could be happy here.

They talked for quite a while in low whispers.

Janet heard how Freda had met Mick and had fallen in love with him. It was when she found she was having his baby that he told her he was married.

'So then me stepdad threw me out.'

'But what about your mother?'

'Me mum? She couldn't wait to get rid of me. She didn't want another mouth to feed. 'Sides, she thought I was a bad influence on the others.'

'You've got brothers and sisters?'

'I should say so. Two brothers and three sisters

23

that were me dad's. He died a long while ago. Then I've got another three sisters—they're me stepdad's. I'm the oldest.'

'That must be quite a houseful?'

'You could say that. In some ways I'm glad I've got this little 'en to love, even if it is only for a few weeks.'

Janet was astounded. She sat up. 'You mean they let us keep them for a few weeks?'

'Sometimes, but only while we're in the hospital. It depends if they've got a family waiting or not to adopt, and they don't like putting 'em on a bottle straight away.'

Janet was grateful she was sharing with Freda. Freda had picked up a lot during her weeks at the home, and Janet knew she had so much to learn.

They talked long into the night. Janet told her all about Sam and her parents.

'Christ, I bet that upset 'em.'

'It did. My father has been really awful about it.'

'Yer, but he must have done it at some time to have got you.'

'But they were married.'

' 'Ere, perhaps you're the result of an immaculate conception.'

Janet put her hand over her mouth and giggled quietly. She suddenly realized she hadn't laughed for a very long time.

Freda told her there were twelve expectant mothers in the home and every day after breakfast and prayers they all had chores to do. Then it was breathing and exercises. The afternoon was for resting and relaxing, then after tea they could stay in the day room for a few hours until bedtime.

When they finally said their good nights, Janet

24

turned over, and for the first time in months went to sleep with a smile on her face.

CHAPTER THREE

For the first few days Janet watched and waited to be told what to do. At the beginning she just had to help out, but towards the end of the week Doreen, another mother-to-be, started labour and was whisked off to the hospital. Doreen's job was to vacuum and dust the day room, so now that became Janet's. Freda was proving to be a good friend and helped her whenever she got behind.

On Sunday morning after breakfast they were to go to church. This was the first time Janet had been outside. The nuns didn't approve of the girls going out alone. Were they afraid they would run away? Where would they go? Every one of the girls said it was her parents that sent her there—out of sight, out of mind.

Janet slipped on her coat and looked out of the window. The wind was blowing the leaves off the trees, swirling them up then tossing them back down. She shivered. Her and Freda's room was at the front; she could hear the traffic but couldn't see beyond the high barrier of trees. At the back of the house was a small garden with a patchy lawn and a few bare straggly shrubs. It had a path that led to the washing line. They each had a set day to do their washing. Houses overlooked the back garden, and the girls only went out there when they had to, as some of the children from the houses sat on the wall and called them names. That upset Janet but

25

Freda told her they didn't know what they were shouting out, it was only what their parents had told them to say.

Janet put her scarf round her neck, pulled her hat on and, gathering up her gloves, hurried down the stairs. She didn't want to be late.

'Miss Slater, don't run. If you fall and injure that child some poor parents will be deprived,' Sister Verity called out.

Janet stood with her mouth open. There wasn't any worry about her falling, just as long as her baby was all right for someone else.

Freda grabbed Janet's arm and almost frogmarched her out of the door. 'Just don't say a word,' she hissed out of the corner of her mouth.

They were at the back of the line with Sister Verity behind them as they were marched in pairs to the church. Janet felt so humiliated as people stood and stared, then whispered amongst themselves. In the church Sister James, a short, round nun with pale blue eyes and a flushed face, ushered them into the two back pews.

As soon as the service was over and the large door opened, the girls were very quickly moved out and sent scurrying along the road. Nobody was allowed to speak to them.

'This happens every Sunday,' said Freda. 'Reckon we've got a sign on our heads saying "Unclean". Treated like lepers, we are. Sometimes I feel like shouting out that what we've got ain't catching unless you're up to no good.' She laughed. 'Come on, cheer up. You'll get used to it.'

Janet smiled, though she didn't think she would get used to it, but then her time at the home wasn't going to last for ever.

26

The weeks went by very quickly and Janet had had only two letters from her mother. They didn't tell her much, just news about the people in the village, those that had died or given birth, or were getting married.

Janet was shown how to make booties and mittens. She enjoyed this, but couldn't believe babies could be so small as to fit into the tiny garments. She saw Dr Winter every week and her pregnancy appeared to be progressing normally. She went to the exercise sessions and had lessons on how to breathe when she was in labour.

As one girl left so a new one arrived. As soon as Janet got to know someone, it seemed she was off. She was dreading the time when Freda would be going.

It was approaching Christmas, and they were busy making paper-chains when Janet told Freda her fears.

'You are daft. You'll be all right. 'Sides, mine ain't due till the end of January and yours is the beginning of March so it'll only be for a couple of weeks. Look, I'm really beginning to show now.' Freda stood up and, resting her hands in the middle of her back, stuck her stomach out, determined to look like the rest of them.

Janet laughed. 'Will you go home after?'

'Yer. I ain't got a lot of choice. Will you?'

Janet nodded.

'I'm gonner miss you.'

'Not as much as I'll miss you. You're the closest friend I've ever had. You must give me your

27

address.'

'Course, and you must give me yours.'

'Mine's easy to remember: The Old Vicarage, Stowford, Near Horsham.'

'Sounds a bit like this place.'

'In some ways it is. I can't always do what I want there either.'

Janet felt her baby move; she loved this feeling of life within her. She sat back and placed her hands on her stomach. 'Next year will be our babies' first Christmas. I wonder what sort of people she'll have for parents. I hope they look after her and love her.'

When the girls had done the ring test on Janet, they'd told her she was going to have a girl.

'Put a sock in it, Jan. You'll have me in tears in a minute.'

Janet knew her friend wasn't joking.

*   *   *

After church on Christmas morning presents were exchanged. A week ago the nuns had taken them out in pairs. Janet didn't go with Freda as she wanted her present of a white petticoat and matching knickers to be a surprise.

Freda's face was a picture when she opened the parcel. 'These are smashing. I can't wait till January when I'll be able to wear 'em.' She held the petticoat against her. 'I hope you like what I've got you.'

Janet held the fluffy pink rabbit to her cheek. 'This is lovely. I've only got an old teddy at home.'

'I know. I remember you saying you'd like something to cuddle.'

'Thank you.'

'I knew I couldn't get you a bloke to cuddle so I thought that might be the next best thing.'

Janet laughed. 'A man is the last thing I need in my life at the moment.'

'Yer, but you wait till this is all over. I bet you start looking again.'

'I'm not so sure, if sex is all they want.'

'They ain't all like that—at least I don't think so.'

'And thank you for the diary.'

'I guessed you'd be needing a new one. You've got a lot to put in it.'

Janet kissed Freda's cheek. 'I'll cherish this for ever,' she said, clutching her rabbit.

The nuns had kept back till today the parcels that had arrived for the girls.

Janet opened her present from her parents. There were three Christmas cards, one from her mother and father in her mother's handwriting, one from the WI ladies—Mrs Scott had signed it and said what a good girl she was giving up her Christmas to look after her aunt—and a card from the children at Sunday school, which brought a lump to her throat. It was wrong to tell them lies. She looked at the scarf and matching gloves they'd sent. It would have been so much nicer if they had come and given her their present. She quickly put them to one side.

'What did your mum send you?' she asked Freda.

'This.' Freda held up a book on baby care. 'Bloody stupid present to give me. She knows I ain't gonner keep him.'

After dinner they sat and listened to the Queen's speech, her first as Queen and very moving. Janet's thoughts went back to the Coronation. That had been a good day. Somehow, even the encounter with Sam she didn't mind now; it had brought her here and she'd found a friend.

Games and carols followed tea, then all too soon Christmas was over.

That night as they were getting ready for bed Freda said, 'It might sound daft but d'you know, this is one of the best Christmases I've ever had.'

Janet looked at her in surprise as she got into bed.

'There wasn't any fights or rows. Just peaceful with a lot of nice people—apart from the nuns, that is.'

'I suppose they aren't so bad. Just got funny ways of thinking they're helping us wicked girls.'

They laughed together.

'D'you know,' said Janet, easing herself up on her elbow. 'It's one of the best Christmases I've had as well.'

'It seems strange, don't it, that next year we'll be in different places. I dunno where I'll finish up; can't see me staying at home for long.'

'I can't see me staying at home after this.'

'They won't chuck you out, will they?'

'No, my father will act as if nothing has happened.'

'But it has.'

'Yes, it has. That's why I think I should move on.'

'But you'll only just be seventeen when you get home.'

'I know.'

'You'll be underage and if you left, they could have the police on you and drag you back.'

30

'Perhaps I'll have to leave it for a few years.'

'Yer, or else get married.'

'Who will have me?'

'You'll find someone.'

'That might be the only answer.' Janet turned over. 'Good night.'

'Good night. And thank you for me present.'

For a long while Janet fondled her rabbit's ears and thought about home and her parents. How different were things going to be? Would she be able to settle down to her humdrum way of life again? She turned over and drifted into a deep sleep.

*   *   *

'Jan! Jan, are you awake?'

She sat up. She was disorientated.

'Jan! Are you awake?' Freda's voice was full of panic.

'Yes, I am now,' she yawned. 'What's wrong?'

'I feel ever so peculiar.'

'What d'you mean, peculiar?'

'I don't know, sick like.' With that she was sick all over the bedspread.

Janet jumped out of bed and put the light on. 'What have you been eating?'

'Only the same as you.' She lay back and groaned.

'You don't look that good. Shall I get someone?'

Freda rolled her eyes, and Janet could see she was drawing up her knees.

'Are you in pain?'

She nodded.

'You haven't started, have you?'

'I don't know.'

'Oh my God.' Janet grabbed her dressing gown from off the bed. 'I'm just going to get—'

The door flew open. 'Just what is the light doing on at this time of night?' Sister Verity filled the doorway like some great black whale.

'It's Freda, Sister. I think she's started.'

'Started? She can't have. She isn't due till the end of January. Look at the state of that bedspread. I'll have complaints from the laundry about this.' In one swift movement it was off the bed and being rolled up. 'It's probably something you've eaten. I did notice that you were devouring those chocolates at an alarming rate earlier this evening.' She started to take Freda's pulse. 'I'll try to get hold of Dr Winter. But if this is a false alarm he will be very cross to be dragged away from his home on Christmas night.'

Janet looked at Freda. She was worried. Beads of perspiration stood out on her friend's pale face and she hadn't come back with any of her bright remarks.

Sister Verity swept out of the room with the offending bedspread under her arm.

'Jan, I'm ever so frightened.'

Janet held her hand. She brushed Freda's damp hair from her forehead. 'You'll be all right.' But Janet too was frightened. Freda had almost another five weeks to go and everybody had said she would probably go over her time as she was so small.

Freda gave out a cry, her brown eyes seemed to sink back into their sockets. She thrashed about in the bed, pulling at the bedclothes. Janet was petrified. She went to look out of the door, hoping

32

one of the nuns was nearby.

'Jan, Jan, don't leave me!' cried Freda, struggling to sit up.

Janet hurried to her friend's side and gently pushed her back down. 'I won't.' She felt so helpless. What could she do? 'Let me go and find Sister.'

'No, no, don't leave me.' She grabbed Janet's hand.

'Try to take deep breaths.'

Freda made a gallant effort but wasn't succeeding.

Janet was living every moment of her friend's pain with her. The girls in the next room heard the noise and came in.

'What's going on?' asked Betty, her shiny face peering round the door.

'I think she's started,' said Janet.

'What? But she ain't due yet,' said Yvonne. 'Have you told Sister?'

'Yes, she's gone to try to get hold of Dr Winter.'

'If you ask me she should get her into hospital,' said Betty. 'She don't look that good to me.'

'Perhaps you could go downstairs and try to find her and tell her Freda's getting worse.' Janet wanted to get rid of Betty. The last thing Freda needed to hear was a lot of horrific tales that she was in a habit of telling.

Betty reluctantly left the room.

It wasn't long before Sister James came in with Betty close on her heels.

'Now back to bed, you girls.' She ushered Betty and Yvonne out of the room. 'And keep your voices down. We don't want everyone to be woken.'

Janet guessed that everyone was awake already, and straining their ears to try to find out what was happening.

Sister James took hold of Freda's hand. 'My, we do feel sorry for ourselves, don't we? You know women have to suffer in labour. It's God's way of punishing them for doing naughty things.'

Janet stared at her. She felt like shouting, 'What a load of twaddle. And what about men? They don't get punished. Besides, how would mankind continue if women didn't have children?' But she decided that this wasn't the time or the place to start that kind of discussion.

'Don't you think Freda should be in hospital, Sister?' Janet tried to keep her voice even.

'We shall see. She isn't the first to have an eight-month pregnancy, you know.'

'But she's so small. Her baby can't be that big.'

Sister James turned and smiled at Janet. 'Time will tell, my dear. Time will tell. This could just be a false alarm.'

Janet looked at Freda. Her heart went out to her. Freda's eyes were darting about, full of fear, and her face was contorted with pain. When she moved Janet saw blood beginning to quickly spread over the sheets. She knew then that this wasn't going to be a false alarm.

Sister Verity returned to the bedroom and, despite Janet's protests, ordered her to go and sleep in Miss Taylor's room. Sue Taylor was very quiet and most of the time had her nose stuck in a book. She had been on her own since her roommate, Barbara, had left.

Janet knew everyone was awake and listening at their doors trying to find out what was happening. When Janet walked into the bedroom Sue sat up and began asking loads of questions.

When finally Janet had finished telling her all she knew, she tried to sleep. But the noise of Freda crying out, and loud urgent voices coming from the passage outside the bedroom told her that something was very wrong.

* * *

The following morning, when the girls were seated for breakfast and Sister Verity had said grace, she went on to say, 'I expect you are wondering what happened to Miss Long last night. Well, she was taken to the hospital and was delivered of a boy.'

Smiles and chatter quickly broke out. But they immediately fell silent when Sister added, 'Unfortunately, the child was born dead.'

Janet took in her breath and asked, 'What about Freda—Miss Long—is she all right?'

'She is very poorly, that's all we know.'

'Can I go and see her?'

The expression on Sister Verity's face had to be seen to be believed. First she went white, then as the colour returned her nostrils flared and she held on to her breath. Janet knew then how Oliver Twist must have felt when he asked for more.

'I'm afraid that is impossible. Once you girls are handed over to the hospital you are out of our hands. Of course we will pray for her at prayer time.'

Janet wanted to scream at her. What was it about these people? They weren't pieces of meat to be handed over. There was her father preaching about the Lord's good works, and these women, who thought they were being righteous by looking after fallen girls, but deep down did any of them

35

have an ounce of compassion? She didn't think so.

Sue gently put her hand on Janet's tight fist. 'She'll be all right,' she whispered. 'She might be little, but she's a fighter. Don't worry, she'll write as soon as she can.'

Janet smiled weakly at Sue and murmured her thanks. Tears filled her eyes. She was going to miss Freda so much. She looked at Sister Verity, who was carrying on as if nothing had happened. What if Freda died? Janet might never know. She would write to her at the hospital. She couldn't wait till prayers; she closed her eyes and silently said her own. 'Please, God, look after her.' She so desperately wanted Him to hear her lone voice.

CHAPTER FOUR

Janet sat in the day room and stared out at the garden. She was so down. It was two weeks since Freda had left. Janet had written to her in the hospital but she hadn't replied. Had she received the letter? Was she all right? Janet didn't have Freda's home address. Would she ever see her again? Was she still alive? All those weeks wasted when they thought they had plenty of time to exchange addresses. She wished with all her heart that she could have gone to see her friend in hospital, but knew only husbands were allowed to visit in the maternity ward. Poor Freda, no husband and now no baby. In many ways that might be for the best; at least she hadn't got the worry of who would be looking after him.

Janet thought about the laughs they'd had

together, the way Freda had taught her to experiment with her make-up and hair. She felt a very different person now, more confident somehow. In the short time they had been together Janet could not believe how strangely happy she'd been, and now it was all over.

'Jan? Jan?' Someone was softly calling her name. She looked round. 'Sue.'

'Sorry, did I wake you?'

'No. What is it?'

'Sister Verity wants to see you.'

'What about?'

'Don't know.'

'Perhaps it's about Freda.' Janet quickly stood up and hurried as fast as her bulk would allow to Sister Verity's office. She gently knocked on the door.

'Come in. There you are, Miss Slater. I want you to put all of Miss Long's things into this bag.' She held out a brown paper bag. 'You can throw out anything like old papers or magazines.'

Janet took the bag. 'Is she all right?'

'I don't know.'

'Could you phone and ask?'

'They are much too busy to be worried about Miss Long. Besides, I expect her family have been informed so she will be going home. By the way, you can stay with Miss Taylor.'

'Thank you.' Janet left the room. She didn't mind sharing with Sue.

Janet sat in the bedroom she had shared with Freda. Both the beds had been stripped down to the mattresses waiting for the new arrivals. It was as though she and Freda had never existed. Tears slowly began to slide down Janet's cheeks and she

37

brushed them away with the flat of her hand.

She began to take Freda's things from the wardrobe; she didn't have much. They must have put her coat on her when they took her to the hospital. Janet looked at the set of underwear she had bought her for Christmas. On an impulse she searched for a piece of paper and wrote her name and address on it, adding, 'Don't forget me', then folded it in with Freda's things. When she'd finished she took the bag to Sister's office.

Every day Janet hoped she would receive a letter from Freda but it never came. On 19 February she eagerly waited for a birthday card from her, but again she was disappointed. The card she had from her parents was flowery and the words affectionate, as all her birthday cards had been. The accompanying letter said they had bought her a dress, which they were keeping as it wasn't worth sending. As usual her mother had done the writing. As she thought about her parents Janet realized how little she knew of them. Although she knew when their birthdays were, she didn't know how old they were; those questions had always been taboo. How strange and sad their lives were.

Janet was sleeping at the back of the house now. Sue had gone and the other girls had been told she'd had a baby girl. Janet now shared with Milly, a nice enough girl, who giggled nervously a lot.

She looked out of the window. If only she could keep her baby, they wouldn't have any secrets. Spring was in the air. The sun was warm in a bright blue sky. This was a nice time of the year to be born. The straggly shrubs were starting to look pretty with bright green leaves beginning to unfold. 'Bit like you,' she said to her stomach. She talked a

38

lot to her unborn baby. She knew she shouldn't think of the baby as *hers,* or form a bond with her, but it was too late. She couldn't help herself.

*   *   *

At the beginning of March Janet's back had been aching all day and she felt tired. Not like yesterday when she'd seemed to be full of energy.

'Reckon you'll be having it soon,' said Milly.

'I hope so. I feel as if I've been expecting for years. I've been here longer than anyone else. I feel like part of the furniture, I've seen so many come and go.'

As she moved a sharp pain made her catch her breath. Was this it? Had she started? Half of her was pleased and the other half petrified.

She sat on her bed and looked at her watch. No point in telling anyone at the moment, not till she was sure. Milly, looking every bit as apprehensive, sat with her, holding her hand.

When the contractions were coming regularly every five minutes she asked Milly if she'd tell Sister Verity.

'Go into the doctor's room and get on the bed. He will be with you shortly.' Sister Verity swept out of the room leaving Milly to accompany Janet down the corridor.

Once there, Janet struggled to get on the bed. 'Why do they have to be so high?' she said out loud.

Dr Winter came in and did his usual poking about. 'Yes, I think we can safely say it's on its way. I'll get my car. Gather your things together and meet me out front.'

39

Milly had been hovering in the corridor. 'Well?' she asked.

'I'm on my way at last,' said Janet with a grin.

'I'll pop up and get your case.'

'Thanks.'

All the girls, as their dates approached, gradually packed everything they possessed ready for their next and last move.

Returning, Milly put Janet's case on the floor and hugged her. 'Good luck.'

'Thanks, and to you too.' Janet smiled and walked away from the place that had been her home for over four months. Up until Christmas she been very happy but since Freda had left it hadn't been the same. She had to hold on to the car's door till another wave of pain passed.

*　　　*　　　*

In the hospital she was put to bed, shaved and given an enema. A nurse took her pulse, blood pressure and temperature and listened to her baby's heartbeat.

'Well, everything seems to be under control, now all we have to do is wait.' She went out of the room, leaving Janet alone.

For what seemed like hours Janet lay moaning in pain. She tossed and turned and held on to the back of the bed. She was frightened, she wanted someone with her. What if something went wrong? She rang the bell behind her bed.

A nurse opened the door and looked in. 'Everything all right in here?'

'Could I have something to ease the pain?' she gasped.

'Not yet. Wait till you're in the delivery room,' came the answer.

When the door closed once again Janet cried. She wanted her mother, Freda, anyone to hold her hand, mop her brow and give her comforting words. She screwed up her face with another contraction, and hated Sam with all her might.

A doctor came and examined her. 'Nurse, you can take Miss Slater along to the delivery room now.'

Her bed was pushed out of the room, down the long corridor and into a cold clinical room. Nurses wearing face masks stood over her. Her legs were put into stirrups and cold metal instruments shoved inside her. She felt faint.

'Gas and air,' she heard someone say and a rubber mask was placed over her face.

Grabbing the mask she took great frantic breaths and held on to it with all the strength she could muster, terrified someone was going to take it away from her, grateful at last for something to cling on to. She drifted into a pain-free world for what seemed to be only a second or two.

The mask was being snatched from her. She fought to hang on to it.

'Come on now, Miss Slater. You have got to start pushing and you can't do it if you are half dopey.'

She closed her eyes, she didn't want to push, she wanted to sleep. Then suddenly the great urge to push was on her.

'That's right. Push,' said a disembodied voice.

Janet was too frightened to open her eyes.

'And again.'

She did as she was told. Sweat was pouring from her forehead and into her eyes. Her hair was wet and sticking to her face; she tried to brush it away. She grabbed the sheet, screwing in up into a ball and, between pushing, felt a pain in her hand where her fingernails were digging in her palm.

'Come now, push.'

Then, as if with an urgent rush to be born, the baby she had been carrying around for nine months was suddenly taking its first breath. She had given birth—given life. She eased herself up when she heard the first snuffly cries, then lay back exhausted.

'It's a girl.'

'Can I see her?'

'After she's been cleaned up.'

Janet opened her eyes just in time to see a nurse hurry from the room holding her baby.

*   *   *

Janet was stitched, cleaned up and her bed pushed back into a ward with other women. She closed her eyes; she didn't want to talk.

'All right, girl?' said a voice close by.

'Yes, thanks.' She turned over. Why didn't they let her see her baby? Was she all right? Was she deformed?

'You don't have to be unsociable, you know.'

'Leave her be,' said another voice. 'Let her get some sleep. Having a baby's bloody hard work.'

'I know that, don't I? I've had enough of 'em.'

'Yer, but it's like shelling peas for the likes of you. She only looks a kid.'

'I was only trying to be friendly.'

All these women were talking about her as if she wasn't there. Janet was worried. She wanted to see her baby and to shut these voices out.

The banging of the tea trolley pushing the ward's door open seemed to be the women's highlight of the afternoon and they chatted excitedly and very loud.

'Come along now, Miss Slater, it's time for tea.' The nurse said it loud and clear and the ward went silent.

Janet turned to face her. She was standing over her with a cup of tea in her hand. Slowly she sat up, aware that all the other women were looking at her.

'When can I see my baby?' she asked.

'Sorry, I can't help you with that. Do you want some bread and jam?'

Janet shook her head.

'Please yourself. You don't get anything else to eat tonight, next meal is breakfast.' She returned to the trolley and pushed it along to the next bed.

The chatter began again and Janet looked around. She was at the end of the ward. The woman who had spoken to her at first was next to her. She was in her thirties. She quickly looked the other way when Janet smiled at her.

After tea, when the cups and plates had been collected, the babies were brought in to be fed. Janet sat up and waited. A nurse came and laid a baby in her arms. Janet looked down at her. This was hers. She wanted to cry with joy at this lovely bundle that smelt of soap and talcum powder. The baby's eyes were closed and she had a screwed up face, a mop of black hair and her mouth was moving. Janet counted her fingers and marvelled at the perfect nails. She had never seen a new-born baby before. She was so small. Janet gently put her baby's hand to her mouth and kissed it. She was trying to unravel the blanket to look at her feet when a nurse came up.

'Now come along. Baby wants her tea.'

Janet felt awkward and embarrassed; she didn't really know what to do. She quickly glanced at the other mothers who were busy feeding their babies and tried to copy them. She put her baby's mouth to her breast, but she fumbled and snuffled and wouldn't suck. Janet looked around frightened; she wanted help.

A nurse came up and forced her baby's head on to her nipple. 'You have to be firm. Have you given her a name?'

'Paula.'

'That's nice.'

Through the pain Janet felt a wonderful feeling going through her when Paula begun sucking, and it was then that she knew deep in her heart she wasn't going to part with her. She was hers and she belonged to her and her alone.

'Nobody is going to have you, you're mine,' she whispered, putting her lips to her baby's forehead. 'That is a promise I am making to you, my Paula.'

*   *   *

When the nurse came Janet told her she didn't want her baby to be taken away again, she wanted to hold her and love her, but she was told it was visiting time and rules were rules. She slunk down in the bed, knowing she wouldn't be having visitors.

Once she peered over the sheet, she found she was the only one with an empty chair at her bedside. She noticed some of the husbands were looking in her direction. Their wives had smug looks on their faces. They must be telling them about this silly girl who had got herself in trouble.

Half an hour later the nurse stood in the doorway and frantically rang the handbell. Kisses were hurriedly exchanged, and most men moved slowly away down the ward, looking behind them, waving and blowing kisses.

Janet wrote in her diary, 'Today I gave birth to a daughter. She is the most beautiful baby in the whole world, her name is Paula.' The date was 2 March 1954, the one day Janet would never forget.

She desperately wanted the night to come. Perhaps Paula would want another feed, then she would be able to hold her again. She smiled and turned over. She closed her eyes and drifted into a land of her own making. A land where the sun shone and she and Paula laughed and played together. Would that time ever come? Janet knew she was going to make it happen one day.

CHAPTER FIVE

The following morning, when Janet was given her baby to feed, she managed to unravel the blanket. She wanted to count her toes; she hadn't seen Paula's feet yet! Janet quickly took a breath when she saw how tiny they were. On the top of her left foot was a brown birthmark. Janet carefully studied it: it was in the shape of a heart.

'Come along now, give baby her breakfast,' said a nurse who was passing.

'Nurse?'

She came over to the bedside. 'Yes, what is it?'

'This mark on Paula's foot, will it ever go away?'

'No. It will probably fade in time, but it shouldn't cause her any problems. Now come on, let her feed.'

Janet smiled down at her baby's face. 'I will be able to find you now,' she whispered.

As the week went on Janet's breasts felt hard and uncomfortable and she found she was prone to tears. At visiting time she desperately wanted someone to fill the empty chair next to her bed. She had written to her mother and told her about Paula, but she hadn't received a letter back. She wanted to show off her lovely new baby. She wanted to be told she didn't have to give her away.

'It's only natural for you to feel down,' said the nurse when Janet was shedding a few tears. 'It's all part of having a baby.'

By the end of the week Janet felt more comfortable. Some of the other mothers had left and when new ones arrived in the ward, flowers and cards decorated their bedside cabinets. Janet never had any cards or flowers. She couldn't bear to watch when it was time for a mother to go home. You could always tell when it was their first born. They walked proudly down the ward with their new baby in their arms and usually the brim of a small bonnet just peeped above a fine cobweb shawl that possibly a grandmother had lovingly made.

Janet buried her head in her pillow. Her baby would never know her real mother, let alone her real grandmother.

One or two of the older women wouldn't talk to her, but the younger ones didn't mind. It annoyed Janet when the nurses called her Miss Slater in a very loud voice.

'Don't worry about it, love,' said the girl who had moved into the bed next to her. 'There but for the grace of God and Bill's father wanting to marry me I might have been in the same position.'

Janet had been in the hospital ten days. In two days' time she would be going home. She had spent most of her time trying to think of ways in which she could keep Paula. Could she steal her away in the night? Where would they go? How could she work and look after her? And Paula didn't have any clothes of her own.

So far there hadn't been any news from her parents. Did she really want to go home? She knew she didn't have any choice.

That morning, when the babies were brought in for feeding, a young nurse came and drew the curtains round Janet's bed.

'Where's my baby?' she asked. 'What's happened to her?' She began to panic.

'She's being put on a bottle and I've got to bind you up.'

'Why?'

'To help stop your milk.'

'Why can't I feed my baby?'

'She's got to get used to a bottle.'

'What for?' asked Janet, her voice rising.

'Her new parents.'

'What? They can't do that. Who are they? I haven't signed anything.'

'That's for the sister to say. I only do as I am told.'

'I want to see Sister.'

'I'll tell her, but you know how busy she is.'

Janet went to get out of bed.

47

'What are you doing?'

She put on her dressing gown. 'Going to find out who is going to take my baby.' She left the young nurse standing with her mouth open.

As she marched along the corridor she felt her bravado slipping away. What was she going to say? As she approached the nursery she saw a nurse giving Paula a bottle. She pushed open the door.

'What are you doing in here, Miss Slater? I told Nurse Gordon to bind you up. Your baby is going on the bottle.'

Janet was looking at Paula, her eyes filling with tears. 'I don't want to give her away,' she said softly.

'Now you know you've got to.'

'I want to keep her.'

'It has all been taken out of your hands.'

Janet's head shot up. 'Who by?'

'Your parents.'

'What have they got to do with it?'

'As you are underage they have signed for Paula to be adopted.'

'They can't do that.'

'I am afraid they can.'

Janet knew her tears were falling but did nothing to stop them. She sat on a chair and took her baby's tiny hand. 'Can I give her the bottle?' she asked.

'No. I think it is better you leave the nursery.'

'But—'

'Please, Miss Slater. It's for your own good.'

Slowly Janet made her way back to the ward. She lay on her bed and thought about her future. She desperately wanted Paula to be part of it.

*   *   *

48

That night, long after lights out, Janet went along to the nursery. She stood by Paula's cot and in the half-light saw that she looked so peaceful. Janet gently ran the back of her finger over her baby's smooth cheek. Paula snuffled and began sucking, turning towards Janet's finger. A smile flitted across Janet's sad face. She lifted Paula from her cot and held her close. The warm clean smell of her baby filled her with a longing she had never known. She put her lips to her soft downy cheek. 'I love you so much,' she whispered. 'I will now make you a promise that one day I will find you and if it takes the rest of my life, we will be together.'

'Miss Slater, just what do you think you are doing?' A nurse had come up behind her.

Janet didn't flinch. 'I was saying goodbye to my baby.'

'You know you shouldn't be in here. Now get back to your bed at once.' The nurse took Paula from her and put her back into her cot.

Janet stood and watched her baby. Paula's head moved from side to side as if she was searching for something.

The nurse took Janet's arm. 'Come along now. You are feeling low, it is quite natural. You'll get over this in time.'

Janet allowed herself to be led away. She knew she couldn't win yet she felt she now had a mission for the rest of her life: to be reunited with Paula. This separation was something she was never going to get over.

*   *   *

Janet arrived back at the village as she had left it—alone. Only her mother was home when she let herself in.

Janet hugged her.

'Janet, Janet darling, let me look at you.' She held her at arm's length. 'You look very well considering. Everybody had been asking after you. They think you are such a good girl looking after an ailing aunt all this time.'

Janet smiled. 'You should have seen her, Mother. She was so lovely; she had dark hair and a little birth mark on her—'

'Please, Janet, I am not interested.'

'I'm sure you would have loved her if only you had seen her. I wish—'

Irene Slater moved away. 'Now, Janet, that is quite enough. It isn't any good wishing. You have to start again. You must forget what has happened.'

'But I can't forget.'

'You will have to.'

'She was my baby.'

'You must think of it as a bereavement.'

'She didn't die.'

'Janet, I don't want you to mention anything about it to your father.'

'She isn't an it, her name's Paula,' she protested.

'Her new parents might decide to change that. Now come along, take your case upstairs and I'll make us both a cup of tea. By the way, your new dress is on your bed. It's blue; we thought blue would suit you.' Irene Slater smiled. 'Also I'm trying to persuade your father into buying a television. I'm sure you'd like that.'

Janet didn't reply, and made her way upstairs.

In her bedroom she pushed the dress to one side

50

and sat on the bed. It was nice in some ways to be home, but she knew she was going to miss Paula. She knew that very soon life would be back to its old boring routine. Janet quickly glanced at the dress. Why didn't they let her choose her own? Once more she was going to have to do the things they wanted her to. She screwed it up and threw it across the floor. She wanted more freedom. It was all right being home but she knew she would miss living with the other girls. She also knew her life could never be the same now.

The dress was in a crumpled heap and, feeling guilty, Janet picked it up. What had happened wasn't her parents' fault. She held up the dress. It wasn't that bad, and after all she should be grateful she still had a home and family, not like Freda. Janet picked up her rabbit and hugged it. She continued to worry about Freda. Was she still alive? If only she knew were she lived. If only she'd written.

Her mother called her to come downstairs. Her father lightly kissed her cheek and welcomed her home.

'You are looking very well.'

'And so do you, Father. Mother tells me you are thinking of having a television.'

'Just thinking about it for the moment, just thinking.'

'It would be nice.'

'We shall see. Now I must get on with a speech I'm giving at the WI.' He went into his study.

Janet knew that her father was an aloof man and it was going to take him a long while to get over what had happened.

'Do you feel well enough to go back to Blakes on Monday?' asked her mother as they sat drinking their tea.

'I don't want to work there.'

'So what will you do?'

'I don't know.'

'Well, there you are then. You'll feel better when you've been to see them.'

'They may not have a job for me.'

'I'm sure they will.'

'But what if they don't?'

'You can cross that bridge if and when you come to it, but I'm sure if Mr Blake knew you'd been away looking after a sick relative he would be pleased to see you back with them.'

'I'd rather work in the village.'

'Now what would you do here?'

'Perhaps Mrs White in the grocers, or the post office might need help.'

'I don't think they do. And I don't think it's such a good idea.'

'Why? Are you frightened I might mention Paula?'

Irene Slater flushed. 'Now, Janet, that wasn't a nice thing to say. It's just that I don't think there is a lot of opportunity for you here, that's all. And I hope that every time something doesn't go your way you don't keep throwing this silly nonsense in my face.'

'It isn't nonsense. I didn't want you to give my baby away.' Janet stood up and moved towards the window. She didn't want her mother to see the tears welling in her eyes.

'Janet.' Her mother's voice was loud. 'I don't want you to mention that child again in this house, do you understand? You are being very selfish. You have put your father and myself though all kinds of anguish, and this must be the end of it.'

Janet hung her head. 'I'll go to see Mr Blake on Monday.'

'Good girl.' Her mother took the tea tray into the kitchen.

Janet sighed. She knew when she was beaten.

*   *   *

She went back to her old job at Blakes. The other employees seemed to be pleased to have her back and, to stop them asking questions, she told them her aunt had finally passed away. After that, the subject was avoided.

Gradually she taught herself to type, but there was little opportunity for advancement, and office life seemed more boring than ever. As she wandered about Horsham in her lunchhour she would look into prams and wonder what kind of pram Paula had. As the weather was warm, babies lay without blankets and she found herself looking at their feet, just in case. If only she had a friend to whom she could talk, go out with. Even her favourite hobby of going to the pictures made her feel lonely for in the cinema nearly everybody was with someone. Then, to upset her more, all the films appeared to be about babies or people getting married and living happy ever after.

*   *   *

It was a warm and sunny Sunday morning in June, and the Reverend Peter Slater's parishioners were gathered outside the church as usual, when out of the blue a motorbike roared up and stopped by the

53

churchyard. Janet couldn't believe her eyes when she saw Freda sitting on the back. She was wearing a short black skirt, which unashamedly revealed her stocking tops as she climbed off the pillion.

Janet rushed up and threw her arms round her. 'It's so good to see you.' Tears filled her eyes.

'Looks like you're pleased to see me,' said Freda, 'even if they ain't.'

Janet glanced across to where the congregation had stopped all conversation and her mother was giving her a very disapproving look.

'I thought you were dead. Why didn't you write?' asked Janet.

'You know me, didn't get round to it, and then I met Charlie here and guess what, we got hitched yesterday. Been on me honeymoon.' She screamed with laughter. 'We stayed the night in Brighton and I suddenly remembered you lived in Sussex, so here we are.'

Janet could feel all eyes on them. She gave Charlie, who was still astride his bike, a slight nod. 'Look, let's move over there.'

Janet took Freda's arm and propelled her towards a clump of trees. Charlie, still on his bike, used his long gangling legs to propel the machine after them.

'You look really great,' said Freda, grinning and, getting closer, added, 'And a lot thinner.'

Janet blushed.

'Don't worry about Charlie here. He knows all about us and where we met.'

Janet looked around. 'He won't say anything, will he?'

'Na. He forgets things as fast as I tell him; he ain't listening half the time.'

54

'So where are you living now?' asked Janet, eager to find out all about her friend.

'Got a couple of rooms, near to Waterloo station. It ain't bad, better than home. I had to go back there even tho' me stepdad had chucked me out. I had nowhere else. Me mum made my life a bleeding misery, though.' She paused. 'You know me baby died, didn't you?'

Janet nodded. 'Sister Verity told us.'

'It was a little boy. What did you have?' Freda added quickly.

'A girl.' Janet wasn't going to say too much about her as it would have been too painful for both of them.

'That was nice. As I was saying . . .' Freda looked across at Charlie who was still sitting on his bike, well out of earshot, casually smoking, '. . . well, when I met him and he said he liked me I thought: this is a good time to get out, so we got married. He ain't a bad bloke though he can be a bit thick at times. Loves that bike.'

Janet smiled. 'It's so good to see you. I really missed you after you left. We mustn't lose touch again.'

'No, s'pose not.'

The congregation was beginning to break up and Janet could see her mother heading towards them. 'Quickly, give me your address.' She took a pencil and hymn book from her bag.

'You ain't gonner write in that, are you?'

'It's the only paper I've got.'

'I'm now Mrs Murrey and I live at flat 6, 21 Bramley Court, Waterloo, and you know that's in London. If you're ever round that way give us a knock.'

55

'I will, and I'll write.'

'Don't expect much of an answer. Writing ain't one of me strong points.'

'Janet.' Her mother was bearing down on them. 'Excuse me,' she said to Freda in a very posh voice. 'Janet, your father is ready to leave so don't be too long, will you, there's a good girl?' As she moved away she gave Freda a sickly smile.

'Good girl.' Freda put her hand to her mouth and began laughing. 'Sorry about that. But you, a good girl after what you did!'

Janet looked around to make sure everyone was out of earshot.

'You ready ter go then?' asked Charlie, grinding his cigarette butt into the ground with his boot. 'Don't forget, gel, we've got to go to work tomorrow, and I needs me sleep.'

'Just coming. Now you look after yourself, and don't forget if you're ever round our way you'll always be welcome.' Freda hoisted up her straight black skirt and cocked her leg over the bike. She threw her arms round Charlie's waist, and they roared off.

Janet stood for a moment or two watching the dust trail. Why did Freda seem so noisy and loud? Was it because now their life styles were so different? They seemed poles apart. She turned and made her way home.

'Who was that young lady?' asked her mother as soon as Janet got in. 'You appeared to be very pleased to see her. Is it someone you work with?'

'No, it was Freda; I met her in the home.'

'And you gave her your address?' Irene Slater looked so horrified Janet wanted to laugh.

'Yes. I like Freda. She's just got married.'

'Well, I hope she isn't going to make a habit of calling on you whenever she feels like it, especially on a Sunday morning and on that noisy thing.'

'Shouldn't think so. They've been to Brighton for the night; they got married yesterday.'

'Married. She doesn't look old enough to know her own mind. Now go on up to the bathroom and wash your hands before Mrs Price brings lunch in, and give your father's door a knock. And, Janet, not a word about where you met that girl.'

'What shall I say if he asks?'

'He won't.'

In the bathroom Janet thought about Freda. Charlie looked a lot older than she. Had she married him just to get away from home? 'I hope everything works out for you,' she said out loud, her voice echoing around the tiled room. Somehow the sound made her feel even more lonely.

CHAPTER SIX

As the year progressed, Janet's life stayed in a rut. Every week was the same; work in the office all week, then every Sunday church in the morning and teaching in Sunday school in the afternoon. Even the children, whom she used to enjoy being with, bored her now. The only joy in her life was when she went to the pictures.

With Christmas approaching Paula filled Janet's mind more than ever. Where was she? Did she have nice people looking after her? Would they buy her generous presents and give her plenty of love?

'Janet, I want you to help me decorate the

Christmas tree in the church doorway, and your father would be glad of a hand setting up the nativity scene. Perhaps it will help cheer you up.' Her mother peered at her. 'I hope you're not going down with something. You've been looking very peaky lately.'

Janet almost asked who'd helped her last year, but knew that wasn't wise. Her thoughts went to last Christmas with Freda. Although Janet had written to her a few times and even sent her a Christmas card, she hadn't received a reply. She remembered that night when Freda had had her baby and shuddered at the memory. Was Freda remembering too?

It was the Sunday before Christmas and the Sunday school had been busy rehearsing their carols and a nativity play, which was to be their contribution to the village concert the following evening in the church hall.

Janet finished clearing away and wished Mrs Johnson, the pianist, goodnight. Outside the wind was bitter and, pulling her scarf tighter round her neck, Janet began hurrying home.

'Janet Slater,' someone called out.

She stopped and turned. 'Mark Scott!'

'Hello, Janet. Haven't seen you around for a while.'

'Well, you've been in the army.'

'Yes, I'm out now.'

'Did you enjoy it?'

'No, I hated it, all that square bashing.'

Janet was pleased it was late afternoon and almost dark so he couldn't see her smile, as she remembered his mother clutching his hand as she walked him to school.

58

'Mind if I walk along with you?'

'No, you're going my way anyway.'

'That's true. Been busy?'

'It's the little ones. I've been getting them ready for the concert tomorrow.'

'Oh yes, Ma did tell me about it.'

'She and her ladies usually do something. Will you be going?'

'You must be joking! No, I expect I'll be in front of the tele.'

'That sounds really exciting.'

'Must be better than you lot singing,' but he laughed when he said it.

They said goodbye and Janet walked to her gate alone. Mark Scott looked different. It wasn't only his short haircut; he seemed taller and broader somehow, more confident, and even, she dared to admit to herself, better-looking than before he went into the army. He definitely wasn't a Mummy's boy now.

She must have been smiling when she went into the house, as her mother said, 'You look happy. Did everything go all right?'

'Yes, thanks. Mind you that little Adam Potter can be a real handful. He's one of the three kings but he keeps pulling his crown down over his eyes and pretending he can't see.'

Her mother laughed. 'I'm so pleased to see you're enjoying yourself.'

Janet was hoping she would say how much they'd missed her last year, but it was almost as if last year had been spirited away.

The following evening a keen audience was seated in the village hall, eagerly waiting for the curtains to part on Stowford's annual Christmas concert.

Janet's youngsters were to go on first, which pleased her, because as soon as their part was all over she could send them back to their parents, sit in the audience and enjoy the rest of the concert in peace.

To Janet's and all the other organizers' relief, the children behaved themselves, even young Adam Potter, and soon Janet was ushering them off the stage.

'I've saved you a seat.'

Janet was surprised to see Mark Scott sitting in the audience.

'Thanks. I didn't think you liked this sort of thing.'

'I don't,' he hissed as the lights went down again and the curtains opened on the WI ladies doing their turn.

During the interval Mark bought Janet a cup of tea.

'Did your mother make you change your mind?' asked Janet when they were back in their seats.

'No. I just thought I'd pop in to see if it had changed that much from when I last saw it.'

'Weren't you here last year?'

'No, didn't get home till Christmas Eve. So you didn't miss me then?'

Janet smiled. 'No, I didn't.' She wasn't going to tell him that she hadn't been there either.

The following day two Christmas cards arrived for Janet; one from Freda and the other from Mark Scott. Janet was disappointed that Freda hadn't said how she was. 'Love from Freda and Charlie' was all that was written on it.

'That's very kind of Mark to send you a card,'

said her mother when she read the name. She didn't mention anything about Freda's card. 'I noticed you and Mark getting on very well last night.'

'He only bought me a cup of tea.'

'He is a very nice young man, and I hope you weren't rude to him.'

'No. Why should I be?'

'Well, you do have this habit of being sharp just lately.'

She shrugged. Her mother seemed to have so little idea of how she felt. 'I'm sorry, but I do feel a bit lonely at times.'

'Well then, if Mark asks you out you should go.'

Janet didn't reply.

*   *   *

A few days later, Janet was waiting for a bus when she saw Mark across the road. He waved when he caught sight of her and ran over to the other side.

'Janet, I'm glad I've seen you. Would you like to go to the local hop on Friday to see in the New Year?'

She felt embarrassed as everyone in the bus queue appeared to be listening and waiting for her answer.

'I don't know,' she said softly, then added in a whisper, 'I can't dance.'

'I'll soon show you. Can you jive?'

Janet shook her head. 'I wouldn't have thought you could dance.'

He laughed. 'You get to do a lot of things in the army.' As the bus came into view he added, 'I'll pick you up about seven.'

It was five to seven when Mark called for Janet, who had been ready a good half-hour before. He was wearing a grey pinstriped suit and with his dark wavy hair he looked rather handsome.

'Janet, remember; don't go getting yourself into any trouble,' her father had said to her earlier.

'Peter, please . . .' tutted his wife.

Janet chose to ignore his remark. Was this how it was going to be for the rest of her life? Was he always going to make some comment every time she went out?

'You look nice,' said Mark when she went to the door.

'Thank you.' She smoothed down the front of the dress her mother had bought her for her last birthday.

'Enjoy yourselves,' beamed Mrs Slater as they left the house.

This was the first time Janet had been out with a boyfriend and she could see her mother clearly approved of Mark Scott.

At first Janet was awkward and embarrassed when they danced, and felt she had two left feet. But Mark was proving to be good company and she was enjoying herself. Over a glass of lemonade he told her he had gone back to his old job at the local garage but he wanted to move on.

'The army taught me there's a big world out there.'

She toyed with her glass. 'I know. I'd like to get away too, but you need money and a job. Where did you go in the army?'

'Spent a short while in Egypt.'

'So that's why you look so brown. Was it hot?'

'A bit. I've got a mate—some bloke I met in the

army—he reckons he's going to start a car-selling business in London.'

'That should be interesting. Would you go with him?'

'Don't know. It might mean putting money into it, and I don't think Ma would approve of me doing that or moving to London.'

'Parents always seem to be telling you what they think is best for you.' Janet looked sad. 'I know mine do.'

'You'll have to wait till you're twenty-one before you can do as you like.'

'How old are you now, Mark?'

'Twenty-one next birthday. It's daft when you think about it; I was old enough to go in the army and get shot at but I still can't get married or start a business without my parents' permission.'

'You're not thinking of getting married then, are you?'

He laughed. 'Not on your nelly. I've got a lot of living to do first. Come on.' He jumped to his feet. 'We came here to dance, not get all melancholy. We'll go over in the corner and I'll teach you to jive.'

By twelve o'clock she had almost mastered it.

As midnight struck everybody began kissing. Mark took Janet into his arms and kissed her gently. It wasn't the kind of passionate kiss Sam had given her, but she liked it.

'Happy New Year,' he said holding her tight.

'And a Happy New Year to you,' she said, pulling away. 'What resolutions have you made?'

'Only to try to start a business.'

The band began to play 'Auld Lang Syne'. Mark took her hand and they joined in the fun.

63

After, when they sat with a cold drink, Mark asked her what her resolutions were.

'I haven't made any.'

'You should. Janet, I've really enjoyed being out with you tonight. I thought you might be like your father.'

She laughed. 'Why?'

'Well, I only know you as the Sunday school teacher. Where do you work, anyway?'

'In an office in Horsham.'

'Ma was telling me you were away last Christmas, that you'd gone to look after an old aunt. Is she all right now?'

Janet could feel herself blushing. 'Yes, thanks.' She was pleased the band struck up the 'last waltz' at that moment, and once again Mark pulled her to her feet.

He was holding her very close. She could feel his breath on her neck.

Would she be able to keep Paula a secret for ever? And did she want to?

*   *   *

After the New Year Janet and Mark saw each other twice a week. During the week they went to the pictures and on Saturday nights they danced at the local hop. For the first time in her life Janet felt really happy—she had something to look forward to. Mark was good-looking, good company and she liked him. They laughed together and she felt at ease with him. Janet was pleased that he didn't make any advances. She wasn't ready for romance. He didn't even put his arm round her in the pictures. At the end of the evenings they just

64

exchanged a quick good night kiss. As far as Janet was concerned that was enough

February came, and as Janet's birthday fell on a Saturday that year, Mark was able to take her to London to see a show. She was so excited. It was something she had always wanted to do. London seemed a million miles away from her life. Mark told her that he also wanted to go and see his friend to find out if he still wanted him to be a partner in his business.

'I'm so pleased that you and Mark are getting on so well,' said her mother. 'Mrs Scott was telling me that Mark has certainly changed since you two have been walking out together.' Mrs Slater placed Janet's clean bedclothes on the bed. 'You can give me a hand to change the sheets.'

'We're not walking out. We just go to the dance and pictures, that's all. He's going to London to see his friend, and as it happened to be my birthday he's taking me along and then we're seeing a film. So you can tell Mrs Scott not to get too gossipy about it. And what did she mean when she said Mark had changed? In what way?'

'I don't know. I think she means he doesn't spend quite so much time watching the television.'

'Is that all? Well, there isn't much else to do round here now, is there?' Janet plumped up the pillow after putting on its clean pillowcase.

'Mrs Scott is a very nice woman. It was terrible when her little Joan died. Don't suppose Mrs Scott ever forgave herself, letting her run off like that. It was a good thing she had Mark so soon after to take her mind off the accident. Not that you would ever forget losing a child.'

Janet knew all about the anguish of losing a

daughter, and could now understand why Mark, an only child, had been so cosseted. Joan had been two years old when she'd drowned in the village pond. Mark had been born a week later. Apparently the Scott tragedy had been the talk of the village for months after; even now Joan's tiny grave always had fresh flowers in the vase.

'Janet.' Her mother broke into her thoughts. 'You will be careful when you go to London, won't you?'

Janet faced her mother across the bed. 'Why? What do you mean?'

'I was just thinking of what happened the last time you—'

Janet was angry. 'I wondered how long it would be before you said something. I won't drag him into the nearest park and make him make mad, passionate love to me, if that's what you're frightened of.'

Irene Slater pulled herself up to her full five foot four and the colour drained from her face. 'How dare you? How dare you speak to me like that? You will apologize at once, young lady.'

Immediately Janet regretted what she had said. 'I'm sorry. But I made one big mistake which I shall spend the rest of my life wishing hadn't happened. So I don't think I'll need reminding every time I go out. Besides Mark and I are just friends.'

Her mother pursed her lips and silently began straightening out the sheet.

Janet knew that if she ever wanted to find Paula she would have to leave this village and her family. There was no way her parents' attitude was ever going to change.

*   *   *

On Saturday, 19 February Janet found herself eagerly waiting for Mark. As usual he was at her door on the dot.

'Happy birthday.' He kissed her cheek and handed her a boxed birthday card and a small present.

'This is lovely. Thank you.'

'It's only a box of hankies, but they do have your initial on them.'

'Thank you. That's very kind of you. But you're taking me to London, I didn't expect anything else.'

Although he had lost some of his tan, when he smiled his dark complexion still offset his even white teeth.

'Don't worry about it. Ready?'

Janet nodded.

They said their goodbyes and left.

On the train Janet remembered her last journey to London. She quickly smiled across at Mark. She wasn't going to let those sad memories spoil today.

By the time they left Kennington underground station it was almost lunchtime. They arrived at a gap in the houses that had a hand-painted sign on two poles announcing 'Danny's Used Cars'.

'Is this it?' asked Janet, looking at the row of highly polished cars.

'Looks like it.'

'But it's only a cleared bomb sight.'

'Most of these places are, unless you've got enough money for a real posh showroom.'

They made their way to the shed at the far end and Mark knocked on the door.

'It's open.'

When Mark stepped inside Danny looked up from his desk and for a moment said nothing. Suddenly he jumped to his feet. 'Well, I'll be buggered. Me old mate Mark.' He clasped Mark to him. 'How are you then, me old mucker?' He gave him a light punch on his arm. 'It's good to see you.'

Janet followed Mark into the tiny office and the heat from the electric fire was overpowering. Through the haze of cigarette smoke she saw that Danny was a few years older than Mark. He had a thin moustache, dark hair and flashing blue eyes. He was good-looking in a David Niven sort of way, slightly taller than Mark, and his very expensive-looking suit was well cut. Hanging over the back of his chair was a tan-coloured sheepskin jacket.

'This is Janet,' said Mark, turning towards her.

'Pleased to meet you, I'm sure. You two walking out then?' He grinned and winked at Janet.

'No, we're just friends.'

'Oh yes. Look, take a seat.' He pointed to a chair behind the desk.

Janet sat down. The desk was strewn with papers, a couple of empty cigarette packets, and an overflowing ashtray.

'So how's things?' asked Mark quickly.

'Mustn't grumble. What you doing up this way? Come to see if it's worth your while putting a few bob in the business then?'

'Still thinking about it.'

'I could do with your expertise up here.' He turned to Janet and, still holding a cigarette between his nicotine-stained fingers, pointed at Mark. 'Did you know this bloke is one of the best mechanics in the business? Half the army trucks wouldn't have got off the ground if it wasn't for this

68

clever sod here.'

Mark looked embarrassed. 'I was only doing my job.'

'Yes, I could definitely do with someone like you.' Danny bent his head closer. 'Have to clock a few of 'em sometimes and patch up a lot of the others. You could earn yourself a fortune up here.'

'I'll have to think about it.'

'Honest, Mark, I'd like you to give it a bit of thought. You can always stay with me till you make up your mind, see how the business is run.'

'Where do you live then?'

'Just up the road, got a couple of rooms. It ain't exactly the Ritz—in fact it's really a bit of a dump—but it'll do for now. Places are bloody hard to get round here, and they cost a bomb, and you have to find a packet in key money. But don't let me put you off. I can always put the word round— that's if you decide to stay.'

'I really will have to think about it,' said Mark seriously.

'So what you doing round this way then?'

'We're going up West. It's a treat for Janet's birthday today. We're going to try and catch a film—*Seven Brides for Seven Brothers*.'

'Happy birthday, my dear.'

'Thank you.'

'I've heard that's a great picture. Now what about a bite to eat?'

'Thanks all the same, Danny, but we want to get on. We hope to get into the afternoon show.' Mark opened the door.

'Fair enough. Cheerio then, mate. Remember to think over what I said. I mean it, you know.' He shook Mark's hand, then took hold of Janet's. 'It's been very nice meeting you, my dear, and when he comes up here again just you make sure he brings you with him.'

Janet could feel herself beginning to blush. Danny was like Sam—a real charmer—and if she did ever meet him again she would have to watch out.

'He seems nice,' said Janet as they made their way back to the underground.

'He's all right, but you'll have to mind your step with him.'

'Why'

'He's a bit of a ladies' man.'

'And you're not?'

'I could be.'

'What are you going to do about the job he's offered?'

'I don't know. But I reckon Danny's right: I could earn a lot up here.'

'But wouldn't you miss the fields and the smell of the fresh air?'

'No, I'd rather have the smell of money.' He laughed. 'But I would miss you.'

Janet didn't look at him and was relieved when they reached the station. As they made their way down to the train she wondered what his future would be here in London, and if he did come here to live and work she knew she would miss him too.

CHAPTER SEVEN

During the week after they had been to London Mark dropped a note into Janet's house and asked if he could meet her the following night after work at a coffee bar in Horsham.

'This is nice,' said Janet, looking round. 'I've never been in here before.'

'Coffee bars are all the go in London. They even have blokes playing in 'em, skiffle they call it. D'you know, they even play on washboards with thimbles on their fingers and they use tea chests as a bass?'

She laughed. 'You're having me on.'

'No, honest. You must have heard of Lonnie Donnegan and Tommy Steele.'

'Yes, of course. Well, I've read about them.'

'That's where they started.'

Janet laughed out loud at the comical idea and they were still laughing when Mark leant across and took hold of her hand.

She pulled away in surprise. 'Don't do that.'

'Sorry.' He looked very hurt.

She felt embarrassed. 'Why did you ask to meet me here? It wasn't to tell me all about skiffle, and I'll be seeing you on Saturday?'

'I'm going away.'

Janet was stunned. 'To London? So soon?'

He nodded. 'I've made up my mind. I phoned Danny yesterday and told him I want to see him and talk it all out. I'm going this weekend so I won't be able to take you to the dance.'

'That's all right,' she said light-heartedly, trying to sound cheerful. 'If that's what you want. After all, it's your future.'

He looked a little happier. 'You're a nice person, Janet, and I'm glad you understand. I was a bit worried in case you thought I was letting you down.'

'Why should I think that?'

'Well, I am the only one you've been out with.'

'Will you be staying with Danny?' she asked, to change the subject.

'Just for Friday and Saturday.'

'Well, I hope his flat's a bit cleaner and tidier than his office.'

'It is a bit of a mess.'

'So can we still go to the pictures next week?'

'If you want.'

'You will tell me what the outcome of all this will be, won't you?'

'Course. Will you miss me?'

'Yes, I will.' Janet looked away. She didn't want him to see in her eyes just how much he had come to mean to her. But what did she mean to him? Was he just feeling sorry for her? He knew she didn't have anyone else to take her out. But she had always made it very clear to him she didn't want any romance in her life—well, not up until now. But had she changed her mind?

'Janet, Janet, you're not listening.'

'Sorry, what were you saying?'

'If I do get settled there perhaps you could come up and see me sometime?'

She laughed. 'You sound a bit like Mae West.'

He laughed. 'I'm really going to miss you.'

'You'll soon forget me with all those posh London girls hanging round.' But, she would have liked to add, not nearly as much as I shall miss you.

*   *   *

On Saturday Janet didn't know what to do with herself and wandered about aimlessly.

'Aren't you going out tonight?' asked her

72

mother.

'No.'

'Oh dear. I do hope you and Mark haven't had a silly quarrel.'

'No. He's gone to London for a few days.' Janet wasn't sure if she should tell her mother his plans—did his own mother know? 'On business,' she added quickly.

'I see. Mrs Scott didn't mention it last night when I saw her at the WI?'

'Perhaps she didn't think it was worth talking about.'

'Yes, I should think that was it.'

By Wednesday, the night they usually went to the cinema, Janet was still anxiously waiting for his news.

His knock on the front door sent her hurrying to open it. 'I'm ready ... Bye!' she called over her shoulder.

As soon as they were outside she said, 'Well?'

He grinned.

'Oh Mark, don't be so annoying. Why haven't you been round to tell me, or ...?' She stopped. 'You're not going then?' She held on to his arm.

'I didn't know you cared.' She quickly drew away. 'I'm just interested, that's all.'

'Well, I am going. I'm not going to put any money into his business just yet, I'm only going to work for Danny. I'll give it a year and then I'll be able to see how the land lies. But don't worry, I'm coming home every weekend even if it's only to keep Ma happy—that's of course unless something urgent crops up—so we can still go to the village hop.'

'What does your mother say about it?'

73

'She's not very happy, but it's Dad I'll miss. He's not that well and I worry about him. His war wound has started to cause all sorts of health problems. Mum will miss my money but I hope I can give her some every week. I'll just have to see how it goes.'

Janet felt happy that he'd be home every weekend, even if she was a little disappointed that it wasn't to see her. Suddenly she realized how she felt about him and how much she was going to miss him.

*　　　*　　　*

On Sunday evening, as they wandered around the village, Janet knew she was going to miss Mark more than she let on. Her life had taken on another meaning since Christmas and now he was going the next day. When he said good night she wished him luck. She wanted him to hold her and tell her how much he liked her, but he didn't.

'You will let me know how you are getting on, won't you?'

He smiled. 'Course. I'll be seeing you on Saturday.'

Janet at least had that to look forward to.

*　　　*　　　*

March 2 was Paula's first birthday. It was Janet's dearest wish that she could have sent her a card or given her a present. Was she having a birthday party? Would there be a fancy iced cake with a candle on? Had her new parents bought her nice things? Did they keep her well dressed? Janet looked at the clock. All day at the office she had gone through every moment of Paula being born again. Once old Mrs Baker told her off for daydreaming. Janet smiled to herself. She'd have a fit if she knew what I was thinking about, she thought. She tried to visualize what Paula would look like with her dark eyes and hair. Was it straight or curly? Short or long? She wanted to cry and felt her heart would break. Was it possible to find out where she was?

Throughout the summer Mark came home every weekend. More and more Janet looked forward to seeing him. Even though he looked tired they still went dancing.

'Danny certainly keeps me busy,' he said in the interval when they were having a cold drink.

'Do you enjoy working for him?'

'I think so. I've certainly learnt a lot about the second-hand car business and the dodgy deals that go on. By the way, I'm getting a car next week.'

'Can you drive?'

'Course, it's part of the job, but I passed my test in the army. If you like I'll teach you.'

'Would you? That would be super.'

'So next week, Miss Slater, we will be coming here in style.'

She giggled.

On Saturday Janet stood waiting at the gate for Mark. She couldn't believe her eyes when he drew up in a gleaming black car.

'Hop in,' he called.

She did so, and sat back, sinking into the soft green leather upholstery. 'This is really lovely,' she said, running her hands over the walnut dashboard.

'Would have liked something a bit flashy, but you can't beat an old Morris for reliability.'

'Did it cost a lot?'

'Na, not now I'm in the trade and in the know. Say, what about we go for a spin instead of the dance?'

'That'll be great, just as long as I get back about the same time. You know what my father's like.'

They sped along the country lanes and laughed at silly things. They stopped to stroll on the downs as the night was just turning. The sunset lit up the sky with fire.

'It's such a beautiful evening,' said Janet as they walked along. 'It's times like this when I wish I could live for ever.'

Mark sat on the grass. 'You don't want to bother with wasting wishes like that. Wish for money and things it can bring.'

Janet sat down beside him. 'Yes, but can it bring happiness?'

'Dunno. But it sure can make life a lot better. Take Danny—it won't be long before he moves.'

'What, the business?'

'No, out of the flat.'

'Why's that?'

'He's making a packet. He's talking about getting a real posh house.'

'What about his flat?'

'I'm thinking of taking it over.'

Janet laughed.

'What's so funny?'

'You. A man of property.'

'It's only a grotty old flat and I'd only be renting it. In fact that's something I'd like to talk to you about, Janet.'

She stiffened. She knew this was going to be a serious conversation. 'What about? Here, you don't want me as a cleaner, do you?' she laughed.

'In a way.'

'Blooming cheek.'

Mark began picking at the grass. He wasn't looking at her. 'Jan, I know this sounds daft but you see I didn't know I'd miss you so much, and I'd like you to come and . . . Oh, what the heck. Janet, will you marry me?'

She stared at him. This wasn't what she'd thought he was going say. She'd thought he might have suggested she go up to London for the weekend, but marriage . . . He had never shown any real emotion towards her. They got on all right but only as friends. They only kissed as friends.

'I don't know,' she finally said.

'You do like me, don't you?'

She nodded.

'Well then.'

She did like him, but did she love him? 'You'd have to ask my father.'

'I know. But what about you?'

'I do like you, Mark.'

'Good, that's settled then.'

'When were you thinking of us . . . you know?'

'What about next year? That'll give me time to save.'

She smiled. 'Mrs Mark Scott. Sounds rather nice.'

'I think so.' He pushed her back on the grass and kissed her. It was a clumsy, searching kiss. He tried to put his tongue in her mouth but she didn't like it. His hand was up her skirt and he began caressing her thigh, but she quickly pushed him away and sat up.

'Stop it.'

'Why, what's wrong?'

'Give me time.'

'Janet, I haven't got time. I'm off in the morning.'

'So?'

'I was wondering if we could . . . You know?'

She quickly stood up. 'No, Mark. Is that all you proposed for? So that you could . . . ?'

'No, course not.' He laughed and stood next to her and put his arm round her slim waist. 'I'm sorry, but you can't blame a bloke for trying now, can you?'

She smiled. 'No, s'pose not.'

They slowly walked back to the car.

'I'm really sorry, Janet. I shouldn't have done that.'

'You didn't do anything.'

He grinned. 'I would have if you'd have given me half a chance. I suppose you do have to behave yourself, seeing you're the vicar's daughter.'

She couldn't bring herself to look at him.

'Janet, I do love you, you know. Sounds silly, but somehow you miss things when they're not there all the time.'

'I miss you too, and I'm very fond of you, Mark.'

He started the engine. 'I'll leave it till next weekend to ask your dad.'

'When will you tell your mother?'

'After I've got your dad's permission.'

Janet laughed.

'What's so funny?'

'Can you imagine it when our mothers get together?'

'I'm glad I'll be out of the way all week.'

'Coward.' Suddenly Janet was beginning to warm

to the idea of getting married.

That night she wrote in her diary: 'Mark proposed and I said yes.' She sat back and chewed on the end of her pencil. She was very fond of him but was it love? The thought of leaving home and going to live in London and being able to do as she liked in her own home was very thrilling. She sat up. Living in London—could she possibly find out who had adopted Paula?

She wrote to Freda, asking her if she would like to be her bridesmaid. Getting married was going to give her a purpose and something exciting to look forward to, even if it was a year away. She only hoped her father would give his consent.

*   *   *

The following Saturday evening Janet was sitting in the garden with her mother. She was nervous; she knew Mark was asking her father.

The Reverend walked across the grass with Mark close behind. 'Did you know anything about this?' His strident voice caused his wife to break off from her knitting.

'About what, dear?' Looking up, she shielded her eyes from the sun.

'These two. Wanting to get married.'

Irene Slater's face went pale. 'No—no, I didn't.'

Janet smiled at Mark, but his face gave nothing away.

'You are both very young,' said Mrs Slater.

'I do have a good job,' said Mark hurriedly.

'That's as may be, but what are your prospects?'

'I hope to have my own business one day, sir.'

'Do you now? Doing what?'

'Second-hand cars.' He looked from one to the other.

'I see.'

'Does your mother know about this, Mark?' asked Mrs Slater.

Mark shook his head. 'I thought I'd ask you and your husband first, just in case you said . . .' His voice trailed off.

Janet felt so sorry for him. He look humiliated, but, trapped in the garden with the Slaters, he'd have to see it through to the end. What if her father refused? Her hope of getting away could be dashed and she would have to wait till she was twenty-one. Three more years.

'So, if I do give my consent, where are you thinking of living?'

'At the moment I share a flat with my boss, Danny, but he's moving and I'm taking over the tenancy.'

'I see,' repeated the Reverend. 'And where is this flat?'

'London, sir.'

Janet smiled at Mark.

'And when were you thinking of getting married? Providing, of course, I give my permission.'

'Next year. When Danny moves out I'll have to get the flat decorated and furnished.' He looked at Janet and grinned.

'Next year. Well, at least you sound as if you'll be taking your responsibilities seriously. I will have to give this some serious thought. A lot can happen in a year. And as your mother said, you, Janet, are very young.'

Janet felt deflated. Was he doing this deliberately? 'I'll be nineteen next year.'

'I still think it's very young to take on such

80

responsibilities.'

'I'm sure Mark is very level-headed,' said Mrs Slater hurriedly.

'We shall see.' Her husband moved away.

'Tea, Mark?' asked Mrs Slater.

'No, thank you. Janet, can we go for a walk?'

'I'll get my bag.' Janet was pleased to get away from any more questions.

When they shut the gate Mark let out a loud sigh. 'D'you know, I think that was the longest half-hour of my life?'

Janet held on to his arm and laughed. 'You should have seen your face.'

'Why? What was wrong with it?'

'Nothing, but you looked ever so worried.'

'I was, and we didn't get an answer, did we?'

'No, I dare say I'll get a grilling when I get back.'

'What d'you think our chances are?'

'I don't know.' Janet was worried in case her father brought up the past. Would he?

'What if he says no?'

'I don't think he will. He's just making sure you squirm a bit.'

'I certainly did that. If he says yes perhaps we could get you a ring next Saturday.'

'I'd like that.'

'Will I have to wait till we're married for . . . you know?'

'Most definitely yes.'

'Thought you might say that.'

'Do you mind?'

'No, not really. It's nice to think that I'll be the first.' Janet couldn't meet his eyes as she didn't have an answer to that. But she knew she had to tell him about Paula soon.

CHAPTER EIGHT

Mark kissed Janet gently. 'I'll see you later.'

She watched him drive away then slowly made her way back into the house.

'Janet? In here.' Her father was calling from his study. 'Sit down.'

She did as she was told.

'This business with Mark Scott has come as rather a shock to both your mother and myself.' He looked at her quizzically. 'You're not in any kind of trouble again, are you?'

Janet felt her face flush with anger as well as embarrassment. 'No, Father. I made one mistake and I won't be repeating it.'

'Very good. He's a nice lad and comes from a well-respected family.' He gave her a rare smile. 'I think we can say you have my permission.'

'Thank you.' She left the room. It was so formal.

Her mother was waiting outside. 'Janet, come with me.'

She followed her mother into the drawing room and sat in an armchair opposite her.

'We have to have a little talk.'

Janet wanted to laugh. Surely she wasn't going to tell her about the birds and bees?

'Are you going to tell Mark about your—shall we call it your discrepancy?'

Janet didn't know how to answer. She was angry. 'How can you call my beautiful baby a discrepancy?'

'Please, Janet.'

'She's my baby and you're not going to change

that.' Her voice was rising.

'It is all in the past and she has new parents so let that be the end of it.' Mrs Slater waved her hands. 'I don't want to hear any more of this. I'm only trying to help and all you can do is shout at me. You can be very hurtful at times.'

Janet looked down at the floor. 'I'm sorry.'

'Well, are you going to tell Mark?'

Janet fiddled with her fingernails. 'I don't know,' was the only answer she could give.

'It's up to you, of course, but most men don't like the idea of . . .' she cleared her throat, '. . . not being the first. You do understand what I am saying, don't you?'

Janet nodded. 'I expect I will tell him.'

'Then don't leave it too long in case he changes his mind afterwards.'

Janet sat open-mouthed. 'Why should he? What was in the past is over.'

'As I said before, give him time. Besides, we don't want to go to the trouble of announcing this engagement only to find it's been called off in a week or so. After all, there will be a lot of preparation and expense involved—that's without people asking what the reason was. So think it over very carefully, my dear.'

Janet couldn't believe what her mother was saying. So once again it was all down to other people and what they thought.

Her mother stood up and made her way to the door. She turned. She looked embarrassed. 'You do understand that he will probably realize he's not the first on your wedding night, don't you?' She quickly left the room, leaving Janet alone with her thoughts.

Should she tell Mark? Would he still want to marry her? Would he help her to find Paula? It was up to her now.

*   *   *

That evening when Mark called for her she quickly told him her father had given his permission for them to get married. They drove round the corner out of sight of the vicarage and Mark kissed her.

'I'm so glad he didn't give you a hard time about it. I'll tell Mum and Dad tonight, then next Saturday I'll meet you somewhere and you can pick out a ring, make it all official.'

Janet snuggled against him. 'I'm so happy.'

At the regular Saturday dance, Mark was in a very loving mood and used every opportunity to hold Janet and kiss her. She did worry that she might not be able to hold him at bay for much longer and she didn't want to make another mistake to spoil everything, and she still had to tell him about Paula.

'I'm so pleased your dad said yes. Cheer up. You don't have to look so miserable about it. Not changed your mind, have you?'

She smiled. 'No, course not.'

'That's good. I can go up to twelve pounds for a ring, but if there's one you really fancy I might be able to push it up a bit more. I can always borrow a few quid off Danny if need be.'

'You mustn't do that. I'll have a look in Horsham during my lunchtime next week.'

He kissed her again. 'I do love you, Janet.'

She felt mean. She wanted to tell him so much. She was unsure of her feelings. What was love?

When she first saw Sam she'd thought that was love. She didn't hear cymbals crash when Mark walked into the room, but did that only happen in books and films? She didn't feel her heart leap when she looked at him, not like when she had gazed down on Paula, but she had read somewhere that mother love was different. She missed him when he was away and if he did find someone else or if anything ever happened to him she would be devastated. Was that love? He was so nice—would she ever get another chance of happiness if she lost him? And what about Paula? When should she tell him about her?

'Are you feeling all right? You look ever so peaky.'

She smiled and touched his hand. 'I'm fine. Come on, they're playing a waltz.'

Mark held her close and they gently swayed to the music. She felt the warmth of him. Yes, she *did* love him, and all she had to do now was tell him about her daughter.

*   *   *

The following Saturday they bought the ring Janet had chosen. It was within Mark's budget.

That evening they showed it to her parents, who smiled benevolently, then Janet and Mark went to his parents'.

'I'm so thrilled,' said Mrs Scott, admiring the ring. 'I'm so looking forward to the wedding. We must have a drink. Tom, get the sherry out.'

Tom Scott held Janet and kissed her cheek. 'Welcome to the family, my dear.'

Janet thought what a kind, gentle man Mr Scott

was.

'You know it will be the wedding of the year here in the village. Are you going to get that clever Mrs Watson to make your dress? And what about bridesmaids?'

'Calm down, Mum. Give us a chance. We've got a year yet.'

'Yes, I know, but a wedding like this will take a lot of organizing.'

Janet looked at Mr Scott standing behind the black plastic-fronted cocktail bar. He took the decanter from a glass shelf behind him and poured sherry into four small liqueur glasses. He smiled at Janet and raised his eyes to the ceiling.

'Only a small one for Janet; remember she is the Reverend's daughter.' Mrs Scott beamed at Janet.

'I am eighteen, you know.'

'You are both very young.'

'Now come along, Mother, don't start.' Mr Scott raised his glass. 'To the happy couple.'

'Hear, hear,' said his wife.

Mark put his arm round Janet's waist and clinked her glass. 'To us,' he said softly.

Janet wanted to cry, she was so happy.

That evening, when Mark was walking her home, she asked, 'Now you've got the car could we go and see my friend Freda one day?'

'Why not? Is that the one who lives in London?'

She nodded. 'She lives at Waterloo.'

'I know Waterloo; it's not that far from Danny's. Look, we could go tomorrow if you like.'

'She might not be in. Her husband's got a motorbike and I think they go out a lot.'

'Tell you what, drop her a line in the week and make some arrangements for a Saturday, then

86

perhaps we could do a show or the pictures later that day while we're in town.'

'That's a lovely idea.'

'Where did you meet this Freda?'

Janet was trying to think on her feet. She wasn't ready to tell him just yet. She crossed her fingers behind her back. 'At the office a long while ago. She moved away.'

'That's a long way from Horsham.'

'Yes, it is. We don't have to go if you don't want to.'

'No, it sounds great.'

Why had she been so stupid? Why had she mentioned Freda? She knew why; she wanted someone to share her happiness with, but she had to tell him about Paula before Freda did.

*   *   *

Three weeks later Janet and Mark were sitting in Freda and Charlie's tiny flat.

'It's really great to see you again. And you've got yourself engaged then?'

Janet proudly held out her left hand and wiggled her fingers for her friend to admire the small diamond solitaire in her ring.

'That's nice. So when's the wedding gonner be?'

'Next year.'

'Not decided on a date then?'

Janet looked at Mark and smiled. 'No, not yet.'

'Right, come out in the kitchen, Jan,' said Freda. 'I've done a bit of tea. It ain't much but I do love playing at being a housewife.'

Janet looked anxiously at Charlie, whom she hoped she could trust not to betray her, then followed Freda, closing the living-room door behind her.

'Now, what's this about? Why did you want to see me? What was so urgent? You up the creek again?'

Janet leant against a green and cream kitchen cabinet.

'No. Freda, Charlie won't say anything, will he?'

'What about?'

'Paula.'

Freda shook her head. 'No, I told him to keep his mouth shut and he usually does as he's told. As I said, what's this all about? Why was you so eager to see me? It wasn't just to tell Charlie to keep mum, was it?'

Janet shook her head. 'I'm always writing to you but I never get an answer, so I thought, now Mark's got a car it would be a good time to catch up on all our . . .' Janet stopped. 'Freda, I'm ever so worried.'

'What about?'

'I don't really know how to tell Mark about Paula.'

'Just come right out with it. I did.'

'I know, but you're different somehow.'

'Why? What d'you mean?' Freda's eyes were blazing. 'You're not saying that I'm some old tart so he expected that from me, are you?'

'No, course not. I don't think that at all. It's just that I'd rather not . . . well, not till after we're married. My mother said he'll know on our wedding night that he wasn't the first.'

'Yes, I expect he will. Has he ever . . . you know, with other girls?'

'I don't think so, but I don't really know. We don't talk about things like that.'

88

'Well, he was in the army, and you know what they say: they have a girl in every port.'

'That's sailors.'

'I reckon they're all the same.'

'What can I do?'

'Your best bet is to find out if he has. If so, he'll know what to expect and you've got some explaining to do. But if he ain't, then you're laughing, and if it seems a bit easier than he expected, just tell him you use these new tampons. That'll surprise him and he probably won't bother about it after that.'

'Are they all right to use?'

'Yer, they're great. But honestly, Jan, I still think you should tell him. Sometimes these things have a horrible way of catching up with you.'

'I want to, but I'm afraid of losing him.'

'He might be a bit miffed at first, but if he really loves you then he'll soon get over it.'

'I hope so.'

'Well, just remember what I said.'

Janet threw her arms round her friend's neck. 'Thank you. Thank you. I only wish we lived closer, then we could see each other a lot more.'

'When you come and live up here in the smoke perhaps we could meet up now and again.'

'I'd like that.'

'So, what's your new name gonner be?'

'Scott. I'll be Mrs Scott.'

'Hmm. From Slater to Scott—change the name but not the letter, change for worse not something better.'

'Who told you that?'

'Dunno. Just something I heard. Me mum was full of those sorta sayings.'

'It's got to be a lot better living with Mark than at home.'

Freda smiled. 'Course it has.'

'Freda, do you think it's possible to find out who adopted Paula?'

'I shouldn't think so. They must keep the records very secret.'

'Yes, but they must be somewhere. She must have a birth certificate.'

'S'pose so.'

'So where would I start looking?'

'Don't ask me. Now come on, take that tray of sandwiches in otherwise they'll be champing at the bit. Tell 'em they're only fish paste.'

'You took your time,' said Charlie when they walked in.

'Girl talk. What you two been talking about then?'

'What we're gonner see. D'you fancy the flicks?'

'Why not? What about you, Jan?'

'That's fine by me.'

'Right then, girl, make us a cuppa and we'll be off.'

'Christ! Let me finish me sandwich first.'

Janet smiled. Married life certainly agreed with Freda. She only hoped she would be half as happy as her.

*   *   *

When they were driving home after the pictures Janet finally got up the courage to ask Mark what she and Freda had been discussing.

'Mark, have you ever, you know—with another girl?'

She noted out of the corner of her eye that he

90

looked at her, but she kept looking straight ahead, glad it was dark and he couldn't see her blushes.

'That's a funny thing to suddenly come out with. What d'you want to know for?'

'Just asked, that's all.'

'Did Freda put you up to that?'

'No.'

'I'm sure Freda isn't the right sort of friend for you. I can't see your mum and dad approving of her.'

'Mark Scott, don't be such a stuck-up snob. I like her.'

'That Charlie said he didn't know she once worked in Horsham.'

Despite the warmth of the evening Janet went cold.

'I don't think she tells him everything.'

'I gathered that.'

Janet began to worry about what else had they been discussing and decide not to pursue that line of conversation again.

'Anyway for your and Freda's information, no, I haven't. Satisfied?'

Janet grinned and held on to his arm. Thank you, Freda, she said to herself. At least he didn't know what to expect.

'Careful. You'll have us both off the road.'

CHAPTER NINE

The date had been set for the wedding. It was to be Saturday, 2 June 1956. At first Janet wanted another date but finally agreed as that day fitted in with everyone else. It would be the third anniversary of the Queen's Coronation, with all the personal associations of that day, and so Janet had thought it rather inappropriate, but had been unable to use this argument against that choice of day.

She still hadn't found the courage to tell Mark about Paula; there never seemed to be the right moment and as the weeks went by it was getting more and more difficult.

By the time winter arrived Mark was very busy at the garage and had to work most Saturdays, which made it difficult for him to get away in time to spend the evening with Janet. Danny's business was growing rapidly and Mark was worried that he sometimes had to cut corners which he didn't approve of just to keep within what Danny was prepared to pay out.

On Friday evenings Janet would phone Mark, standing shivering in the village phone box to guard her privacy from her parents.

'Are you coming home tomorrow?'

'No, I don't think I'll be able to. I've got this rush job on. Some bloke's been giving Danny hell and I said I'd stay and get it sorted.'

Janet's mouth went down. She was glad he couldn't see her sulking. 'If it's Danny's problem then he should see to it.'

'It's not as easy as that. Besides, Danny isn't that good a mechanic.'

'I get fed up without you.'

'Do you? Do you really?'

'You know I do.'

'Tell you what, why don't you come up here tomorrow? We could have a bite to eat somewhere

92

when I finish, and then perhaps go to the pictures.'

'So why can't you come home when you finish?'

'He wants me to do a job on Sunday and I can't let him down. He's bought the house next door and intends to make the forecourt bigger.' Janet felt cross. 'I want you here with me.'

'Do you?'

'Yes.'

'Look, you come up here and we can have a great evening together.'

'All right.'

'Well, now that's settled I'll see you about four. I should be finished by then.'

'OK.'

'Janet, I love you.'

'Me too. See you tomorrow.' She put the phone down and opened the door. The wind was blowing and she pulled her headscarf tighter at her throat. She didn't care how cold it was: she was happy, she was going to London for the day.

'Just make sure you don't miss the last train,' said her mother when she told her parents what she was doing. 'And don't go back to his flat.'

Janet knew that was coming. 'We are going out straight from his work.'

'Is that man still living with him?'

'I think so, but I'm not really sure.' Janet knew Danny had moved out months ago. Mark had told her he'd bought a nice house on Clapham Common, but she wasn't going to tell her mother otherwise she would stop her from going.

'You know time is moving on and you should both be sorting out the list of people you want to come to the wedding.'

'We'll do that when Mark comes home.'

'You mustn't leave it too long as the invitations have to be printed.'

'I know.' A few months ago when they had decided on the date it seemed a long way away. Since then her mother and Mrs Scott had been beaming and buzzing around like bees organizing everything. It was all being taken out of their hands. She'd had that feeling before.

*   *   *

'This is a nice surprise,' said Danny when Janet pushed open the door of his office. 'Mark said you might be coming.'

He jumped up and to Janet's surprise kissed her cheek. His overpowering aftershave almost took her breath away. He was wearing his expensive thick, light-coloured sheepskin jacket, even though the office was stiflingly hot from the electric fire and stuffy with cigarette smoke.

'He should be finished soon. Fancy a cuppa?'

'Please.' Janet was secretly admiring one of his three rings in which the diamond was very large and sparkled when it caught the light. It made the jewel in her engagement ring look very insignificant. She could guess how well his business was doing.

'Pop into the workshop while I play mum.' He smiled and she noticed again how very good-looking he was.

Janet made her way to the corrugated, single-storey building behind the office. She pushed open the door. The radio was blaring.

'Yoo-hoo. Mark, it's me,' she shouted above the music.

94

The sound of ball bearings being run along the concrete floor made her look at the back of a car that had been lifted up on blocks.

Mark was lying on a wooden platform; he pushed himself up. 'Jan, you've arrived.' He stood up. He was wearing a navy-coloured knitted bobble hat, which he quickly pulled off, ruffling his dark hair. His overalls were dirty and greasy and he had oil smudges on his face. He moved over to the bench and turned the radio off. He went to kiss her cheek.

'Get off.' She grinned. 'You're ever so dirty.' Janet quickly cast her eyes round the workshop. 'It's freezing in here. How can you work in a place like this?'

'You get used to it.'

'Why is he sitting in the warm office and you're out here?'

'He's the boss.'

'Will you be long?'

'No, just got to test these brakes, then we can go.'

'What shall I do?'

'Sit in the car and press the brake pedal while I bleed the brakes.' He opened the car door.

Janet sat inside and did as Mark told her. She'd never driven but she knew which was the right pedal to press.

'Right, that's it.' Mark took a dirty piece of rag from his pocket and wiped his hands. 'Danny should have a cuppa ready by now.'

They went into the office.

'All finished?' asked Danny.

'Yes. But tell him to watch it.' Mark put the car keys on the desk. 'It could really do with new set of

95

linings.'

'I ain't splashing out for those. He wants to be bloody lucky I'm doing his brakes.'

'Now come off it, Danny. They were dodgy when he bought it.'

'He bought it tried and tested, and at a good price.'

'If you say so.' Mark took a mug of tea Danny had offered.

'So where are you two off to?'

'Going home first for a bath, then out for a bite, then off to see a film. I'll probably take Janet home and I might be a bit late in on Monday.'

'Don't make it too late. There's plenty of work here.'

'I thought you were working on Sunday?' said Janet curiously. Had Mark got her here for another reason?

'I was, but he's decided to leave it this weekend.'

'I'm waiting to get the house next door knocked down. Then we can start straightening the place. Thought they might have been here be now.'

'They would have if you hadn't spent so much time haggling over the price.'

Danny laughed. 'That's business, me boy.' He turned to Janet and gave her another of his beaming smiles. 'You'll have to get him to bring you over to my place one of these weekends. Got plenty of rooms with beds. Think about it.'

'Won't your wife mind?'

He laughed. 'I ain't married.' He gave her a strange look. 'Well, not yet, anyway.'

Mark and Janet left Danny's and walked to Mark's flat. It was part of a three-storey house that had been converted into flats, and was only a few

96

streets away from the garage. Opposite was a cemetery. The front door was open and they went into a large hall. Janet was very apprehensive as they climbed the stairs, the brown lino cracked at the edges, to Mark's flat. 'Where's your landlord?'

'He doesn't live here, he just rents the places out. At least we all have our own front doors.'

Janet looked around the room they had entered. It felt cold and damp. It was large and had a high fussy painted ceiling. The walls were covered with red striped wallpaper and Janet noted that in a few places it had started to lift. There was only one long thin window; the faded red velvet curtains were drooping where some of the hooks were missing. Placed in front of an electric fire, which was wedged in the grate of the ornate fireplace, were a sofa and two armchairs, their colour undistinguishable through grease and dirt.

'I'll just put the fire on. Costs a bomb to heat this room; spend all my time feeding the meter. I'll show you where everything is in the kitchenette and you can be making a cuppa while I have a bath.'

'Where's the bathroom?'

'Just along the corridor. The bedroom is in there.' Mark quickly moved across the room and closed the door. 'It's a bit untidy at the moment.'

'Where did you sleep when Danny lived here?'

'On the sofa. It's a bed as well and it's quite comfortable. This is the kitchenette. They call it that 'cos it's so small.'

Janet could see that for herself; with the two of them in there it was overcrowded. Under the window with its green and white check curtains was a sink with an enamel draining board. A glass-fronted cabinet was on the opposite wall, and Janet could see a few tins and packets inside as well as some crockery. A drop-leaf table stood below it, with two stools tucked under. A small cooker was next to that.

'There's not a lot of room in here.'

'No, but then it don't matter that much.' He put his arm round her. 'When you're Mrs Scott and take it over you'll make it look like a palace.'

He took her in his arms and went to kiss her.

'Get off, you're all dirty.'

He grinned. 'I'd like to be.'

'Mark, I hope you haven't got me here to . . . you know?'

'Now, as if I would.'

'Well, I can tell you now, it won't work.'

He laughed. 'Didn't think it would.'

They moved back into the big room.

'The view's not bad.'

'It's a bit morbid, looking over a cemetery.'

'I don't know, there's always plenty of flowers out there. I was thinking of getting a radiogram. It would look good in that corner, don't you think?'

Janet smiled, suddenly full of enthusiasm. 'I'd really love that. I've always wanted a record player but my father wouldn't hear of it. We could buy a record every week.'

'We'll have to see about that.'

She knew Mark was going to make her happy. She wasn't that thrilled at the thought of living here in this flat, but at least she'd be in London and her own mistress, and she could probably make the place look a lot better. 'Go and have your bath.' She gently pushed him away.

'You going to come and scrub my back?'

98

'No, I'm not. How many use that bathroom?'

'Don't know. Must be about four of us.'

Janet almost shuddered at that. 'Are they all men?'

'Don't know. Don't see much of them as we're all at work.'

She was dreading to think what the bathroom looked like.

'I'll see to the tea.'

*   *   *

The following weekend, Mark was home and after collecting Janet from her Sunday school class, he took her to his parents' house for tea.

The Reverend and his wife weren't very pleased that Janet wouldn't be attending church that evening but, as she pointed out, they had to see about the wedding invitations and this was the only time Mark had.

'I feel like a naughty girl, not going to church,' said Janet as they sat in the front room of the Scotts' house.

'Well, you have got a good excuse. Sad, isn't it?' said Mark, chewing the end of his pencil and looking at the list.

'What d'you mean?'

'Look at it.' He flicked the paper with his finger. 'The only friends you've got are Freda and Charlie while I've only got Danny to invite.'

She laughed. 'And Freda's my bridesmaid and with Danny being your best man, there will only be Charlie sitting in the pew.'

'I've only got old George from the garage. Should have kept in touch with some of my army

99

bods,' he said pensively. 'No, joking aside, I still reckon it's sad.'

'It doesn't matter. There will be enough there. Most of our relations and lots of people in the village have been invited by our parents between them.'

'It seems wrong that we're only going to be on parade for the village and relations.'

'It's only for a day.'

'We could run away to Gretna.'

Janet laughed. 'That would really put the cat amongst the pigeons.'

'Be a laugh, though, wouldn't it?'

'Don't even think about it.' Janet put her pencil down. 'Mark, do you like children?'

'Can't say I've ever thought about it.'

'I'd like some.'

'It'll have to be when we've got a proper house. I wouldn't fancy bringing my kids up in London. 'Sides, I want us to enjoy ourselves a bit before we settle down. Got plenty of time for kids.'

Janet took a deep breath. 'Mark. I've—'

'Mark, Mark, quick!' Mrs Scott came racing into the room.

'What is it?'

'Your father. He's ill.'

Janet looked bewildered. 'What's wrong?'

Mark ran from the room.

In the kitchen Mr Scott was sitting on a chair. He looked a dreadful colour and was having difficulty breathing.

'Get a doctor,' said Mrs Scott.

'No, I'm going to take him straight to the hospital. Janet, will you be all right going home?'

She nodded. 'Don't worry about me.'

'I'll get the car, Mum.'

Mark left the house and Janet took her hat and coat from the hall stand. She waited with Mrs Scott until Mark had brought the car round, then helped get his father into the back. When they had all driven off, Janet slowly made her way home.

She was upset about Mr Scott and also the lost opportunity to tell Mark about Paula.

*   *   *

Mark took his father to hospital. He told Janet later that he'd had a very bad bout of flu coming on, and couldn't get his breath.

By Christmas he was back home and seemed to be a lot better. Janet was in charge of the nativity play again. This time Adam Potter was a year older and better behaved.

As they walked home after the concert, Mark said, 'Don't seem possible, does it, that it was only a year ago we started going out together?'

She squeezed his arm. 'And now we're planning our wedding.'

'Not us doing the planning, our mothers.'

She laughed. 'Well, it gives them something to do.'

'What happened to that old aunt you was looking after a couple of years ago? I haven't heard about her lately. She dead?'

Janet froze. What could she say? She sniffed and to her relief Mark didn't wait for an answer and took her silence as yes.

'That's a shame. Sorry, I shouldn't have asked. You must have been very close? Here, guess what? I was talking to a customer the other day and he was selling his car 'cos he was going to live in Canada.'

'That's a long way away.'

'He reckons there's no end of prospects for blokes over there, and he said they're calling out for mechanics. Would you fancy living in Canada, Jan?'

'No, I would not. It's freezing over there.'

'But just think—we could live in a nice house with heating and in the summer it's warm and with all that space we could do all sorts of things.'

'I'm not moving to some place that's the back of beyond.'

'I just thought you'd like a challenge, and this bloke says—'

'He's really brain-washed you, hasn't he?'

'No, but let's face it: anything's got to be better than that poky flat.'

'Not to me it isn't. I'm looking forward to being in charge of my life for a change.'

'You could still be in charge of your life in Canada.'

'But it's too far away. And what about your mum and dad? You mother wouldn't want you to go that far away.'

'That's true.'

*   *   *

That night when Janet filled in her diary she thought about the Christmas before last when she'd been expecting Paula.

She wondered if Mark was serious when he spoke about Canada. He did seem very excited at the prospects over there. She sat back and mulled it over. If he was serious she would have to tell him the real reason she'd gone away and why she wouldn't go to Canada with him. So many times she had tried to tell him about Paula but it had never seemed to be the right moment. Canada was too far away for her to be able to begin her quest, looking for Paula.

Would he understand? She remembered the fuss when she'd told her parents she was expecting, but Mark was different; he was of her generation and he loved her. He might even help her to find Paula. Then they would have a ready-made family. He'd said he didn't want children just yet, but Paula was different.

She suddenly felt hopeful about a happy ending to the problem of her secret. She decided to wait till after Christmas and when Mark asked her what her New Year's resolution was as he had this year, she would tell him. To find my daughter, Paula.

CHAPTER TEN

It was Christmas Eve and Mark had been very quiet all evening.

'Are you all right?' asked Janet as they made their way home from that evening's celebratory dance.

'I think I'll go on home, if you don't mind.'

'I thought you were coming to midnight mass?'

'I'll give it a miss. You don't mind, do you?'

'Yes, I do. I don't ask you to do much but just this once I . . .' She didn't finish the sentence. She felt like saying that she minded very much, but

103

didn't want to start having words, not tonight.

When they reached her gate he quickly kissed her cheek and hurried away.

'See you tomorrow.' Janet's voice was taken by the wind. She was angry. There had been none of his now familiar kisses or cuddles and they'd had very few dances. He had sat and hardly spoken. Was something on his mind? He said he thought he had a cold coming. Janet did have to admit to herself that he didn't look that well, but men could be such wimps sometimes. He was lucky; she knew Mrs Scott would make a fuss of him.

Janet walked into the hall where her mother was standing in front of the mirror putting on her hat.

Mrs Slater turned to face her daughter. 'Isn't Mark with you?'

'No, he's gone home.'

'I thought he would have made some kind of effort this year. I know he doesn't come to church but the midnight mass is different somehow.'

'I don't think he feels that well.'

'Oh dear,' said her mother. 'I hope it isn't anything serious or catching. Are you ready then?'

'Yes.'

They walked the short distance to the church in silence.

Mrs Scott raised her eyebrows when she saw Janet enter without Mark, and quickly slid along the pew to sit beside her. 'What's happened to Mark?' she whispered. 'Why isn't he here?'

'He's gone home,' said Janet in a low voice.

'Why?'

'He doesn't feel well.'

'Oh dear. I hope he hasn't got the flu. I am anxious about him in that flat on his own. I worry in

104

case he isn't eating properly. I hope he's being careful; I don't want him giving anything to his father and Tom finishing up in hospital again.'

Janet half smiled. Mrs Scott was a pillar of strength in this village to most people but when it came to Mark she was just like any other doting mum. Poor Mark, perhaps he wasn't so lucky after all to have his mother fussing round him. Janet resolved to go and see him first thing in the morning.

Her father began the service. As she stood with her head bowed her thoughts and prayers, as always at this time of year, went to Freda, and especially to Paula. She would be two in March.

*   *   *

Early the following morning, after breakfast, presents were exchanged in the Slater home. Janet wished her father would unbend, just a little. He gave her a brief smile, a quick kiss on the cheek and thanked her for the gardening gloves. In these past two years they had said less and less to each other. It made her unhappy to think it was her doing, but surely she had been punished enough. She wanted to scream at him, 'Where is your Christmas spirit and the goodwill to all men?'

When she'd finished helping her mother wash up she said, 'I'm going round to see Mark.'

'Don't be late for this morning's service,' called Irene Slater as Janet put on her hat and coat.

'I won't. Bye.'

The Scotts lived the other side of the village and Janet enjoyed the brisk walk in the bright crisp morning sunshine.

'Merry Christmas, Mrs Scott,' said Janet when the front door was opened.

'Merry Christmas, Janet.' She kissed her cheek. 'Mark is still in bed. He doesn't feel too good. You can go on up if you like. First door on the left.'

Janet thanked her and slowly went up the stairs.

She gently pushed open the door. 'Hello. It's me.'

The curtains hadn't been drawn back so the room was dark and stuffy. Even when her eyes got accustomed to the gloom all she could see was a lump in the bed. He turned over.

'Janet,' he croaked.

'Merry Christmas. How are you?'

'I feel like death.'

'You look like it. Do you want anything?'

'No, thanks.'

She stood in the doorway, not knowing what to do. 'I'll leave your present downstairs.'

'OK.' He turned over again.

Down in the kitchen Mrs Scott was preparing the dinner.

'Go in the other room, Janet, and Mr Scott will pour you a sherry.'

Janet wandered into the front room.

'Hello, Janet love.' Mr Scott lightly kissed her cheek. 'He doesn't look too good, does he?' He raised his eyes to the ceiling. 'I'm a bit worried about him. It's not like him to be ill. Sherry?'

'It's a shame.' Janet took the glass that was offered. 'Thanks.'

'I'll just pop one out to the little woman.'

Janet sat and thought about Mark upstairs. She didn't like him being ill. She wanted to nurse him, hold him close and kiss him better. She looked at

106

her watch, then wandered out to the kitchen. 'I'm sorry but I must go—church service. I'll come back this afternoon, if that's all right with you?'

'Be pleased to see you,' said Mr Scott. 'Don't worry too much about him, he's a strong lad,' he added as they moved towards the front door.

But as Janet walked home she did worry.

The next day Mark was worse and Mrs Scott called for the doctor.

'It's bronchitis,' said Mrs Scott, who looked really anxious when Janet visited in the afternoon.

'Is he going into hospital?'

Mrs Scott shook her head. 'Dr Lake said he would probably be better off here, but we must be careful as it could lead to pneumonia.'

'That's awful.'

'I blame all that smog in London.'

'It can't be very nice. Can I go and see him?'

'Of course.' Mrs Scott gently took Janet's arm and said in a low voice. 'I don't know what I'd do if I ever lost him.'

'He'll be fine in no time, you wait and see, so don't worry.'

'Yes, I'm being silly, but after losing one . . .' She suddenly stopped. 'You don't want to hear about all that; it's history.'

Janet peered round Mark's bedroom door. Her heart jolted when she saw him lying there. His eyes were closed and his face pale. He began to cough and as he clutched his ribs he opened his eyes.

'Hello, Jan. I didn't know you were there.' He coughed again.

She moved towards him and held his hand; it was cold and clammy. 'Don't talk.'

He lay back and closed his eyes again.

107

Janet felt close to tears. She didn't like to see him ill. She knew then how much he meant to her.

* * *

Throughout the first half of January Janet would hurry home from work just to sit with Mark every evening.

As the month dragged on Mark felt much better and some days he even managed to get down the stairs. On Saturday and Sunday between church she would spend the day with the Scotts. It was a happy house with music and laughter.

'Can you send a postal order to my landlord?' Mark asked Janet. 'I'm frightened I'll lose my flat.'

'Don't worry about it. I phoned Danny and told him you were ill and he's seen to it, and said get back soon as the work's piling up.'

A smile lifted Mark's pale face. 'Thanks. What would I do without you?'

'Is there anything else you want me to do?'

He grinned and tapped the bed. 'You could join me.'

She moved away. 'I thought you were ill?'

'I am. Guess I'll have to wait till I'm better.'

She quickly kissed his cheek. 'Even then you'll have to wait.'

He pulled a face. 'Till we're married, I suppose?'

She smiled and nodded. 'Then I'll look after you.'

'It should be me looking after you.'

'Who's looking after who?' asked Mrs Scott when she entered the room with a steaming bowl of soup.

'Me, looking after Janet when we get married.'

'Janet, I don't like the idea of Mark going back to work for that man Danny. I'm sure it isn't a healthy place to work in.'

'Mum,' he sighed. 'I'm grown up and I can make up my own mind where I work.'

'I know, but lying about on a cold floor. It doesn't do you any good.'

He grinned. 'I'll ask Danny to put in underfloor heating.'

'And what about that flat? I bet it's damp.'

'Yer. I grow mushrooms in there.'

Mrs Scott tutted. 'You're beginning to get cheeky. Sure sign you're getting better.' When she left the room Janet and Mark burst out laughing.

*   *   *

The following week Mark showed Janet a letter he'd had from Danny. The workload had become desperate and Danny had had to get in some help. When was Mark coming back, he wanted to know.

'What are you going to do?'

'Dunno. The doc said I'm not fit enough to go back just yet.'

'Can't he wait a few more weeks? The weather will be a bit better then.'

'Not according to that. He's got so much work.'

'So he'll have to tell this new fellow he's only temporary till you are on your feet.'

'I'll suggest it. But what about the flat? I don't want to lose it as they are so hard to get.'

'If the worst comes to the worst you can go back to your old job here and we might be able to get somewhere to live in the village.'

He screwed up his nose. 'You don't want that, do

109

you?'

She shook her head. She was looking forward to getting away, and now their plans were in jeopardy. Perhaps *she* could go to see Danny, persuade him to hold Mark's job open, even give him the flat rent money herself. Danny had always been so approachable.

'I still think Canada would be great,' Mark interrupted her thoughts.

'Don't start on that again.'

'I don't know why you're so against it.'

'It would upset my parents.'

'What about mine? My mum would hate it after losing Joan. But we can't let them run our lives.'

'Let's get the wedding over first, shall we?'

'If you say so.'

By the end of that week, Janet had mustered both the money and the resolve. On Friday she told Mark she had to go shopping the next day.

'So where're you going?'

'It's to see about material for my dress so don't ask too many questions.'

'Who's going with you?'

'Me, myself.'

'I'll miss you.'

'I may be late home so I might not be round till Sunday.'

'I suppose I'll have to put up with that.'

'You will if you want to see me all dressed up at our wedding.'

*   *   *

'What a lovely surprise,' said Danny, jumping up when Janet pushed open his office door. He looked

110

outside. 'Where's Mark?'

'He didn't come; he's not well enough.'

'So, what do I owe this pleasure to?' His face dropped. 'He's not any worse, is he?'

'No. Mark's worried about his flat.'

Danny sat down and put his fingertips together. 'I told him I've seen to it.'

'You said in your letter that you've got someone else in to work for you so now he's worried he'll lose his job and the flat.'

'This bloke's only temporary, and as for the flat, I told you that's been seen to. If you like I'll take you round to see the landlord and he'll tell you the rent's been paid.'

'I've brought twelve pounds for the month's rent money.' Janet pulled an envelope out of her handbag containing some of her savings.

'Put it away. It's been taken care of.'

'Yes, but how long for?'

'Till the end of January.'

'But that was last week.' Janet began to panic. 'What if he lets it before—'

'Calm down. He won't do that.'

'But you don't know that. I'd better go and see him. Do you have his address?'

'Look, I'll tell Rob—that's the bloke I've got in—that I'm off out for a while. Then we can go round and you pay off another month yourself.'

She smiled. 'Thanks. Why are you doing this?'

'I think a lot of Mark and I don't want to lose him. Come on, we'll go now.'

'You sure you don't mind?'

'When you smile at me like that I'd do anything. That Mark's a lucky bugger. You've got a lovely smile.' He took a set of keys from off the peg board behind him.

Janet turned. She didn't want him to see her blush.

'Right, let's do it in style. We'll take the Vauxhall.'

Outside he opened the passenger door of a gleaming two-tone grey car. The chrome was shining and the tyres had been painted white. It was lovely.

'Hop in.'

Janet felt like a queen. The engine purred into life and they slowly moved out.

'Nice little car this, don't you think?'

'It's lovely, but not very little.'

'Do you drive?'

'No.'

'You should get Mark to teach you.'

'I will when he's better.'

'So when is it you two are getting hitched?'

'June, the second. You should know that; you're going to be his best man.'

'Just teasing. Is he taking you anywhere nice for your honeymoon?'

'We haven't talked about that yet.'

'Now if it was me I'd take you somewhere really posh.'

She laughed nervously. 'Oh yes, and where would that be? Blackpool?'

'There are worse places than Blackpool, young lady. And with me lying beside you in the honeymoon bed you'd feel like you was in heaven.'

Janet was beginning to feel uncomfortable. As he swung the car round a corner, she slid along the bench seat and was now very close to him.

He laughed. 'Good cars these for getting the girl up close.'

112

She quickly moved away.

As he'd promised, Danny took her to see the landlord and Janet paid February's rent.

'Right, now where to?'

'Thanks all the same but I'd better go home.'

'Don't be daft. Let's go and have a bit of lunch. I know a nice little place not too far from here.'

'I don't know . . .'

'Look, Jan, I wasn't trying to get fresh or anything, it's just my way. 'Sides,' he laughed, 'I wouldn't want Mark to come at me with a monkey wrench.'

As Janet was hungry she agreed. 'But I must go after that.'

'No problem. I'll run you to the station.'

'Thanks.'

Danny was the perfect host in the restaurant, recommending dishes to her. Janet felt very grown up and special.

'Would you like a port and lemon or something?' he asked when they'd finished.

'No, just a cup of tea, thank you.'

'I like Mark and I feel he's wasting his talent just being a grease monkey.'

'What do you mean?'

'He should start selling 'em. The game's getting very good, especially now I'm going a bit upmarket.'

'You want him to sell your cars?'

'Yer, we could split the profit. He could make a bit more than he does now, and not get dirty.'

'Have you asked him?'

'A couple of times.'

'I thought he would have to put money in your business.'

'That was at the beginning. No, now I'm up and running he could work on commission.'

'He never told me that. So why doesn't he want to?'

'He reckons you have to be a bit of a shark,' he grinned. 'I must admit you do have to bend the truth sometimes.'

'Mark wouldn't do that.'

'I know. But you could perhaps try to persuade him.'

'I wouldn't want Mark to do anything he didn't want to.'

'But think of the money. I like you, Jan. You're not like the other girls I find meself stuck with.'

She laughed. 'Well, that's up to you.'

'I know. But most of 'em are gold-diggers. They think that just 'cos I've got nice clothes and me own showrooms I'm worth a few bob.'

'And aren't you?'

He leant forward. 'Well, yes, I am and so could Mark be if he played his cards right. But there you go, so don't tell anyone. You and Mark will have to come and look at my pad one of these days.'

'That would be nice.'

He beckoned the waiter over for the bill, then turned to Janet. 'We could go now if you like?'

'No. No, thank you. I really must get back.'

'Please yourself.'

As he drove her to the station she could feel him continually looking at her and it made her feel very uncomfortable. What was going through his mind? And would it affect Mark's job? And what if she did try to persuade Mark to sell cars, could they finish up in a nice house?

She felt flattered that a man like Danny could be

114

interested in her—or was it all show?

As she sat on the train she looked at her reflection. In a week's time she would be nineteen. She wasn't bad-looking and hadn't lost her figure after having Paula. But she knew now that Mark was the one she wanted to spend the rest of her life with.

She had to tell him about Paula soon. There shouldn't be any secrets in their relationship.

CHAPTER ELEVEN

Mark was pleased Janet had been to see Danny and that she had paid his rent, but he warned her again to be careful of Danny, as he was a ladies' man.

This year Janet's birthday was on a Sunday, and after church and her Sunday school they spent the evening quietly at Mark's house. They sat in the front room with his parents watching television. Mark had his arm round her and in the dark he would gently brush his lips against her cheek. She was thrilled with his touch and wished they could be alone.

The next day he was going back to work at last so she would have to wait till the end of the week before she saw him again.

On Friday when Mark came home he was full of Danny's house, which his boss had taken him to see that afternoon.

'You should see it, Jan, it's great. He's got four bedrooms. I ask you, what does he want with four bedrooms?'

'Perhaps he's going to take in lodgers.'

Mark laughed. 'No, can't see him doing that.'

'Who does his cleaning?'

'Seems he's got some old dear who comes in, she keeps it looking good.'

'Lucky old Danny.'

'It's an investment, he's just making sure his money grows. Clever bloke is Danny, and that's made up my mind. I'm going to sell cars. You wait and see, we'll have a house just like it in a few years' time.'

During the past few weeks they had spent many hours talking about their future but never once did Janet feel it was the right time to tell him about Paula. At times she felt weighed down with guilt, and because she feared she might lose him and after a lot of soul searching, she decided that it might be better to leave Paula unsaid. This grew to a firm decision not to tell him.

Now that Mark had made up his mind to give selling cars a go, he didn't get home till late on a Saturday evening. He would be full of how much money he'd made. It seemed everybody wanted to buy a second-hand car and he was surprised at some of the wrecks they managed to get rid of. Danny's business was growing. As the old buildings alongside were being pulled down so the area that held the cars was getting bigger and the cars more expensive.

Janet was pleased that Mark appeared to be happy and he told her that he much preferred sitting in the office and driving about looking for cars than, in his words, 'tarting them up and selling them on'. Having sold his own as soon as he went back to work, he came home in a different one

116

every weekend, which he borrowed from the forecourt. He only chose the good-looking models and some of them were very smart and slick with the chrome shining. They certainly turned a few heads when they drove by. He had also bought some nice clothes; smart crepe shoes and a new suit. Janet was glad it wasn't a teddy boy suit. He said he had to keep up the image, like Danny. She did have worries about his role model and hoped he didn't become too much like him. She also hoped he was saving more so they could decorate the flat. She would have liked one of the new contemporary three-piece suites she had seen in a furniture shop. It would look lovely along with the radiogram they were getting.

When they saw the news at the cinema of Grace Kelly and Prince Rainier's wedding, Janet squeezed Mark's hand.

'Our wedding will be just as wonderful as theirs.'

He smiled and kissed her cheek. 'I'm glad it won't be as expensive.'

By May, Janet was being swept along with all the preparations their mothers were making for the wedding.

With just two weeks to go everything was beginning to get exciting. Janet was so happy. The banns were being read and even her father managed a smile when he read out their names in church. The two-tier wedding cake was being iced and decorated with fancy roses and lattice work. Her lovely dress hung behind her bedroom door and all the village was looking forward to this grand event.

Janet had been trying to work out how much it would cost to go abroad for their honeymoon. They

117

still hadn't made any decision and she was beginning to get cross with Mark lately, trying to pin him down to some answers.

One Friday evening, when Janet had left her lists and calculations to join her mother who was watching television, their peace was shattered by someone banging on the front door.

'Who on earth can that be at this time of night?' said her mother, looking at the clock.

'I'll go,' said Janet, and she hurried to open the door.

'Mark!' She threw her arms round his neck.

He held her for a few seconds, then stepped back.

'What are you doing here on a Friday?' In the porch light she noticed how pale his face was.

'Who is it, dear?' Her mother's voice came from the drawing room.

'It's all right, Mother, it's Mark.'

'Well, ask him in.'

He shook his head.

'No, we won't stop,' Janet called. She lowered her voice. 'Are you all right?'

He ran his fingers through his hair. 'I had to see you, Jan.'

'Is something wrong?'

He looked round nervously.

'I'll get my cardi and we can talk outside.'

They walked down the path in silence, till they were away from the house.

'What are you doing home tonight?'

'Jan, there's been a bit of trouble.'

'Trouble? What kind of trouble? You've not had an accident, have you?'

'No, not me.'

'It's Danny. Oh, poor Danny. How did it—'

118

'It wasn't Danny.'

Janet's mind was reeling. It couldn't be anything to do with his mother or father. That kind of news would have spread round the village quicker than the plague.

'Let's sit in the car.'

'Have you been home yet?'

'No. Look, Janet, I've got to get away.'

'What?' It was like an explosion. 'Where to?'

'I don't know at the moment.'

'When?'

'Now. I can't go back to work for Danny.'

'Oh my God, you're not in any trouble with the police, are you?'

'No.' His reply was quick and sharp.

'But why now? We get married in two weeks. Mark, what's wrong?'

He gripped the steering wheel with both hands, his knuckles white. 'I sold a car.' He wiped the perspiration from his top lip. 'I knew it wasn't in good condition and . . .' He turned to Janet, his eyes full of tears.

She sat with her mouth open. 'What happened?' she whispered.

'It was a family. The wife and two kids . . . They're all . . . The car went up in flames and they couldn't get out.'

'And the husband?'

'He's badly injured. Janet, I can't go back to the garage. The family will kill me.'

'But if it was an accident . . .'

'But I sold them the car.'

'It wasn't your fault.'

'I don't know that. It wasn't as roadworthy as it should have been.'

119

'So how do you know all this?'

'Rob told me.'

'How does he know?'

'The police came to the yard.'

'Why didn't he fix the car before it was sold?'

'It was a cash job and they wanted it quick. They were going on holiday.'

'So it *wasn't* your fault. What did Danny say?'

'Told me not to be so sensitive. He reckoned the bloke must have been a bad driver. But what if the police find the car's to blame?'

'As Danny said, you only sold it to them.'

'Yes, but it'll be on my conscience for the rest of my life. What if the police blame me? I could be had up for manslaughter. I could go to prison.'

'Oh no.'

'What am I going to do?'

Janet didn't know how to comfort him.

'I'm not going back. I'm getting out of this business. I haven't got the stomach for it. I know Danny cuts corners, but I was the one who sold it. It's those kids. What if that bloke lives? His family's all gone.' His voice shook. He took hold of her hand. 'You do understand, don't you?'

'My poor love. Of course.' Janet put her arms round him. 'You don't have to go back there. We can manage for now, and after the wedding we can find somewhere round here to live.'

'After the wedding we're going to Canada.' It was a demand not a request.

Janet took a deep breath. 'What?'

'Don't you see? We can go to Canada and start a new life. Start afresh.'

'I don't want to.'

'I thought you loved me.'

120

'I do, but I can't go all that way away.'

'Why not? You don't get on that well with your parents so what's stopping you?'

'I'm sorry but I don't want to.'

'Give me one good reason.'

'I thought you'd given up that idea.'

'No, it's always been at the back of my mind. So, what d'you say?'

Janet sat and stared at him. What could she say? She turned her head and closed her eyes tight. She'd thought to hide it but this was the moment she had to tell him the truth. The moment she had been dreading. 'Mark, I'm really sorry but I can't go with you. You see I have to find someone.'

'Find someone? What're you talking about?'

'I've got to find my daughter.'

'What did you just say?'

'If I went to Canada I wouldn't be able to look for my daughter,' she said softly.

The silence filled the air for what seemed to Janet for ever.

He turned and faced her. 'Did I just hear you right? A daughter?'

'Yes. I have a daughter, Paula. She's two years old now and—'

'You've got a kid?' Mark looked at her long and hard, his face filled with anger. 'You were going to marry me and not tell me …? You, a vicar's daughter?' His voice was beginning to rise. 'You who's always been so prim and proper and wouldn't even let me put my hand up your skirt? So, when did this happen? And how many blokes have you had it off with then?'

'It was only one.'

'I bet.'

'It's true.'

'I don't believe this. You were going to make me wait till you got me well and truly hooked, then calmly announce it one day, I suppose?'

'It wasn't going to be like that.'

He sat staring out of the window.

'I'm sorry, Mark, but there never seemed the right time to tell—'

He turned on her like a caged animal. 'The right time. Don't give me that. Course there's been times. Ever since we started to go out. So how long ago did all this happen?'

She didn't answer.

'So how old were you?'

'Sixteen.'

'Does my mum know?'

She shook her head.

'How come you managed to keep this so quiet?'

'I was sent away.'

'Who sent you away?'

'My mother and father.'

'You could have said something before we got—'

'I couldn't, nobody knows.'

'I bet they don't. And you didn't trust me enough to tell me?'

'It wasn't like that.'

He gave a nasty laugh. 'Well, you certainly fooled all of them and me. So what did you do with the kid?'

'I had her adopted.'

'So that should be the end of it.'

'No, you see I promised her I'd find her one day.'

'When?'

'When she was born.'

'And she said, "Oh good, Mum. I'll look out for you." Don't talk so bloody daft.'

122

'I need to find her.'

'Why?'

'I must. She's mine and I love her,' she said softly.

'And what about me?'

'Mark, can't you see, I must find out if she's happy.'

'And what about me?' he repeated. 'I don't believe I'm hearing all this. I thought you loved me.'

'I do.'

'Well, you've got a bloody funny way of showing it.'

'I'm so sorry.'

'I bet you are. Sorry I found out about it.'

'I've got to find her.'

'And how do you reckon to do that?'

'I don't know. I thought that if we lived in London—that's where she was born—I might stand a better chance.'

'And I was the patsy who was going to look after you, feed you and clothe you while you were swanning about looking for your long-lost kid. Spare me the hearts and flowers, will you?'

'Mark, it wasn't going to be like that.' Tears filled her eyes.

'I bet your mum and dad nearly had a fit when you told 'em. Who's the lucky bloke who got your knickers off then?'

'Mark, you're being horrid.'

'I feel horrid. Bloody horrid. I don't need all this. It hasn't exactly been a good day. So who's the father then?'

'A fellow I met in London, at the Coronation. His name was Sam.'

123

'Why didn't he marry you?'

She didn't answer.

'Does he know?'

She shook her head.

He banged the steering wheel. 'I loved you, Janet. I thought you were sweet and when I heard about that awful accident this morning I thought: Janet will understand. We'll get married and fly off into the sunset together. It all seemed like a dream, but now it's turned into a bloody nightmare.'

Tears trickled down her cheeks. 'What are you going to do?'

'I'm going to Canada. On my own.'

'What about the wedding?'

'I'm not marrying you, you little tramp. What if I find out you've got other dark little secrets you're hiding from me? She isn't black, is she?'

Janet shook her head. 'I thought you'd understand. I made one silly mistake and it seems I'm going to suffer for it for the rest of my life.'

'That was your decision. There was me thinking I was marrying Little Miss Innocent.'

'Would it have made any difference if you had known about Paula?'

'Well, I wouldn't have been so quick to marry you, that's for sure. Now if you'll kindly leave my car I'll be off home. Don't bother to get in touch.'

'I thought you loved me.'

He didn't answer.

'What about all the preparations for our wedding?'

'That's your problem.' He started the engine.

'I didn't think you would be like this,' she cried.

'And I didn't think I'd be marrying someone else's cast-off.'

'Mark, please don't go. I love you.'

'But not enough to tell me the truth about yourself. Goodbye, Janet.'

She got out of the car and Mark roared off.

She sat on the wall and cried. What would happen to her now? She knew she loved Mark and she didn't want to spend the rest of her life alone. Tomorrow she would go and talk to him. Perhaps he would feel different after he'd had time to think about it. He wouldn't let her down. She had chosen a bad time to tell him about Paula but she couldn't go to Canada with him.

She wiped her eyes. She didn't want to go in and face her parents. She would go for a walk. Tomorrow she would see Mark, and, with luck, everything would turn out just fine.

CHAPTER TWELVE

Janet called out her good nights and managed to get to her bedroom without her mother noticing her red eyes.

She stood behind the closed door and gently ran her hands over her white brocade taffeta wedding dress. With its long sleeves and sweetheart neck it was just perfect. Her veil and headdress were in a brown cardboard box on the floor. Would she ever wear them?

Her thoughts ran to the reception in the flower-decked church hall and that lovely two-tier cake—could all that be wasted? Surely Mark would have second thoughts after he'd had a night to think about it. Tomorrow she would go to see him. If his mother found out what had been said she would also try to make him see sense. But what if he'd made up his mind and really didn't want to marry her? What would her parents say? Was she about to bring them more disgrace? How could she stay and hold her head up in this village now? What was going to happen to her?

She sat on the edge of the bed and, burying her head in her hands, let her tears fall unchecked. Why had she let this happen? It was her fault. She knew she loved Mark and didn't want to lose him. Was she being stupid? Should she let her obsession with her daughter stand in the way of a lifetime of happiness? Would she ever find her? She had no idea how she'd even start looking for her. Had she set herself a hopeless task? The great idea was beginning to seem ridiculous.

Tomorrow she'd tell Mark that she would abandon her idea of finding Paula and go to Canada with him. But would he still want her? And could she ever really forget her little girl?

After getting undressed and into bed, she began to write in her diary. She knew sleep wouldn't come easily. Her mind was in a turmoil. This had been a terrible day. That one night with Sam was going to haunt her for the rest of her life. She had gone over and over in her mind the words she would use when telling Mark about her daughter. But the answers she thought she'd get from him had borne no resemblance to reality.

She slid down the bed and cuddled her rabbit, wondering what Freda would have to say if Mark decided not to marry her. She felt sick—all the expense her parents had had, and she'd let down Mr and Mrs Scott too. She buried her head in the pillow and, once again, cried.

*   *   *

The banging on her bedroom door startled her. The bright sunlight streaming through the window made her blink. She had difficulty opening her puffy eyes.

'Janet, Janet? Are you awake?' Her mother's voice was loud and urgent.

'Yes, Mother.'

The door opened and her mother stood in the doorway. Janet could see Mrs Scott right behind her.

'My dear God. Just look at your face.'

She didn't have to, she knew her eyes were red and swollen.

Mrs Scott pushed past Irene Slater, waving a piece of paper. 'He's gone,' she shouted. 'My Mark's gone. What's happened between you two?' Her hand was trembling, causing the paper to rustle.

Janet began to cry again.

'Please, Mrs Scott. You can see Janet's upset. Give her a chance to answer.' Irene turned to her daughter. 'Have you two had a silly quarrel?'

Janet couldn't answer.

'It's all just pre-wedding nerves,' Janet's mother tried to soothe.

'Not according to this note. He's gone. He's taken his things and gone.'

That statement brought forth more tears from Janet.

'Gone? Where? When?' Irene Slater stood wide-eyed.

127

Mark's mother read from the paper. 'All it says is the wedding's off and I was to ask Janet to explain. Well? I'm waiting.'

Janet looked up at them. They looked like two lions waiting to pounce. What could she say?

'Could I talk to my mother on her own?' she said in a low broken voice.

Mrs Scott looked put out. 'Why?'

'I need to.'

Mrs Scott tutted and left the room, closing the door behind her.

'So?'

Janet blew her nose. 'The wedding's off because I told him about Paula.'

'Oh my God. You told him about that?'

Janet nodded.

'When?'

'Last night.'

'That was very silly of you, especially at this stage. Why did you wait till now? I told you to tell him earlier!'

'He wants to go to Canada.'

'So what's wrong with that?'

'I won't be able to look for my baby.' Tears flowed again.

Her mother seemed to grow before her eyes. She looked at the closed door and hissed. 'I have never heard anything so ridiculous in all my life. You threw away the chance of a lifetime of happiness on some silly whim.'

'It's not a silly whim.'

'Of course it is. Have you given a thought to the people . . .' she lowered her voice, 'the people who adopted your child? Do you think they would want you poking your nose into their affairs, that's of

128

course if you could find out where she was? Those kind of documents are very secret.'

'I must find her.'

'Stop talking nonsense. What if she doesn't want to be found? You can't go round ruining people's lives just because you feel like it.'

'I *must* find her.'

'Janet. Stop being so melodramatic and face facts. That is all in the past. You must think of her as dead.'

'I can't. She's not dead.'

'I'm beginning to lose my patience with you. Don't you think you've given your father and myself enough problems and now we've got this to contend with? You are a very selfish girl. Now what are we going to tell Mrs Scott?'

'The truth—'

'Oh no we are not. We will say that Mark got cold feet. That way the blame will not fall on your shoulders.'

'Mother, you are a wicked hypocrite.'

'How dare you? You have brought more than enough disgrace to this family. I am not going to stand by and see us all dragged into the gutter. Now you will do as I say.' She opened the door. 'You'd better come in and hear it from Janet.' She gave her daughter a sweet sickly smile.

Janet let out a deep sob and the tears fell. She looked at her mother. 'Mark had a bad day at work yesterday, and he wanted to get away. He wanted to go to Canada but I didn't, so he said the wedding's off.'

Mrs Scott sank on to the bed. 'Is that it? Is that the only reason?'

Janet nodded.

'Why wouldn't you go with him?'

'She has her reasons,' interrupted her mother.

'But why did he want to go that far away?' Mrs Scott sniffed and dabbed at her eyes. 'What has he done?'

'There was some kind of accident. It wasn't Mark's fault.'

'So why did he run off?'

Janet didn't answer.

Panic filled Mrs Scott's face. 'Oh my God. He hasn't killed somebody, has he? Are the police involved? Is he running away from the police?'

'No.' Janet was filled with guilt.

'He is all I had,' Mrs Scott wailed. 'He was my only child.'

'I know. I know how you must be feeling. I would have been upset too if our Janet had gone that far away.'

Mark's mother turned on Irene Slater. 'Did you know about this? Did you stop her?' She pointed to Janet.

'No, of course not. I'm just as upset as you. After all my daughter has been jilted.'

Janet couldn't stand it any longer. 'Go away!' she screamed. 'Leave me alone.' She threw herself back down on the bed and buried her head in the pillow.

With a look of disbelief they left the room.

*   *   *

It was late afternoon. Janet was still in bed. She lay staring at the window but not seeing anything. Her mother hadn't been back to her room. Janet's mind was going over and over last night. She loved Mark,

130

and now she had lost him. Outside the birds were singing, it was a warm sunny day, but Janet felt nothing. All their plans, their future—all of it gone, and it was her fault. What would happen to her now? Would she ever find happiness again?

Her mother brought in a cup of tea. She stood at the foot of the bed. 'So. What happens now?' she asked.

'I don't know.'

'Your father is a very unhappy man.'

'*He's* unhappy? How do you think I feel?'

'Don't answer back. He has been trying to comfort Mrs Scott.'

'I do feel sorry for her.'

'Let's face it, my dear child, it has been all your doing. All these people you have made unhappy—I don't know how we are going to face the village after this.'

Janet looked at her mother and knew she had to get away, away from these narrow-minded people. But where would she go? London was her only hope, and the only people she knew there were Freda and Charlie, and Danny. Aunt Rose was no good to her in the circumstances. She'd be bound to betray her to her mother.

'Janet, I think it's about time you came down and apologized to your father.'

'Yes, Mother.' When her mother left the room Janet got dressed and, after packing a few of her belongings into a small case, she scribbled a note. She stood and looked around her bedroom, wondering if she would ever see it again. She gently ran her fingers over her wedding dress and inwardly sobbed. Then quietly closing her bedroom door she crept down the stairs and left the house

131

that had been her home for all those years.

CHAPTER THIRTEEN

Once again Janet was on the train to London. This time she knew it would be for good. She could never see herself returning to Stowford; she knew her parents wouldn't want her back.

Her mind was churning. She couldn't believe Mark had gone. They could have sorted something out. Tears stung her eyes, she slumped in her seat and turned her head to look out of the window, so that no one would see her crying.

She had to be practical. Her first priority was to get a job and somewhere to live. She had fifty pounds in her Post Office savings book, but that wouldn't last long.

A sudden thought came to her. Had Mark gone to his flat? If he was there perhaps they could talk this through. She began to feel a lot happier at the idea of seeing Mark again and how she would greet him brought a slight blush to her cheeks. She wouldn't say no to any of his requests this time.

She sat up, feeling better. He had had plenty of time to mull over all that had happened and if they sat and talked it might all work out for the good. The thought of seeing him again filled her with longing and she knew that when they were alone she would love him with every part of her body. There was even a slight spring in her step as she made her way to his flat.

Luckily she didn't have to pass Danny's car sales. She wondered if Mark had been there to see him.

She didn't think so. What had happened yesterday had really upset him.

Mark's flat was the middle one in the large three-storey house. There wasn't a car outside, and when she rang the bell there was no reply. She rang again.

'If you're looking for the bloke that lived there you're too late. He left very early this morning,' a young man with a mass of hair and a beard said as he came up the stairs. He continued on up the next flight of stairs.

'Did he say if he would be back?'

The young man peered over the banisters. 'I didn't speak to him, just saw him loading up his car and driving off. Looked like he was going for good.'

Janet felt as if all the air had been taken from her body. She wanted to collapse. Mark had gone. 'Excuse me,' she shouted. 'Is there any way I can get hold of the key?'

'You can try number two. I think he keeps a spare in case of a fire,' came the now disembodied voice.

'Thanks.' She hurried down the stairs and banged on the door of number two, which was quickly opened.

'Yes?'

'Do you have a spare key to number four? You see my fiancé has gone out and forgotten to give me his.'

'Nice try.'

'I beg your pardon?'

'Christ, you ain't let the grass grow under yer feet, have you? I don't know what kinda grapevine works round these parts but as far as I'm concerned it ain't to let.'

'I know that, don't I? Mark Scott lives there.'

'He don't any more. Went this morning, and if you wanner rent the place you'd better see the landlord quick. I can give you his address if yer like?'

'No thanks. I do know where he lives.'

'Do yer now? Well, in that case I suggest you go round and see him a bit smartish—that's if you wants the place.'

'Did Mark leave any messages?'

'No.'

'Thank you.' She turned and walked away.

Mark had really gone. Gone from her life for ever. She moved across the road and sat in the cemetery. What was to become of her now?

The sun warmed her back as she sat there. She still couldn't think straight. Mark's leaving dominated her thoughts. Where had he gone? Could he get a plane to Canada just like that? She knew he had enough money for the sixty-pound fare he'd once told her about.

Gradually she began to realize she had to take care of herself. Should she go and see Freda? Maybe she would put her up for a few days till she got herself sorted out and pulled her thoughts together. She stood up. A party of mourners came through the gates to place flowers on a new grave. Their sad faces made her realize life was very short. She had lost Mark through her determination to find Paula. Now, looking for her daughter was all she had left and that gave her strength for the task that lay ahead.

*   *   *

134

'Jan! What're you doing here?' Freda had come to the door with pipe cleaner curlers sticking out all over her head.

'Can I come in?'

'Course.' She looked quizzically at Janet's small case. 'Bloody hell, what's gone wrong?'

Janet threw her case to the floor and, crying, hugged Freda tight.

'Oh my God. You'd better come in and tell me all about it.'

They moved into the living room.

'Is Charlie—'

'Na, he's tinkering with his other love, his bike. Now, what's this all about?'

Janet blew her nose. 'Mark has left me.'

'What? You've only got two weeks to the wedding.'

'I know.'

'What did he go and do that for?'

Freda didn't interrupt when Janet went into great detail about all what had happened the previous day.

'You must admit you did leave it a bit late to tell him about . . .' said Freda, giving Janet a knowing look.

'I know, but I can't go to Canada.'

'Jan, don't you think you're letting this thing about Paula get out of hand?'

'No. I was . . . I don't know.'

'Well, I think you have.'

'You sound like my mother.'

'She's right in some ways.'

'I don't need you to lecture me.' Janet was beginning to wish she hadn't come here.

'I feel sorry for Mark.'

135

'Why? He left me, remember,' said Janet sharply.

'Yes but he'd had a rotten day all round. You say he's left his flat an' all.'

Janet nodded.

'And you think he's gone to Canada?'

'Yes. He was very determined.'

'He had to be. Jan, if you don't mind me saying so I think you've been a silly cow.'

'Shut up. I don't want to hear.'

'Well, I think you should. This business with Paula is getting ridiculous.'

'Stop it. Stop it. First Mark, then my mother. I thought you might have had a bit of sympathy.'

'I have, but you've probably just chucked away a lifetime of happiness.'

'It might not have lasted a lifetime.'

'You know what I mean.' Freda was getting cross. 'You can't blame him. It must have been a quite a shock, poor bugger.'

'But what about me?' Janet stood crying. 'What am I going to do?'

Freda held her friend close.

'I came here 'cos I thought you'd be on my side.'

'I am.'

'Doesn't sound like it.'

'I don't suppose your mum's that happy about all this?'

'No, and as I said, it's poor Mrs Scott I feel sorry for.'

'It's rotten for all of you. Now take your coat off and I'll make us a cuppa. I expect you could do with one?'

'Yes, please.' She wiped her eyes.

As Janet followed her into the kitchen, Freda

136

turned and said light-heartedly, 'I'm bloody annoyed with you two. D'you know you've just done me out of wearing that lovely bridesmaid's frock.' She filled the kettle. 'I was really looking forward to tarting meself up and swanning down the aisle in me long frock. Bit different to me and Charlie's wedding.' She laughed. 'Here, what shall I do with it?'

'Please yourself.'

'Could keep in it case he comes back.'

'I don't think he will.'

'You never know, me girl. You never know.'

Janet gave her a slight smile. 'I was wondering if I could stay with you for a few days, just till I get myself sorted out.'

'I'd say yes, but I'll have to ask Charlie first. I know he's the strong silent type but he can be a bit of a funny bugger sometimes.' Freda noted Janet's sad face. 'But I'm sure it'll be OK. Say, couldn't you take over Mark's flat, just for a month or so till you got on your feet?'

'I don't know. The rent's twelve pounds a month.'

'So have you got any money?'

'Yes.'

'Enough for a month's rent?'

'Yes, but I've got to eat and I haven't got a job.'

'Well, you won't have any trouble getting a job round these parts. Do you know where the landlord lives?'

Janet nodded. 'Danny took me there once when Mark was ill.'

'If I was you I'd go and try to see him. Places are like gold dust round here.'

Janet looked at her watch. 'It's too late now. I

could go and see Danny on Monday. Would you come with me?'

'Sorry, I can't. I have to go to work.'

'Yes, of course. Freda, do you think Charlie will mind if I stay till say, Monday?'

'I'm sure I can twist his arm. Now drink up and wash your face. I'll make you a quick sandwich.'

Janet suddenly realized she was very hungry. She hadn't eaten anything all day.

'I've got to get ready after that as we're going over to see Charlie's mum. She ain't that well.'

'Look, if it's any trouble . . .'

'I'll pop down and have a word with his nibs.'

Freda was soon back. 'Charlie said that's OK. We don't know what time we'll be back. You can kip down on the sofa. Is that all right?'

'That will be fine.' She kissed Freda's cheek.

'What's that for?' asked Freda as she put her hand to her face.

'Thank you for being my friend.'

Freda grinned. 'Daft 'a' p'orth.'

Janet was still awake when Freda and Charlie came home but she pretended to be asleep. She didn't want to talk any more and risk another lecture.

The next day Charlie tinkered with his bike and after dinner Freda said she wanted to do her washing, so Janet went for a walk. The conversation was a little strained when Charlie was around—as Freda had said, he was the strong silent type, which made him difficult to know—and Janet was pleased when it was time for bed.

*   *   *

138

It was ten o'clock when Janet walked into Danny's office.

'Jan! What on earth are you doing here?' He was swinging back in his chair and quickly sat up. 'Is he outside?'

Janet shook her head.

'Look, if you've come to ask me to take him back, well, I'd have to think about that. We had a big bust-up on Friday and he said some bloody awful things.' He stopped. 'What's wrong?'

Janet stood clutching her handkerchief. She wiped her eyes.

'I haven't come to ask for Mark's job back. I need some help.'

Danny got to his feet and hurried round his desk. He put his arm round her shoulders. She buried her head in his chest and cried.

'There, there.' He patted her back. 'Now tell me what this is all about.' He led her to his chair, while he sat on the corner of his desk.

She told him about everything, including Paula. She had nothing to lose now. When she'd finished he let out a long low whistle.

'Bloody hell. What a mess. I must say you are a bit of a dark horse. Got a daughter then?' He smiled. 'So, how can I help you?'

'First I've got to find somewhere to live. Now that Mark's gone I thought about taking over his flat.'

'That could be a start. You'd have to watch out, though. I think only blokes live there.'

'It will only be for a while till I can get a job and find a more suitable place of my own.'

'That shouldn't be too hard. There's plenty of work round here. What did you do?'

139

'I worked in an office.'

'What, typing and that sort of stuff?'

She nodded.

'I might be able to help you with that one.'

'I was wondering if you wouldn't mind taking me to see Mark's landlord so I can take over the tenancy?'

'Why not? We can go now, if you like. Things slow down a bit on Monday mornings. He'll want a month in advance. Do you have enough?'

She shook her head. 'Not in cash, but I've got money in my Post Office book. Do you think he'll want key money?'

'He didn't from Mark.' He looked at his watch. 'Don't worry about that for now. I can lend you the rent. You can pay me back when you've got it, OK?'

She nodded. 'Thanks, Danny. This is really kind of you.'

'That's what friends are for, and I hope I can be your friend, Jan.'

She gave him a slight smile.

'Right then, let's be off. Where are you going to stay tonight if we can't get the keys?'

'I'm staying with my friend Freda at the moment—we met in the home for unmarried mothers. I was there last night but it's not a lot of fun sleeping on a sofa.'

'So you went to her first?'

'I didn't have any choice.'

'You had me.'

'I don't know where you live.'

'We will have to rectify that, won't we?'

She didn't reply.

140

*　　　*　　　*

Janet clutched the rent book with her name on it. She almost gave out a sigh of relief when he didn't mention key money as Mark had once told her that sometimes it could be as much as fifty pounds. This was her first hurdle over.

'If you can hang on till I close up, I can take you to your friend's to collect your things, then bring you back,' said Danny as he drove to the flat.

'Thanks all the same, Danny, but you've been more than kind and I couldn't put you to any more trouble.'

'It's no trouble. In fact I would enjoy it. It ain't always fun being a bachelor and living on your own.'

'I can't see you being on your own for long. You must have plenty of girlfriends at the pubs and clubs you go to.'

'Don't always want that.'

They reached the flat.

'I'm all right now. I'll just get the keys from the man downstairs, and tidy the place up before I go over to Freda's.'

'If you hang on till about five I'll call back and take you. In fact I insist, and we'll go for something to eat as well.' He leant across and opened the car door. 'See you at five.'

She stood on the kerb and watched him go. Then she walked up the stairs and knocked on number two's door.

When the man she'd seen earlier opened the door she said confidently, 'I have come for the key to number four. I have the rent book to prove I am renting the flat.'

141

'Certainly, love. I'm Frank and you are . . . ?'

'Miss Slater.'

'Don't make too much noise as you're right above me, and I don't like a lot of noise.'

'Don't worry. I intend to be very quiet.'

'Very well, Miss Slater.' He handed her the key.

As she opened her door her heart began pounding. She closed the door and leant against it. Tears filled her eyes as she stood and looked round the room. She should have been sharing this with Mark.

She was now in charge of her life, but was this what she wanted? She knew one thing: she didn't want to be on her own.

She began to clear away some of Mark's mess. The ashtray was overflowing and the room smelt musty. She opened the window to let in some fresh air. The flowers in the cemetery were bright and colourful. The bedroom was untidy with bedding all over the floor. She had to get some new sheets and cleaning materials. 'But first things first,' she said out loud. 'The kitchen and a cup of tea.'

She was so engrossed in her cleaning and sorting out that when the bell rang she jumped out of her skin.

'Danny,' she said on opening the door. 'What are you doing here so early?'

'It's five thirty, and you've got a dirty face.'

She laughed and looked at her watch. 'So it is, you'd better come in and wait for me to get ready.'

'I've brought you a house-warming present.'

'That's very kind of you, but you shouldn't have.'

'Well, I have. Open it.' He handed her a cardboard box.

'A radio. My very own radio. Oh Danny, thank

142

you so much.' She lightly kissed his cheek.

'Thought you might need something to cheer you up. Right, now go and tart yourself up, then we can be off.'

'Have you seen the state of that bathroom?'

'I used to live here, remember?'

*   *   *

Freda was overjoyed at Janet's news.

'I can lend you a pair of sheets for now.'

'Thanks. I can go shopping tomorrow.

'Look, I was going to take Jan out for a bite to eat,' said Danny. 'So how about you and Charlie coming with us?'

Freda grinned. 'We don't wanner play gooseberry.'

'It'll be a kind of thank you for looking after Jan.'

'Well, if you insist.'

'We going in that posh car you've got outside?' asked Charlie.

'Why not?'

'I like those Vauxhall Crestas. Very smart,' said Charlie.

'Is that all right with you?' Janet asked Freda.

'I should say so.'

Janet felt a pang of guilt when they were sitting in the cafe Danny had chosen, laughing and joking. She had just been jilted and here she was enjoying herself. Freda caught sight of her as her expression changed.

'I'm off to the ladies. Coming?' she asked Janet.

'What are you suddenly looking like you've lost a tanner and found an 'a'penny for, my girl?' Freda peered into the mirror and rubbed her little finger over her bright red lips.

'I feel guilty. I don't know where Mark is and here I am having a good time.'

'Well, that was up to him.'

'I know, but it was all my fault.'

'So, are you going to spend the rest of your life carrying all this burden on your shoulders and worrying yourself into your box then?'

'I don't know.'

'If you want my advice, for what it's worth, you wanner start thinking of yourself and your future for a change.'

'I do know that.'

'Right, let's start with tonight.' Freda went into a cubicle. 'By the way, that Danny's a bit of all right. Not bad-looking and worth a bob or two. You could do worse,' she called out.

'A man like Danny's the last thing I'm looking for.'

CHAPTER FOURTEEN

For two weeks Janet had been shopping, hunting out bargains, and cleaning. During the day she was happy, but at night when she went to bed cuddling her rabbit, the bed that she and Mark should have been sharing and she found it hard to control her tears. She hadn't realized how much she loved him, and she missed him so much. Had he gone to Canada? How would she ever find out? Did his mother know?

It was Saturday. This should have been the

happiest day in her life, her wedding day. She felt so miserable, and mooned about all morning. At two o'clock, when she should have been walking down the aisle, she wondered if Mark would be thinking that, too. Were her parents upset? And what about Mr and Mrs Scott? In some ways they had lost a son. Tears trickled down Janet's cheeks. She had to get out of the flat, so she went and sat in the cemetery.

Sitting in the warm sunshine, Janet watched lonely people putting flowers on the graves of their loved ones. Some did a little tidying up, while others stood quietly and dabbed at their eyes. Although she felt as if she'd had a bereavement she knew she had to cheer up, as Danny had promised to take her, Freda and Charlie out to a show tonight and a meal after.

*   *   *

'Thanks, Danny, that was a really smashing evening,' said Freda as they said their good nights. She pulled Janet to one side. 'You wanner hang on to him. He's all right, and so thoughtful,' she whispered.

Janet was on her guard when Danny took her home, even though she needed a shoulder to cry on. She knew that if he was kind and loving she would let her heart rule her head and probably give herself to him. That could cause a lot of complications. He must have sensed her feelings because he behaved like the perfect gentleman, and didn't even ask to come in for a coffee.

'Did he go back home with you?' asked Freda eagerly when they met up the following Saturday.

'No. I must start to look for a job soon,' said Janet, changing the subject.

'Where?'

'I don't know. It'll have to be in an office.'

'Remember that Danny said he'd help.'

'I can't let him help me any more. He's been very good already.'

'He's got a soft spot for you, you know.'

'I like him, but that's all.'

'Funny, ain't it? All that time you was with Mark and you didn't tell him about Paula, yet you told Danny almost at once.'

'Well, I was very vulnerable when that happened.'

'He didn't cast you aside, though, did he?'

'But it was slightly different; he wasn't going to marry me.'

'Not then he wasn't, but give him half a chance and I reckon he'd be there.'

Janet blushed. 'Don't talk daft. That's the last thing I want right now. Besides, he's a confirmed bachelor.'

'What, with all the tarts that hang around him?'

'He's not interested in getting married.'

'That's what you think.'

'What's he said to you?'

'Nothing.'

Twice now they had been out as a foursome and now Janet was worried in case Danny had confided in Freda. 'Has he said anything to you?'

'No, course not. It's just me matchmaking.'

But Janet wasn't so sure.

'Look at the place he lives in.'

They had been to his house at Clapham once when he had to pick up some papers. He had

146

showed them around. It was a lovely house with a large garden and it overlooked the common but, as Freda had said, it needed a woman's touch.

*   *   *

The job Janet found was in the office of a large West End department store, and the money was twice what she had been getting in Horsham.

The girls were friendly and helpful and it didn't take her long to settle down.

She wasn't happy in Mark's flat and a year later found herself a flat in Wandsworth. It was very basic, almost the same size as Mark's. She did worry at the time that if he ever came back he wouldn't know where to look for her. Would he go to Danny to try to find her? She knew that could never be and he might even be married by now. She often thought about her parents and would have liked to find out how they were getting on but her pride prevented that. She had sent them birthday and Christmas cards, and included her address, but had never received any replies.

As she looked round her new home she knew this wasn't for ever. She was going to save hard and one day buy herself a house.

On Saturday afternoons the big West End shops shut, so Janet would meet Freda, and they would have a sandwich together.

'Seen much of Danny lately?' Freda asked one day.

'Not for a few weeks.'

'You know you shouldn't keep giving him the elbow. He could be your way to a life of luxury.'

'You know I'm not looking for any relationship

147

at the moment.'

'Still, it don't hurt to keep your options open, does it?'

'No, I suppose not.' But Janet knew that wasn't what she wanted in her life. She was enjoying her freedom, such as it was, and didn't want to be tied down to anyone, not while she still thought about Mark. And besides, she had a task; she was determined to find her daughter, but where to start?

As time moved on, more and more Janet found herself drawn to Southwark.

She felt she needed to be near where Paula was born. On Sundays she would stand outside the place she and Freda had called home for all those months. It was still run by the nuns and, keeping out of sight, she would watch Sister Verity and Sister James walk the mothers-to-be in twos to church. There weren't so many girls there now; perhaps that was because being pregnant out of wedlock wasn't such a sin these days.

She would also go to the park and watch the children playing round the pond. She would look at little girls' bare feet, hoping to see a heart-shaped birth mark on their left foot. Sometimes if she saw a child whom she thought could have looked like Paula she would even call out her name. But was her daughter still called Paula? And did her adoptive parents live in this area? At times her quest seemed nothing more than a hopeless dream.

*　　　*　　　*

Over the next four years Janet blossomed and became more confident. She worked hard and saved, all the time planning and searching. When she found a neat terraced house to buy in Southwark she was ecstatic. It had two bedrooms, a front room, dining room, kitchen and bathroom. Everything she had ever wanted, except there was no Mark or Paula to share it with.

'It's lovely,' said Freda, as they moved from room to room. 'And look at that garden.'

'It's a bit overgrown but I'll soon get it into shape. I was so lucky to get it.'

'That's as may be, but I still reckon it's a bit of a millstone round your neck. Couldn't see my Charlie ever buying a house and landing himself with a lot of debt.'

'It's what I want.'

'Na. My Charlie would rather have a landlord look after the repairs.'

It wasn't long before her house contained many things some people considered luxuries. She had a television, fridge and a record player. She would go to the pictures, buy Cliff Richard and Pat Boone records, but she was always alone at night.

During these years she had been out with men whom she'd met at work, or girls in the office had persuaded her to go along with them on blind dates, but she knew deep down nobody could take Mark's place.

Danny had taught her and Freda to drive. They had had a lot of fun together and he was just as pleased as Janet when she passed her test first time. Freda had to have a couple of tries, but she got there in the end.

'Could teach you a lot of other things as well,' he had said to Janet at the time.

She had laughed that off. Now when she looked

149

out of her front room window and saw her dear little Mini in the road, she was very proud. She was concerned when Danny sold it to her, remembering his past reputation and the accident that had sent Mark running away.

'Mark was daft over that affair. The cops said it was the driver's fault. Seems he only had a provisional licence; he hadn't even passed his test. Besides that, I've got a bit more respectable since then. This is a good clean little motor, and it's in very good condition,' he had assured her.

Janet had to admit he did now have a showroom, a new office and an office cleaner. He was almost respectable.

Janet didn't like to get involved too much with the girls at work, and in the beginning, whenever possible, she kept her distance from Danny. But as the years went on she went out more and more with Danny, Freda and Charlie in a foursome. They spent many Christmases and New Years at Danny's, and he'd use any excuse to have a party. Janet was very fond of him and he was always the perfect host but she had made it perfectly clear she would never stay at his house alone.

At first he had asked her why, and she told him she didn't want to get into another relationship.

'You still carrying a torch for Mark?'

She didn't reply.

'I would never hurt you, Jan.'

'I know.'

'Give it time; you may change your mind.'

He was kind, but she knew she wouldn't. They went to see shows and have a meal occasionally, just the two of them, but that was as far as she would allow their relationship to go. She was very

150

fond of him as a friend and that was what she wanted him to stay.

Freda still shared Janet's life and most Saturdays would find them spending the afternoon shopping and chatting.

'I went to the hospital the other day,' said Janet one Saturday when they were sitting in a fashionable new coffee bar.

'Why? What's wrong with you?' asked Freda, her voice full of alarm.

'Nothing. It was the place where Paula was born. I told them me and my husband wanted to adopt a baby.'

'And what did they have to say to that?'

'That I would have to go to the welfare office.'

'And did you?'

Janet nodded.

'And?' said Freda, eagerly sitting forward.

'I had to fill in a form and send it back to them, including my marriage certificate.'

'Well, you could easily get one of those.'

'How?'

'Marry Danny, of course.'

'Don't start on that again. Besides, he's got that Tina on his arm now.'

'Yer, but how long will that last?'

'I think he's quite serious.'

'One good thing—she don't have to worry about getting pregnant, not with this 'ere pill everyone's talking about.' Freda continued stirring her frothy coffee.

'Don't you like Tina?'

'I think she's great. Charlie likes her and she does enjoy a good laugh. Just so long as she's not leading Danny on or is after his money.'

151

'I think Danny's too wise to fall for anyone like that.'

'I hope so.'

'Would you go on the pill?'

'Wouldn't have to.'

'Why's that?'

Freda sat back. 'Funny, ain't it? Me mum could have 'em like shelling peas. I have one and muck up me works.'

'I didn't know that.'

'I only found out after I went for tests. We wanted a kid and nothing happened. Charlie said it wasn't him. That's when they told me.'

'I'm really sorry,' said Janet with genuine concern. 'Was Charlie very upset about it?'

'You should know Charlie be now. He don't get upset about anything; takes it all in his stride. He just said what is to be will be and left it at that. Except he was bloody annoyed at all the money he'd spent on French letters.' She laughed.

'It's still sad, though,' said Janet.

'Got over it now.' Freda continued drinking her coffee, but Janet could see it still distressed her to talk about it.

*   *   *

It was a chance remark in the staff cloakroom one lunchtime that excited Janet and sent her looking for Paula in another direction.

'Which one of you is getting married on Saturday?' asked Janet to a bunch of giggling juniors.

'Me,' said a girl with the new short hairstyle.

'Are you having a white wedding?'

152

'No. Well, yes, in a way. Me mum ain't very pleased about it.'

'Why's that, are you . . . you know . . . ?'

All the girls laughed.

'No, nothing like that,' said the bride-to-be. 'It's just that my Wayne's a teddy boy and I've got this smashing little white mini and white boots, and we're getting hitched in the registry office over at Southwark. Wayne's sister used to work there. Mum wanted me to have it in the church, but we ain't like that.'

Janet stopped applying her make-up and looked at the girl. 'That must have been a very interesting job your future sister-in-law had.'

'Dunno, never asked her.'

'What did she do?'

'Just filled in forms, I think. Something to do with births and deaths.'

'It must be real sad having people sitting telling you about someone who's died,' said one of her friends.

'Dunno, didn't ask.'

'I live near there. What time are you getting married?' asked Janet.

'Eleven.'

'I'll come and wish you luck.'

*   *   *

'I'm changing my job,' said Janet out of the blue to Freda on Saturday as they wandered around the shops.

'So where you off to?'

'I'm going to work in Southwark's registry office.'

'Is it a good job?'

'I don't know.'

'You'll miss your discounts.'

'I don't care about that.'

'What's brought this on? You've been in that office for years.'

'I know. I feel I need a change.' Janet felt she had to tell her the real reason. 'Freda, I might be able to find out who adopted Paula.'

'What? You're becoming obsessed with this bloody thing. First you move to Southwark, now you're going to work there. I hope you're getting good money. Don't forget you've got a mortgage to worry about.'

'I know that.'

'I tell you, Jan, you'll finish up like some silly old maid that's gone out of her mind over something that happened in the past,' said Freda. 'You'll end up like that potty woman in that film, you know, the one with John Mills in.'

'Thanks. I think you mean like Miss Havisham in *Great Expectations*.'

'If you say so. What if you do find out about Paula—do you think they want you interfering in their lives?'

'Don't start on that again.'

'She's what, eight, now?'

'Nine.'

'So they might have all moved away. They might even have gone abroad, there's a lot going to Australia now.'

'You're a right wet blanket.'

'I'm only saying.'

'Well, at least I might be able to find out her name,' said Janet defiantly.

154

'And what good will that do?'
'It's a start.'
'You ain't gonner give up, are you?'
'Never.'

*   *   *

Janet was nervous on her first day at her new job. The building was Victorian and from the outside looked elegant and overbearing, and inside, with the grand staircase and stained-glass window, it had an air of elegance and forboding. The staff seemed friendly enough and were eager to show her her duties in the typing room. At the end of the first week she felt more relaxed and was able to ask a few questions.

'Are all the birth certificates kept here?' she casually asked Helen, a fellow worker, in their tea break.

'Most of 'em.'

Janet had to be on her guard and choose her words carefully. She didn't want to arouse any suspicions.

'A lot of stuff goes on to Somerset House for storage,' volunteered Helen.

'Oh, I see. I bet they get musty.'

'Them that's kept in the basement do, and damp. It's so bloody cold down there in the winter. I hate it when I'm sent down there to look for something. You could be in there for days and the spiders are as big as me hand.' She shuddered. 'It musta been really awful in the war when they had to go down there if there was a raid on.'

'It might have saved a lot of lives.'

'Yer. Even so, I reckon old sourpuss knows what

I think of it and that's why she always seems to pick on me.'

Janet could hardly contain herself. How could she get into the basement? Spiders and the cold wouldn't put her off!

Old sourpuss was the name the girls had given the supervisor, Miss Wilson, a tall thin woman in her mid-forties, who stood very upright and peered over her half-glasses at the girls under her.

Every time she came into the room holding a slip of paper, she would glance around, her sharp eyes seeking out one of the girls to send her off to the basement to look for something that was wanted. Janet was always hoping to catch her eye. She had to find out more about the layout of the floors below. But she had to bide her time.

*   *   *

Two months later Janet took her Mini to Danny's to be serviced.

'Got some good news,' he said when Janet walked into his office. 'I'm marrying Tina.'

'I'm so pleased for you,' said Janet, throwing her arms round his neck and kissing his cheek. 'She's a nice girl.'

'She's up the duff.'

Janet laughed. 'I never thought you'd get caught.'

Danny smiled. 'I don't mind really. She's not a bad looker.'

'She's lovely.' She liked Tina and they'd got on well on the few occasions they had met. She was good fun and good for Danny.

'Yer. It was that blonde hair and baby blue eyes

156

that did it, not to mention those lovely long legs. She was the greatest thing to walk into me office, but I never thought I'd end up marrying her.'

Janet laughed again. 'I'm really very happy for you. When's the great day?'

'Can't leave it too long. She wants a white wedding and all the trimmings.'

'And why not?'

'We thought in August, August the eighth. She shouldn't be that big be then.'

'When's the baby due?'

'Beginning of February.'

'My birthday's in February.'

'When?'

'The nineteenth.'

'I'll tell her to make it then.'

'I can't see you as a dad.'

'Why not? I'll make a very good dad.'

'I'm sure you will.'

'I'm taking her to Jersey for our honeymoon.'

'Lucky old Tina, but does she know what she's letting herself in for?'

'Don't worry, she keeps me in check. It's her family that I'm scared of.'

'You, scared? I never thought I'd hear that.'

'No, they're not bad really. Just keeping an eye on Tina.'

'You can't blame them.'

Danny straightened his tie. 'Mind you, if you'd played your cards right it could have been you.'

'I am very fond of you, Danny, but I don't think I would like to spend all the rest of my days with you.'

'Fair enough. But you and Freda and Charlie will come to the wedding.'

'Just you try and keep us away.'

*   *   *

It was a few days later that Janet got the chance to go to the registry office basement.

Miss Wilson walked in and looked around as usual, holding a slip of paper.

Janet held her breath and smiled sweetly at her.

'Miss Perrin, you could take Miss Slater with you to help you,' she said, handing the paper to Helen.

Janet jumped up.

Helen sighed as she took the note from Miss Wilson.

'And don't take all day,' they heard her call as they left the room.

Their high heels clattered down the stone stairs. With every step it got colder, and Helen's face got longer.

Helen pushed open the large door and switched on the light. A single lightbulb, hanging from the ceiling on a brown flex lit up the room. It cast eerie shadows round and the room felt chilly and dismal. The walls had water stains running down them and Janet was sure stalactites were beginning to form on the brick ceiling.

Her heart sank as she stood and looked at the rows and rows of shelves lining the walls. They were full of boxes and bundles of paper tied up with different coloured tape. Metal filing cabinets with deep drawers filled one wall along with the cobwebs that hung like curtains. In the middle was a large table. You could see where people had put the boxes by the marks left in the dust.

'Where do you start?' she asked.

158

'You wouldn't believe it but this lot are in years, then in quarters.'

'What name are we looking for?'

'Miller. It's a death certificate.' She looked at the paper. 'Dated June the sixth 1949. The bloke who's asked for it probably wants to find out if he's been left a fortune.'

'Are all the birth certificates in here as well?'

'Those from this parish are in the other part of the basement.'

'So what do we have? You know, the ones we have at home?'

'Dunno. Think they might be copies.'

Helen began looking and pulling out different boxes.

Janet began wandering along the shelves.

'You're suppose to be helping me,' shouted Helen. 'Now start by going through this lot.' She threw a bundle of folders on to the table, making the dust fly.

Janet began looking through them, but her mind was elsewhere. Was Paula's birth certificate somewhere down here? Where were her adoption papers? Was she still called Paula or had they changed her first name? She wanted to ask Helen about adoption papers but she had to gain her confidence first. She felt sick with anticipation. She was so near, but at the same time her mission still appeared to be an impossible task.

How could she get down here alone?

CHAPTER FIFTEEN

The sun was shining and everybody was in a happy mood when Tina, looking lovely, walked down the aisle. The long train on her dress was held up by the two smallest of the six bridesmaids. Their dresses were a delicate shade of blue. Although Tina only had one sister there were plenty of cousins, and she had told Janet that she dare not offend anyone.

Freda and Janet were quietly shedding a tear.

'What are you crying about?' asked Janet, keeping her voice very low.

'Thinking about the wedding we didn't have. What about you?'

'The same. But you did get married.'

'Just about.'

For a moment or two they held each other's hands and, after giving them a squeeze, exchanged smiles.

The reception was on a grand scale. Janet met Danny's parents, who were quiet and very nice. Tina's parents were real cockneys, very loud, and determined to enjoy themselves.

''Allo, love,' said Tina's mother, plonking herself next to Janet. 'It's Jan, ain't it?'

'Yes.'

'I'm all outta breath. Still, I do like a dance.' She was a rather large lady. 'My Tine tells me you're a friend of young Danny?'

'Yes, I've known him for years. I'm very fond of him.'

'I'm pleased about that. Got a lovely house.

She's done all right. Pity she's up the duff, but just as long as he looks after her that's all I worry about. And Gawd help him if he don't. As you can see we're a large family.'

Janet smiled and nodded. 'Don't worry. Danny will look after her.'

'He'd better. Don't they make a lovely couple?' Tina's mother smiled as she watched Danny and Tina dancing together. 'I'm really looking forward to being a granny. They're off to Jersey, you know?'

'Yes, Danny told me.'

'Flying as well. You wouldn't get me up in one of them there things. I'd be worried to death it'd fall out of the sky.'

'I think they're very safe.'

Tina's mum sang along with the band a bit, then suddenly said: 'I hear your feller as good as left you at the altar. That must 'ave been rotten.'

'Yes, it was.'

'Went off to Canada then, didn't he?'

Janet winced. Had Danny told them everything?

'My Tine said it was something to do with a car. Silly sod. And you wouldn't go with him. Couldn't have been up to much to run off like that. He couldn't have been the right one for you.'

'I'll never know.'

'Never mind, love.' She gently tapped Janet's hand. 'You're a nice-looking girl. One day someone will come along and sweep you off yer feet.' She looked across at Danny and Tina and inclining her head towards them added. 'Mind you, if 'e had done anythink like that my lot would have killed him.'

'You don't have to worry about Danny.'

'I hope not—for his sake.'

161

'Jan, want to dance?' Danny was standing over them.

'Why not?'

When she was in Danny's arms, she said, 'You've married into a great family.'

'They ain't bad.'

'But beware.' She laughed. 'Tina's mum's just been telling me what they'll do to you if you don't behave.'

Danny laughed. 'Don't. Even the thought of it brings tears to me eyes.'

Janet laughed with him. 'I know you'll be good to her. You've always been a good friend to me, Danny.'

'And I always will be. Me being married won't make any difference.'

* * *

It was another six months before Janet was able to get into the basement at the office on her own. She had worked hard to get promotion and win Miss Wilson's approval. Her excitement had increased when she'd learnt that some adoption papers were held here. Every time someone went downstairs Janet asked to go with them. She would glance around and poke about, trying not to arouse too much suspicion.

Miss Wilson did ask her once why she was so eager to go down to the records and she had told her she wanted to learn all aspects of the job, which fortunately seemed to satisfy her. Miss Wilson also stressed that whatever she saw and read should be treated with the strictest confidence.

As Janet managed to work her way up through

162

the system she was soon in charge of her section and able to move about freely. Then the day came when she was asked to find a birth certificate for 1954. She could hardly contain her excitement as she went to the basement alone.

She didn't care about the cold; she was flushed with elation. Pulling her cardigan round her she went to the 1954s and took out a file. Quickly she rummaged through it. Paula had been registered under the name of Samuel. There were a lot of Samuels.

The clatter of shoes on the stone stairs made her put the file back.

It was Helen. 'Ain't you found that yet?' she said, bursting into the room. 'Old sourpuss is yelling for you.'

'Yes, I was just coming.' Janet had made sure she found what she had been sent down for before she started looking for herself. She put the precious box that could hold all the secrets back on the shelf. She knew which one to go to next time.

'D'you know, I reckon you're up to no good down here,' said Helen as they made their way upstairs.

'Why? What d'you mean?' asked Janet in alarm.

Helen laughed. 'Don't sound so worried. I reckon you're starting a witches' coven down here, and sneak down here to chant all sorts of wicked things and stick pins in dolls of people you don't like.' She screamed with laughter at her joke.

Janet also laughed. 'Damn. I've been rumbled.'

*   *   *

It took another two weeks for Janet finally to get

163

her hands on Paula's birth certificate. And when at last she did, she stood looking down at the paper in her hand. This was the only thing to tell her her daughter did exist and that she was her mother. She quickly put it into her pocket.

At home she studied it. She noted the adoption number in the corner. She had to find those papers now.

That took another week, but the task wasn't hard as she knew that all the adoption papers were numbered.

With trembling hands she found what she had been looking for and without even glancing inside the envelope she quickly put it into her pocket. She felt sick and her heart beat fast and loud, so loud she thought everybody would hear it when she returned to her office. She wanted to shout out, tell someone. She secretly curled her fingers round the priceless papers. She knew what she was doing was wrong but she had come this far and she wasn't going to let this opportunity pass.

The rest of the day seemed to go on for ever and she couldn't wait to get home.

Once there, she quickly closed her front door and, without removing her coat, sat with tears in her eyes as she studied the paper in her hand. Paula had been adopted by a Mr and Mrs Brook. She was still Paula and they lived in Streatham. Janet eagerly waited for Saturday when she could show Freda.

*   *   *

'You took a bloody chance pinching this. What if you'd got caught?' Freda was reading the certificate.

'Well, I didn't.'

'So what you gonner do?'

'I'll put it back when I've finished with it.'

'I meant now.'

'I'm going over there.'

'What, just knock on the door and say, "Oh, by the way, I'm Paula's real mum and I'd like to take her home"?'

'Don't talk daft.'

'Well, what then?'

'I'll go and make sure they still live there first. If not, perhaps a neighbour will know if they've moved. I'm so excited. I'm going tomorrow, will you come with me?'

'I can't.'

'Why not?'

'Me and Charlie's got to go and see his mum.'

Janet felt deflated. Nine years she had waited to get this far.

'Why can't you go on your own?'

'I just need moral support.'

'Can't you wait till the Sat'day after?'

'No.'

'Well, please yourself, but be careful.'

*   *   *

Janet peered through the windscreen of her Mini as she slowly made her way along Dover Road, looking for number twenty. They were nice houses, expensive-looking. Her heart leapt when she drove slowly past it. She stopped and sat looking behind her.

Now she was here what should she do? What

165

could she say? All these years she had carefully worded her first sentence to her daughter but now she had cold feet. What if Paula was happy? Should she upset her life?

She got out of the car and made her way up the path. She knocked on the door.

'Yes?' A large plump woman had pulled open the door and stood in the doorway. 'Yes?' she said again.

'I'm sorry to trouble you,' said Janet, feeling her bravado slipping away. 'But I was looking for a Paula Brook.'

'The Brooks moved away years ago.' Janet wanted to sink to the ground. 'Do you know where they went to?'

'Allan!' she screamed out. 'Where did the Brooks go to?'

'Dunno,' came the answer from within. 'Up Lewisham way, I think.'

'Yes, that's right,' said the woman. 'He moved with the job, bank manager or something. Bit of a stuck-up chap; the little girl seemed nice enough, though.'

'Do you happen to know which bank he works for?' asked Janet.

'Can't say I do. Sorry I can't be of much help.'

'That's all right. Thank you.' She made her way back to her car. Was that Paula she was talking about? Janet smiled. She said was a nice kid.

She would have the day off tomorrow and go to every bank in Lewisham.

*   *   *

Janet was up early on Monday morning and made

166

her way to the High Street. She had gone over her plan a hundred times. At ten o'clock she was going to start at one end of Lewisham High Street and gradually work her way along. It shouldn't be that difficult and she had till three o'clock. She would go up to the counter and ask if a Mr Brook worked here. If the answer was yes, she would try and see him, then at the end of the day she would follow him home. It was going to be that easy.

Her step was light as she began at the first bank.

The banks were very busy and she had to wait in line. By lunchtime she hadn't had any luck, and was only halfway along the road. Then it happened.

'Yes,' said the young lady at the counter. 'We do have a Mr Brook here. Have you an appointment?'

Janet shook her head. 'No. But will he be free at all today?'

'I'll find out for you.'

Janet was trembling. She couldn't believe how well it was going, and if he couldn't see her today she would come back tomorrow.

The teller returned. 'Mr Brook has a few minutes at two thirty, would that be convenient?'

'Yes, yes, that will be fine.'

'Could I have your name, please?'

'Slater. Miss Slater.' Paula's name hadn't been Slater so that shouldn't arouse any suspicion. 'Thank you,' she said cheerfully, walking away. She felt like singing out loud. A clock chiming told her she had two hours to wait, so that called for a cup of tea.

At two thirty she was ushered into Mr Brook's office. He was seated behind a large desk and looked up when she entered. He raised his thick bushy eyebrows and looked at her very intently.

Janet felt uncomfortable. 'Take a seat,' he said, recovering his composure. 'Now what was it you wanted to see me about?'

He was a very upright man. There was something about him that reminded Janet of her father.

'I was told by a friend to see you as I want to open an account. You see, I hope to be moving to this area soon.'

'You didn't have to see me; any of my staff could arrange that for you. I'll just get the relevant papers for you to fill in and sign.'

Janet waited for him to leave the room, then she too left. Now she had seen him, there wasn't any point in staying.

At the end of the day she sat in her car and waited for the staff to come out. Mr Brook must have been one of the last to leave. He retrieved his car from the parking area to the side of the bank, and drove away, with Janet following.

After about twenty minutes he turned into a drive. Janet continued on past, then turned her car round and stopped a few houses away.

She sat trembling. Could this really be it? Was she going to see her baby at last? She had been searching for nine years, now the end was almost within her grasp.

She left her car and, dreamlike, walked up the path and rang the bell.

A short, thin mousy woman opened the door and poked her head round. 'Yes?'

'I'm sorry to bother you, but does a Paula Brook live here?'

'Yes.' Her grey-blue eyes darted over Janet and Janet noted a look of surprise, almost a sense of

168

fear in them. 'What did you want to see her about?'

'Who is it, dear?' Mr Brook pulled the door open wider. 'You? What are you doing here at my home?'

'Who is she?' Mrs Brook asked her husband.

He pushed his wife to one side. 'I said, what are you doing here?'

'You know her?' asked Mrs Brook.

'She came into the bank today. Did you follow me home?'

'What did she want?' Mrs Brook's voice was high and out of control.

'She said she wanted to open an account, but that wasn't it, was it?'

Janet shook her head.

'Are you . . . ?' Mrs Brook stopped. 'Don't you see the likeness, dear?'

'Of course. I noticed it as soon as she walked in. How dare you follow me? Now get away before I call the police.'

'What do you want?' screamed his wife. 'You're not going to take her away. You can't.'

'What's all this racket out here?' Paula stood in the hallway. Janet felt her tears running down her face. This was her baby. It was like looking at a mirror image of herself when she was young. She wanted to push past these people in her way, and kiss her and hold her, tell her how much she loved her and ask her forgiveness, but her path was blocked.

Mrs Brook turned and hurried to Paula, ushering her away. Mr Brook leapt forward and roughly took Janet's arm.

'Now you listen to me,' he hissed as he propelled her down the path. 'You stay away from Paula. She

169

belongs to us and I don't want you upsetting her.'

'I only want to know how she is.' Janet's tears fell.

'You gave her away.'

'I didn't have any choice.'

'Is this your car?'

She nodded.

'Now you listen to me,' he said again angrily. 'And you had better listen carefully. If I ever see it in this area again I shall call the police. And if you so much as try to see my daughter again, then I won't be responsible for my actions. So stay away.' He pushed Janet hard against her car and walked away.

Blindly she opened her car door where she sat and cried bitter tears. She had seen Paula. As she drove slowly past the house she saw her daughter was looking out of the window. She wasn't smiling.

*   *   *

Paula stood at the window and, narrowing her eyes, watched the car slowly drive past. Was that woman her mother, the woman who had given birth to her? Paula knew she had been adopted; her father had told her many times. What did this woman want with her now? She was the person who had given her away. Paula wanted to shout and hit her like she had been hit herself. Paula hated her and wanted to tell her. Why had she come here?

'Paula,' her father was calling her. He walked into the room with her mother behind. 'I think you know who that woman was.'

Paula nodded. 'How did she know where to find me?'

170

'She was very devious. She came to the bank.'

'But how did she know my name?'

'It must have been a fluke. Perhaps someone had told her. But don't let it upset you. If you spoke to her she would probably tell you a lot of lies.'

'What if I see her out somewhere?'

'I forbid you to see her.'

'Why?'

'Because we have brought you up.'

Paula looked at her mother, whose face gave nothing away. Why didn't she say something? Was she so terrified of her husband? Paula often heard him shouting at her. Did he hit her as well?

'There's promotion going at the bank,' her father was saying. 'I'm going to apply for it. It will mean moving away.'

Mrs Brook took a sharp intake of breath. 'I thought we were settled here.'

'You know me, always on the look out for promotion, and this has come at just the right time.'

'What about Paula's schooling?'

'She's adaptable.' He left the room.

Paula went to speak but her mother put up her hand to stop her. Paula could see the hurt in her eyes.

'Just do as he says, my dear.' She too left the room.

Paula turned back to the window and looked up and down the road. That was her mother, the woman who had given her away. She had the nerve to come here and cause more problems. She was going to have to leave her school because of her. How she hated her. She loved her school. Paula had wanted to tell her to go away and leave them

171

alone. She had upset her kind mother and that made her hate that woman even more.

CHAPTER SIXTEEN

Janet felt utterly miserable as she drove away. Tears ran down her face. This had been her hope, the thing that had driven her on all these years. The reason she hadn't married Mark. But she had seen her daughter, and through her tears she managed a slight smile. Was this now the end? Would she ever see her again? Was life worth living now?

She wasn't concentrating on her driving when a wheel hit the kerb. She fought to control the car but couldn't stop it from slewing across the road. It mounted the kerb and hit a bush, then a wall.

Janet sat for a moment or two with her head on the steering wheel. She was dazed and trembling. She sat back. Thank goodness the road had been empty. If a car had been coming the other way, she could have killed somebody. Although she was shaking and her legs felt like jelly she got out to survey the damage. She pulled twigs and bracken from the radiator and fortunately, as far as she could see, only the bumper was bent. On closer inspection she could see there was a dent in the wing but the car still looked driveable.

She didn't want to go home and brood on the day's events alone, but where could she go? Freda was still at work and Charlie wasn't the greatest of conversationalists. She looked at her watch. Danny would still be at the showroom; she would go and see him. He always had a broad shoulder for her to cry on, and he would see about getting her a new bumper and the wing straightened.

Danny was just locking up his office when Janet drove in.

'Jan, what you doing here?'

She got out of her car.

'My God. What's happened to you? And what have you done to the car?'

She knew her face was tear-stained and her mascara had run for she had been crying all the way there. 'I've had a bit of an accident,' she sniffed. 'And could an old friend cadge a cup of tea?'

'Course, come in.' He unlocked the office again and put the light on. 'Would you like to go somewhere and have something a little stronger?'

'No, tea will be fine, if that's OK with you? 'Sides, I can't go anywhere looking like this.'

'That's true. Now I'll just put the kettle on then you can tell me all about it.'

'Is Tina expecting you home?'

'Not to worry, she gets used to me walking in at all hours, just as long as I get to see her before she goes to bed.'

'How is she? She's not got much longer to go now, has she?'

'About two weeks. I can't wait.'

'Never thought I'd ever see you as a family man.'

'We all change. Look, I'll tell you what, I'll give Tina a ring and if it's all right with her you could come over for the weekend.'

'I'd like that, but are you sure she won't mind?'

'Course not. Look, you ain't come here to talk about me and Tina, or that bumper, so I'll make

173

this tea and you tell me what's wrong.'

They sat drinking tea and Janet told him all that had happened. Danny was a good listener and didn't interrupt even when she stopped to wipe away her tears.

'So, after all this time you've found her,' he said softly.

She nodded. 'She's quite a tall girl for her age.' Janet dabbed at her eyes. 'It's her birthday in March.'

'The old man sounds a nasty bit of work—mind you, I don't like any bank managers, not when they want money. But looking at it from his point of view I know how I'd feel if someone came to take my daughter away.'

'Do you think I was wrong?'

'Dunno. It ain't for me to say. So what you gonner do now, Jan?'

'I don't know. This is what I've spent years of my life looking for and now I've found her . . .' She sniffed and blew her nose.

Danny put his arm round her. 'And you lost the chance of marrying Mark.'

'I know. Why was I so stupid?'

'You wasn't stupid. You was a mother. I think I know how I'd feel.'

'If only Mark had understood.'

'You should have told him right at the start, give him a chance to think about it.'

'I know that now, don't I?'

'Would you see him if he ever came back?'

Janet's head shot up. 'Has he been in touch?'

'No. It's just that . . . well, you never know, do you?'

'I don't know how I'd feel. Time makes you

174

mellow, doesn't it?'

Danny nodded.

'He's probably married with a couple of kids now.'

'Yer, could be. Let me give Tina a ring.' He went back to his desk and picked up the phone. 'Hello, love, it's me. Look, I've got Jan in the office. No, there ain't nothing wrong with her car. Well, there is . . .' He looked at Janet, raised his eyes to the ceiling and tutted. 'No, she's had a little bump, nothing to worry about. Tine, have we got anything lined up for the weekend? Christ, I clean forgot about that. What about the weekend after?' He put his hand over the receiver. 'That all right?'

Janet nodded.

'Tine, that's great, Jan will be coming then. No, just Sat'day night and Sunday. OK, see you later.' He put the phone back on the cradle. 'Sorry about that but it seems we've been invited to a birthday party. It's one of Tina's lot and we can't let 'em down.'

'I understand.'

'But make it the weekend after. Put it in your diary.'

She smiled. 'Don't keep one now. Thanks, Danny, for the tea and sympathy.'

'It's my pleasure.' He kissed her cheek and held her tight. ' 'Sides, that's what friends are for.' He handed her a set of keys. 'Take that one,' he pointed to a blue Ford. 'And I'll get yours seen to. I'll get Rob to give it the once-over while it's in.'

They walked to the cars together. 'Give my love to Tina.'

They said their goodbyes. Janet went home feeling exhausted but she did not sleep much that

175

night. She had an awful lot to think about.

*   *   *

Janet didn't go into work the next day with her usual enthusiasm. Now she'd found what she'd been looking for, her life didn't seem to have any purpose.

On Saturday she met Freda in the coffee bar and told her all that had happened.

'What did she look like?' asked Freda.

'She's got long dark hair that's done in a ponytail and she's quite tall. I would have loved to have talked to her. I wonder if she's doing well at school.'

'You'll never find out now, not if the old man has anything to say about it.'

'No.'

'So, what you gonner do now?'

'I don't know.'

'You could fly off to Canada and try to find Mark.'

'Don't talk daft. Even if I wanted to I wouldn't know where to start looking.'

'You could go and see his parents. They must know, he's sure to have kept in touch.'

'I couldn't go back there, not now.'

'Have you ever been back?'

Janet toyed with the spoon in the saucer. 'Once, but I didn't stop. I just sat in the car and watched my parents walk back from church. I saw Mark's mother as well, but she didn't talk to my mother.'

'So, what you gonner do with your life?'

'I've got to start again.'

'You're not going to move, are you?'

'No, I love my dear little house too much, but I am going to change my job. I couldn't work there now. I wouldn't want to go down in that records room again; I'd get too upset.'

'What d'you fancy doing?'

'I'm not sure. It'll have to be office work.'

'I'm always surprised you ain't ever worked in a hospital, especially with babies.'

'I couldn't do that. I couldn't be a nurse.'

'No, not a nurse. In the office.'

Janet sat back. 'D' you know, that might not be a bad idea.'

*   *   *

The following day Janet went to the local hospital, which was always crying out for staff. She was offered a job as receptionist in the antenatal clinic.

That weekend she didn't go to stay with Danny and Tina as Tina was rushed to hospital. She had a baby girl whom they called Emma. And when they asked Janet to be godmother she was overwhelmed.

At last she was going to get to hold a baby, even if it wasn't hers.

*   *   *

As, over the years, Janet watched her goddaughter grow into a little girl, and then into a big one, she was aware that her own life was slipping by. She often wondered where Mark was.

Was he happily married and settled in Canada with children? She knew she could find the answer to that just by going back to Stowford, but that part of her life was over. Her parents had never answered any of her letters and she couldn't face Mr and Mrs Scott, not now.

And when Janet did go out with other men she found them either shallow and uninteresting, or overbearing.

'What's happened to whatsisname? Jack?' asked Freda, after yet another short-lived boyfriend bit the dust.

'He wasn't really my type. I know, it's me. I seem to attract the wrong sort.'

'Too bloody fussy, that's your trouble,' was Freda's comment when Janet told her she'd finished with Jack Murdoch, a commercial traveller, when he'd got drunk one night and, rather crassly, tried to get Janet to sleep with him.

'I've still got my rabbit to cuddle in bed,' Janet joked.

'Hummh. Fat lot of good that is.'

As the decades moved on Janet settled down to her comfortable lifestyle. In 1977 the Queen's Silver Jubilee brought back the most poignant of memories for her, disturbing the careful balance of her existence. She was melancholy as her thoughts went back to the Coronation and the night Paula was conceived.

Where was Sam, Paula's father, she wondered. Her curiosity sometimes made her look for him in films and on the television. Had he ever made the big time?

For years she had tried to put the past behind her, but still she found herself glancing into cars, hoping she would see Paula, although she had no idea what she looked like now she was a woman. When Janet saw her all those years ago she thought

178

she looked like her, but who knew now? Could she be married? Was Janet a grandmother?

In the end, she decided her job was the most rewarding thing in her life and with promotion found she could afford almost anything she liked. Except the one thing she wanted more than anything else and that was to see her daughter again.

PART TWO
1979

CHAPTER SEVENTEEN

Paula couldn't believe the look of horror on Trevor's face. She took hold of his hand. 'Aren't you pleased, darling?'

He nervously looked round the restaurant. 'Paula.' He coughed and smiled, not meeting the loving look in her warm brown eyes. 'I don't know. No. I don't know. I think so.'

Paula could see immediately that he didn't mean it.

He continued. 'It's just that it's come as a shock and, let's face it, it does cause one or two problems.'

She pulled her hand away. She felt hurt. 'I thought you loved me.'

'I do, darling, you know I do.'

'But you said . . .' She stopped.

'Paula, perhaps we'd better go home and discuss this quietly over a drink.' He beckoned the waiter over. 'My bill, please.'

After paying the bill he gently took her arm and led her from the restaurant. She looked up at him for he was taller than she, even in her fashionable high heels. He was so good-looking that her heart beat faster. To her he was perfection. His thick dark hair, slightly greying at the temples, and his brown eyes could melt her with just one look. He was always immaculately well dressed and well spoken. She couldn't wait for his phone call asking to take her out. She loved him, but knew he didn't love her in the same way. If only she had found him first.

In the car Paula's head was reeling. His clenched jaw told her he was angry. This wasn't the reaction she had expected from him. She wanted him to be as thrilled as she was that they were going to have a baby.

Inside Paula's flat Trevor poured himself a large whisky. 'Have you forgotten to fill the ice tray again?' he asked curtly.

'No.'

'Thank goodness. You know how much I like ice in my drink.'

In the kitchen Paula put the ice in the bucket. She was upset: this wasn't how she thought he would react.

'Thanks, darling.' He put some ice in his glass and sat on the sofa. 'Come and sit with me.'

She sat next to him. He put his glass on the coffee table in front of him and pulled her close. He kissed her soft full mouth with all the passion she had come to expect from him. His hand travelled over her breast and as he kissed her neck he whispered, 'Paula, are you sure about this thing?'

She pulled away from him. 'Are you talking about our baby?'

He visibly winced. 'You don't have to go through with it, you know. Are you really sure this is want you want?'

She jumped back, almost as if she had been stung. 'Of course.'

He too sat back. 'But what about your career?'

'It isn't that important.'

'How can you say that? Have you thought about money? These things go on for ever, you know.'

'Yes I do know, and I also know we can't get married but I thought I could sell this flat and buy

184

a small house with a garden, perhaps somewhere in the suburbs—this place is worth a great deal now—then you could come and go as you please, just like now. Things will be the same except you'll have a child. Oh, don't you see, it will be lovely? I wouldn't have to worry about—'

He stood up. 'Come on now, Paula, be practical.' A deep frown filled his forehead. Why was he so angry?

'I don't want to be practical.' She tossed her head, pushing the soft brown hair from her face. 'I want a baby. Is that so wrong?'

'This was something we should have discussed.'

'Why?'

'I'm a businessman, not a family man.'

'You can learn.'

'You know I can't divorce Glenda. I can't leave her to fend for herself.' He moved over to the fireplace and, taking a cigarette from the onyx box on the mantelshelf, lit it with the matching cigarette lighter and blew smoke into the air. He pointed a finger at her. 'Paula, I'm very disappointed in you. You said you were on the pill.'

Paula visibly shrank. 'I was, but I stopped,' she said weakly.

'That was very selfish of you.'

Paula was in shock. This wasn't what she wanted to hear. She stood up. 'I thought you loved me.'

'I do, darling, I do.'

'But not more than your wife?'

'That's different.'

'Why?'

'You know why. I love you. I can't have the fun with Glenda I have with you.'

'You mean she can't perform in bed as well as

185

me?'

He smiled. 'Now you know that isn't the only reason. We get along very well together. Dinners, weekends away, the theatre and countless other things, so don't let's spoil it by having a baby and all the mess that goes with it.'

She looked up at him. She knew she would miss going abroad with him, staying in elegant hotels and eating in the best restaurants. She had also been aware right from the start that their affair wouldn't last for ever. She was always afraid he might toss her aside one day, but now she was going to have a baby and that would be hers to love for ever.

He held her close and the smell of his expensive aftershave filled her nostrils. 'Come on now, darling, be sensible.'

She didn't want to be sensible. She knew if she didn't stand her ground he would, as usual, get his way.

He was taller and fifteen years older than she but he had a fine body and was so good-looking in a mature way. His few grey hairs gave him a distinguished look and his deep brown eyes never failed to thrill her whenever he looked at her. He was a perfectionist and appearances meant everything to him. She knew when she first met him that he was married and his wife confined to a wheelchair. He never took Glenda out; always said she preferred to stay at home. In the beginning Paula had refused to break her golden rule and go out with him; she never went out with married men. But then, after countless refused invitations, he had told her that he was waiting for a divorce. Her first reaction had been that he was heartless

186

but he'd said that was what Glenda wanted. She didn't want him to be tied to her for ever and he was financially in a position to provide for her very well.

It wasn't until Paula was head over heels in love with him that she found out his wife was in a wheelchair after a car accident involving a drunken driver on their way home from a masonic do. As their affair grew she realized he had lied to her and wasn't going to divorce Glenda. She had received a large amount in compensation and money was very important to Trevor. Paula knew then he would never leave his wife, but despite all of this she was by then so hopelessly in love with him, she was prepared to agree to anything if it meant having him around.

'You know I can pay for an abortion.'

'I don't believe you just said that. Trevor, I was twenty-five last month. I can't and I don't want to leave it much longer. This is something I desperately want. I'm going to have this baby with or without you around.'

A look of total disbelief filled his face. 'What did you just say?'

'I think you heard.' Even as she said the words her resolve hardened.

He grabbed her hand. 'Paula, what can I say to make you change your mind?'

'I'm going through with this.' The more he argued the more determination she had to show.

'Why, Paula? Why? We are happy enough as we are.'

She didn't answer. She knew that if he kept on, despite her current show of single-mindedness, she would be putty in his hands and he might be able to change her mind. She had to stand up to him over this.

'Well, I suppose if you've made up your mind about this idiotic thing then I'll have to give you any financial support you need, but don't expect me to be a father to it.'

'Why not?'

'I'm not the fatherly type.'

'Trevor, don't you see I need something of my own to love?'

'You have me.'

'You will never be mine.'

He looked away and stubbed out his cigarette in the large ashtray. 'How will you manage all this?' He waved his arm around her expensive flat.

'I told you, I'll sell it.'

'And what about when you're fed up at home all day changing nappies and all the other revolting things that go with babies, and you start to crave the bright lights? You can't give children away, you know.'

Paula blanched. 'That will be my problem,' she said softly.

He stood behind her and, folding her into his arms, held her tight.

She smiled and almost purred with delight. She felt warm and safe with him. Why didn't he want to be a father?

'Look, it's getting late and you're tired. I'll come round tomorrow and we can talk this thing through.'

Paula didn't answer.

He picked his keys off the coffee table. 'Don't bother to see me out.' He kissed her cheek. 'Bye, darling. Love you.' He closed the door.

Paula sat on the sofa and hugged her knees. She knew he wouldn't divorce his wife but she hadn't stopped taking the pill to trap him. She wanted a baby, something of her very own to love.

Since she was a seventeen-year-old she had strived for perfection. That's what had made her climb the ladder of success in the estate agency business where she worked. She was now chief mortgage negotiator for all the firm's ten London branches and apart from commission she had an excellent salary, but she was prepared to give it all up for the love of a baby.

She sat reflecting on her life. Nothing had ever been her own, not even her parents. Trevor doesn't know I was adopted, she said to herself. When he talked about her giving her baby away he didn't realize how much that statement had hurt her.

She knew she had been adopted almost as soon as she could understand. Her father, who had a good position in the bank, had told her. He was a very strict disciplinarian and she had to do everything he told her to, otherwise he was going to send her back to the home they had taken her from. He had said her mother had been a wicked woman who had babies and left them to fend for themselves. Paula was terrified of him, the things he said and the threats of what he would do to her. He had abused her mentally and physically, made her feel inadequate and useless. But she only realized that after she had run away, when the woman she had called Mum for all of those years had died. Paula was just sixteen. Her mother had been a quiet woman and Paula had never been sure if she knew what had been going on and whether he had been a bully to her too. During her childhood, Paula had hated her real mother so much that she'd vowed if she ever found out who she was she would physically harm her, just as she had been all these years.

Paula shuddered at the memories.

At college she had made friends with Sue. It was her friend's mother who had taken Paula in when she left home. She spent three years with them and they were some of the happiest she had ever known. Sue knew all about Paula's life. Her father never came looking for her; Sue said he was probably afraid she would spill the beans. Sue was now happily married and had twin boys. She'd met Harry at a dance and within a year they were married. Paula still saw Sue, who lived nearby, but Sue never made a secret of the fact that she didn't approve of Paula seeing Trevor. What will her reaction be when I tell her about the baby? mused Paula.

There had been other men in Paula's life but they all seemed young and immature. Trevor was different. From the moment he walked into the estate agents asking to look at some of the most expensive property they had on their books she knew he was a cut above the others. He was confident and, in addition to his stylish clothes, he had a certain air about him. When she showed him round a vacant house he told her about his wife and how they needed wheelchair access. He often popped into the office on some pretext or other and Paula soon realized he was pursuing her. As time went on Paula knew she was falling for him; he was charming and attentive and brought her expensive gifts, which at first she refused. Then he mentioned the divorce which she knew now to be just a ploy. Gradually, and after a lot of soul-searching, she let him share her bed. Now he had a key and would come and go when it suited them both.

Paula brushed a tear from her eyes. Why was she getting upset?

The baby was something she wanted more than anything else. Something that was going to be hers and only hers.

Her thoughts went to her real mother. Who was she? She must have been a very selfish woman to have given Paula and her other children away. Had she been reunited with her other offspring? Why had she had Paula adopted?

She sat up. Her mind went back to when she must have been about nine. There was a terrible row with a woman who said she had come to see Paula. Her mother had ushered her away and told her it wasn't anyone important. The woman was crying and her father was shouting as he took hold of the woman's arm and practically dragged her from the house. Had that been the woman who had given birth to her? Had she come looking for her? Was she going to take her away and then make her live with her in a life of squalor with all her other children, as her father had always told her she did? She didn't look scruffy and she had a car.

Her father had been promoted just after that and they'd moved. Paula remembered not being very happy at having to go to another school.

These things hadn't bothered her for years. True, there had been times when in her depths of despair she had been angry at her mother for giving her away. She was still angry with her—leaving me to that monster, she thought. All the hate from the

191

past began to rise again. But was history repeating itself? Had her real father been married to someone else? If he had been then she couldn't have been much of a mother to give her baby away, whatever the circumstances.

She needed to talk to someone, but it was eleven o'clock, too late to phone Sue. Perhaps they could have lunch together. Would Sue approve of the situation? Paula didn't think so.

She gently touched her stomach. 'I will never part with you whatever happens,' she said softly. 'Never.'

CHAPTER EIGHTEEN

Twice during the following morning Paula had telephoned Sue but she wasn't at home. She was anxious to speak to her, so when Sue walked into her office Paula leapt up to greet her.

'Sue, I'm so pleased to see you.' She held her close for a moment.

Sue laughed. 'What have I done to get a welcome like this?'

'Can you stay and have a bit of lunch?'

'Only if you're paying.'

'It can go on expenses. I'll just get my jacket.'

They walked out into the late April sunshine.

'I love this time of year,' said Paula, closing her eyes and holding her head up to feel the warmth of the sun on her face. 'It's a promise of what's in store for us. All the buds are beginning to open to start a new life.'

Sue laughed. 'Hark at you. I must say it's

certainly given you a spring in your step and you look positively blooming. Mind you, can't say I like the light nights that much. I have a job to get the boys to bed when the sun's still shining.'

'Is that what being a mother is all about?'

Sue nodded. 'That and countless other things, but then I wouldn't change any of it.'

They reached a restaurant where Paula knew they could sit quietly and talk.

They studied the menu and ordered.

'How are the boys getting on at school?'

'They love it. I think they tell their teacher all that goes on at home.'

'That could be embarrassing. How long have they been there now?'

'Since September. I do miss them through the day, though—no mess and no one to shout at.'

'Don't worry, they'll be on holiday soon so you'll be able to make up for it then.'

'So, what's this all about? You didn't bring me here to discuss my kids.'

Paula smiled. 'You can read me like a book.' She sat forward and said in a low voice, 'I'm pregnant.'

Sue's pale blue eyes opened wide. 'Are you sure?'

Paula nodded.

'How far gone are you?'

'About six weeks.'

'I thought you were on the pill.'

'I was.'

'Is it . . . his?'

Paula sat back. 'Of course. What do you take me for?'

'Just asked, that's all. Does he know?'

'Yes.'

'Are you pleased?'

'Over the moon.'

'And what does he say about it?'

'He wants to pay for an abortion.'

'What?' yelled Sue.

'Shh,' said Paula looking round at the raised heads.

Sue quickly put her hand to her mouth. 'Sorry about that, but he's such a bastard. I don't like what he's doing to you and his wife. Talk about having your cake and eating it.'

'She knows about us.'

'Does she? You've only got his word for it. You've never met her.'

'Well, hardly. He can't go up to her and say, "By the way, this is my bit on the side."'

'So . . .' Sue stopped as their food was put in front of them. 'Thank you,' she said to the waiter and picked up her knife and fork. 'So,' she repeated, 'what's going to happen?'

'How do you mean?'

'*Are* you going to have an abortion?'

'No, course not. I stopped taking the pill because I want a baby.'

'Are you sure?'

'Yes.'

'What about your job and your flat and a thousand other things—that's without not having a husband in tow.'

'I have thought very carefully about this and it's what I want.'

Sue smiled. 'Good. I know you're sensible and would have thought this through. So when's it due?'

'December. It could even be a Christmas baby.'

'That's bad timing. Poor little mite won't have

any birthday presents.'

'Yes, it will. Sue, I'm so thrilled about it.'

Sue touched her hand. 'So am I. You'll make a smashing mum and I'll always be around to help in any way I can. Now I think we should have a glass of wine to wish you both good health.'

Paula smiled. She knew she had done the right thing.

'What are you going to do about his lordship?'

'I don't know. I suppose he'll get fed up with me when I start getting fatter.'

'Are you upset about that?'

'I was last night, but now, strangely, no. I knew he might find a younger woman one day, but I thought he might have been a little more enthusiastic about being a father.'

'Will he help to support it?'

Paula shrugged her shoulders. 'I'll have to wait and see about that.' She looked at her watch. 'We'd better be quick. I have a client at two.'

'Yes, of course. When are you seeing him?'

'Tonight.'

'Well, give me a ring after he goes if it's not too late.' She gave her a sly grin. 'And if you've got any energy left.'

'Don't be cheeky.'

Outside they kissed each other's cheek and went off in different directions.

Paula felt happy. She knew she could always rely on Sue, even if Trevor did desert her.

*   *   *

That evening while Paula sat waiting for Trevor she was trying to evaluate how she felt towards him. At

195

least, despite his early talk about divorce, he would never leave his wife. She admired him for that, while acknowledging he had lied at the start of their affair. Perhaps he'd come in this evening with a bottle of wine and a bouquet of flowers, tell her how much he loved her and wanted their baby. Then they would make love.

She got her usual tingle of anticipation when she heard his key in the lock, and jumped up from the sofa to greet him.

There were no flowers or wine. He came to her and holding her tight kissed her willing mouth.

'I wasn't sure you would be here tonight,' she whispered as he kissed her neck.

'Why?' He held her at arm's length.

'I thought that after last night . . .'

'That's why I'm here. Let's sit down.' He took her hand and led her to the sofa. He sat in the armchair opposite and leaned forward.

'Paula, I've been giving a great deal of thought to what you told me and, well, I don't think it's such a good idea.'

She wasn't sure what she was expecting him to say.

'I will make the necessary arrangements for you to go away. You will, of course, go to a private clinic. You can tell people you are going on holiday—that way no one will be any the wiser. We can go abroad for a week when it's all over. A week in the sun will do you good.'

She sat staring at him. 'You don't understand, do you? I want this baby. I don't want to be sent away like some silly adolescent.'

He stood up. 'Well, I think you are being very selfish. You are throwing away not only your

196

happiness, but mine as well. We enjoy a wonderful life together but we won't be able to if you go ahead with this . . . this stupid half-baked thing.' He stood up and took a cigarette from the box on the mantelshelf.

Paula watched him blow smoke into the air. 'Trevor, I'm sorry this has upset you, but I am determined to have this baby and if you don't like it then I'm afraid it's over between us.'

He looked stunned. 'I don't believe this. You would put a baby before me? After all we've meant to each other?'

Paula could feel the tears stinging the backs of her eyes. She wasn't going to cry in front of him. She didn't want to turn him away, but what choice did she have?

He ground his cigarette into the ashtray. 'In that case you'd better have this.' He dived his hand into his jacket pocket and threw her door key on to the coffee table. 'I'll always love you, Paula, and if at some time you see things my way I would be pleased to start all over again.'

She didn't see him out. The door slamming echoed round the silent flat. Tears began to fall. Was she being stupid? Is this what she really wanted? Why couldn't he see things her way? Why couldn't she have a baby and Trevor?

The shrill ring of the telephone made her jump. She wiped her eyes with the back of her hand.

'Hello,' she said into the receiver.

'My God, you sound awful. Is he still there? Just answer yes or no.'

'Sue.' Paula began to cry.

'Paula! Paula, are you all right?' Sue's voice was full of anguish.

Paula sniffed. 'Yes. Sorry about that.'

'Has he gone?'

'Yes.'

'Right, I'm coming round.'

'You don't have to.'

'Yes I do. That's what friends are for. See you in a bit.' The phone was replaced.

Paula went into the bathroom to repair her make-up. She blew her nose. 'Oh, what the heck! I don't have to put on a show for Sue,' she said to her reflection in the mirror. 'She'd rather I put the kettle on.'

Sue was round in less than half an hour.

'Right, what's happened?' she asked, removing her jacket.

'He's gone.'

'For good?'

Paula, fighting back the tears, nodded. 'I think so. I've made some coffee.'

'Good. We have got some talking to do. After we've had coffee, of course.'

'Yes, Mum,' Paula laughed half-heartedly.

They went into the kitchen together.

'Now have you been to the doctor?'

'Yes.'

'So it's definite?'

'Yes.'

Sue suddenly threw her arms round Paula. 'I'm so pleased for you. I know this is what you want.'

'Don't. You'll have me in tears again.'

'You can blame that on your hormones. How long do you intend to work?'

'As long as I can. I'm going to sell this flat and get a small house. I thought of round your way. Kennington's nice and the properties there hold their prices.'

'And we've got the lovely park. You know I'll give you any help and advice I can.'

'I know that.'

'If you like I'll come to the hospital with you.'

'That'll be nice. Don't fancy those blood tests— might pass out on them.'

'Well, you let me know. I can always get Mum to look after the boys, and she can bring them home from school if need be. She doesn't mind, in fact she thinks it's great to look after them. I don't like to put on her, but I know she gets lonely since Dad went.'

'That was very sad.'

'It was quick, just the way he wanted to go.'

'But not so good for you and your mum.'

'True. But hey, come on, cheer up. I'm here to talk about your forthcoming event.'

Paula felt happier telling Sue her hopes and fears and they talked for hours.

'Look at the time,' said Sue. 'Harry will think I've left home.'

'Well, if he's locked you out you'll have to sleep here.'

'He's not that daft. There's no way he could cope with getting himself and the boys ready in the morning.' She laughed. 'No, I know I'm indispensable.'

'You're very lucky.' They said their good nights and Sue left. When Paula closed the door she smiled to herself. She was so fortunate to have such a good loyal friend. This wasn't the first time in her life that Sue had come to her rescue but this time Paula was a lot older and a lot wiser, and she was in charge of her own destiny.

She gently patted her stomach. 'At least you'll be

all mine. Come on, my little darling, it's time for bed.'

CHAPTER NINETEEN

The next four weeks, apart from slight morning sickness, Paula felt fit and happy. At first she had been hurt and upset that there hadn't been any word from Trevor, but she knew she had to accept that his part in her life was now over, and was surprised how easy it was getting to live without him. Having Trevor around had always been a hit-and-miss affair. Some nights she would prepare a meal and wait for his key in the door; most times he didn't even bother to phone to say he couldn't make it. On two of her birthdays when he had promised to take her out she had sat dressed up waiting, but he hadn't turned up. She couldn't phone him at home as he had told her she mustn't worry Glenda. On both occasions when she had phoned his office the following day he had said he'd been out of town and hadn't been able to make it. She had loved him and they say that love is blind. Now she knew she had been silly as well.

They all knew about the forthcoming baby at the office and her boss said she could stay as long as she wanted to, which was good news as she would need all the money she could get.

She was going to put her flat on the market and had been looking at houses near to where Sue lived. She was now ready to move forward.

Sue had been with her on her first visit to the hospital and everything appeared to be fine.

Janet looked at the notes she was holding and carefully read them over again. Could this be really happening? Was this patient really a Miss Paula Brook? Could it be her Paula? She was cross with herself; Brook was a common name. But to have the same Christian name—it was too much of a coincidence. When she checked her date of birth, 2 March 1954, Janet felt her knees buckle. She knew then that all her years of searching, and the anguish and secret hopes since first seeing her daughter so briefly, were over. Now Paula was about to walk into her life.

The memory of that dreadful day sixteen years ago when she finally found her, and her adopted father was so angry he almost threw her out, was still with her. Seeing Paula's sad face at the window was something she would never forget. Was she ever told who I was? Janet wondered.

She knew the family had lived in this area once but they had long moved on and the trail had gone cold. Since that terrible scene, Janet had never tried to find them again. But that had never stopped her hoping.

She was contented in her own way and had never married. She'd finally realized she couldn't love anyone the way she had loved Mark. She had often thought about him, but even those memories were beginning to fade. Freda said she'd been daft to turn Danny down, but he was happy with Tina and they now had two lovely children.

She sometimes wondered about her parents. Twice since she left she had driven down to

Stowford, the last time just a few years ago when she suddenly felt she wanted to see them. Everything had looked the same. Part of her had wanted to announce herself, knock on their door, but at the time she had worried that she might be rejected. She had sat and watched as the congregation left the church. She saw Mrs Scott but not her mother and father. She had been tempted to go into the church but didn't think that was very wise; someone might have recognised her. She would have loved to have gone up to Mrs Scott and asked about Mark. Did they still hear from him? Was he married?

All the memories of these past years came flooding back.

Mary, the young girl whom Janet worked with, was talking to her. 'Are you all right? You've gone a funny colour.'

'Sorry, I was looking at these notes.'

'Any problems?'

'Not that I can see.'

Janet read through the notes again and memorized Paula's address. She smiled to herself. Paula wasn't married but that wasn't the sin today that it had been when Paula had been born. She was going to be a granny. It would be wonderful if Paula could accept her. Tears filled Janet's eyes. Miss Brook was due to have another checkup next week, Janet would make sure she was in reception at that time.

*   *   *

'Miss Brook,' said Janet politely, trying to keep her emotions under control when Paula came up to the desk and gave her name.

Janet saw Paula's friend quickly glance from one to the other.

'If you would like to go along to the waiting room, you will be seen soon. There aren't many in front of you. You have got your sample with you?'

Paula nodded. 'Yes.'

Janet smiled. The paper she was holding was shaking in her trembling hands. This was her daughter; in her mind's eye she could see the sad little girl at the window. Janet wanted to rush from behind her desk and hold her. She wanted to touch her, just to reassure herself she was real.

'Come on,' said the friend, taking hold of Paula's arm.

Janet stood and watched them walk away. She had to find an excuse to speak to her. But would Paula want anything to do with her? Had she even been told she was adopted?

*   *   *

Sue and Paula wandered into the waiting room and sat down.

'Did you have a good look at that woman?' asked Sue.

'No. Which one?'

'The one on reception. There's something about her. She looks familiar.'

'Can't say I noticed.'

'Well, you look when we go out. I'm sure I've seen her somewhere.'

After Paula had seen the doctor and had been told everything was in order, she and Sue left. As they went through the main reception Paula looked around but the receptionist wasn't there.

Paula was deep in thought as Sue drove her home.

'You're quiet. What's up?'

'It's funny really. All the years I knew I was adopted and it didn't really worry me, except that I hated my mother. But it's only now you start to think about it.'

'What brought this on?'

'It was when the nurse was filling in my records and she asked if there was any history of family illness. I felt—I don't know—as if I've lost my roots, I suppose. I had to tell her I didn't know as I had been adopted. Am I being daft?'

'I don't think so. I can understand that's exactly how you must feel.'

*   *   *

As soon as Janet got home that evening she was on the phone to Freda.

'Freda, you're never going to guess what's happened today, not in a million years.' Janet was finding it hard to control her tears.

'Bloody hell. That's a right turn-up for the book,' she said when Janet had finished telling her what had happened. 'What you gonner do about it?'

'I thought I'd go and see her.'

'Is that wise?'

'What have I got to lose?'

'Nothing, but it could mean more heartbreak.'

'But I can't see her every month at the hospital and not tell her who I am.'

'What if she rejects you?'

'I don't know. What can I do? It's fate. It was

meant to be.'

'Jan, I can't tell you what to do. All these years you've been looking for her and now in a way she's found you. P'rhaps you're right, p'rhaps it is fate. You have sacrificed a lot to find her; now you can only tell her the truth.'

'Yes, I've got to.'

'Well, you know I wish you all the luck in the world. Let me know how it goes, won't you?'

'Of course.'

'But, Jan, give her time.'

'I will.'

'Bye for now, Granny Slater.'

'Bye,' croaked Janet. She replaced the receiver and let her tears fall. For the first time in her life they were tears of joy.

*   *   *

Paula lived not far from Janet and on Sunday afternoon Janet was sitting in her car looking at Paula's flat when she came out. Janet quickly put her head down. She didn't want her to see her; she might think she was behaving suspiciously.

It was a lovely day and Paula had obviously decided to walk to wherever she was heading.

When Paula had passed, Janet left her car and, keeping her distance, followed. When she saw she was heading for the park she grinned. That was the perfect place to talk to a stranger.

She saw Paula sitting on a park bench watching the ducks and children round the pond. She sat next to her.

'It's a lovely day, isn't it?' said Janet.

'Yes, it is.'

205

Janet gave a little laugh. 'Don't I know you from somewhere?'

'I don't think so. You may have come to the office at sometime. I work in Trads, the estate agents.'

'No, I haven't been in there. I work at the hospital so unless you've been there lately I must be mistaken.'

Paula laughed. 'I was at the hospital only last week. I'm having a baby.'

'That's it then. Congratulations. That's probably where I saw you.'

They spent about an hour chatting. Janet dearly wanted to tell her who she was.

Paula looked at her watch. 'I'm afraid I must go. It's been very nice talking to you.'

Janet panicked. She didn't want her to leave just yet. What could she say? 'Look. I know this might sound silly, but you look very much like my daughter.'

Paula laughed. 'Poor girl. Where does she live?'

'I don't know. You see, she was adopted as a baby.'

The colour left Paula's face.

Janet was worried she was going to start screaming or faint. 'I'm sorry. I didn't mean to upset you. I shouldn't have said anything.'

Paula regained her composure. 'No, that's all right. Now I really must go.' She stood up and hurried away without giving Janet a backward glance.

Janet sat for a long while just staring into space. What had she done? Paula didn't admit she had been adopted. But by her reaction she knew. Perhaps she was ashamed of it, or of her mother.

*　　　*　　　*

Janet's phone was ringing as she walked in.

'Well?' said Freda, on the other end of the line. 'What happened?'

Janet told her.

'So you think she knows?'

'By her expression I'm sure she does, but she didn't want to admit it.'

'What you gonner do now?'

'I don't know. I'm getting tired of running around in circles.'

'You giving up? Never. Not now you've found her.'

'I must confess that after spending half a lifetime looking it does seem a shame to be rejected.'

'Well, let's face it, you didn't expect her to welcome you with open arms, did you?'

'I don't know.'

'You've got to give her time to come to terms with it. After all, it must be a bit of a shock to see your mother in the flesh, so to speak, for the first time.'

'I suppose so. We do look a bit alike.'

'That's nice.'

They said their goodbyes and Janet sat all evening with her thoughts. She didn't want to change her job again—she was happy working at the hospital—but if it was going to cause a problem for Paula she didn't have any option.

*　　　*　　　*

Paula was on the phone as soon as she got home.

'Hurry up, Sue,' she said to the ringing tone. 'Sue? You'll never guess what's happened, not if you guessed all night.'

'Is everything all right?' asked Sue, her voice full of alarm. 'You're not miscarrying, are you?'

'No. Listen. I think I've just met my real mother.' Although it was only a second or two the silence seemed to go on for ever.

Finally Sue said, 'What did you just say?'

Paula repeated the sentence.

'Where?'

Paula told her what had happened.

'So she was the woman at the hospital?'

'Yes.'

'I thought she looked like you.'

'You didn't say.'

'Well, I didn't make the connection at the time. And you say she lives near here?'

'Yes.'

'What are you going to do?'

'I don't know. I think I hate her even more for her smarmy way of getting to see me. I'm sure it was deliberate.'

'Do you want to see her?'

'Of course I don't. We don't have anything in common.'

'Does she want to see you?'

'I don't know. Can I come round? I need a bit of company.'

'Of course. It's a bit of a shambles, and they've got to have a bath, but you know you are welcome at any time.'

'I'll be round in a short while.'

Paula put the phone down. She went to the cupboard in her bedroom where all her papers were kept. She took out the box with her birth certificate in and, sitting on the bed, studied it. She knew her surname had been Samuel. Was that woman's name Samuel? Why did she give her away? On the surface she seemed a nice person. She quickly put the birth certificate in her handbag and made her way to Sue's.

*   *   *

Paula helped get the boys to bed and then she sat and read them a story. When she went downstairs Sue called her into the kitchen.

'They've gone down now.'

'You can come again.'

'It's getting me in practice for when I have to read bedtime stories.'

Sue smiled. 'You're going to be a smashing mum.'

'I hope so.'

'We'll sit out here and talk. I'll make some coffee. Harry wants to watch tele, anyway. Now what's this all about?'

'What should I do?' asked Paula, sitting on the stool at the breakfast bar.

'What about?'

'This woman.'

'Wouldn't you like to talk to her?'

'No I would not. Can I go to another hospital?'

'I don't know. You'll have to ask your doctor.'

'I'll do that. I don't want to see her again.'

'Why?'

'She abandoned me, remember.'

'No, she didn't abandon you. Don't be so dramatic. She had you adopted. You were only

saying the other day you didn't have any roots—
well, now's your chance to find out who you really
are.'

Paula looked into her mug. 'I don't know if I
want to,' she said softly.

'What are you frightened of?'

'What if I've got brothers and sisters and she still
sees them? How will that make me feel?'

'Would you like me to have a word with her?'

'No. I don't want her to know I'm interested.'

'Well, I think you should see her. After all, you
can always tell her to keep away from you.'

'I suppose I could.'

'So, shall I have a word first?'

'Would you?'

'Why not? It could be quite intriguing. That's if
you want me to know all about your mother's dirty
linen.'

'Sue, you've been my friend for a long, long
while, and you and your mum kept me sane,
remember? So whatever happened in that woman's
life perhaps I would like you as well as me to know
about it.'

'OK. I'll go along to the hospital tomorrow and
perhaps she and I could go and have a coffee
somewhere and a little chat.'

'Who would have thought this was going to
happen? What would I do without you?'

Sue smiled, though she felt anxious. Would
Paula be happy knowing about her mother? And
was her mother prepared to talk to a complete
stranger?

'I think I've seen her before,' said Paula,
casually.

'You have? When?'

'It must have been when I was about nine or ten. She came to the house.'

'Did she say who she was?'

'No. My father threw her out, but I guessed it was her.'

'That sounds like your father.'

'I remember she was crying.'

'So she was upset?'

'I suppose so.'

'Did she ever try to see you again?'

'No, we moved just after that.'

'She must have been searching for you.'

'Do you think she was? I've never thought about it in that way before.'

'She might be very upset when she knows how you were treated.'

'Good.'

'Oh come on, Paula, that's not a nice thing to say.'

'I want her to suffer like I did.'

'Have you ever thought why she gave you away? How she might have suffered?'

'No, I've always been too angry. Every time my father hit me I vowed that if I ever met her I would do the same to her.'

'She looks quite young, so she must have been very young when you were born—and remember things were a bit different in the fifties.'

'I suppose they were.'

'They weren't as broad-minded as we are today.'

'Are you going to make me forgive her?'

'I wouldn't do that—well, not till we hear her reason for having you adopted.'

'I don't want to talk to her.'

Sue touched Paula's hand. 'Remember, she will

be your baby's only grandmother.'

Paula didn't have an answer to that. Instead she said softly, 'The name on my birth certificate is Samuel.'

'So that's who I'll ask for.'

'Don't let her tell you a lot of lies.'

'How can she do that?'

'I don't know.'

'Aren't you excited?'

'No, why should I be?'

'I just thought it must be rather nice to find a—'

'I don't want to know.'

'Well, we'll both be a lot wiser tomorrow.'

Paula looked into her coffee cup. Part of her wanted to find out the truth, but part of her didn't want to be hurt any more.

CHAPTER TWENTY

When early the following morning Sue got to the hospital reception desk, she suddenly realized she didn't after all know who to ask for. Paula had told her that the name on her birth certificate was Samuel, but what if that woman was married?

'Name, please?' a young lady asked, looking up when Sue approached her.

'Excuse me, but do you have a Miss or Mrs Samuel working here?'

'Not to my knowledge. Now could I have your name?'

'Perhaps you could tell me the name of the lady who was here on this desk yesterday?'

'If you wish to see the doctor I have to have your

name.' The receptionist was getting a little cross.

'No, I'm not pregnant, it's just that I would like to talk to the person who saw my friend yesterday, a Miss Brook.'

'I'm afraid I can't give out any information regarding other patients.'

'I am aware of that.' Sue was beginning to get a bit ruffled with this slip of a girl. 'I just need to talk to her, that's all.'

'What about?'

'It's personal.'

She tutted. 'Wait here.' With a toss of her head she disappeared into the room behind the desk.

'Janet, there's somebody out here that wants to speak to a Miss or Mrs Samuel. Do you happen to know her?'

Janet jumped up. 'Did she say what she wanted?'

'No.'

'Thanks, Mary.' Janet touched the back of her hair nervously and smiled. Her daughter had come to see her.

Sue almost gave a sigh of relief when Janet came out.

Janet recognized Sue at once and quickly looked round for Paula. 'Is Paula . . . Miss Brook . . . ?'

'No. I am on my own. Can I have a word?'

Janet was beginning to panic. Why wasn't she here? 'Look, let's go over there.' Janet pointed to two chairs that were against the wall away from the rest of the patients.

When they sat down Janet said, 'I hope I didn't upset Miss Brook yesterday. That's the last thing I want to do.'

'No—well, yes, you did in a way.'

'I'm very sorry. Are you a relation?'

213

'No, a very good friend.'

'I see. What did you want to talk to me about?'

'So many things. What time is your lunchbreak? Perhaps we could talk then?'

'Yes. If you think it would do any good.'

'I think so.'

'I can go off at twelve if that's OK with you?'

'That will be fine. I have some shopping to do this morning. Where shall I meet you?'

'At the entrance.'

Sue stood up. 'We have a lot to talk about.'

Janet watched her walk away. What was she going to tell her? It was obvious her daughter didn't want to see her otherwise she would have come with her friend. Janet slowly made her way back to her office. Was this going to be another sad day—the day her daughter was going reject her completely?

It seemed every five minutes Janet looked at the clock. Mornings usually flew by but today was going so slowly and it was unusually quiet. The ticking of the clock was loud and overbearing, and even noise from children shouting and yelling would have been welcome. Finally it was twelve and she hurried from the office, her heart beating fast. Would Paula be with her friend?

Sue was waiting alone.

'Hello,' said Janet. 'There's a quiet place round the corner. I thought we could go there.'

'I don't mind.'

They walked along in silence. It wasn't until they were in the restaurant and had ordered that Sue spoke.

'I hope you don't mind but I'd like to write a few things down. Paula asked me to.'

214

Janet was surprised. 'No, no, I don't mind. Did she know she was adopted?'

'Yes, her father told her almost as soon as she could understand.'

'I see. What is it she wants to know?'

'The first thing is why did you have her adopted?'

Janet felt uneasy. 'I would rather tell Paula that, if you don't mind.'

'She doesn't want to see you, but she does want to know about you and why you gave her away.'

'I didn't have any choice. You see, I was sixteen when I became pregnant and we lived in a small village. It was a terrible disgrace in the fifties and my parents sent me away.'

'Didn't Paula's father want to marry you?'

'I didn't want to marry him.'

'Did he know about Paula?'

'No. I didn't want to give her up but as I was underage it wasn't my decision. I've tried to find her. I did manage to see her once, but her adoptive father made me promise not to worry them again. He threatened me with the police and I didn't want to upset Paula.' Janet, using her fork, pushed her sausage and chips round the plate. She wasn't hungry.

'That sounds like her father,' said Sue.

Janet quickly looked up. 'Did they treat her all right?'

'I think so.' Sue wasn't prepared to tell her the truth; that was up to Paula.

'Are they still alive?'

'Her father is; her mother died quite a while back.'

'Does she live with her father?'

215

'No.'

'Is she getting married?'

'Look, I'd rather not say anything about Paula. Is there anything you would like me to tell her?'

'No. Just that I regret what happened. I've spent a great many years looking for her.' Janet could feel the tears stinging her eyes. 'I've looked at girls who I thought might have resembled Paula. For years I studied little girls' feet in the park, looking for a birthmark.'

Sue almost gasped.

'I looked twice at cars when I thought the drivers could have been her.' She wiped her eyes.

Quickly regaining her composure Sue asked, 'Are you married?'

Janet shook her head. She blew her nose. She wasn't going to tell this stranger about Mark.

'I would really like to talk to Paula. Do you think she would give me a ring?'

'I don't know.'

'Here's my phone number.' Janet wanted to know if Paula was getting married. Did she have enough money? From the outside her flat looked very expensive; did she rent it? So many questions were buzzing around her head.

'I must go. Here's my share of the bill.' Sue put some money on the table.

'I'm sorry. I was miles away.'

Janet stood up. 'I don't know your name.'

'Sue.' She held out her hand. 'I do hope we meet again.'

'I expect we will for a few months at least, at the hospital.'

Sue didn't have the heart to tell her Paula was thinking of going to her doctor for her checkups.

As soon as she could, Paula left the office and hurried to Sue's.

'Well?' she asked, when Sue opened the door. 'What did she say?'

'She's a very nice person.'

'She might be now.' Paula followed Sue into the kitchen.

'I've got her phone number, it's there on the worktop. Paula, I think you should give her a chance to tell you why she did what she did.'

'Why?' Paula turned the piece of paper over, then stuffed it into her pocket.

'She was sixteen when she was expecting you. She said she has been trying to find you all these years. She knows about your birthmark.'

'She does?' asked Paula in surprise.

'She used to go to the park looking at little girls' feet on the off chance she might see you.'

'Stop it, you're breaking my heart,' said Paula sarcastically.

'Well, at least she's genuine. She came to your house once, but your father, not your real one, threatened her with the police if she came looking for you again.'

'That sounds like the old sod. Who was my real father?'

'I didn't ask. I think you should ask that.'

'You're being very cagey, Sue. What was really said?'

Sue handed Paula a cup of coffee. 'Not a lot. She's very fond of you.'

'She doesn't bloody well know me.'

217

'Paula, keep your voice down. I don't want the boys picking up the wrong words.'

'Sorry. It's just that I'm so angry.'

'Why?'

'I don't know. I don't want this woman interfering in my life.'

'Just bear in mind that you're on your own.'

'I've got you.'

'I might not always be there when you need me. You could do with someone around who has your welfare at heart.'

'So who do you suggest? There's Trevor and now my long-lost mother. Not much of a choice, is it?'

'Don't be silly. Trevor's the last person you can rely on. And before you start on about the past, remember nobody can turn the clock back.' Paula was angry with Sue for talking to her as if she were a child. She felt angry at this strange woman who was now causing a rift between her and her best friend. 'I think I'll be going.'

'You don't have to. Stay and have a bit of dinner.'

'No, thanks. I feel a bit tired.'

'Please yourself. I don't think fish fingers with my two sound that exciting anyway.'

'I'll give you a ring tomorrow.'

'Paula, don't let this upset you. Give the woman a chance.'

'I'll see myself out.' She kissed Sue's cheek. 'Bye, boys,' she called as she passed the lounge, but she didn't think they heard her above the television.

All the way home she thought over what Sue had said. She was all alone.

Arriving home she took the paper with Janet's

218

phone number on it from her pocket and, screwing it up, threw it in the bin. She wasn't going to call her. This woman was now winning Sue round. She must be really selfish.

Paula's thoughts kept going to Janet. She should phone her and tell her what she thought of her and how much she hated her and wanted her to stay away from her.

When her phone ran she jumped, and then carefully picked up the receiver. 'Hello,' she said softly.

'It's Sue. Have you phoned her yet?'

'No.'

'Well, I think you should.'

'I don't want to.'

'Are you all right?'

'Yes, and thanks, Sue, for talking to her.'

'That's OK. She does seem a nice person.'

'I'll phone her if it's going to make you happy.'

'It isn't me I'm worried about.'

'I'll do it. Bye.'

Paula went to the bin and took out the paper. Smoothing it straight she put it beside her telephone. Did she want this woman in her life? But the idea of finding out about her own background was beginning to intrigue her. Twice she went to dial the number but changed her mind.

*   *   *

As soon as Janet got home from work she phoned Danny. She had to tell someone and Freda always went to the launderette on Monday evenings nowadays.

'Hello, Tina, it's Jan. Is Danny home yet?'

219

'No, not yet. Is it the car?'

Janet laughed. 'No.' She had recently bought another from Danny. 'You haven't got a lot of faith in your husband, have you?'

Tina also laughed. 'No, I suppose not. Do you want him to give you a ring when he gets in?'

'If he's not too busy.' She could hear the children shouting in the background.

'Be quiet, you two. Sorry about that. By the way, when are we going to see you?'

'I don't know.'

'Come over at the weekend. That's if you can put up with the kids.'

'I might do that. I'll let you know.'

Janet put the phone down and reflected on Tina and Danny. She loved them both dearly, but she didn't want Danny to hear her news from Tina; she was busy with the children and perhaps he wouldn't be told everything.

As she walked away the phone rang. 'Hello.'

'Is that Mrs Slater? Mrs Janet Slater?' Paula's tone was sharp.

Janet held her breath. It was Paula. 'Yes,' she whispered. She didn't bother to correct the Mrs.

'My friend has been telling me about your meeting.'

There was a long pause. Janet was waiting for her to say something. 'Yes. I think it went well.' Janet didn't know what to say, but she suddenly knew she had to see her. 'Paula—may I call you Paula?'

'Yes.'

'Could we meet? I would like to talk to you.'

'Why?'

'I feel I have a lot to tell you.'

'Why, is there some medical problem I should know about?'

Janet could hear the panic in Paula's voice.

'No. It's just that I thought you might like to know things, like who your grandparents are and where they live.' Janet was clutching at straws. She was trying to make herself sound interesting.

'Not really. Who was my father?'

'Paula, I would rather tell you these things to your face. Would you like to come round to my house?'

'No. Is there any point in me meeting you?'

'Only if you feel you want to.'

'I don't know. I've done without you all these years.'

'I know and I only wish I could turn the clock back.'

There was a long silence.

'I'm sorry if I am upsetting you,' said Janet.

'No, you're not.'

'Well, thank you for calling.'

'Wait. I'll meet you somewhere.' Paula wanted it to be on neutral ground; that way she wouldn't feel intimidated.

They made arrangements to meet in a quiet local pub in half an hour. When Janet put the phone down she was almost dancing with happiness.

*   *   *

In the pub Janet sat nervously watching the door. She didn't like sitting there on her own. She began to wonder if Paula might have got cold feet and changed her mind.

Paula stood outside. Part of her wanted to go in and tell this woman what she thought of her, and part of her wanted to walk away. What could she say to this woman? What should she call her? Certainly not mother. The door opened and a man walked out. Paula tried to see in but the door closed too quickly. Was she in there? 'If I don't meet her I'll only have Sue nagging me. So it'll be just a quick hello then I'll be off,' she said to herself.

She took a deep breath and pushed open the door.

When Paula walked in Janet felt so much joy she wanted to hold her close. It took all her strength to remain composed.

'Hello,' she said, when Paula came towards her. 'What would you like to drink?'

'Just a shandy.' Having seen her in white coat at the hospital Paula was taken back by the smart way Janet was dressed. She looked almost too young to be her real mother.

As it was Monday the pub was practically empty and Janet was back quickly.

'I've never been in here before,' said Janet, looking round.

'I come with Sue sometimes. You know, my friend who you met this morning.'

Janet nodded and smiled. 'Yes, she seems a very pleasant person. Have you known her long?'

'Since we went to college together.'

'That's nice.'

'I lived with her and her parents for a few years.'

'Why was that?'

Paula was on her guard. She was cross with herself for letting that slip. Should she tell this

222

woman about her father? That would make her feel guilty. 'It was more convenient.'

'Paula, is there anything you would like to know about me?'

Paula was determined not to like this woman. She had to be on the defensive all the time. 'Who was my father?'

Janet looked at her. This was the moment she had been waiting for: to tell her daughter all the things that had happened in her life. She took a deep breath and, looking into her daughter's brown eyes, began her story.

CHAPTER TWENTY-ONE

At first the conversation was very stilted. It was mostly Janet answering Paula's questions. Janet was nervous; she wanted to ask questions without appearing to be nosy. She wanted to know everything about her daughter's life over these past twenty-five years.

'Did you bring any photographs of you as a child?' asked Janet tentatively.

'No.'

Janet could see Paula wasn't going to be gushing and she knew she would have to bide her time.

As they sat quietly talking the atmosphere gradually began to feel easy.

*   *   *

Paula was studying Janet. She seemed a pleasant woman with a ready smile, and appeared to be genuinely pleased to see her. If she was telling her the truth perhaps all these years she had been wrong about her. Even the deep hate she had had was slowly lifting a little as Janet told her about her life, but Paula was still on her guard. She didn't want to be hurt again.

Paula was told about Sam. She heard how Janet's parents had sent her away when she was pregnant.

'Why didn't you marry my father?'

'At the time I was only sixteen and he wasn't for me. He was very ambitious.' Janet had to be careful it didn't sound too much like a one-night stand.

'Does he know about me?'

Janet shook her head.

She told Paula about the home and the nuns and where she was born and how she met Freda, who, after all these years, was still a very good friend.

She then decided to tell her about Mark. She wanted her to know everything; she had nothing to lose.

'He went to Canada two weeks before you were due to be married? That must have been heartbreaking!' said Paula.

'Yes, it was.'

'You didn't tell him before then that you had had a baby?'

Janet ran her finger round the rim of her glass. 'It sounds silly today, but then it was considered such a disgrace.'

'Did you have any other children?'

'No.'

Did she believe this woman? If this were true then Paula knew her father had been telling her lies. 'So you never married?'

Janet shook her head. 'No, when Mark went to Canada he never even got in touch with Danny, a great friend of his—well, he was till the trouble over a car.' She went on to give her a brief outline of that episode in her life.

'What about this Mark's parents?'

Janet looked away. 'I don't know. I've never spoken to anyone in Stowford since I left.'

'So my grandparents don't know about me?'

'Only that you exist. I would go back if you ...' Janet stopped. She didn't want to rush things. 'They may not be alive now.'

Paula looked uneasy. 'All those years ago, would you have gone to Canada if you knew where to look for Mark after you saw me?'

'I might have done, but by then it was too late. Besides, he was probably married with children by then.'

'Did you ever regret it?'

'In some ways. I loved Mark, but you see I'd made you a promise when you were born. I was determined to find you.'

'And it has taken you twenty-five years,' said Paula softly.

'Yes.' Janet could feel the lump rising in her throat. She swallowed hard. 'Have you still got a birthmark on your left foot?' she asked light-heartedly.

Paula laughed. 'Yes, I have. Fancy you remembering that.'

'I used to walk round the park in the summer looking at little girls' feet, just in case.'

'You did?' Paula was careful not to let her know Sue had told her this. 'I bet that caused a few stares?'

225

'I was very discreet.'

The landlord was calling time.

Janet began to panic. 'I haven't had the chance to ask about you and the baby. I'm so pleased about it.' She wanted to add that being a grandmother was going to be wonderful, but would Paula let her share her life now? 'Look, would you like to come back to my house?' Janet didn't want this evening to end.

'No, I have to go home. I've got a busy day tomorrow.'

'Please, could we meet again sometime?'

'I don't know.'

'Please, Paula.'

'Perhaps. I'll think about it.' Now Paula had heard about her past she was beginning to mellow just a little towards Janet. 'Here's my phone number.'

*   *   *

That night Janet couldn't sleep. She was so happy. She had seen and spoken to her daughter. She was so proud of her. She wanted to hug her, to make up for all the years. She knew Paula had a good job and she was clever as well as very attractive. Janet wondered what sort of effect their meeting had had on her. Would she see her again socially? She hadn't said very much about herself. When Janet thought about it, it was just her job she had talked about. Janet knew Paula's adoptive mother was dead, but she hadn't said anything about her father; she hadn't even talked about the baby, or its father.

She lay looking at the ceiling. Could they become a family? But what about the baby's father? Would he let Janet into their lives? Janet smiled to herself. There was nothing to stop her hoping. Tomorrow she would buy her a small present for the baby. After all, she had twenty-five Christmases and twenty-five birthdays to make up for.

*   *   *

Paula too was finding sleep difficult. As she tossed and turned so many thoughts filled her mind. Had she been wrong all these years? Believing her father had been easy, as she needed someone to hate, but now after meeting this woman she wasn't so sure. Had he told her all those things because he loved her and didn't want to lose her? Paula's mind was in a turmoil. I was this woman's only child, she thought. She said she had given up her own happiness, her own chance of marrying, just to find me. But was that the truth, or was the woman just trying to sound like a martyr? Would Paula ever learn the truth? Tomorrow she would tell Sue all about Janet. She knew Sue liked her and would be pleased the meeting had gone so well. But was this going to change her life?

*   *   *

The next evening Janet phoned Paula, but she was out. She wanted to tell her about the pram set she had bought. It was white. Did Paula want a boy or a girl? Did she want to marry the father? She hadn't said anything about him. Janet knew she must take things one step at a time, but she was impatient.

She phoned Freda, who was thrilled with her

227

news.

'So when you seeing her again?'

'I don't know.'

'Does she want to see you?'

'I hope so.'

'What did you tell her?'

'Everything.'

'Blimey, that must have taken all evening. And what about her?'

'We never got round to that.'

'Is the father married?'

'I don't know.'

'Well, you'd better let me know all the grisly details when you find out.'

Janet smiled. 'Of course.'

For the rest of the week Janet waited for a phone call from Paula, but it never came. Was she avoiding her? Did she want to see her again? On Friday night Janet was due to go and stay with Danny and Tina for the weekend. She had so much to tell them, she was always sure of a warm welcome there and Tina knew all about Paula.

*   *   *

On Friday Paula was at work when Trevor walked into her office. She wasn't sure if she wanted to throw her arms round him, or sock him one. She could see by his clenched jaw that he wasn't in a good mood. He closed the door behind him.

'Trevor. What brings you here?' she said, smiling.

'I thought that perhaps you might have phoned me over these past few weeks.'

'Why? I thought we had discussed everything.'

228

She was cross that he hadn't even bothered to ask how she was feeling.

'I've been away and I didn't want you to think I hadn't returned your call. My office does have problems passing on messages at times.'

She never phoned him at home as he had told her it upset Glenda. 'No, I haven't phoned you. I've not had any reason to.' She went to a filing cabinet and began looking through some files.

'Can't you stop working for a moment?'

'Trevor, I have a job to do.'

'Can we meet somewhere?'

Paula knew she had to be careful. She knew she hadn't really got over him and she still wasn't sure if she wanted him back into her life.

'I need to talk about our situation.'

'I thought we had said all there was to say.'

'I mean about Glenda.'

Paula was stunned. 'You're going to tell her about the baby?'

'Well. I think it's something we need to discuss.'

'I thought we had.'

'I've been giving it a lot of thought. We must talk about it.'

She wanted to throw her arms round him and kiss him, but she had to be sure this wasn't just another ploy to get her into bed, and anyway, did she want him now she was beginning to feel confident on her own? 'I'm not sure.'

'We can go for a meal.'

'When?'

'Tonight if you can make it.'

'OK. Pick me up about eight.'

The phone was ringing when Paula walked into her flat. 'Hello. Sue! No, I can't stop, I've got to get

229

ready. I'm going out with Trevor.'

'You're what? What for?' Sue sounded shocked.

'He's asked me out to dinner.'

'And what else?'

'I'll have to wait and see.'

'Be careful. Remember the things he said.'

'Yes, Mum.' Paula put the receiver down. Sue meant well, but she wasn't on her own, and if Trevor was going to come round to the idea of the baby, who knew? She might find a place for him in her heart again.

*　　　*　　　*

Janet, on her way to Danny's, drove round the corner to Paula's flat, singing and tapping the steering wheel in time to the music on the radio. She drew up behind a large grey car that was parked outside the block where Paula lived. Janet was going to drop a letter into her flat if she wasn't home. She just had to see her again.

But before she had chance to move, Paula came out smiling and laughing, looking up into the face of an older man. She didn't see Janet and they got into the car and drove away.

Was that the father of her baby? He was very good-looking. Was he going to marry her? There was so much she had yet to learn about Paula's life.

When they were out of sight Janet put the letter through Paula's letter box.

*　　　*　　　*

There hadn't been any flowers or gifts when Trevor walked in. Paula had wanted him to ask her how

230

she felt, if she was well, but he only talked about himself. In the flat he was on about his job and the fact he had been sent away for a few weeks and he didn't like the hotel or the people he was dealing with.

She was laughing at him when they got into the car and as soon as they pulled away he began grumbling about the traffic. When they were seated in the restaurant he complained about the menu.

'Doesn't anything please you these days?' Paula finally asked.

'People and shoddy service certainly don't.'

'I thought we were here to discuss you and Glenda.'

His head shot up from the menu. 'No, my dear, not me and Glenda, that isn't the issue.'

'But you said—'

'Paula, I still love you,' he whispered. 'And what I want to know is, are you still going ahead with this . . . this baby thing?'

Paula felt hurt. It wasn't what she wanted him to say. 'I thought you were going to tell Glenda about the baby?'

'I was. But she was so upset about my being away that I didn't have the heart.'

'But you've been away before.'

'Yes, I know. We've had some lovely times together, you and I.'

'Yes, we have.' She was getting cross with herself; she was weakening under his spell again.

He touched her hand and she felt a thrill. 'And we can again,' he whispered.

'So what was different about this time?' she asked quickly, pulling her hand away.

He looked embarrassed. 'I met this girl. It was

231

only a dinner date,' he added quickly. 'She phoned Glenda and asked for me. She said she wanted to thank me for such a wonderful night.'

Paula's eyes were wide open. 'You gave her your home phone number?'

'She must have taken one of my personal cards from my pocket.'

'Was that when you had your clothes off or on?'

'Don't be bitchy.'

'So what did Glenda have to say about that?'

'She nearly went mad. Accused me of having an affair behind her back.'

'But Glenda didn't mind about me?'

'Well, darling. Not exactly.'

'You told me Glenda knew about us.'

'She did up to a point. That you accompanied me at the firm's dos and the like. I told her you were a friend of the boss's wife.'

'I don't believe this. All this time you've been lying to me and your wife. You told me Glenda knew all about me.'

'Be sensible. I couldn't really tell her about everything, could I? Besides, I owe it to Glenda. Now you've got this other problem.'

'Like what?'

'This baby thing. I don't want you making waves.'

'Me, make waves?'

'Shh, Paula, keep your voice down.'

'Trevor, I am not going to get rid of my baby.' She sat back. Although she was hurt and tears were stinging her eyes, she smiled. 'Shall I tell you why I'm going to have my baby?'

'Is it to trap me into marrying you?'

She laughed. 'What? I'm just beginning to find

232

out what a selfish bastard you are. No, it's because I want someone to love, someone of my very own to love me with no strings attached. Very recently I have found out what it is to really love someone so much that you are prepared to give up your life for them.'

'That was a very dramatic speech. Now, shall we order?'

'I have discovered the real meaning of love. I was adopted when I was a baby and my real mother has spent twenty-five years of her life looking for me.'

'Very touching.'

'Now she's found me. That's love, true love.'

'So you were adopted? I didn't know that.'

'Never had any reason to tell you.'

'And now this woman has told you you're her long-lost daughter and you believe her? What's she after?'

'How callous can you get?'

'Please, let's order.'

Paula stood up and threw her napkin on the table. 'I'm going home to phone my mother.'

Trevor stood up. 'Please, Paula, sit down, people are looking.'

'I don't care. And don't try to get in touch with me again, will you?' Paula walked away. Her knees were shaking and she was having difficulty walking straight. What had she done? She knew now she would never see him again.

She glanced over her shoulder and was upset that he hadn't made any attempt to follow her.

Paula knew at that moment that she, her baby and her mother could be at the very beginning of a wonderful life together.

CHAPTER TWENTY-TWO

It was a bright June Monday morning and Janet went to work with a spring in her step. She'd had a lovely weekend with Danny, Tina and the children. The weather had been wonderful and she had spent many hours playing with the children in the swimming pool Danny had recently had installed. Danny and Tina were thrilled with her news about Paula, and said they wanted to meet her as soon as possible. The only cloud that Janet could see on her horizon was that Paula might not want her and could reject her completely.

Janet was thrilled but very surprised when Paula phoned that evening.

'Hello. This is Paula. I got your letter.'

'Paula, how lovely of you to phone.'

There was a silence as each waited for the other to speak.

Janet broke the silence: 'Can I meet you?'

'Of course.'

Janet was taken aback at the eagerness of the reply.

'I did phone you at the weekend.'

'I was at a friend's.'

'I was wondering if you would you like to come to my place?' Paula's voice was soft.

'I'd love to. When?' Janet was having trouble trying to contain her excitement.

'How about tonight?'

'I can be there in about half an hour.'

'I look forward to it.'

Janet wanted to jump in the air, she was happy

beyond words. Her daughter was inviting her to her home. When she sat back she suddenly realized this might not be the kind of meeting she was expecting or wanted. What if Paula was going to tell her to stay away from her, stay out of her life. 'No,' she said out loud. 'She would have told me over the phone. And her voice sounded kind and friendly.'

But Janet's mind was full of doubts as well as hope as she drove to Paula's. As she walked up the stairs to Paula's flat her daughter was standing at the open door.

'I saw you out of the window.'

'This is very kind of you.' Janet was careful not to show her real feelings. She quickly glanced around at the expensive fittings and furniture. On the stack deck was a photograph of a young girl whom Janet guessed was Paula, with her mother. There was another of Sue and her family, but there weren't any of men. Everything in the flat was very tasteful. 'This is very nice.'

'Thank you. Please, sit down. Would you like coffee or a drink?'

Janet sat on the edge of the sofa. 'Coffee would be fine. I've bought this for your baby.' Janet handed her the pram set. She emphasized the word your. 'I hope you like it. It's white.'

Paula was smiling. 'Thank you. This is baby's first present.' She held it up. 'It's lovely, thank you.'

'Do you want a boy or girl?'

'I don't mind, just as long as it's healthy. But a girl would be nice. And I think you would like that, wouldn't you?'

Janet felt the tears well up. She was being included. Her daughter wanted her to be here. She

235

had trouble controlling her voice. 'Yes, I would.'

'I'll make the coffee.'

Janet followed Paula into the kitchen. 'I must tell you I was worried that you wouldn't want me in you and your baby's life.'

Paula turned, and leaning against the worktop said, 'Janet—do you mind if I call you Janet?'

Janet shook her head. She knew she would never be called Mum.

'I didn't want you at first, but now . . . When the coffee's ready I'll tell you about my life.' She smiled. 'We certainly seem to have a lot in common.'

'Oh, what's that?'

Paula laughed. 'Our choice of fathers for our babies for one thing.'

Janet was careful not to probe.

They sat in the lounge and Paula brought out a photograph album. They laughed at the pictures and fashions as Paula told Janet about her adoptive parents.

Janet wanted to take the photographs and relish the childhood she'd missed out on. She knew Paula's mother had passed away and wanted to hit the father when she heard what he had said about her. 'I'm so sorry. If only I'd known.'

Paula brushed that aside and went on to tell her about Trevor.

'Did you love him?'

'I thought so, but I knew right from the start he would never be mine completely.'

'He doesn't sound the type to stay with a disabled wife.'

'I think it's a way of saving him a fortune. If he left her she would probably demand everything he's got in the divorce settlement.'

Janet couldn't comment on that so she asked, 'Will you be able to manage on your own?'

'I should think so. I earn good money and over the years I've put a lot by, and when he or she starts school, with my estate agent's qualifications, I'll be able to go back part time.'

'You are very sensible. If I can help you know I will.'

'Janet, I must admit when you first came into my life I hated you, but now I would like us to be friends.'

'So would I, and remember I'll always be here for you. I let you down once and I promise it will never happen again.' Janet wanted to hold her close and kiss her, but she knew she had to take everything at her daughter's pace.

*   *   *

Soon they were shopping, or eating out or in each other's homes. It was exciting sharing and exploring each other's lives and tastes. Paula was introduced to Freda, Charlie, Danny and Tina and their children; Janet met Sue's family. There was so much to see and do together and everything always seemed to be accompanied by plenty of laughter.

Paula was blooming. She was beginning to show but she felt happier than she had for years. Janet couldn't believe that after twenty-five years all the dreams she had ever wished for had finally come true.

'Jan, what are we doing this weekend?' Paula called from her kitchen towards the end of a week in July.

'I don't know. Did you have anything in mind?'

Paula walked in carrying a tray of iced lemonade. 'I was wondering, as it's such lovely weather, would you mind very much if we went to see your parents?'

Janet was stunned. 'Why?'

'I just would like to, that's all. I want to see where you were brought up.'

Janet stood up and walked to the window. 'I don't know. What if they reject me again? I couldn't bear that.'

Paula came up and put her arm through Janet's. 'We could just go to the church. You said a lot of my ancestors are buried there.'

'Yes, they are.'

'Could we just go and look at the gravestones?'

'Well yes, I suppose so.' Janet would have given her the top brick off the chimney if she'd asked for it.

'I would like to find out more about my background. It's a pity you don't have any photographs of them.'

Janet knew photographs had come to mean a lot. She hadn't taken her album when she left home. These past weeks she had been pleased to have studied and had copies made of pictures of Paula when she was a little girl. It was her attempt to capture the childhood of the daughter she had been denied.

'We don't have to go and see my grandparents, not if you don't want to.'

Janet smiled. 'Yes we will. We'll go on Sunday. We can sneak in the back of the church when my father's taking the service and sneak out again before the end.' She laughed. 'It's a bit like when

238

me and Freda used to go to church with the nuns.'

'The difference is that it's me that's expecting now.'

'And I definitely won't send you away.'

*   *   *

On Sunday morning, Janet, who was driving, felt very apprehensive when they left the main road and were approaching Stowford. She hadn't been there for many years.

'I know it's silly, but I'm really excited. Coming face to face with people whom I've never met, but who are part of my life.' Paula turned to face Janet. 'I'm so pleased you found me.' She was like a child.

Janet was glad she was wearing sunglasses so that Paula couldn't see the tears in her eyes.

The sound of the church bells filled the air. Janet parked the car and surveyed the congregation slowly making their way inside the church.

'We'll sit here for a while,' said Janet. Everything looked exactly the same. To her as she sat and watched, it was as if time had stood still.

'It's very pretty round here. Do you know any of those people?' asked Paula eagerly, leaning forward to peer through the windscreen.

'No. No, I don't think so, but it is a long while ago and some of the children have grown up and others must be pretty old by now.'

'Would your mother be inside?'

'She could be.'

'Would you know Mark if he was here?'

Janet was silent. She hadn't thought that he could have come back. She couldn't face him, not after all these years. Possibly she wouldn't even recognize him. 'I don't know,' she said softly. Suddenly she put her hand to her mouth and took a sharp intake of breath.

'What is it?' asked Paula. 'Are you all right?' Her voice was full of concern. 'You've gone a funny colour.'

Janet nodded. 'I'm all right, it's just a shock.' She felt sick. 'That old lady holding on to that young woman's arm is my mother.' Paula was intrigued. 'My grandmother. How old would she be now?'

'I don't know exactly. She must be in her late sixties, at least. She looks like she's having a lot of trouble walking.'

Guilt was beginning to fill Janet's head as she watched them go through the church doors. She should never have left like she had. She should have made some effort to see them on the two occasions she had been here. What if they had needed her all these years?

'Can we go in now?' asked Paula, interrupting her thoughts.

Janet smiled. Her heart was bursting with love and happiness for her. Paula was like a child waiting for a treat.

'Yes.'

In the church they sat at the back. The service had started. The congregation was very sparse and the vicar was a young man whose loud voice filled the building. Where was her father? Janet sat looking at the backs of heads. One or two people she thought she recognized, but she wasn't sure.

After the service she and Paula quickly left the church.

'Are you going to speak to your mother?' asked

240

Paula.

'I don't know. I wonder where my father is. Let's wait over there by that tree and see where my mother goes. I lived at the vicarage over there.' Janet pointed to the red-brick building.

'It looks a nice house. Do you miss the country?'

'I didn't, but now, with all the hustle and bustle in London, I don't know. Would you like to live in a place like this?'

'A few years ago I would have said no way, but now, now I haven't got Trevor and with a baby on the way, I don't know either.'

'It's a lot cheaper. Look, here comes my mother. She seems to be going to the vicarage.'

'I think we ought to go and see her,' said Paula, moving forward.

Janet hung back. 'I'm not so sure.'

'What if your father's old and infirm? They can't harm you now.'

'No, not any more.' She put her arm through Paula's. 'Come on then, let's go and meet your grandmother.'

'I only hope the shock doesn't kill her.'

Janet stopped. 'Don't say that.'

'I was only kidding. Come on.' They made their way to the house and Janet took a deep breath and rang the doorbell.

The young woman who had been helping Mrs Slater walk to and from church opened the door. She smiled. 'Can I help you?'

'Do the vicar and Mrs Slater live here?'

'Mrs Slater does, and also my husband, Mr Thomas. Who did you want to see?'

'What about Mr Slater?'

'He died about six years ago. Did you know

241

him?'

Janet nodded.

Paula could see her mother's anxiety and, coming forward, quickly said, 'He was my grandfather.'

Mrs Thomas frowned. 'I didn't think he had any children. Are you sure you're in the right parish?'

'Yes,' said Paula. 'We have just seen my grandmother come into this house.'

'Just a moment.' She disappeared inside.

'I'm sorry, Janet, but I could see you were upset. Shall we go?'

'No, not now we've got this far.'

Janet couldn't describe the look of surprise on her mother's face. She wasn't sure if it was disbelief, anger or total bewilderment.

'Janet.' She drew herself up. 'After all these years you have finally returned.'

'Yes, Mother.' Janet felt like a naughty girl who had run away from home.

'What do you want?'

'I came to see you.'

'I'm not sure I want to see you.'

Paula took Janet's arm. 'Come on. You were right.' She turned to Mrs Slater. 'I would have thought that after all these years you would have forgiven her.'

'And who are you, young lady?'

'I'm your grandchild.'

Irene Slater held on to the door post. Her face turned a deathly white.

Janet broke free from Paula and rushed to her mother's side. 'Quick,' she called to Paula, 'go in and get a chair. The dining room's the first door on the left.'

242

Paula hurriedly opened the dining room door and took a chair, much to the astonishment of the vicar and his wife, who were sitting at the table.

After looking from one to the other they quickly followed Paula with the vicar calling, 'Young lady, where do you think you are going with that chair?'

When they caught sight of Janet gently lowering her mother on to the chair they rushed to her side.

'What has happened? Are you feeling unwell, my dear?' The vicar knelt in front of Mrs Slater and gently tapped the back of her hand.

'I'll get a glass of water,' said his wife after giving Janet and Paula a long look.

'I'm Janet Slater and this is my daughter, Paula.' Mrs Slater groaned and the vicar stood up.

'We've come to see my mother.'

Mrs Thomas returned and Mrs Slater took the glass of water that was held out.

The Thomases looked stunned.

'We didn't think you had any children,' said Mrs Thomas to Irene Slater.

In a funny way Janet was enjoying this conversation, even if it did upset her mother. 'I was banished years ago.'

'You weren't banished, you left of your own accord. You never even bothered to write.' Irene Slater's voice was beginning to rise with anger.

'I sent you birthday and Christmas cards with my address on, but you never replied.'

'You didn't even know your father had passed away.'

'I'm very sorry about that.'

'So, why are you here now? What it is you want of me?'

'Nothing. I thought you might like to see your

243

granddaughter, and to tell you you are going to be a great-grandma.'

'Are you married?' she curtly asked Paula.

'No.'

'I thought as much. The daughter's turned out like the mother.'

'That's not a nice thing to say,' said Paula. 'My mother has given up a lifetime of happiness to find me, and I'm very pleased she did.'

Janet felt so proud of Paula. She was acknowledging that she was her mother.

Mrs Slater ignored Paula's remark and said smugly, 'Mark has done very well for himself, he's married, of course.'

Janet winced and felt hurt. But if he was happy . . . ? 'How are Mr and Mrs Scott?'

'You knew them?' asked Mrs Thomas with doubt in her voice.

Janet nodded. She decided that as she had nothing to lose now, so she might as well let all the dirty linen come out. 'Many years ago I was going to marry their son, Mark, but he jilted me two weeks before we were due to be married.'

Mrs Thomas's eyes were wide open. Janet could see she was trying hard to keep the surprised look on her face under control.

'Mark had very good reason,' said Mrs Slater.

'Mrs Scott is fine,' said Mrs Thomas, recovering her composure. 'Mr Scott has a bad chest.'

'He's had that for years. When did my father pass away?' Janet was talking to Mrs Thomas.

'About six years ago. He had a heart attack.'

'It was six years and three months, to be exact,' said her mother very quietly. 'And I blame you for that.'

244

'Me? I wasn't even here.'

'Your father never got over your going.'

'He didn't make me very welcome when I was here. He didn't show me a lot of affection.'

'No, because you preferred to behave like some loose woman.'

Paula giggled and began to shuffle.

'Would you both like to come in for a cup of tea?' asked the vicar.

Janet looked at Paula, who only shrugged.

'That would be very nice, that's if it isn't causing you too much trouble.' Janet wanted to see inside her old home again.

'It's no bother.'

They followed Mrs Thomas, with the vicar taking Mrs Slater's arm and coming behind them.

'How long have you both been here?' asked Janet.

'Just over six years. We were very lucky to get such a lovely parish,' said Mrs Thomas over her shoulder. She was beaming. 'It is so pleasant round here. Where do you live?'

'London,' Janet and Paula answered together.

'And when is the baby due?'

'Christmas,' replied Paula. 'This is a lovely house.' Paula was standing in the lounge looking over the garden. 'It must have been a great place to grow up in.'

'It was very lonely,' Janet whispered. As she looked about her, suddenly, out of the blue, she wondered what had happened to all her possessions—what about her wedding dress? Probably ended up as dusters, she thought sadly.

'It's certainly worth a good deal of money today.'

'Paula is in the estate agent business,' said Janet,

trying to smile.

'Well, it isn't mine to sell,' said Mrs Slater. 'It belongs to the church.'

'I know that,' said Janet.

'But did she?' A stick was pointed in Paula's direction.

'My daughter was only passing a comment.'

'Just as long as she doesn't think it will be hers one day.'

Paula gave a funny laugh.

'Is that what you've come here for, just to find out who owns this place?'

'I know it belongs to the church. We only came so Paula can see who her relatives are.'

Mrs Thomas came in with the tea.

'Tell them to go. I don't want them here upsetting me.'

'But I've made the tea.'

'I don't want her here. I shall end up having another one of my attacks. Get her out,' Mrs Slater shouted. 'Get rid of her.'

'That's not very Christian of you,' said Paula.

'I don't feel very Christian towards her.'

Janet stood up. 'Come on, Paula.'

Outside Janet began to cry.

'Please, please don't.' Paula put her arm round her mother. 'This was all my fault. I didn't know she was going to be like that.'

Janet stayed in the comfort of her daughter's arms. She was happy about one thing: at last she had someone who cared for her.

CHAPTER TWENTY-THREE

After the meeting with her mother Janet took Paula for a gentle stroll around the cemetery, looking at the names on the gravestones.

'Some of these women died quite young, didn't they?'

Janet was wandering silently along beside Paula, not really taking that much notice of what she was saying. She was busy thinking about her mother. Why had she behaved like that? Why hadn't she been pleased to see her after all these years? Did she really hate her and blame her for her father's death?

Janet stood and looked at his grave.

'The Reverend Peter Slater.' Paula was reading the stone. 'Peter's quite a nice name.'

Janet noted that fresh flowers filled the vase. She wished she had some to give him. Tears filled her eyes. Why did all this have to happen? Why couldn't her mother accept that she had made a silly mistake when she was young? Janet looked at Paula standing at her side. Her dark eyes shining, she was glowing with health and vitality. Her dark hair gently moved as she turned her head. No, at the time Paula might have been a mistake but now, to Janet, she was the most precious thing in the world. Janet looked at the slight bump that was partly hidden beneath Paula's loose-fitting jacket and tried to smile. Now, to add to her joy, she was going to make her a grandmother. Tears ran down Janet's cheek.

'I'm so sorry,' said Paula, a worried look filling

her pretty face. 'I didn't think this would happen. I thought they would be pleased to see you. It must have been awful for you when you were expecting me, and yet you were still determined to find me.'

Paula put her arm round Janet's shoulders. Janet needed love and comfort, so she buried her head and cried.

Paula held her close and when Janet pulled away, she said, 'This is all my fault. I feel terrible making you come here.'

Janet wiped her eyes. 'No, you mustn't. I'm glad I did. At least I know now how my mother feels and that my father has gone.'

'Would you like to go and see Mark's mother and father?' asked Paula softly.

'No. I don't see any point. Besides, after upsetting my mother I think we should leave it at that.'

'It was just a thought.'

Janet knew Mark wasn't in this country and didn't want to hear about his marriage all over again, this time from his mother. And what if there were children too? Would Mark's parents blame her for Mark going away? She couldn't stand any more rejections today.

As they made their way back to the car, Janet said, 'What about your father? Shouldn't you tell him he's going to be a grandfather?'

Paula laughed. 'I don't think so. I think he would react rather like your mother. They have such funny ideas, everything must be done the right way and me not being married is not the right way.'

'But things are different now.'

'Not as far as he's concerned. Besides, we never saw eye to eye all the years I lived there. I was so frightened of him, I couldn't wait to get away. It would have been different if Mum was still alive.'

Janet began to smile. 'This isn't much of a day out, is it? Come on, let's go and find a pub and have lunch.'

*　　　*　　　*

It was the beginning of August and Paula was at the hospital for her checkup.

'Everything all right?' she asked Janet who was glancing through her notes.

'Looks like it.'

'I was wondering, would you be able to come with me when I go into labour?'

Janet smiled. 'You've got almost another five months to go yet, but I would love to be with you.'

'That's good.'

'Are you seeing Sue this weekend?'

'Yes, do you want to come?'

'No. I can see you another day. Besides, I must go and see Freda.'

'Perhaps we could all have a get-together. What about a barbecue one weekend?'

'That sounds a great idea. I'll ask Danny, he likes doing that, and his garden has been purpose-built for it.'

'Sue's two love the pool. Are you sure he doesn't mind?'

'He revels in it. Tina said it's the only time he's willing to cook.'

'They are a lovely couple. They always make me so welcome.'

'Well, you're part of their family now. I'll give you a ring tonight after I've got in touch with

Danny.'

Janet stood and watched Paula walk away. Over these past few months Paula and Janet had been invited to Danny's house and, along with Freda and Charlie, they had treated Paula like a long-lost child. When Paula was asked to invite Sue and Harry along Janet felt as if they had all been friends for years.

Janet decided to get on the phone right away. With the bank holiday coming it would be a lovely time for them all to get together and sit around drinking and talking.

*   *   *

When Janet and Paula arrived at Danny's he raced up and, putting his arm round them, kissed their cheeks.

'My favourite girls—well, after Tina and Emma that is. This was great idea of yours. Even Tina's parents are here. Sue and Harry's two are in the pool already. You going in, Jan?'

'You know I can't swim.'

'Now's a good time to learn.'

'Not with you around it isn't.'

Freda, who was deep in conversation with Elsie, Tina's mum, jumped up and kissed Janet when she walked in.

'And how's our baby?' Freda asked gently tapping Paula's stomach.

'Great.' Her smile lit up her face.

'I was just telling young Freda here,' said Tina's mum, 'it's our ruby wedding at the end of October and we're having a bit of a do and I'd like you both to come.'

250

'That would be lovely. Where's it going to be?'

'Here. I ain't got the room at my place and I don't like halls—too empty—and Tine don't mind. I'll get her to send you both an invite. Got to do it all posh, like. You will be able to come with your mum, won't you?' she asked Paula.

Janet winced.

'Of course. Thank you.'

'You must be ever so pleased that your mum found you. I notice you don't call her Mum. Still, give it time. Mind you, it must have been a shock. Did you know you was adopted?' Elsie only knew straight-talking.

'Yes.'

Janet took hold of Paula's arm. 'We must go and say hello to Sue.' They moved on.

'Sorry about that,' said Janet.

'That's all right. She's a nice lady.'

'She means well.'

They had a few words with Charlie, and Sue and Harry, when they could make themselves heard above the children's squeals of delight. Everybody was having a wonderful time.

Paula sat down. 'Thanks for bringing me here.'

Janet sat beside her. 'I'm so pleased you're enjoying yourself.'

'My baby's going to have a lot of playmates,' she said, looking around. 'You know some lovely people.'

Janet smiled and let her eyes take in the scene. She was surrounded by people she loved and laughter was coming from every corner. 'Yes, I am very lucky,' she said.

*   *   *

251

The following morning Paula was in the shower getting ready for work. The radio was loud as she listened to the reports of Earl Mountbatten's death. Yesterday everybody had been very shocked and angry at the news and it had brought a sadness to Danny's party.

As always when she ran her hands over her stomach she talked to her baby.

'Today I'm going to take a very important man to see a very expensive house. So I don't want you dancing and jiggling about.' She gently soaped her breasts and her thoughts went to Trevor. Why hadn't he bothered to get in touch? After all, this baby was his. She missed him touching her and making love. Had he loved her? She knew when she made the decision to have a baby that he wouldn't be pleased at first, but she thought he would have seen it from her point of view. He had Glenda. Had she made the wrong decision? No, she smiled to herself. This baby was going have so much love.

She suddenly stopped massaging her breasts. There was a lump. Fear filled her and she let the warm water cascade over her shoulders. 'No, stop being silly,' she admonished herself. 'There can't be anything wrong, I feel so well.'

That evening when Paula got home from the office she quickly leafed through the books on pregnancy she had borrowed from the library.

She began to read out loud, almost as if to reassure herself. ' "Sometimes the breasts feel lumpy due to the milk ducts." See, I knew there was nothing to worry about.' She tapped her stomach.

252

*   *   *

Every morning while showering or having a bath Paula was half afraid to touch her breast. Every day she wanted to tell someone but fear made her stop; if she said nothing perhaps the lump would go away.

As her breasts grew larger she convinced herself the lump had disappeared.

At the end of September Paula was due at the hospital and she casually mentioned the lump to the doctor. He confirmed what she'd read in the book and was told it was nothing to worry about.

Paula and Sue were having a coffee later that day when Sue said, 'Are you feeling all right? You've been very off for a few weeks now.'

'I'm fine,' she answered rather too quickly.

'No regrets?'

Paula laughed. 'No, course not.'

'Has Trevor been worrying you?'

'No. I haven't seen him for months. I don't think he'd be interested in me, not with this.' She placed her hand on her stomach.

Sue smiled. 'You're really beginning to show now. Looks like it could be a big baby.'

'Not too big, I hope.'

'Are you sleeping all right?'

'Yes.'

'You've got bags under your eyes.'

'Thanks, that really makes me feel good. Can't you say anything nice?'

Sue wasn't convinced everything was fine and decided to call Janet when she got home.

'Janet, it's me, Sue. Is there anything wrong with

253

Paula?'

Janet was filled with alarm. 'Why? What do you mean?'

'I don't know. I can't put my finger on it; she seems worried somehow. She looks like she isn't getting a lot of sleep.'

'I'll have a word with her.'

'She's very snappy and argumentative, which is not like her. I'm worried it might be Trevor bothering her.'

'She would have told you.'

'I don't know about that. She knows how I feel about him. Don't let her know I said anything.'

'Course not.'

When Janet put the phone down she sat and thought about these last few weeks. Yes, there was something not quite right. Paula seemed tired and had lost her sparkle, and she had been inclined to be a bit touchy but Janet had put that down to her hormones. Tomorrow she would look up her records at the hospital just to see if she was hiding something from them.

*   *   *

The next day Janet read through Paula's notes very carefully and as far as she could see there weren't any problems.

That evening she phoned Sue and told her that everything appeared to be fine.

Janet was going to see Paula later on the day the invitations to Tina's parents' ruby wedding party arrived. That evening she rang the doorbell of Paula's flat and waited, then rang again, becoming fidgety. Paula knew she was coming tonight; it had been arranged at the weekend. Her car was outside and she didn't walk anywhere these days. Janet rang the bell again, this time keeping her finger on the bell.

'I'm coming.' Paula pulled open the door. 'Oh, it's you. Sorry about that,' she said, quickly turning her head.

'Is everything all right?'

'Yes.' Paula desperately wanted to tell her about the lump and that it had returned.

'I've got the invites.'

'Invites? What to?'

'The ruby wedding do. Have you forgotten?'

'Yes. No. Sit down, I'll make a coffee.'

Janet could see she wasn't listening. 'Paula, are you sure you're all right?'

'Yes, yes I told you. Don't fuss.' Her voice was raised as she went quickly into the kitchen. Paula stood and looked at the kettle. She couldn't think straight. She touched her breast. Should she tell Janet? But what if it was a false alarm? She was confused. Was she getting upset over nothing?

Janet sat down. There was something wrong, but she didn't like to ask if Trevor been round upsetting her.

'Kettle's on,' said Paula, returning to the lounge.

Janet could see she had been crying. She jumped up. 'Paula, what's wrong?'

'Nothing,' she said abruptly, and turned to fiddle with a bowl of fruit that was on the coffee table. 'It's just that I'm fed up with you and Sue keeping on at me.'

'I'm sorry. I didn't realize we were.'

'I just feel a bit under the weather, that's all, and I get you and Sue on at me all the time, watching

255

me like a hawk. I can't move without one or the other of you. I want to do my own thing for a change. Make my own decisions.'

Janet didn't know what to say. 'I'm sorry. Would you like to be left alone then?'

'Yes,' she snapped. 'Yes I would. Just go, leave me. I should never have let you come into my life.'

Janet was speechless. 'I can't leave you in this mood.'

'I said go,' screamed Paula. 'I never want to see you again.'

Janet had tears in her eyes. She picked up her handbag and slowly walked out of the room. Every step she took she wanted Paula to call her back, but she didn't.

Tears were dimming her view as she drove home. What had happened to bring this about? Why was she being pushed out? Had she been too overbearing? She couldn't stand being rejected again.

*　　　*　　　*

Paula stood at the window and watched her go. Why was she doing this to Janet? She knew the answer. Fear.

*　　　*　　　*

When Janet arrived home she wanted to tell someone, but was afraid Paula wouldn't like it if she phoned Sue, so she phoned Freda.

'Why did she react like that?' she cried to Freda.

'Perhaps she's right. Perhaps she is feeling stifled with you and Sue round her all the while.'

'I'll stand back.'

'I think that'll be wise. She'll phone you when she's calmed down.'

'I hope so. I couldn't stand to be tossed aside now.'

'Don't worry, I'm sure everything's all right. Just give her a bit of time.'

'Thanks, Freda. What would I do without you?'

'Dunno. By the way, did you get your invite to Elsie's do?'

'Yes.'

'I'm really looking forward to that. We'll have to think of something nice to buy them.'

'Yes, we will.'

They said their goodbyes.

Janet knew the last thing on her mind at the moment was Tina's mum's wedding anniversary.

*　　　*　　　*

Paula, through her tears, watched Janet drive away. Why was she being so silly? Janet was the one person she should be able to confide in. Fear had been making her angry. She needed Janet and knew she had to ask her to come back. She had to talk to her.

Paula dialled Janet's number, but it was engaged. She would be telling Sue and in a few minutes Sue would be round here banging on the door.

She sat and looked at the phone. She had made up her mind that tomorrow she would go and see her doctor and then this thing would be all behind her. She felt her baby move. Please don't let it be anything dreadful, she prayed.

The following evening Paula was surprised that Sue hadn't been round. Perhaps Janet *hadn't* phoned her.

After seeing her doctor she still needed comfort, and phoned Janet. She knew she should apologize, and sooner rather than later was better for everyone.

'I'm sorry about yesterday,' said Paula. 'Could you come round?'

'I'll see you in about half an hour.'

When Paula opened her door she said, 'I tried to phone you last night but you were engaged.' Janet felt angry at being on the phone when Paula had wanted her. Why had she bothered to tell Freda? 'I'm sorry about that. I was talking to Freda; we were discussing the present for Tina's parents.'

'I'm so sorry for what I said, but you see I was really worried.' Paula sat down and tears began to stream down her cheeks.

Janet sat beside her. 'What about? Is it Trevor?'

Paula shook her head.

Janet gave her a tissue and Paula blew her nose.

'Please tell me what's wrong.'

'I was just being silly. You see, I've got this lump, and well, I thought it was getting bigger.'

'Where?' asked Janet in alarm.

Paula pointed to her left breast.

Janet sat stunned. 'Have you told your doctor?'

Paula nodded. 'I went to see him today.'

'What did he say?'

'Said it was nothing to worry about. It was probably my milk ducts.'

258

'He could be right.'

'I know. But somehow ... I'm very worried about it.'

'How long have you felt it?'

'About six weeks now.'

'Six weeks!' screamed Janet. 'And you've kept it to yourself?'

She nodded. 'At first I didn't see any point in making a fuss. But it is getting bigger.'

'No wonder you've been a bit sharp. Paula, you should have said something.'

'I didn't want to make a fuss.'

'Can you get tomorrow off work?'

'If need be. Why?'

'I'll try and have a word with Dr Parker.'

'What will he do?'

'He'll have a look and confirm what your doctor has told you.'

'Is he a mother and baby doctor?'

'No. But he's very patient and good at sorting out things.'

'What kind of things?'

'He looks at all sorts of lumps and bumps.'

Paula sat very still and quietly asked, 'Is he a cancer doctor?'

'No. Well, in a way, yes.'

'Is that what you think it might be?'

'No, I don't,' said Janet forcefully. 'But that's what you're thinking, isn't it?'

Paula nodded.

'Well, in that case we had better make sure you can put that idea right out of your mind.'

'But what if ... ?'

'I'm sure it's nothing to worry about.'

Paula put her arm round Janet. 'I'm so glad I've

got you to talk to. I feel awful about last night. I didn't think you'd want to see me again.'

Janet smiled. 'If you think one little outburst is going to put me off, then you don't really know me.' Janet held her close. She was fighting back her tears. 'Now, what about this coffee?'

*   *   *

It was well into the night before Janet reluctantly left. All the way home her mind was going over and over the evening. What torment had Paula been going through? Why had she kept this to herself for so long? At least now she was able to share her anxieties.

Janet would go in to work early tomorrow and see Dr Parker before he started his rounds. He was a very busy man but she knew she could get him to see Paula, who had decided to go to work and wait for Janet's call, just in case the doctor couldn't see her right away.

They had to know for sure.

Janet's mind was in a muddle. All kinds of thoughts kept coming into it and she tried to banish them away. God couldn't be that cruel to take . . .

'Please,' she said out loud. 'Please don't let it be . . .' She couldn't say the word.

CHAPTER TWENTY-FOUR

Danny looked at his watch: six o'clock. Mondays were always dead, and he'd promised Tina he'd try to get home early. It was hot and he felt tetchy.

He'd been dealing with a difficult supplier all day and still hadn't got the part he wanted.

He was just locking the office door when a car drew into the courtyard. He cursed under his breath. He didn't want anybody wasting time looking over cars they had no intention of buying.

The driver got out and for a moment he stood looking at Danny. Then the man, who was slightly greying at the temples, came up and shook Danny's hand. Danny was speechless.

'Hi there, me old mate. Long time no see,' he said with a slight Canadian twang.

'Mark! What the bloody hell are you doing here?'

'That is just the sort of welcome I'd expect from you.' To Mark the years just fell away; it was as though he had never left. 'So, you still own this place then?'

Danny threw his arms round Mark's shoulders and held him close. 'It's good to see you, me old mucker. Why didn't you let me know? How're you doing then?' Danny was pumping his arm up and down.

'Not bad. Not bad at all.'

'So what you doing over here, and why ain't you ever written?'

'It's a long, long story.'

'Where are you staying? Can you spare the time to come and have a drink?'

'I thought you'd never ask.'

'Look, I'll just go and phone the wife.'

Mark grinned. 'So you're married then? Who's the lucky girl?'

'Tina, you don't know her. Come in the office.' Danny opened the door.

'I must say you've certainly tarted the place up a bit since I was here last,' said Mark, looking around. 'Wasn't sure you'd still be here; thought you'd be in the nick by now.'

'Thanks. I might tell you I'm a respectable trader now.'

Mark laughed. 'Wasn't sure I was at the right place. Even the office looks smart.'

'I had to get a new one; the last one was falling down.'

'You've got some pretty good cars out there.'

'Gone a bit upmarket.'

'I can see that. Got a partner yet?'

'Na. Rather go it alone. You're looking good, Mark.'

'So are you.'

'Getting a bit grey round the edges now.'

'Aren't we both?' Mark ran his fingers over his hair. 'Still, you look very prosperous.'

'I mustn't grumble.' He picked up the phone and dialled. 'Hello, love, it's me. Look, I'll probably be home late tonight. Yes, I know I did but something's come up. Do you remember Mark? Janet's Mark.' Danny noted Mark's head shot up at Janet's name. 'Yes, that's the one. Well, he's here, bold as brass and twice as handsome. We're going for a drink.' There was a long pause. 'That's none of our business,' he said, turning his back on Mark. 'Yes, I'll get a cab. Kiss Jason good night for me. Bye.' He replaced the phone and turned to Mark. 'Right, that's settled.'

'You've got kids?' asked Mark.

'Two, a boy and a girl.' He proudly handed Mark one of the pictures on his desk. 'That's Jason—he's six—and that's Emma. She's fourteen now and a right little madam.'

'They look great kids and your wife is certainly a stunner. How did you manage to get one as good-looking as that?'

Danny laughed. 'It's me charm and you can keep your eyes off her.'

'Well, I never pictured you as a family man.'

'What about you, you got any kids?'

'No.' Mark's reply was short. 'Now, how about this drink?'

'Leave your car here. We can walk round the corner. Where're you staying tonight?'

'Don't know yet.'

'Why don't you come back to my place?'

'I can't do that.'

'Why not?'

'Your wife might not like it.'

'She won't mind. I'll give her a ring later and tell her.'

When they were finally seated in the pub with their drinks, Danny began asking questions.

'Anyway, what you doing back here?'

'I came over this time for my dad's funeral.'

'You've been back before this then?'

'Once or twice.'

'I'm sorry to hear about your dad.'

Mark shrugged. 'It happens to us all. Anyway, I thought that after all these years I'd bury the hatchet and come and look you up. Not that I really thought you'd still be at the same place.'

'Well, I'll be buggered, after all this time. I never thought I'd see you again after the to-do we had when you left here. By the way, that bloke didn't have a driving licence; he couldn't drive. He got sent down.'

'I was a bit hasty over that.'

'And leaving Jan. That was a rotten thing to do.'

'You know about that?' Mark looked surprised.

'She did tell me.'

'I never thought I'd ever hear of her again. She left Stowford and nobody knew where she'd gone.' He looked into his glass and gently swirled the beer round.

'Did you try to find her then?'

He nodded. 'I made a few enquiries some years back.'

'Well, it's all water under the bridge now.' Danny decided he had better not pursue that line of conversation and quickly said, 'So, are you married? Have you brought the missis over here?'

'No, I'm not married now. I was, but it didn't work out.'

'Sorry to hear about that.'

'I've got a good job, though.'

'Still in the car game?'

'Yes. I'm a manager of a big firm, leasing and that sort of thing. They've got branches in the States. We do a lot of business down there.'

'So, how long you over here for?'

'About six weeks all told.'

'Blimey, that must be a good firm. With pay?'

Mark nodded. 'I had a lot of holidays due, and at this time of the year when the weather starts to turn, that's when I normally go to the States for them. This year they didn't mind me coming back over here first.'

Danny noted he didn't say home. 'Where're you living then?'

'Toronto.'

'Is it all right?'

'It's great. Don't think I could live back here, not now. How long have you been hitched then?'

'A few years.'

'Still living in the same house?'

'Yer. Had quite a bit of work done on it, had an extension added, and a swimming pool.'

Mark gave a low whistle. 'A pool, now that has to be something. Is it indoors?'

'No, worse luck, but I might see if I can get a dome or something over it so we can use it all year round. What's your place like?'

'Just a town house, but I've got a cabin in the mountains that I use at weekends. It's great in the summer and good for skiing in the winter.'

'Sounds good.'

'You'll have to come over sometime. The cabin's by a lake and in the summer the swimming and the fishing's fantastic.'

As the evening wore on the drinks set them off reminiscing. They talked about their days way back in the army where they met, and then when Danny first started his car business.

'You had some right old heaps in those days,' said Mark.

Danny laughed. 'It paid off, though.'

'And what about the grotty flat?'

'You should have seen it when Jan lived there.'

'Jan lived in it? She came to London?' Mark had been deliberately avoiding asking about her. 'Do you still see her?'

'We're good mates.'

'How is she?'

'Very well. She never married.'

Mark looked into his glass. 'Where is she now?'

'Not far away. Got a nice little house and she

265

works at the hospital. Her and Paula come over quite a bit.'

'Do you know why I went away?'

'It was over the car thing and Jan looking for her daughter, wasn't it?'

'You knew she had a daughter?'

'Not till you went off.'

'She told you?' Mark put his drink down in surprise.

'You were a bastard over that and she needed a shoulder to cry on. She came up here to live and work and to track down Paula. It took her a long time.'

'She found her?' His voice was full of astonishment.

'It took years, but yes, she found her. Jan is a very determined lady.'

'Is she keeping well?' he asked softly.

Danny smiled. 'I should say so. She still looks good and she's gonner be a granny. Look, why don't you stay up here for a day or two, then I can get her to meet you somewhere?'

'No. No, I can't. I don't want to intrude on her life, not after all this time.'

'Don't be daft. She'll be pleased to see you, and I'm sure she don't hold any grudges. Jan's not like that.'

'You seem to know her pretty well.' Mark drained his glass.

'As I said, I was there when she needed a shoulder to cry on. I've got a very soft spot for Jan, and I would have married her at one time if she'd given me half a chance.'

'What does your wife think of that?'

'She loves Jan, and Paula. All the family do. I

266

still think Jan's carrying a torch for you.'

'Don't talk daft. After all these years?'

'She never married. She's a smashing person.'

'You sound as if you're carrying the torch.'

'I did for a good many years, before Tina came on the scene, but no, not now. Look, I'll phone Tina and we can go home and finish our drinking there.'

When Danny went to the phone Mark sat and thought about Janet. What did she look like now? She would no longer be that slim young girl he knew and had loved. Danny had said she was going to be a granny. Had her daughter been pleased to see her? Did her son-in-law approve of what she had done all those years ago? Was she still angry with him after the way he had treated her? His mother had told him that she had left Stowford the day after he did and nobody had heard a word from her since. Did she know her father had passed away? Had she lived in London all this time? He would like to see her again, but did she want to see him?

'Right, that's settled,' said Danny. 'I've called a cab.'

'Will my car be all right on your forecourt?'

'I should think so.'

'It's a hire car.'

'Don't worry about it.'

'Does your wife mind?' asked Mark as Danny downed his beer. 'No, she's a good 'en.'

'D'you know, this beer's going to my head.'

'Now that's one thing Tina don't approve of.'

'What's that?'

'Blokes chucking up all over the place.'

'No fear of that. It's too good to waste.'

They left the pub laughing, but both were thinking about Janet.

They sat in the taxi, each with his own thoughts.

Danny wanted to phone her secretly and tell her Mark was here, but would she want to see him?

Mark was keen to see Janet again. He needed to ask her forgiveness. Danny had said she hadn't married. He smiled to himself. After all these years did he stand a chance? She had found her daughter. She had to be admired for that. He now knew he should never have been so stupid—and that deep down he had never stopped loving Janet even though he had married Babs. Janet was so different: when she loved she gave it her all, as looking for her daughter had proved. He would so much like to be part of her life again, to show her his new way of life, but would she want to share it with him? He knew he had to see her before he returned to Canada.

* * *

As soon as he set eyes on Tina, Mark knew what had attracted Danny. She was a tall blonde with laughing blue eyes, and even after having two kids she still had a great figure. She gave her husband a big hug but stood back when Danny introduced her to Mark.

'Hello,' she said offering her hand. 'I've heard a lot about you.'

Mark felt ill at ease. 'And I know it's not all good.'

She didn't answer and turning to Danny said, 'I only hope you two haven't been drinking too much.'

268

'No, love, just a couple of pints.'

'I've made a bed up for you in the spare room,' she said to Mark abruptly and without hiding her feelings.

'Thank you. I hope I'm not putting you out.'

'Would you like a cup of coffee?'

'I'll put the kettle on,' said Danny.

'You've done wonders with this house. I would never have recognized it,' said Mark, looking around.

'That's Tina's good taste. You wait till morning and get a shufty at the garden.'

'This room is really smart.' Mark was sitting on the floral sofa in the lounge. Soft lighting added to the room's charm.

Mark sensed Tina didn't like him and that made the conversation stilted. He was glad when they finished their coffee and everyone agreed it was time for bed.

Mark lay stretched out on his back with his arms behind his head and looking up at the ceiling, reflected on his life. It was something he had done many times since going to Canada. At first he was so homesick and never thought he would stay.

He could understand Tina's opinion of him, he knew what he'd done had been very cowardly. If only things had been different . . .

He could remember every moment of that day, all those years ago, when he'd left Stowford. As he drove home from Danny's that evening he was so very upset and never imagined that Janet wouldn't go to Canada with him to start a new life. And he could never in his wildest dreams have guessed that her reason for not going was to look for her long-lost kid.

After he had left her standing at her gate with tears running down her face he had driven about the village, trying to get his head round the thought that she had a child. Why hadn't she told him about it before? He should have given her another chance to explain and himself a few days to cool his heels, but that wasn't his way. After collecting his things from his flat he spent the night at the airport. He managed to get a flight to Toronto, but if the only flight available had been going to Tibet he probably would have taken it. He thought about Jan and the hurt he felt and at the time part of him had been reluctant to board the plane, but he couldn't go back.

When he arrived in Toronto he felt out of place, but he got lucky in finding a job as a mechanic. Babs worked in the office and before long they were dating and were married within the year. There were long hours with the job, but he had stuck with it and when promotion was on the cards he was put forward. He was their main traveller now, but it meant many days and sometimes even weeks away from home. He didn't mind that, as he and Babs weren't hitting it off, and it was no surprise when she left him for another bloke and they moved away.

Mark turned over. He was pleased Janet had found her daughter. He would love to see her again. Danny said she had never married and he felt guilty at letting her down. How did her family react to the news that he had jilted her? He shuddered. That was a horrible word, but then it was a horrible deed and he felt full of remorse. Many times he had thought of trying to find her, but where would he look? Now he knew where she was and he had to see her and ask her forgiveness. But would she forgive him? He was angry with himself for throwing away all these years.

It had taken the death of his father to realize life was short and you shouldn't have hang-ups. It was those thoughts that brought him back to London and to Danny, but in any case he now felt unsettled and wasn't sure what he wanted out of life. He was pleased his mother was going to Canada with him for a holiday. How many times had he asked them both to come over? With the money he was earning he could afford to pay their fares, but it was too late for his dad now.

His eyes began to feel heavy. It had been a long day. He knew that when sleep did come he would, as he had many other nights, be dreaming of Janet.

CHAPTER TWENTY-FIVE

Paula had spent the night drinking coffee and reading, but the words on the page hadn't registered. Every time she got back into bed she'd pummel her pillow, turning this way and that, trying to get comfortable, but sleep wouldn't come. So many questions were going through her mind. What if it was cancer and she died? What would happen to her baby? What would Trevor's reactions be to all this? She quickly dismissed that thought as she knew he couldn't handle another problem. What did return to her mind over and over again was, thank God Janet had found her. She knew now how much her mother had come to mean to her and she would need all her support.

271

Janet was someone who had her interest at heart and would look after her. Tears filled her eyes. What will I do if I'm told the worst? she wept. She needed to talk to Janet. Paula looked at the clock; it was three o'clock. She couldn't phone her, not at this time of the morning.

*　　　*　　　*

Janet was glad to see the dawn finally break. Most of the night she had been awake, tossing and turning, worrying about Paula. Had Paula managed to sleep? What was going through her mind? She wanted to be with her. At three o'clock this morning Janet had been making more coffee. She would dearly have loved to have phoned Paula, to talk to her and try to reassure her, but decided against it, just in case she was sleeping. When Janet looked in the mirror she knew her dreadful night was showing.

Having arrived at the hospital early she managed to track down Dr Parker, who was in his consulting room having a coffee before starting his long day. She carefully explained about Paula.

He sat listening intently, then finally asked, 'When can I see your daughter?'

'As soon as you can arrange it.'

'You know it doesn't have to be cancer. Pregnant women get all sorts of lumps.'

'She said it has grown.'

He looked at her and said gently, 'I'll draw off some of the cells and we'll know better when they've been examined.'

'How long will that take?'

'A few days for the results to come through.'

272

'But what if—'

'Please, don't start worrying too much at this stage. If it is cancer, remember today we have a good recovery record—not the best in the world, I grant you, but we are making strides.' He called in his nurse. 'Make arrangements for Miss Slater's daughter to have an appointment for a biopsy as soon as possible.' He turned to Janet and smiled.

She gave him a faint smile back and, following the nurse, left the room.

'I didn't know you had a daughter,' said the nurse as she leafed through the appointment book.

Janet didn't reply.

'Could she come in next week?'

'Oh,' said Janet in alarm. 'Nothing sooner? I was hoping it would be today?'

'He's a very busy man, you know.'

'I expect he is.' Janet knew how fiercely loyal some of the nurses were to their doctors and would do anything to keep their lists down. 'You understand we would like to know the answer soon,' she said meekly.

'I'll find out. I can only do my best.'

'Thank you.'

She went back to the doctor and within a few minutes came out smiling. 'You must have some sort of charm. He said if you can get her here today after his rounds he'll see her then, not for the biopsy, just to see if it's needed.'

Janet wanted to throw her arms round him. At the end of today would all their fears be dismissed?

Janet was on the phone immediately, telling Paula to meet her at the hospital before six.

She asked Paula how she felt and she said fine and gave a little laugh, but Janet could detect fear in her voice. Unfortunately Janet couldn't say much over the phone so the conversation was cut short.

When Janet put the phone down she sat and reflected on the morning so far. What if the consultation brought news neither of them wanted to hear? Dr Parker hadn't made any comments when Janet had been explaining the situation to him. The phone ringing made her jump. It was still a bit early for appointments to be booked.

When she answered it she was surprised to hear Danny's voice. He never phoned her at work.

'Danny. What's wrong?'

'I've been trying to get hold of you at home.'

'What is it? Is something wrong with Tina?'

'No, nothing like that. I've got some good news. Well, I think it is.'

She sat stunned as he went into great detail of what had happened the previous evening. When he stopped she asked, 'Is Mark still in this country?'

'Yes, he's staying at our place for a few days, so, can you come over this evening?'

'No. No, I can't. I'm busy.'

'Can't you put it off?'

'No, I can't.'

'Well, what about tomorrow night?'

'I'll have to see. I'll ring you and let you know.'

'Jan, he said he'd like to see you.'

Mark wanted to see her. She felt her knees go weak. 'How is he?' she whispered.

'Fine and still as good-looking. Do try to get over, Jan.'

'I'll try.' She played with the phone cord, winding it round and round her fingers. 'How long is he staying?'

274

'Only for a few days. I know it might be a bit awkward, but see if you can make the effort. I know he really wants to see you.'

'I'll think about it. At the moment it is a bit difficult.'

'Well, give me a ring.'

'I'm sorry, but I must go.'

They said their goodbyes.

Janet sat staring at the phone. Mark was in this country. Was he married? Danny had said he would like to see her, he hadn't mentioned that he was with anybody. He said he was only here for a few days so he hadn't come back for good. Janet knew that at that moment the most important person in her life was Paula, and Mark would have to wait. She wanted to laugh and cry together. Once again she was going to have to make a choice, but once again she knew where her priority lay and Mark would have to take second place.

*   *   *

The day dragged for Paula. After Janet's phone call first thing this morning she had decided to go to her office. That might take her mind off things and help to pass the time.

Although she was busy, Janet also thought the day seemed to be going on for ever and she was so pleased when Paula walked in at five thirty.

'I know I'm early, but I couldn't go home,' said Paula.

'Don't worry. I've finished so we can go along and see if Dr Parker is in his office. I'll just get my things.'

They walked in silence to the doctor's room.

275

Janet gently knocked on the door.

'Come in.'

Janet took a deep breath and walked in, Paula right behind her.

'So, this is your daughter?'

'Yes.'

'Now, young lady, you have a lump?'

'Yes.'

'Well, I'd better have a look at it.'

'I'll wait outside,' said Janet hastily.

'You don't have to,' said the doctor.

As he didn't know their circumstances and Janet wasn't sure if Paula wanted her that involved with something so personal, she decided to leave.

Impatiently she sat outside wondering what was happening. Why does time sometimes appear to stand still? she was thinking.

At last the door opened and Paula called her in.

Dr Parker was writing. He looked up. 'Your daughter has a lump that I'm not that happy about.'

Janet quickly looked at Paula, whose face gave nothing away.

'I am arranging for her to have a biopsy. I shall be drawing off a few cells.'

'When?' said Janet rather louder than she wanted to.

'Nurse tells me I can fit it in tomorrow.' He leant back in his chair and put his fingers together. 'You know it doesn't have to be malignant. Most lumps are benign and as Paula is pregnant that could be the reason for it, but we shall see. I hope that the biopsy will put both your minds at rest.'

Paula gave Janet a slight smile that lifted her pale face.

'I'll bring you,' said Janet, worried at the urgency of it.

'Thanks.'

Outside Janet took Paula's hand. 'Would you like to come home with me?'

She nodded. 'Could I stay the night? I don't want to be on my own.'

'Of course.'

'I'll have to go home first to get some things.'

'I'll follow you, then you can leave your car at your place.'

'Thank you, Janet.' She threw her arms round Janet, who was trying desperately to stem the tears that were about to fall.

'You must tell Sue all that's happened.'

'I will.'

'She's very worried about you.'

'I know. I have been giving her a hard time.'

'When she knows the reason she'll understand.'

*   *   *

At first Sue wanted to see Paula but she said she was spending the night with Janet and that put Sue's mind at rest.

'I'll tell you everything that happens.'

'You'd better.'

All evening Janet and Paula talked about their pasts, little things they both felt they needed to know about each other, things that had been left unsaid before. They carefully avoided the subject that was uppermost in both their minds. Finally they went to bed. After another fitful night they were up and about early, getting ready for the trip to the hospital.

277

The nurse told Janet she would phone down when the biopsy was all over. She also told her they wouldn't know the results for a few days.

Janet tried to concentrate on her work but it was very difficult and she was pleased when Sue walked in.

'I couldn't wait at home. Is she all right?' asked Sue, her face ashen with concern.

'I don't know.'

'When did they do it?'

'I think she was one of the first in, but you know how long some of these things take. We won't know the results for a little while.'

'Can't you pull any strings?'

'I shall have a go, but you know what some of these departments are like.'

'I'll hang around for a while. I'll go and have a coffee.'

'As soon as I hear anything I'll come and get you.'

'Thanks,' Sue smiled.

Every time the phone rang Janet was on tenterhooks.

Then at long last the nurse told Janet that Paula was in the waiting room. She hurried along to the coffee shop to collect Sue and they made their way to find Paula.

'How are you feeling?' asked Janet, sitting next to her.

'A bit sore.'

'Do you hurt anywhere?'

'Only under my arm.'

Janet looked anxious. 'Look, I can't leave just yet. Sue, could you take Paula home?'

'Of course.'

'Would you like to stay with me tonight?' asked Janet.

'No, thanks all the same but I'll be all right.'

'When you're ready I'll take you home,' said Sue. 'Mum's looking after the kids so it's a good excuse to stay out of it for an hour or two.'

'Thanks, Sue,' said Janet.

*   *   *

Once she'd arrived home after work, Janet first rang Paula and when she was reassured that she was all right she sat and looked at the phone. Throughout the day all thoughts of Mark had gone out of her head. But then he began to fill her mind. Should she phone Danny? Did she really want to see Mark?

She finally decided she needed someone to talk to and it had to be Freda.

She told Freda everything, including the news that Mark was over here, which left Freda breathless.

'I'm coming over now,' she said.

'No, you don't have to.'

'I want to.'

'Leave it for tonight. I'll let you know how things turn out.'

'OK.'

Janet looked at her watch: it was seven. She dialled Danny's number.

Tina answered the phone. She quickly decided not to tell them about Paula, there wasn't any point at this stage.

Tina told Janet that Danny and Mark had gone out. 'He's a bit of all right. I was a bit off at first,

279

after what he done to you, but he seems a really nice bloke.'

Janet smiled. 'Is he back here for good?'

'No, he's just come over for his dad's funeral. Sounds like he's got a really good job in Canada.'

'Is he with his wife?' Janet asked tentatively.

'He ain't married. He was once, but not now. Jan, he's still got a soft spot for you, you know.'

Janet laughed. 'That's all in the past now.'

'Look, why don't you come over tomorrow evening? You can have a nice long chat.'

'No, I don't think I can make it.'

'Jan, don't leave it too long, he's only here for a few days.'

'I'll try not to. Tell him I called and that I'm sorry to hear about his father.'

She replaced the receiver and wept. She was crying for Paula, her baby and now Mark. What future did they all have?

CHAPTER TWENTY-SIX

Days later Janet was sitting in the corridor outside Dr Parker's consulting room, waiting for Paula, who was there for the results of her biopsy. As she hadn't been recalled, gradually, as the days went by, their fears had receded, they'd relaxed and had carried on as usual.

Janet sat back and began thinking about her meeting with Mark last week. She smiled to herself. Somehow he seemed taller and more good-looking than ever, in a mature way. He was certainly more self-assured. Tina had told him Janet had phoned and he'd returned the call, and had asked to take her out for a meal. As Paula was back at home and appeared fine, Janet had readily agreed.

*   *   *

When they'd first met he had hugged her and she'd been full of mixed feelings. It had been difficult to talk at Danny's and in the car they had only exchanged a few words. Janet had been pleased they were going to spend an evening in a restaurant and as the evening wore on they relaxed and soon were laughing and talking over old times.

He'd told her about his life in Canada. She had listened spellbound when he described Toronto.

'It has the longest street in the world. And it can be very cold in winter, but our homes are built for it. You would love my cabin in the mountains. In the summer you can take the boat out on the lake or just sit on the bank, then at night when we have a log fire it's warm and cosy. In the autumn the trees are full of colours that you'd never believe—it's a wonderful sight. We also get the great brown bears wandering around. I can ski now. I tell you, Jan, it's a different world over there. You'd love the shopping malls, and you should see the different ice-cream flavours they've got.' He was bubbling over with enthusiasm.

Although she knew he was divorced she had to ask. 'So who's the lucky person who shares all this with you?'

He began to fiddle with his fork. 'No one now. In some ways I wasn't sorry when Babs left. She wasn't what I wanted. She was just there when I needed a shoulder to cry on.'

281

'I know the feeling,' said Janet softly.

'I know now that in many ways I was a fool to go off like I did. Don't get me wrong, I don't regret going to Canada one bit, but I do regret leaving you.' He leant forward and touched her hand.

'Don't, Mark.' She quickly pulled it away.

'Jan, can you ever forgive me for what I put you through?'

'We were both to blame. I should have told you about Paula.'

'I shouldn't have been such a hothead. I know now I was stupid, but my pride was hurt.'

'I was very upset at the time.'

'You've never married?'

'No.'

'Do you think we could ever pick up the pieces again?'

'I don't think so. We are both very different people and live in different parts of the world and all that happened a long while ago. Things have changed.'

'But have our feelings?'

Ignoring that question she asked, 'So has Stowford changed that much?' She hadn't told him she'd returned and had seen her mother.

He sat back. 'No, not really. I told you about my father?'

She nodded.

'I'm taking Ma back with me for a holiday.'

'That'll be exciting for her. How long will she be there?'

'I'd like her to stay till after Christmas, but she might not like that; she's a bit shaky on her pins these days. I'll have to go to the States at some time so if she didn't come with me she would be left on

282

her own.'

'When do you go back?'

'Next week. You know, Jan, if you and your daughter ever want a holiday you'd be more than welcome and I'd love to show you the sights.'

Janet laughed. 'We'll have to wait a while till the baby's a bit older.'

'Fancy you going to be a grandmother.'

She smiled and would have liked to have said, 'And you could have been its grandfather if you hadn't run away.'

'I do admire you for all your perseverance.'

'It paid off in the end.'

'You must be very proud of her.'

'Yes I am.'

'I would like to meet your daughter.'

'Perhaps the next time you are over here. Now you've broken the ice you can always keep Danny informed.'

'Will you ever forgive me, Jan?'

She looked down. She couldn't look him in the eye. In some ways she would never forgive him, but in others she knew in her heart that she would have loved to have shared all those years with him. She looked up. 'That's all water under the bridge now.'

'I will write to you.'

'That will be nice.'

As he drove her back home he said that as it was late he didn't think he'd come in for a coffee.

They sat in the car for a moment or two and Mark put his arm round her. When he pulled her close and kissed her lips she felt herself melting. She was flustered; she pulled away and quickly said good night. Once again she was standing watching him drive off alone, knowing that she could never be part of his life now, but she was also aware that all her old feelings for him had returned.

*　　　*　　　*

The noise in the hospital brought Janet back. She looked at her watch. She was beginning to get a little concerned. Paula had been in there a long while and she noticed the nurse seemed to be deliberately avoiding eye contact. Was anything wrong? No, she would have been recalled if they had found . . . Janet instantly dismissed that thought.

'Are you Paula's mother?' asked a sister who had come out of the room.

'Yes.' Janet could hardly get the word out. Fear was racing through her mind.

'Can you come in?'

Janet followed her into the room. Paula was sitting on the bed crying. She held out her arms to Janet.

Janet took hold of her and held her close. Paula's sobs racked her body and filled the air. Janet didn't have to be told, she knew the news was bad.

Dr Parker's voice was very soft: 'I'm very sorry, but I'm afraid the tumour is malignant.'

Janet felt as if a knife had been thrust into her. This wasn't happening. She heard herself saying, 'No, no, it can't be.'

Someone said something but it wasn't registering in Janet's head and she asked, 'What happens now?'

'Well, I am waiting for Paula's doctor. We are going to discuss the baby. You see, I need to remove the growth, do a mastectomy and give Paula radiotherapy treatment, but I'm afraid Paula is adamant about not having it.'

'I'm not putting my baby at risk,' yelled Paula.

Janet was looking from one to the other, bewildered. 'What's going to happen?'

'I need to give Paula radiotherapy treatment but because of the baby it isn't possible.'

Janet felt sick. She wanted to pick up Paula and run away with her.

Dr Parker was still talking. 'As Paula is so far advanced I'm sure we can arrange for her to have a Caesarean section safely.'

'But she's got another two months to go.'

'Seven-month babies do survive.'

'And then what?' asked Janet weakly.

'We will discuss the removal of her breast, then we can start with the radiotherapy.' He sounded very optimistic.

'When can all this be done?' asked Janet softly.

'As soon as possible. I don't want to leave her treatment for too long.'

All this time, after her first outburst, Paula, who was cradled in Janet's arms, was silent. Only her gentle sobs and wet tears spreading across Janet's blouse told of the terror she was going through.

One by one doctors, nurses and the radiotherapy doctor came and went, each one discussing Paula almost as if she wasn't there.

Finally they were told they could go. The hospital would notify Paula as soon as it was possible to move the lists round.

'Don't worry about it,' said Paula, and her voice sounded so small and far away. 'I'm not having my baby put in any danger.'

'It won't be,' said Janet.

'I shall wait till it's born.'

'You can't,' said Janet.

'It's my body and my baby.'

'Paula, you can't.' Janet wanted to crumple in a heap. 'Please, Doctor, tell her she's wrong.'

'I'm afraid she's right. It is her decision although I think she is putting her own life at risk. The longer we leave the treatment the larger the growth will become.'

'Paula, listen to the doctor.'

'I want to give my baby every chance.'

'It will have.' Janet wanted to shake Paula. 'Please, Doctor, can't you make her see sense?'

'See how she feels in the morning. Come and see me when you've decided.'

Janet helped Paula from the bed. She suddenly seemed like a little girl, small and vulnerable.

Slowly they walked in silence till they reached the car park, then Paula began to laugh. It was a loud hysterical laugh and at the same time tears were running down her cheeks.

'Paula, what's wrong?'

'Me and you. We really are of the same mould. Both cursed.' She leant against the car and cried. They were bitter, angry tears. 'Don't you see? You spend your life looking for me, then when you find me I'm going to die on you. Now my baby is going to be like me, it'll have no mum to love and look after it.'

Janet felt as if she'd been shot. All the hurt she'd suffered these past years was bearing down on her. This shouldn't be happening. What could she say? 'Paula, don't say such things. Don't be such a pessimist.'

286

'What else can I do, start singing "Always Look on the Bright Side of Life"?'

'Now you're being silly.'

'Am I? I don't want to die.'

Janet felt herself tense. She wanted to scream out, 'You are not going to die.' Instead she said softly, 'Remember what they said. Let's take one step at a time and see how you feel tomorrow.'

Paula's mind was racing when she got into Janet's car. What was going to happen to her baby? How much time did she have? Suddenly she knew she had to be positive. She mustn't think about herself; she had to make plans for her baby's welfare. Tomorrow she would see about making a will.

*　　　*　　　*

At first Paula moved in with Janet but after a week of tears, frustration and worry, the arrangement was not working. Paula decided she wanted to go home. She had completely dismissed the idea of having a Caesarean and Janet knew that if she kept nagging she would lose her. Sue also gave up as she too knew Paula had made up her mind.

Two weeks passed in which Janet hadn't seen Paula. She phoned but the conversation was always curt and cut short. Janet tearfully phoned Sue, who told her Paula was keeping herself to herself. Sue hadn't seen much of Paula and she was also very worried. On Sunday morning they decided to meet outside Paula's flat. They went up the stairs together and rang her bell.

Janet gasped when Paula opened the door.

'What do you two want?' Her eyes had lost their

sparkle and had dark rings under them. Her hair was lank and untidy.

'Oh, that's very nice,' said Sue, pushing past her and walking in.

'Paula, you don't look well,' said Janet, following Sue.

'Have you forgotten I'm pregnant and I've got cancer?'

'No, of course we haven't. We're both very worried about you.'

'I'll make a cuppa,' said Sue, moving towards the kitchen. 'My God,' she called out. 'The state of this place.'

Paula looked guilty. 'Well, I didn't feel like doing any clearing up.'

'I can see that,' said Sue, standing in the doorway.

'What's the point when I'm going to die anyway?'

'I do love your positive attitude,' said Sue. Janet could see her hands shaking. 'But what about that little bundle you're carrying? Do you intend to bring it home to this pigsty?'

Janet felt uncomfortable. She could see the lovely flat was in turmoil. Only Sue could talk to Paula like this.

'Right, Jan, can you give me a hand to clear up this mess?' said Sue.

Janet quickly moved to the kitchen.

'You don't have to, you know,' said Paula.

'I'm not drinking tea here till I wash some of this lot. You can't live like this. What on earth has got into you? You've always been so fussy.' Sue began to fill the sink with water and dirty crocks.

Paula stood and looked at them and suddenly

288

tears ran down her face. 'What's going to happen to my baby?'

Janet threw the tea towel on to the unit and gathered Paula into her arms.

'Have you decided yet what you're going to do?' asked Sue softly.

Paula nodded. 'As I'm now over seven months I've decided to go ahead with the Caesarean.'

'Thank God for that,' said Sue.

'And the mastectomy?'

Paula shook her head. 'I don't think I could bear to look at my body after that. Besides, who would want me then? I know Trevor couldn't bear to look at me.'

'Has Trevor been in touch then?' asked Sue quickly.

'No.'

'I can tell you that any man that was worth his salt would love you as you are,' said Sue.

Paula looked at her. 'It's all right for you, you've got a good man.'

Janet felt ill at ease. 'Look, you have a rest, then we'll pack your case and you move in with me. We can sort anything else out later.'

'We'd better get this flat in some sort of order first,' said Sue, pulling on rubber gloves.

*   *   *

A week later Janet and Sue kissed Paula goodbye and left her in bed waiting to be prepared for her Caesarean. Despite all the talking and nagging she was still adamant, she wasn't going to have a mastectomy. Dr Parker was going to do a wedge operation to remove the growth a few days after she'd had the baby.

Janet sat with Sue as they waited in the coffee shop.

'I'm so worried,' said Janet, playing with the spoon in the saucer of her third cup of coffee.

'I know,' said Sue.

'This has been the longest week of my life.'

'It's a good thing she's got you to turn to. She told me she had phoned Trevor and told him the baby was going to be born today.'

'Yes. She didn't tell him why and he didn't ask.'

'She said he was very offhand.'

'Yes, he was, and that really upset her.'

'That sounds like him. Is he going to give her any financial support?'

'She said she wants nothing from him.'

'But how will she manage?'

'Don't worry, we will. It gives me a chance to make up for all the lost years.'

'If you ask me I think she's better off without him.'

'I don't know. Do you know if she loves him?'

'She did once but not now.'

'A bit like me in some ways,' said Janet wistfully.

'You managed to get to see Mark then?'

Janet nodded. 'Only the once on our own.' Sue knew that Mark had been staying with Danny and everybody knew their story. 'He's back in Canada now.'

'Are you sorry you didn't get a chance to meet him again?'

'In some ways it would have been nice, but there you go, that's the story of my life.' She gave a little laugh. 'I'll phone Danny and Freda as soon as we know about the baby.'

'Just think, today you're going to be a grandmother.'

Although tears were stinging her eyes, somehow Janet managed to smile. 'Friday, the ninth of November. We shall soon know if it's a boy or a girl.'

'Do you mind which?'

Janet shook her head. 'I hope they are both going to be all right.'

Sue gently touched Janet's hand. 'I'm sure they will be. Paula is very much like you, a very determined young lady, and like you she will go to any lengths for what she wants.'

'I hope so. I was worried when she started saying she wasn't going to have a seven-month baby.'

'She was determined to hang on a little longer, just to give it a better chance.'

'What about her? What chance does she have?'

'I'm not going to even think about that.'

'D' you want another cuppa?' asked Janet.

'Why not? I'll get them.'

When Sue walked away Janet's thoughts went to Freda and the baby she'd lost. She'd been eight months. Janet hadn't told anyone of her fears. She closed her eyes and said a silent prayer for Paula.

*   *   *

At long last a nurse came up to them.

'Miss Slater?'

'Yes?' said Janet, jumping to her feet.

'You have a dear little granddaughter. As she only weighs four and a half pounds she is in intensive care, but you will be able to see her soon.'

'How is my daughter?'

291

'As well as can be expected.'

'Can I see her?'

'As soon as we've tidied her up. By the way, have you got a name for the baby?'

Fear gripped Janet. 'Why? Is something wrong?'

The nurse smiled. 'No, it's just that we like to know if there's a name we can put on her wristband.'

'Is the baby all right?'

'Yes. She's beautiful.'

Janet slumped back down on to the seat.

Sue, who all this time had been silent, said, 'Well, that's the first hurdle over.'

Janet put her head in her hands and cried.

Sue sat beside Janet, staring into space. As a mother she knew what it was to love a child. She put her arms round Janet's shoulders. 'Has Paula thought of a name?' she asked.

Janet shook her head. 'Not really. She was thinking of Peter—that was my father's name—if it had been a boy. She said she couldn't make up her mind about a girl's name.'

'Well, it takes time to get it right.'

When the nurse came and told them they could go and see baby Brook they both leapt to their feet and followed her. Although Janet worked at the hospital in reception she was well away from the maternity unit and the layout and the staff were new to her. Both she and Sue were very apprehensive as they walked into intensive care.

'You must stay this side of the glass,' said the nurse as she disappeared through a door.

The bleeps and sounds from the monitors attached to the babies filled the air ominously. They moved closer to the glass partition, and Sue clutched Janet's hand when the nurse smiled and pointed to a incubator with a very small baby inside.

'This is baby Brook.' They could just about make out what she was mouthing.

'Welcome to the world,' said Sue softly.

Janet stood and gazed at this tiny pink bundle that had a couple of wires attached to her. She was wearing a pretty little pink bonnet and a nappy. Her thin, sticklike arms were moving about in jerky movements. Janet was having difficulty in seeing as tears fell from her eyes.

'She's lovely,' she whispered.

They stood looking almost hypnotized. At last the nurse came out and said they could go and see Paula.

Janet blew the baby a kiss. 'Sleep tight, my precious. We're going to see your mummy.'

Once again Janet and Sue were hurrying along the many corridors. They didn't speak till they were in the lift.

'She's lovely,' said Sue, leaning against the wall.

'Yes, she is.' Janet was beaming. 'Somehow Caesarean babies' heads always seem to be pink and round.'

'They don't have such a struggle to get into this world,' said Sue.

'That's true.'

Janet felt a little apprehensive when they got out of the lift and made their way to Paula's room.

They were told she was in a side ward and they carefully pushed open the door.

Paula was lying on her back with her eyes closed.

When Janet and Sue walked in she opened her eyes.

'Hello,' she croaked. 'Have you seen her?'

Janet nodded and, pulling a chair closer, took hold of Paula's hand. 'How are you feeling?'

'Numb at the moment.'

'What does she look like?'

'She's lovely and she's got a mop of dark hair,' said Sue sitting next to Janet.

'Thank you for such a beautiful granddaughter. You are a clever girl.'

Paula gave a little grin. 'It wasn't all that hard.'

'Have you thought of a name yet?' asked Sue.

Paula nodded. 'I've given this a lot of thought. How do you like Janie?'

Janet swallowed hard. 'Janie sounds lovely.'

'In a way I wanted to call her after you. When do you think they'll let me see her?' asked Paula.

'I don't know,' replied Janet, swallowing back a sob. 'As soon as possible I should think.'

'It's shame I can't feed her.'

'Why's that?' asked Sue.

'Because I'll be having that radiotherapy.'

'Of course,' said Sue softly. To Janet suddenly the joy of the moment had gone. They now had this big problem to overcome. They would face it together head on.

CHAPTER TWENTY-SEVEN

Three days after Janie was born Paula's wedge operation was performed. They were going to start her radiotherapy treatment a week later.

At first Paula felt sore and miserable, but Janet was there whenever possible with a soft word and a

294

small treat.

Every morning before she went to work Janet would hurry along to the intensive care unit to see Janie, and then when she'd finished for the day she would go and sit with Paula.

One afternoon Paula was sitting in the intensive care unit beside Janie's incubator holding her baby's tiny hand when a nurse came up.

'You'll be able take her home when you go. She's gaining weight nicely.'

Paula was suddenly filled with both panic and pleasure, but when she looked down at her beautiful daughter, these feelings were replaced with despair. Would she ever see her grow up, go to school, have boyfriends and perhaps marry? Tears streamed down Paula's face.

'Are you all right?' asked the nurse, putting a comforting arm round her.

'Could she get cancer through me?'

'All possible tests have been done, and of course she will be monitored, but it's very unlikely.'

Paula fished in the pocket of her dressing gown for a tissue to wipe her eyes. 'I can't wait to hold her and cuddle her.'

The nurse stood next to Paula and looked at Janie. 'She is lovely. And I think you can have that cuddle now.' The nurse lifted Janie out.

Paula smiled at the tiny arms and legs waving about. She held her close to her, savouring her lovely baby smell. Janie turned her head and nuzzled against her. Paula then realized what a dreadful wrench it must have been for Janet to part with her all those years ago.

*   *   *

When Janet proudly brought her daughter and granddaughter home, Janet was thrilled when Paula asked if she could stay with her for a while till she got on her feet.

As Paula was going to have go to the hospital every morning for her radiotherapy treatment a rota had been planned between Sue, Tina and Janet to take her or look after Janie, with Freda coming over and helping out at the weekends.

At first the treatment made Paula very sick but as the weeks progressed she found she was feeling less ill.

Every evening Janet would hurry home from work, eager to see her daughter and granddaughter, who was so small and delicate that at first Janet was almost afraid to hold her.

She was such a good baby and to Janet the thrill of feeding, changing and bathing her and doing all the other wonderful things she never did with Paula was marvellous. Even burping her at two in the morning was a joy. Many times Janet was pleased to have Sue around to give a helping hand and to use it as an excuse to bill and coo over the baby if Paula wanted to rest in the afternoon while her mother was at work.

Janie Paula were the names Paula had chosen, and on Sunday, 16 December, Janie was christened. Freda, Sue and Danny were her godparents and everybody went back to Danny's where Tina, as usual, had put on a wonderful spread. Janet thought her heart would burst she was so happy, but they all knew about the dark cloud that was hanging over them.

Everybody was fussing over Paula and the baby

and at last Janet found a quiet moment to have a word with Tina to thank her for what she'd done. 'This is a lovely spread, and the cake is super. I can never thank you enough, and her christening gown was perfect.'

'Well, we knew you wouldn't have time to do much. 'Sides, it's the least we can do, and both of mine wore that for their christenings.'

'What would we do without you?'

Tina laughed. 'Don't, you'll have me in tears soon.'

'I'm very sorry we never got to your Mum and Dad's party.'

Tina touched Janet's hand. 'Don't you go worrying about it. We all understand the reason. By the way, Mum sends her love. Did you see that lovely baby record book she sent over for Janie?'

'Yes, I did. That was most kind of her.'

'She was very upset to hear the news about Paula. Life's so bloody unfair. After all you've been through as well.'

'I'm glad I'm here to help take some of the burden off her.'

'Mind you,' Tina nodded towards Paula, 'she looks very well and I love her trouser suit. She's got her figure back nice and quick.'

Janet smiled proudly across at her daughter, who was talking to Harry and Sue. She looked lovely, so tall and slim in her smart new navy suit. 'Yes, she's pleased about that.'

'She looks so happy. You'd never think she had ... We're all keeping our fingers crossed for her.'

'Thanks. All we can do is hope. So many women do get over it, so let's hope Paula is one of the lucky ones.'

'We hope so. When does she finish her treatment?'

'Not till after Christmas.'

'She seems to be coping very well.'

'Yes, she does. I was hoping it would have been finished before, but there you go.'

'What happens then?'

'I don't know.'

'What are you doing for Christmas?'

Janet smiled. 'For the first time in my life I am having it at home.'

'You know you're both welcome here if it gets too much for you.'

'Thanks, Tina. Danny was very lucky when he found you.'

She laughed. 'I keep telling him that.'

'Mum,' said Emma, coming up to Tina, 'Jason's gone and pinched one of those chocolate things and he's stuffing it in his mouth like a wild animal.'

'Talk about no rest for the wicked. Why don't you tell your father?'

'He's busy talking to Uncle Charlie and he told me to tell you.'

'Typical,' said Tina with a toss of her head.

'She's growing up, quite the young lady now.'

'And saucy with it, but she can't do any wrong in her father's eyes. I'd better go and sort it out. Don't want Jason sick all over the place.'

Janet laughed. She loved these people. They had been her salvation for so many years.

Janet found Paula sitting alone in the dining room. 'Where's Janie?'

Paula managed a smile. 'She being spoilt by young Emma. Don't worry, Tina's with her.'

298

'You look tired.'

'I feel it a bit. Everyone's so good to us. Have you seen all the lovely presents Janie's had?'

Janet nodded.

Paula took a hanky from her pocket and blew her nose. 'I've made out my will.'

Janet was stunned. 'Don't think about things like that, not today.'

'I told the solicitor I was going to ask you to look after Janie if anything happened to . . .'

Janet looked around, almost willing someone to come in so this conversation would stop. 'Please. Don't even think about things like that.'

'I must. Will you?'

'You don't have to ask that question.'

Paula sniffed. 'I feel a lot better now.'

Emma came running in. 'Auntie Paula, Auntie Paula. Your Janie's been sick all over my mum.'

'Oh dear, I'd better come and tell her off. Shall I smack her bottom?'

Emma's face was full of alarm. 'No, don't do that. She didn't mean to. I expect it's something she had for her dinner.'

Laughing, Paula, put her arm round Emma's shoulders. 'I expect it is.'

'I didn't like that priest pouring water all over her—did he do that to me?'

'I expect so.'

'Is Janie a good girl?' asked Emma, stopping and looking at Paula.

'Yes.'

'That's good.' She looked around, then whispered, 'I don't believe, of course, but Jason does and we have to pretend, so,' she raised her voice so that Jason could hear, 'does Father
299

Christmas know she's been born?'

'I would think so. He's very clever,' said Paula out loud and very pointedly.

'You'll have to write him a note just in case he don't know, as she can't write yet and she might not get any presents.'

'I'll write a letter for her.'

'Great. I've done one for me and Jason,' she laughed.

Janet's eyes filled with tears as she watched them leave the room hand in hand. How could life be so cruel? Everything she had ever wanted and wished for was here and it could all be taken away from her. Her life seemed to be full of both wishes and tears.

Freda came and sat beside her. 'You all right?'

Janet nodded.

'Well, me old mate, we never thought we'd see this day, did we, all those years ago—you at your granddaughter's christening?' She gently tapped Janet's hand.

Janet shook her head.

'She's a lovely baby. Does she look like Paula when she was born?'

'Yes, she does.'

'I never really got over losing mine, you know.'

'Oh Freda, what can I say?'

'Not a lot really. It would have been better if me and Charlie could have had one, but there you are, what will be will be. Mind you, it was a long hard struggle for you but I'm glad you found her in the end. I was a bit worried when you said she was going to have it when she was just eight months.'

'I know. I thought of you and that terrible night too.'

'Well, things have got much better nowadays and the babes stand a better chance. What about Janie's father, has he seen her?'

'No. Paula phoned him but he's not interested.'

'The bastard. Does he know about, you know, the other?'

'No. She didn't want his sympathy.' She paused, 'Freda. I'm really worried sick about the future.'

'Of course you are, but she's a strong girl, a bit like her mum. Don't worry, she'll pull through.'

'God, I hope so.'

'Just you remember, we're all here to help you.'

Janet smiled. 'You have always been there when I needed you.'

'Well, we go back a long way. I can't believe me and Charlie have been married twenty-five years.'

'I can still see you coming to Stowford on the back of his motorbike, showing all your legs.'

'Always been a bit of a brazen hussy, ain't I?' She laughed. 'Thank Gawd he's into cars now. Can't see me cocking me leg over the pillion these days.' She sat back and smiled. 'Just think, I was a June bride. That was some honeymoon we had, one night in Brighton.'

They laughed.

'Still, we made up for it on our anniversary.'

'Two weeks in California, that can't be bad.'

'It was magic. If I don't have another holiday I'll remember that for the rest of me days. Me going in a plane—mind you, I was scared stiff. I shut me eyes and hung on to that seat for grim death when it went up. Thought me life was gonner flash before me eyes. But it was really great. And all that sunshine and Disneyland—we was like a couple of kids.'

Although Janet had heard all this before she didn't stop Freda, as she said it had been a trip of a lifetime and she deserved something to remember and to talk about.

'Yer know, Charlie ain't a bad old stick, a bit on the quiet side, but a good 'en.'

They both sat in silence for moment, reflecting on the past.

* * *

The day after the christening Paula said she wanted to go back to her own home. Janet wasn't happy about that but decided it was her life and she mustn't interfere.

'I've got to learn to stand on my own two feet,' said Paula as she folded the washing.

'But I love having you both here.'

'I know. But just let me give it a try. Sue and Tina will have Janie when I go to the hospital, and my treatment's not for much longer.'

'OK, but you will come back if it's too much for you, won't you?'

'Of course.'

'And leave any washing and ironing for me to do.'

'Now that's what I call a good offer.'

'Have you thought about what you're doing for Christmas?'

'I must admit I've been too scared to do so up till now.'

'Will you be going away?' asked Janet, dreading the answer.

'No. I was hoping we could spend it with you.'

'Yes, please. This will be the happiest Christmas

302

of my life.'

'And mine,' said Paula softly.

*　　　*　　　*

It had been settled that Paula would be going to Janet's on Christmas Eve, which this year fell on a Monday. She hadn't told Janet, but she was finding it hard to manage, what with night feeds and all the responsibility of being a new mother with a tiny baby. Also she felt constantly tired. Sue came round to give her a hand whenever she could, but Paula knew she had to learn to be independent. And in some ways she was pleased to go to the hospital for a rest even if she was being bombarded with radio waves.

'This flat and these stairs don't help,' said Sue on the Saturday before Christmas, when she called on Paula unexpectedly and found her crying. 'What's wrong?'

'I feel so tired and so low.'

'Well, look what you've been through. Why don't you go and stay with Janet? You know she's more than happy to take some of the worry off you.'

'I know, but I can't keep leaning on her.'

'She loves it. Don't you see, she's trying so hard to make up for all the years she wasn't around?'

'Yes, I know.'

'Well, then?'

'I was going on Monday, but do you think she'd mind if I went today?'

'Give her a ring and then let me help you get your things sorted out.'

*　　　*　　　*

Janet came struggling in with a large Christmas tree just as the phone rang. She could hardly contain herself when Paula asked if she could come round today instead of Monday.

'Do you want any help?'

'No, Sue's here with me. I'll be round as soon as I can.'

When Janet put the phone down she sat and reflected on past Christmases. She had always spent them either with Danny and Tina, or Freda and Charlie. She had always enjoyed them but this one was going to be the best ever. It would be special, even though they still had a cloud hanging over them. She was going to have her daughter and granddaughter with her in her own home. She had never bought a Christmas tree or put up decorations before. She was crying with happiness, excitement and anticipation at what lay ahead. They all had a wonderful future together. 'I only hope this isn't just a dream,' she whispered to herself.

The bang of the postman pushing the letters through the door brought her back. She wiped her eyes with the flat of her hand and picked the letters from off the mat. There was one from Mark. He had written when he'd first returned to Canada, but she hadn't bothered to write back; at the time she had had too much to cope with. As she opened it she felt guilty; she hadn't even thought to send him a Christmas card.

The card was lovely, and the letter was about how much his mother was enjoying her stay. He was going to bring her home sometime in January. He said he was hoping to be in England for about two weeks. He'd give Janet a ring and perhaps they could go out for a meal.

She sat staring at the paper. Was he trying to come back into her life? Did she want him back? The only thing she was certain of was that she would never leave Paula and the baby to go to Canada.

She quickly put the card and the letter to one side. The tree had to be put in a pot and the lights and all the baubles she had bought were waiting to transform the tree into something magical. This was a job she had been waiting all her life to do. A job that she could only do now she had found her daughter.

*　　　*　　　*

Paula, with Sue close behind, came struggling in with all of Janie's paraphernalia.

'I'd forgotten how much stuff one little bundle creates,' said Sue, putting the bags she was carrying on the floor.

'You didn't mind me coming here today, did you?' asked Paula.

'Mind?' said Janet. 'I'm only happy when you two are around. Sue, can you give me a hand taking some of this upstairs?'

In the bedroom Sue said, 'She's feeling a bit low.'

'I gathered that.'

'I suggested she came here today. I hope that was all right.'

'You know it's what I want, but I must let her make the first move, I mustn't force myself on her.'

'She'll probably feel better when her treatment's

finished.'

'I hope so. I'm just keeping my fingers crossed that everything will be all right.'

'Thank God she's got you.'

When they returned to the lounge Paula said, 'I love the tree.'

'After we've had something to eat, that can be a job for you to do while I put up the decorations. This is going to be the best Christmas I've ever had.'

'Let's hope it won't be my last,' said Paula softly.

For a moment or two both Sue and Janet were speechless.

Then Janet said angrily, 'Don't talk like that. You've got everything to live for.'

'Yes, I have, but at the moment I don't know if I've got the strength.'

'I'll make a cup of tea,' said Sue, leaving the room. When she was in the kitchen she stood and cried; it was with a strange mix of sorrow and gratitude for them both. They had been so brave through all of this. Thank God they had each other to help them carry on.

CHAPTER TWENTY-EIGHT

Despite the nagging fear they were both feeling, Christmas had exceeded their expectations, though, much too soon, it was all over.

'You don't have to go home tomorrow, you know,' Janet said to Paula as they sat round the fire on Boxing Night.

Paula was feeding Janie, and Janet was holding

the tiny fingers, marvelling at the tight grip she had on her.

'Perhaps I could stay for a few more days, just till after the New Year.'

'You'd like that, wouldn't you?' Janet said to her granddaughter. She was sure she gave her a smile, despite the bottle's teat in her mouth, although Paula would have said it was wind.

'I don't know how I would have managed without you,' said Paula.

'Don't even think about it.'

'When I first thought about having a baby I just assumed that Trevor would have been as happy as I was. I knew he would never be a full-time father but I thought he would at the very least have been a bit interested. We got on so well together. I never expected him to react like he has and I never thought I'd get ill. I just assumed my life would be perfect.' Paula fished in her pocket for a tissue to wipe her eyes. 'He didn't even send me a Christmas card. I was very hurt about that.'

'Perhaps he had a good reason.'

'It can't be his wife. That's never stopped him before. Especially when he wanted to share my bed.'

'Now don't start getting upset over it. It's all in the past.'

Paula looked down at her baby. 'He doesn't know what he's missing, does he?'

Janet smiled. 'No, he doesn't.'

'I would never ask him for money, you know.'

'You don't have to.'

'I am still thinking of selling my flat and getting a small house.'

'You don't have to hurry to do anything.'

'It wouldn't have hurt him to send his daughter a Christmas present.'

'Does he know he's got a daughter?'

She nodded. 'I phoned him and told him.'

'What did he say?'

' "That's nice." '

'Was that it?'

'Yes. Just two words.'

Janet could think of more than two words to call him, but they weren't very ladylike.

'You didn't tell him about the treatment you're having, then?'

'No. He would think I was trying to worm my way back into his affections.'

'Do you love him?'

'I did once, but I knew he could never be mine.'

'Didn't you have other boyfriends?'

'Yes, but they weren't a patch on Trevor. He was so worldly and mature. But that's all over now.' She took the empty bottle away from Janie and put her over her shoulder.

Janie gave a loud burp and they both laughed.

'I'm enjoying this so much,' said Janet.

'So am I,' said Paula with genuine pleasure. She turned to her baby. 'And we don't need your father to help us, do we?'

Janet felt tears pricking, and she had to look away.

*　　　*　　　*

After quietly celebrating the New Year, and with just one week left before her treatment finished, Paula went home. She appeared to be a lot happier and was beginning to cope.

Janet was feeling very lonely and the house seemed empty without a baby, her washing and her feeding bottles around. She knew she shouldn't go round to Paula's as it would seem she was always interfering.

On the Monday evening, when Janet came home from work, her phone was ringing. She was hoping it was Paula, ringing to ask to come round.

'Hello.' Janet felt her heart quicken when she heard Mark's voice. 'Where are you?'

'At home. At Ma's. I was wondering if I could come and see you on Wednesday. I've got a car— perhaps we can go out for a meal.'

'I don't know.'

'Please, Jan. I'm only here for two weeks.'

'Well, all right. Look, give me your mother's number and if I find I can't make it I'll give you a ring.'

'OK.' He read out the number, which she wrote down. 'Jan, don't let me down.'

'Will you be seeing Danny?'

'No, I won't have time. I'm sorting out some business over here.'

'That's a shame, he and Tina would have liked to have seen you.'

'Yes, but give them my regards, won't you?'

'Of course.'

'Jan, you will come out with me?'

'Yes. I'll be ready about seven, is that all right?'

'That'll be fine. Did you get my card?'

'Yes, thank you. I'm sorry I didn't send you one, but, well, life has been a bit hectic.'

'Is that because of the new baby?'

'Yes.' She wasn't going to burden him with her problems.

'Ma was really surprised when I told her about that.'

I bet she was, thought Janet. I bet all the village knows now. Poor Mother, all her dirty linen will really have come out of the closet.

'Janet, since I saw you last there's a few things I'd like to talk to you about.'

'Oh, what's that?'

'I'll leave it till Wednesday. Bye.'

She replaced the receiver and stood looking at it. What did he want to talk about? Why couldn't he tell her over the phone? Perhaps his mother was there and he didn't want her to hear. Had he been to see her mother? Did she know she was a great-grandmother? Did she want to see Paula and Janie?

Janet was excited about seeing Mark again and found herself singing. She smiled to herself—she was behaving like a young girl. Then her thoughts went to Paula. What news would she be given on Friday when her treatment was concluded?

*   *   *

Janet told Paula that Mark was back here and she was going out to dinner with him.

'I'm so pleased for you.'

'I can't wait to tell him about Janie.'

'What if he wants you to go back with him?'

Janet laughed. 'What, and leave you two? You must be joking.'

'Janet, you shouldn't keep putting us before your happiness. What if I met someone and wanted to move away, how would I feel about that?'

Janet was stunned. It had never crossed her

310

mind that Paula might want to marry. 'I would never stand in your way, whatever happened,' she said softly.

'So,' said Paula, 'that's how I feel, too. Now you go out and enjoy yourself.' On Wednesday Janet eagerly waited for Mark. He arrived a little early but she had been ready for almost an hour.

When she opened the door he kissed her cheek.

'I'm ready,' she said, moving forward and closing the door behind her. She didn't want to ask him in; she wanted him at a distance.

'You look lovely. How's your family?'

Janet smiled. That was a wonderful phrase. Your family. 'We have had a few ups and downs.'

'You'll have to tell me about it.'

They got into the car and headed for the restaurant they had been to before.

'What was it you were not saying on the phone?'

'I couldn't say too much with Ma breathing down my neck, but I went to see your mother. I told her about your daughter and your granddaughter. She said she knew, that you'd been there.'

'Yes, we went back last summer and she told us to go, she didn't want to speak to us.'

'Why didn't you tell me?'

'Didn't see the point. It wasn't any concern of yours. You live in Canada and I'm over here and I didn't think I'd see you again, and besides, my mother made it perfectly clear that she didn't want to see us. I think she was worried what the village would say.'

'I think she's changed her tune now. She's in a rest home. I don't think she's that well.'

Janet was filled with guilt. 'You've seen her?'

He nodded. 'Yes.'

'But why?'

'I don't know really. In a way I wanted to find out if I was in any way to blame—why you had rejected her. But now I know it was the other way round. She said she wanted nothing to do with you.'

'That's nice.'

Mark drove into the car park. 'It's a shame.'

They had a drink and ordered their meal.

'Did your mother like Canada?'

'Yes, very much. I think she's coming out for good.'

'So we won't be seeing you over here any more then?'

'That depends.'

'On what?'

'Two things really. First, my firm maybe opening a place over here, and the other is you.'

Janet looked up from her plate. 'Why me?'

'I'd like you to come to Canada with me.'

'Please, Mark, don't spoil the evening. We've been through all this before, twenty-five years ago, remember?'

'That was when you were looking for your daughter, but now you've found her it's about time you started to think about yourself.'

'She needs me more than ever now.'

'You can't run her life. What if she meets someone and wants to get married? She won't want you in tow then.'

'It isn't only that.'

'Well, I think you're being very silly.'

'Thanks.'

'What is so important that would stop us from

312

being together?'

Janet sat back. Tears filled her eyes.

'You do still have some feelings for me, don't you?' Mark gently put his hand on hers.

'Yes, I do.'

'So what's stopping you from giving it a try?'

'Mark, I don't know what the future holds for Paula.'

He gave a hollow laugh. 'Do any of us?'

'At the moment she's having radiotherapy treatment for cancer.'

Mark visibly sank into his chair. 'Oh, Janet. I am so sorry. What can I say? You must think—'

'You weren't to know.'

'How long has she . . . ?'

'She has till the end of the week and then she finishes her treatment. Then we will have to wait and see.'

He poured her a glass of wine. 'My poor darling. All these years—'

She raised her hand to silence him. 'I know. I didn't want to tell you.'

'Me and my big selfish mouth. Jan, please forgive me.'

She smiled. 'I shall feel a lot better after Friday. We should know something then.'

'Let's drink to her good health.' He lifted his glass. 'To Paula.'

'To Paula and Janie.'

'Is that the baby's name?'

Janet nodded. 'She's so lovely. It's marvellous when she stays with me. I get to do all the things I missed out on with Paula.'

'I bet you make a smashing gran.'

'I hope so.'

'You've certainly been through it one way and another.'

'Let's hope it's all plain sailing from now on. When are you going back?'

'The end of the week. Got to be at work next week. If Ma does decide to come over I'll be back to give her a hand.'

'So I might be seeing you again?'

'Could well be, could well be.' The rest of the evening was taken up with small talk about Stowford and Canada.

Janet looked at her watch. 'I really must be going. I've got a long day tomorrow.'

'That's all right. I must admit I didn't expect the evening to turn out like it did. I'm glad you told me about Paula, Jan. At least now I can understand how you feel.'

Janet smiled, but deep down she knew nobody knew how she felt. Every moment of the day and night Paula filled her thoughts and until they had a good result it would always be the same.

When they were in the car he put his hand in his pocket and brought out a small box. 'This is for your birthday.'

'My birthday? But it's not till—'

'I know, the nineteenth of February.'

'Fancy you remembering.'

'I never forget the nineteenth and as I won't be here I thought I'd help you celebrate a month early.'

She laughed. 'I didn't expect—'

'Go on, open it.'

'Thank you.' She was smiling as she opened the jewellery box. Inside was a small gold watch. 'Mark, this is lovely.' She kissed his cheek. 'What can I

314

say?'

'I would like to make up for all the years I've missed.'

'Mark. I'm sorry, but you know—'

'I understand. But you can't blame me for trying.'

They laughed.

Janet was happy and relaxed with Mark, but she knew the best birthday present she could have would be to hear that Paula was cured.

*　　*　　*

Janet waited with Janie when Paula had her last lot of radiotherapy. They had to go and see the doctor afterwards.

'Well, Paula. It looks like everything is fine.'

'Am I cured?'

'We will see you in six months.'

Paula threw her arms round both Janie and Janet.

Janet, who was holding the baby, could hardly control her tears. 'I can't thank you enough, Doctor,' she blurted out.

Outside they sat in the car and Paula, making a fist, shouted, 'I've done it. I've conquered it.' She kissed Janet's cheek loudly. 'Thank you for being with me.'

Janet dabbed at her eyes. 'I think this is the best day of my life.'

'And mine,' said Paula softly. 'And mine.'

'It's another early birthday present.' When they arrived home, first Paula and then Janet was on the phone telling Tina, Freda and Sue the wonderful news.

'I bet we've left a few tears in our wake,' said Janet cheerfully when they'd finished all the calls. Her thoughts went to Mark. She would have liked to phone him, but decided against it. She didn't want Paula to know they had been discussing her. She would phone him tomorrow. He wasn't going back to Canada till Sunday.

'Tomorrow I'm doing a very special meal for you,' said Paula. 'I can't upstage Mark's present, but I can cook.'

'You don't have to. Your news is the best I could have.'

'In the afternoon you take Janie over to see Freda and then when you get back everything will be ready.'

That night, for the first time in months they slept soundly and it was Janie wanting her feed that woke them.

The following afternoon Janet went to see Freda. There were plenty of hugs and tears, and a great deal of chatting.

Freda tutted as she admired the watch. 'Looks like he's setting his cap at you again.'

Janet laughed. 'What, with him over there and me here?'

'There's planes, you know.'

'I'd never leave England, not now.'

*   *   *

The meal Paula cooked was great, and afterwards, they sat and talked. Janet was a little upset that Mark hadn't phoned but guessed that as tomorrow was his last day he must be busy.

'I'm going home tomorrow,' said Paula, out of

316

the blue. 'I feel so fit that I can face anything now.'

'Only if you're sure.'

'I'm sure.'

'Well, don't forget: I'm at the end of the phone if ever you need me.'

'That's something I'll never forget.'

Sunday was moving day and by the end of it Janet was alone once more, but this time she was happy. Although she wasn't sure what time he was leaving, she decided to phone Mark; she wanted to share the good news with him.

'Who is that?' asked his mother.

'Is Mark there?' She was excited at the thought of talking to him again.

'No, I'm sorry he went back to Canada yesterday. Who is this?'

Janet realized she must have misunderstood what he'd meant by the end of the week. She didn't want to talk to Mrs Scott and as she hadn't recognized her voice, Janet put the phone down. He hadn't called her, and now she was a day too late to speak to him.

CHAPTER TWENTY-NINE

Paula looked out of the window at the snow falling in large flakes. It was beginning to settle. February was such a bleak month but at least spring wasn't that far away, and after getting the all-clear from the hospital a month ago she felt that life was good. She loved having a daughter and enjoyed every minute of being near her, and at the moment she didn't have any plans to return to work. When she thought of what might have been she was scared.

Paula turned to Janie, who was in her cot waving her chubby legs in the air and gazing up at Paula. 'Just you wait till the spring, young lady. We'll go out and see the ducks and lambs; you'll like that. There's so much to show you.' She bent over the cot. 'You smell.' She lifted Janie up and felt a sharp pain in her back. 'You are getting such a weight now, you've just done my back in.' She held her baby close.

Paula was seeing her life in a new light and her baby meant everything to her. Tonight Janet was coming round and bringing a takeaway. She was so good to them both. If she wasn't showering Janie with gifts she'd come and take all the washing and it would come back neatly ironed. Many times Paula wished Janet had never parted with her when she was born; she would have made a wonderful mother. Paula sat on the bed. She sighed. 'If only I could call her Mum, that would make her so happy.' Janie smiled back at her. But Paula knew she couldn't, not yet.

That evening, when Janet arrived she could see Paula wasn't feeling so well.

'I've done my back in,' said Paula, hobbling round the room.

'You lie down, I'll see to Janie.'

'Thanks.'

'Have you suffered with your back before?'

'No.'

'I'll give Sue a ring and see if she can pop round tomorrow.'

'No, don't bother her, she has enough to do. It will probably be all right in the morning. I've taken a couple of asprins.'

318

A week later Paula was still suffering and Janet suggested she have an X-ray. 'You'll have to get a letter from your doctor first.'

'I'll do that.'

Janet became worried as she watched her daughter. Every move she made was with great difficulty.

A week later, after her X-ray, Paula, went to the hospital reception desk to see Janet.

'Well?' asked Janet.

'I've got to go back to my doctor for the results sometime next week. I had to laugh, she suggested I rest. I ask you, how can you rest with a three-month-old baby?'

'Why don't you come and stay with me?'

'No, I'm all right. Besides, you're at work.'

'Well, come for the weekend.'

'I could do.'

*　　*　　*

On Sunday afternoon, just as the washing machine had overflowed, Paula was lying down, Janie was becoming fretful and Janet was dashing about trying to get everything under control, the phone rang.

'Hello,' Janet abruptly picking it up.

'Oh dear, seems I've caught you at a bad time,' said Mark.

'Mark, sorry, but yes, I'm afraid you have. Where are you?'

'Canada.'

'Canada? You're phoning me from Canada?'

'Yes. I wanted to know how Paula was. What happened, has she finished her treatment?'

Janet sat down. 'Yes, she has, and she's got the all-clear.'

'Oh, Jan. I'm so pleased about that, I really am. I'm sorry I didn't get the chance to phone you before I left.'

'Not to worry.'

'I wanted to, but something came up and—'

'I said, don't worry about it.'

'So everything's great then?'

'We're keeping our fingers crossed. It was kind of you to phone.'

'It's nothing.'

'Please don't think I'm being rude but I really must go. The baby's crying.'

'I can hear her.'

'Paula isn't feeling that good.'

'Nothing serious, I hope.'

'No. It's her back.'

'Oh, I see. Well, take care, Jan.'

Janet sat for a few moments. Why had he phoned? Was it just to ask how Paula was?

Janie's screams got louder and Janet knew it was time for her bottle.

During the course of the evening, Janet casually mentioned to Paula that next Sunday was 2 March. As this was going to be the first birthday she had spent with her daughter she wanted it to be special. 'What would you like to do on your birthday?'

'I hadn't really thought about it.'

'This is the first we've had together.'

'I know. Let's wait till Thursday, when I get the results from my X-ray.'

'Are you worried about anything?'

'No, not really.'

'I'll try and think of something for your birthday treat.' Janet was worried: Paula looked tired even though she had spent the weekend with her and had been resting.

On Thursday Paula phoned Janet to tell her the doctor had said her back pain was due to wear and tear.

'What? What are they going to do about it?'

'Nothing. She's given me stronger painkillers.'

'I see.'

'I've been thinking about my birthday. Why don't we go and see your mother, my grandmother?' said Paula out of the blue.

'What? No, not again.'

'It's my birthday treat, remember.'

'Yes, I know. But look at the reception we got last time. It was hardly a treat. No, I couldn't stand that again.'

'If the weather's fine it'll be a nice ride out.'

'That's as maybe. No, I'm sorry, Paula.'

'I'd like her to see Janie,' said Paula softly. 'Now she's in a rest home she might have mellowed.'

'Not my mother.'

'Don't you think you should give it a try?'

Janet felt all her old hang-ups return. She didn't want her mother to upset her again, but if it was something Paula really wanted to do, well then, she knew she would fall in with her wishes. 'What about your back?'

'Now I've got these stronger painkillers I should be able to cope. You said Mark said she was in a home, and old ladies get very lonely in those places. Couldn't you just go this once?'

'I suppose it would be worth a try.'

'Would you know where to look?'

'Not really, but that woman at our old house should know.'

Since they'd been to Stowford Janet had dismissed that part of her life, but when Mark had told her her mother was in a home her conscience had started troubling her and she'd told Paula about it.

'Look, why don't we all go down there on Sunday?'

'What if they throw me out?'

'That's a risk we'll take. Oh come on, it'll do you good to do something different for change.'

'I can think of a thousand better things to do.'

'Perhaps we could have a birthday lunch out, then go and see her. We could even take her some flowers and some for your father's grave.'

'It's a funny birthday treat.'

'I know, but I feel I should try to see my grandmother again.'

'Why?'

'I don't know. I just do.'

'Well, if you really want to . . .'

'It'll be nice.' Paula put the phone down and went over to Janie, who was lying in her carrycot. 'You're going to see your great-grandma next Sunday.' Then added, 'Let's hope the weather's kind to us.'

*   *   *

On Sunday the weather was kind and although Janet wasn't very happy at the thought of seeing her mother again, the drive to Stowford was pleasant.

When they arrived at the church the morning service was over and the congregation were in little groups quietly talking. Janet and Paula sat in the car while Janie had her bottle.

'That looks like Mark's mother,' said Janet, pointing out a woman who was wearing a large black hat.

'Do you want to go and talk to her?'

Janet shook her head. 'No.'

'Didn't you get on with her?'

'Yes, I did. She's a nice person and Mr Scott was a lovely man; they always made me so welcome.'

'So why don't you go and have a word with her?'

'I'd rather not. Besides, she might not recognize me.'

Paula laughed. 'You haven't changed that much.'

'No. I'll wait to see the vicar's wife.'

'There she is,' said Paula.

As she was moving towards the vicarage alone, Janet decided that was probably the best place to have a word with her. She left the car.

'Excuse me.'

The vicar's wife turned round. 'Yes.'

'I don't suppose you recognize me, I'm Janet Slater, Mrs Slater's daughter.'

The woman straightened her back. 'Yes, I do remember you. You came here last year in the summer. And I seem to remember you upset Irene. Well, what do you want?'

'I understand my mother is in a home.'

'Yes, she is. Who told you?'

'That doesn't matter.'

'What do you want her for?'

'I would like her to see her great-

323

granddaughter.'

'I see.'

'Could you tell me where she is, please?'

'She is very poorly.'

'I would like to see her.'

'She isn't dying.'

'I'm sorry?'

'In case you thought you were going to inherit her savings, I have to tell you she isn't dying.'

Janet knew her mouth had dropped open. 'I beg your pardon. I came here to get an address, to go and see my mother, not to be accused of trying to get her money.'

'I just thought I would make it clear to you.'

'Well, you've certainly done that. So, could I have her address?'

'She's in the residential home the other side of the village. You can't miss it; it's the old manor house.'

'I know where that is. Thank you.' Janet turned to walk away.

The vicar's wife put a hand on Janet's arm. 'I'm sorry if I sounded a little put out, but we've just had a problem with another parishioner whose son went abroad and now he's back just to get his hands on his mother's money. You see, we do have a duty to protect our elderly.'

'Who would do a thing like that?' asked Janet softly.

'I couldn't possibly tell you. It was told to me in strict confidence.'

Janet stood and looked at her in amazement. What sort of church woman was she that she was ready to pass on gossip to a virtual stranger? 'I shouldn't think I would know who you're talking about anyway. It's many years since I lived in this village.'

'Yes, I know.'

Janet turned and walked away.

'What was all that about?' asked Paula.

Janet laughed. 'She wasn't going to tell me where my mother was as she thought I'd only come to take her money.'

'What?'

'It seems a man has come back from abroad and he's only interested in his mother's money and all the village are ganging up on him. She wouldn't tell me who it was.' Janet was keeping any thoughts as to his identity to herself.

'How many men have left the village?' asked Paula.

'I don't know.'

'Do you think she was talking about Mark?'

'Of course not,' said Janet, surprised the same thought was running through both the minds.

'Why did Mark go and see your mother?'

'Please, Paula, stop trying to make something out of it. It can't be Mark, his mother's not in a home, we've just seen her and besides, she might be going to live in Canada, and from what I gathered he doesn't have any money worries.' Why had these fears come to her?

'Is he the only child?'

'Yes, she lost a little girl many years ago, she was only two, she drowned in the village pond.'

'That must have been really awful.'

'I don't really know much about it, except that for years my parents forbade me to go anywhere near the pond.'

'See, they did love you once.'

'I suppose so.'

325

'That poor woman. It must take a long while to get over something like that.'

'For ever, I should think.'

'Did you find out where your mother is?'

'Yes, it's just the other side of the village. Come on, let's go and see what sort of reception we get there.'

Paula laughed. 'D'you know, there's more intrigue in this small village than in the whole of London.'

'I shouldn't think so. It's just that everybody knows everybody else's business, and if they can't find it out, they make it up.'

They drove down the tree-lined drive to the manor house.

'This looks very grand,' said Paula.

'It was once. It was owned by the local squire. They used to ride to hounds from here. I would come and watch them go off fox-hunting.'

'That must have been quite a sight.'

'Yes, it was. Then once a year they had the hunt ball. As the vicar's daughter I would be asked to go. It was all very smart and proper—long frocks, the lot.'

'Did you have all the young men fighting after you for a dance?'

'No, they were all too frightened of the vicar.'

'Didn't you have any dances?'

'Only with the old men and I reckon some of them would have been right dirty old men if they'd been given half a chance.'

Paula laughed. 'See what I mean about these small villages?'

Janet parked the car then removed the bouquet of flowers she'd brought, from the boot, and

326

handed them to Paula. She took Janie from the car and they walked to the front door.

The door was opened by a young woman and they told her who they had come to see.

'You'd better come in. Rene's in the lounge.'

'Is there somewhere I can talk to my mother in private?' asked Janet.

The young woman's eyebrows lifted. 'You're Rene's daughter? Rene Slater's?'

Janet nodded.

'She's always said she's all alone, didn't have anyone after her husband, the vicar, died.'

'I haven't seen her in a while.'

'You'd better come and have a word with Miss Baker first. She's in charge here.'

Miss Baker was a formidable-looking woman in her late fifties, tall and slim, with glasses that made her dark eyes look big and round.

'This lady says she's Rene Slater's daughter.'

'I wasn't aware she had any family. What is it about you people? You're not the first to come here to see if your parent is dying,' said Miss Baker.

Janet pulled herself up to her full height. 'I can assure you I haven't come just to see if she is dying.'

'We had a young man and his wife come here and poor Mrs Coleman was in a bad state when they left.'

So that's who the vicar's wife had meant. Janet smiled to herself. She remembered Peter Coleman from school, he'd been a bully and she wasn't surprised to hear he hadn't changed. 'I was told that my mother was in a home and I would like to speak to her in private, if you don't mind,' said Janet softly.

327

Janie began to whimper and Janet, who was holding her, patted her back and rocked her to and fro. 'And to show her her great-granddaughter.'

'I see. You do understand we have to be on our guard? We're responsible for these old people, and some are very vulnerable and confused.'

'I can understand that, but I can assure you that Mrs Slater is my mother.'

'Sarah, as lunch has now finished you can take these visitors to the dining room, then go and get Rene.'

Janet squirmed at them calling her mother Rene. She had always been so proud of the name Irene Slater; somehow it had stature and now she was known as Rene.

Janet looked round the dining room. It was sparse but clean. Two large tables dominated the room, with a number of nonmatching chairs pushed under them. In the centre of the tables, which were laid for tea, were small vases with a few sorry-looking flowers in them.

The door opened and her mother stood there, leaning heavily on a stick. She had shrunk and looked frail, she was an old woman but to Janet, standing in front of her mother, the years just fell away. She suddenly felt like a nervous little girl who had done wrong.

Sarah helped her mother to a chair.

'Mother, this is Janie, your great-granddaughter.' Janet bent down at show her Janie.

Irene Slater looked up at Janet with her faded blue eyes. On recognizing her daughter she straightened up and her face became angry.

'What do you want?'

'I don't want anything. I thought as today is

328

Paula's birthday you might like to see her and my granddaughter.'

'Where's her husband?' She waved her stick at Paula.

'Is that important?'

'It is to me.'

Paula smiled at her. 'We've brought you some flowers.'

'I don't want flowers.'

Sarah moved forward and took them from Paula. 'They're very nice.'

'Sarah, d'you mind if I sit down? I've got a bit of back trouble.'

Sarah shook her head. 'No, go ahead.'

'Mother, I can't turn back the clock. We have to look to the future.'

'And what kind of future do I have? You left me and your father, we didn't leave you. You've always been a selfish girl, only thought of yourself.' She looked up at Sarah. 'She's never been to see me in years.'

'I wasn't exactly welcomed last year.'

'Well, what do you expect after I don't know how many years? Go away and leave me alone. I'm happy here. They look after me so I don't need you. And by the way, if you're after my money you're going to be unlucky. I've left it to the cats' home.'

Paula laughed.

Janet turned and told her to shush.

Janet was beginning to get angry. 'I don't need your money.'

'That's what they all say. Take me back to the day room, Sarah.'

Sarah put down the flowers and took hold of her

329

arm as she struggled to stand up. They shuffled from the room but not before Mrs Slater had pushed the flowers to one side with her stick.

Janet sat down. 'I'm sorry, Paula. That wasn't very successful, was it? And on your birthday as well.'

'Don't worry. It was my fault for insisting we came here, but I thought she might have been pleased to see us.'

'Not my mother.'

'At least you know where you stand now.' Tears filled Janet's eyes. 'I hoped that after all this time she would have mellowed a bit.'

Paula put her arm round Janet's shoulder. 'She doesn't know what she's missing, does she?'

Janet shook her head.

Sarah came back into the room. 'Miss Baker wants to see you.'

They followed Sarah and as they passed the day room Janet felt a great sense of guilt as she caught sight of little old ladies with shawls round their hunched shoulders sitting dozing in their high-backed chairs. This was her mother's life now.

Miss Baker was looking out of the window when they entered. 'Please, sit down. I don't know what you expected from your mother.'

'I just wanted her to see my family.'

'Well, she wasn't happy about it. Do you live far away?'

'London.'

'I see. Would you mind if I took your address?'

'No, you might need to contact me.'

'I don't think you should come to see your mother, at least not for a while. We'll talk to her and perhaps in the future she may change her mind

330

and ask to see you.'

Janet gave Miss Baker her address. 'Is my mother well?'

'Yes, apart from some arthritis.'

'Did Mark Scott come to see my mother?'

Miss Baker's head shot up. 'Is that Mrs Scott's son, who lives in Canada?'

'Yes.'

'He did come along with his mother once. Do you know him?'

'Yes.'

'A nice young man. Very pleasant. I understand Mrs Scott will soon be going to Canada to live. Your mother will miss her, she often comes to see her.'

Janet guessed that over the years, possibly because they had both lost their husbands, they had settled any differences they might have had, so why wouldn't her mother forgive her? 'Thank you,' said Janet. 'And if you feel you'd like to get in touch with me you have my address.' Janet looked at her fingers. 'You will let me know if anything . . .' She couldn't say the word.

Miss Baker smiled. 'Of course, my dear.'

Janet and Paula left the house, with its smell of disinfectant, and walked out into the warm spring sunshine.

They sat in the car and Janet looked at the house.

'Are you all right?'

Janet nodded. 'You're right. She really doesn't know what she's missing.'

CHAPTER THIRTY

The page of Janet's reception appointment book announced the day to be Monday 31 March.

'I wonder what today will bring,' she said to Mary, the young girl who shared the desk with her.

'Same as always, I should think. Mums-to-be will be waddling in, and those that bring their kids will have 'em running all over the place with the other mums yelling and shouting at them to be quiet.'

Janet laughed. 'That sounds about right.'

'Did you see your daughter over the weekend?'

'No. I don't like to keep going round there, in case I seem like an interfering old mother.'

'I'm sure she doesn't think that. Her baby's lovely and she's getting on a treat.'

Janet smiled. 'Yes, she is, and she's getting quite a weight.'

'When you think what a tiny little thing she was.'

'Yes.'

'And Paula's looking well,' said Mary, gathering up the files.

'I am worried about her back. It's giving her a lot of pain and for a couple of weeks now she's been off colour and a bit tetchy. D'you know, she even gave Sue a telling off for something ever so trivial, which is not like her.'

'I can't imagine Paula being like that.'

'She's been complaining that she's putting on a bit of weight.'

'Aren't we all?'

'It was her stomach she was going on about.'

'But she got her figure back very quick.'

332

'Yes, but you can see now she's having trouble fastening her skirts and trousers.'

'Is she going back to work?'

'Not yet. I don't really want her to, but she says she may have to. She's put her flat on the market and she is looking at a smaller house. That way she'll have a few thousand to live on, but it won't last for ever.'

'The father doesn't help, then?'

'No. She doesn't want him to.'

'When's she looking at the house?'

'Today. She's going with Sue.'

'Where is it?'

'Just up the road from Sue. Streatham way.'

'It's nice round there.'

'Yes, and it's not too far from me.'

The morning proceeded without any great traumas and it was lunch time when the phone rang.

Mary handed Janet the receiver. 'It's for you. It's Sue.'

'Hello, Sue, everything all right?' Janet was on her guard. Sue never phoned her at work, but nonetheless she was taken back when Sue told her Paula wasn't feeling very well and that she had called the doctor.

'What's wrong?' she asked, trying to hide the panic in her voice.

'I don't know. When I came round this morning she didn't want to go out. She keeps being sick and she looks terrible. We're waiting for her doctor. It seems she's been very sick all over the weekend.'

'Why didn't she call me?'

'You know Paula, she likes to be independent.'

'Yes, but that's all very well if you're feeling all

333

right.'

They discussed what they thought could be the matter and finally Janet said, 'As soon as I finish I'll be round.'

'I'll stay with her till then.'

'Thanks.' Janet put the phone down.

Mary looked concerned. 'What is it?'

'I don't know. Paula's not feeling too good. I'm very worried.'

*   *   *

As soon as she could Janet left the hospital and rushed over to Paula's. Sue was still there and when she opened the door Janet could see Sue had been crying.

'What is it? Has the doctor been?'

Sue nodded. 'Come into the kitchen.'

Janet followed her.

'Sit down.'

Janet did as she was told.

'She may have to go back into hospital.'

Janet leapt to her feet. 'Why?'

Sue took hold of Janet's hand. 'First she's got to have some tests.'

'Why?'

'The doctor thinks it might be jaundice.'

'Well, that's not too bad.'

'Or,' Sue hesitated, 'she said secondary cancer can't be ruled out.'

Janet felt her legs crumble. The room was swaying. She held on to the worktop. She wanted to be sick. She tried to let the words sink in. She wanted to scream out, No! No! It can't be true! Not my baby. Not my daughter. 'But she had the all-

334

clear just a short while ago.'

'I know.'

'The doctor must be wrong.'

'Let's hope so.'

'Janie. What will happen to Janie?' she gasped.

'Don't worry. We'll make sure everything is taken care of. You go and see Paula. The doctor managed to get her in to see the specialist tomorrow.'

'What can I say? Oh Sue, what has she done to deserve this?'

Sue had tears running down her cheeks. 'If only we knew.'

'Where is she?'

'Upstairs. Lying down.'

When Janet walked into the darkened room she could see Paula was lying on top of the bed. Janet's movement made her look round.

'Jan. Oh Jan, what am I going to do?'

Janet sat on the bed. Paula sat up and put her arms round her. 'I don't want to die.'

Janet held her close. 'You're not going to die. You have too much to live for.'

'The doctor said—'

'Shh. You've got to have some tests, so don't let's start being defeatist.'

'When I go for the tests tomorrow, will you come with me?'

'Of course.'

Paula sniffed and wiped her eyes. 'Sue said she will have Janie.'

'Now stop worrying about it. We will take care of everything. If you want I can stay the night with you.'

'Thanks. I'd like that. I don't want to be on my

own.'

'You don't have to.'

'I think I'll get up now.'

'Are you sure?'

She nodded. 'I'd better, but I feel so weak.'

'Do you want something to eat?'

'No, I keep being sick.'

When they moved to the kitchen Janet saw how yellow Paula looked. Janet silently prayed that her face hadn't revealed her emotions.

*   *   *

Once again Janet had a sleepless night. Over and over she prayed that the doctor was wrong about the cancer. She was thankful when morning came and she and Paula could do something positive.

After the tests at the hospital Paula and Janie came back to Janet's. All evening Paula and Janet tried to be cheerful but they both knew i' was a sham. Neither would tell of her real fears. That night Janet lay listening for any sound that would give her the excuse to get up. Her mind was going over all what had happened that day.

First Paula had had blood tests, then more X-rays. Paula told Janet the doctor had prodded her stomach, then had told her it would be a day or two before they had the test results.

Then Sue, who was looking after Janie, had taken Paula for a cup of tea, while Janet had been asked to remain behind so the doctor could speak to her alone. Janet could recall his every word. They were pounding relentlessly in her head.

'I'm afraid things don't look as good as I would have hoped,' he'd begun.

336

'But you gave her the all-clear a short while ago. It can't be secondary, can it?'

'It can happen very quickly.'

Janet had sat stunned while he'd told her he would let them know the outcome of the tests as soon as possible.

Now, she turned on her back. 'Please let him be wrong. Please don't let it be . . .' Her tears ran into her ears. Her mind was going over and over so many things . . .

A sound disturbed her. Janie began to whimper. Janet leapt out of bed, disorientated. She must have dozed off. She didn't want Janie to disturb Paula.

Picking her granddaughter out of her cot she held her close and whispered soothing noises. 'Come on, let's go down and get your bottle.' As she padded down the stairs she was surprised to see the kitchen light on.

'Paula. What are you doing down here?'

'I couldn't sleep.'

'Are you in pain?'

Paula shook her head and held out her arms for her daughter. 'I've taken the new painkillers.'

'What about a sleeping pill?'

'I don't fancy getting hooked on those.'

Janet was busy warming Janie's bottle. 'It won't be long before we get the results.'

'I don't want to know what they are going to tell me.'

'Now how do we know it isn't good news?'

Paula took the bottle from Janet and popped it into Janie's eager mouth. 'I think we both know the answer to that.'

'You can't be sure.'

Paula smiled down on her daughter. 'You're like a little bird in the nest, all you do is open your mouth and think about your tummy.' The tears fell gently on to Janie's face, causing her to blink. 'Janet, please promise me that you'll look after Janie?'

'I do wish you wouldn't talk like that.'

'I must. I must know she'll be loved and brought up with plenty of love around her.'

'You've nothing to fear there,' sniffed Janet.

'I wish you had been around all my life.'

Janet stood up and walked to the sink. 'So do I. Would you like a cup of tea?'

Paula nodded. 'You are a wonderful mother.'

'Don't.' Janet tried to laugh it off. 'You'll have me blubbering all over the place.'

'I'm so glad we've got to know each other.'

'Come on now, back to bed. I'll finish seeing to Janie and then bring your tea up.'

'I'll finish feeding her, then you can change her.'

'Thanks. Why do I get all the rotten jobs?'

Paula looked up at her. 'Can I call you Mum?'

Janet's throat felt tight and she swallowed hard. She wanted to throw her arms round Paula and hug her close but she would have squashed Janie. 'I've waited all these years to hear that,' she said softly.

Paula gave her a smile that, despite her tiredness and pain, was radiant.

Janet knew this was a night she would remember for the rest of her days. The night she was finally accepted as Paula's mother.

*   *   *

When it was confirmed that the cancer was in

Paula's bones and liver Janet knew she had to make the most of every precious day they had left together. She took extended leave from work and Paula and Janie moved into her house. The garden was looking lovely and on days when it was warm Paula would sit watching her baby trying to sit up when she was put on the grass.

Sue came in every day. Danny, Tina and Freda were told, and they would phone Sue almost daily for news. Sometimes, when they knew it was convenient, they would call in and always came with gifts or would take Janie out for an hour or so.

Janet had left it till the end of April before she wrote and told Mark the news. Soon after flowers had arrived from him, and every other week there was a letter. Janet had told him not to phone as she didn't like to talk in front of Paula. It seemed he phoned Danny every week for news.

Spring was giving way to summer. Mark had told Danny that he was coming over at the end of May to help his mother pack, as she was going to Canada. He said he wanted to see Janet but she had written to put him off.

'When's Mark coming over?' asked Sue one day when she was busy preparing Janie's bottles. She knew he was due in England.

'He's been and gone.'

'What? Is that why Danny and Tina wanted you to go over to their place for the day last week?'

'Who told you that?'

'Tina told Paula and she said you'd refused.'

That statement worried Janet. 'Did she know Mark was here?'

'I don't think so, she didn't say. You should have gone. I would have managed here.'

339

'I know. It's just that I don't want to leave her.'

'I understand that, but you're stuck in day and night looking after them both. You look terrible.'

'Thanks.'

'You only go out for the shopping when I'm here.'

'I know.'

'Paula would be very upset if she knew that Mark had been here and you hadn't see him.'

'She won't know, unless someone tells her.'

Sue smiled and put her arm round Janet's shoulders.

'I can't leave her,' said Janet.

'I bet Freda will have something to say about this.'

'I expect she will.'

'Will he be over here again?'

'I shouldn't think so, not now his mother's in Canada.'

'Looks like you've missed your chances again.'

Janet nodded. 'Looks like it.' She shrugged and smiled. 'You're beginning to sound like Freda.' She turned and looked through the kitchen window at Paula. She was lying back in the garden chair looking peaceful and relaxed in the warm sunshine. She even had a tan. Janie was in her pram waving her little brown legs in the air. Every now and again one would disappear as she put it in her mouth. It was such a wonderful tranquil sight nobody would guess the trauma that was being lived out. 'She looks so well. You can't believe she's . . . I wish the doctors were wrong.'

Sue joined Janet and she too gazed on the restful scene. 'It's not fair. It's such a bloody wicked world.'

A week later the doorbell rang unexpectedly. Janet was very cross. All their friends knew that she liked to have a warning if they were coming just in case Paula was having a bad day, and when they did arrive they always used the back gate.

The bell rang urgently again. If it's a damn salesman I'll give him a piece of my mind, Janet thought. She pulled open the door. 'Yes? What do you want?' she said abruptly.

To her surprised a tall good-looking man was standing on the doorstep holding a huge bouquet of flowers.

'I'm sorry, but I've been given to understand that a Miss Paula Brook is staying here.'

'Yes, she is.' Although Janet guessed who he was she still had to ask. 'Who wants to know?'

'I'm Trevor.' He had a smug expression on his face. 'I'm a very good friend of hers and incidentally, her baby's father.'

Janet felt her knees buckle. 'What do you want?'

He smiled and Janet could see why her daughter had fallen for this man.

'I'd like to see Paula and her child.'

Janet wanted to scream at him to go away but she was worried Paula, who was in the garden, might hear her and come to find out what the shouting was about. She stepped outside and pulled the door to behind her. 'Why? And how did you know she was here?'

'The junior in her office told me. So I thought I'd come and take her out for a meal.' He looked round. 'I don't like discussing my business on the

341

doorstep. Could I come in?'

Janet could kill that silly office girl. She hadn't been here so she didn't know how ill Paula was. 'No. Not till I've asked Paula.'

'So who are you?'

She pulled herself up to her full five foot two inches and said proudly, 'I'm Paula's mother.'

He grinned. 'Oh yes, I remember, she did say something about finding her long-lost mother. Now if you don't mind I'd like to speak to Paula.'

'I do mind.'

He laughed. 'I do have my rights.'

'What rights?' She disliked his arrogant attitude.

'The rights to see the child.'

'I don't think you have.'

'Do you want me to make a fuss?'

Janet looked at him and realized he was a man who was used to getting what he wanted. There wasn't any way she was going to let him take Janie from Paula. 'I hope you haven't come here with the idea of taking Paula's daughter away from her?'

He laughed again. 'I can't think of anything more distasteful than a screaming infant.'

'So why are you here?'

'I would like to see Paula in private and what I have to say I don't want to discuss in front of a complete stranger.'

Janet couldn't think straight. What could she say? 'Wait here, I'll see if it's convenient.' She went inside, closed the door and leant against it for a few moments, trying to compose herself. She was shaking from head to toe. What did he want? She would kill him if he attempted to take Paula and Janie from her. What was he here for?

Paula looked up and smiled when Janet walked

into the garden. 'Who was that at the door?'

Janet was pleased she was having one of her good days, and went to sit on the bench next to her. Janie was asleep in her pushchair.

'Paula. Trevor is at the front door.'

Janet watched the colour drain from her daughter's face.

'What does he want?'

'I don't know, he wants to see you.'

'Does he know I'm . . . you know?'

Janet shook her head. 'Do you want to see him?'

'Why not?' She stood up.

'Are you sure? What if he wants to . . . ?'

Paula gently touched her hand. 'Don't worry about Janie. She hasn't got his name on her birth certificate so he hasn't any claims on her. Besides, he can't stand children.'

'So what does he want?'

She laughed. 'Perhaps he wants to whisk me away to some foreign climes. Bring him in and let's find out.'

Janet reluctantly did as Paula asked. She stood at the kitchen window watching him, while arranging the flowers he'd brought. First he kissed Paula but he didn't make any attempt to look at Janie. Perhaps she had misjudged him. He put his arm round Paula and they were soon deep in conversation. Then Janet noticed Paula's face change. It was suddenly full of anger.

She stood up and screamed, 'Get out! Get out! Mum, come quick! Get him out of here.'

Janet raced from the kitchen. 'What have you said to her?'

He stood looking cool and calm and slightly amused.

343

Sobbing, Paula fell into Janet's arms. 'He wants his wife to adopt Janie.'

'What?'

'She can't have any children as I was telling Paula here. I told her I knew of this girl who was in trouble and Glenda was good enough to say she'd love to adopt the baby. She'd have a nanny and wouldn't want for anything.'

'Get out,' shouted Janet. 'I can't believe you've just said that. To come here with such a . . .' Janet couldn't think of the right word. 'Now get out of my house at once.' Janet broke away from Paula and began pushing Trevor along the path.

'Kindly take your hands off me, woman.' He brushed the sleeve of his jacket.

Janet looked round for something to hit him with. She bent down and picked up a flowerpot full of bright red cascading geraniums.

When she raised it above her head a look of horror spread across his face and he ran out of the back gate as the flowerpot crashed against the post, leaving a trail of earth and plants behind him.

Paula, despite her tears, began to laugh hysterically. 'I can't believe you've just done that,' she sobbed.

'Paula, I'm so sorry. I would never have let him in if I'd thought he was going to upset you. Why has he suddenly turned up?'

They sat down again.

'He's got a bloody nerve. For some unknown reason he was telling Glenda—that's his wife—about Janie. It seems she's been a bit broody and fretful lately and decided she would like a baby. Anyway, he told her he knew of someone who'd had a baby and wanted it adopted. He said he was

344

willing to pay.'

'What?'

'That's Trevor. He thinks he can buy anyone and anything, and to him Janie is just another commodity.'

'He didn't tell his wife the baby was his?'

'No. He did say I could go and see her whenever I wanted and that would be a good excuse for us to start over again.'

Janet sat with her mouth open. 'I can't believe you've just said all that.'

Paula began to cry. 'Promise me that you'll never let him take her from you.'

'I promise.'

'He has a lot of powerful friends.'

Janet held her close. The thought that quickly flitted across her mind was, so has Danny.

Janie stirred.

Paula smiled and, with the tears glistening on her cheeks, looked at her daughter. 'It seems our little bird will be wanting feeding again.'

*   *   *

That night Janet lay thinking about Trevor. She was worried. Could he take Janie from her when Paula was no longer . . .? Her brain wouldn't let the words form in her head. He had upset Paula, and Janet knew stress was bad for her. Could he have any hold over her?

The next day Trevor's name was not mentioned, but just as Janet had predicted, Paula was having a bad day. She was in pain and only wanted to sleep. Even Janie failed to bring a smile to her sad face. Janet was angry that Trevor could think he could just waltz back into her daughter's life, causing her so much stress. Did he know about the cancer?

That morning Sue came round and Janet managed to tell her what had happened, while Paula was sleeping. She was so angry.

'So what's going to happen?'

'Nothing. I'm going to phone Danny. He has a lawyer and he can find out what rights Trevor has, but I don't think he has any.'

'Then what?'

'I think Danny will find a way of keeping him away.'

A smile filled Sue's angry face. 'Now that's something I'd like to see.'

After Sue left, and while Paula continued to sleep, Janet phoned Danny at his office.

He was outraged and demanded Trevor's address.

'No, don't do anything that would upset Paula.'

'The bastard. He can't go round saying things like that. Does he know how ill she is?'

'I don't know. Yesterday she had a good day and you know how well she looks sometimes.'

He didn't reply and Janet knew he was too choked to do so.

She continued, 'I'm sorry if I've upset you but I just had to tell someone.'

'I'm glad you did.'

'You must have very soggy shoulders after all the tears I've shed on them.'

'That's what friends are for. How is she today?'

'Not too good.'

There was a pause on Danny's end of the phone. 'I could get him done over, Jan.'

'No, you mustn't. Look, I was wondering if you

346

could see your solicitor and get things straight.'

'I'll do that right away.'

'Thanks. Why don't you and Tina pop over one evening?'

'We'd like that. We'll give you a ring first, just to make sure it's OK. I'll find out a few things, then we can talk this through properly. I don't think he's got any rights to Janie, but I'll find out.'

'Thanks. I look forward to seeing you both. Love to Tina. Take care.'

'Bye, Jan.'

Although Danny was a big tough guy on the outside, Janet knew that when she'd replaced the receiver he would have a quiet smoke and be deep in thought. He was a true friend, always there when she needed him and she loved him dearly.

*   *   *

Even though Danny had tried to reassure Paula that Trevor couldn't take Janie, Janet could see it was still worrying her.

Tina told Janet that it had upset Danny when Paula had told him to drive carefully when they left.

'D'you know, we sat in the car round the corner and had a good cry? How could she worry about us when she's . . . ?' Tina couldn't finish the sentence.

Over the next month it broke Janet's heart that she could only sit and watch her daughter deteriorate. She was in so much pain. Her back had been playing her up and she was often very sick. Now the doctor called every few days and a nurse came in every day.

'She may well have to go into hospital as she gets

near the end,' said the doctor one day, as he and Janet stood in the kitchen.

'No, I don't want her to.' Janet's voice was full of fear.

'It might be better.'

'I can look after her.' Janet wasn't going to let anyone take her daughter away.

'You have the baby to look after as well.'

'I get a lot of help.'

'It will have to come.'

'I don't want to lose her.' Tears filled Janet's eyes.

'I'm afraid that is inevitable.'

'I want her with me.'

The doctor gently tapped Janet's arm. 'I'll see myself out.'

After he had left Janet sat and looked at Paula, who was sleeping. She wished with all her heart she could perform a miracle and cure her. If only she could turn the clock back twenty-six years. There would have been no way she would have parted with such a precious gift as her daughter.

CHAPTER THIRTY-ONE

It was Sunday 29 June and Janet had been up and down the stairs all evening. Janie was teething and very fretful, and Paula, who was in a lot of pain, was getting upset. It was almost midnight when Janet decided to phone Sue for help.

Janet hurried down the stairs with Janie in her arms when she saw Sue's car pull up outside the house. 'I hope you didn't mind me calling you out at this time of night but I'm at my wits' end,' she said softly.

Sue quietly closed the front door behind her. 'I would have been furious if you hadn't. Give Janie to me.'

'She's teething, poor little mite. Look at her red cheeks. I was worried Paula might get too agitated and restless if she hears her.'

Sue gave a slight smile. 'Don't worry, I'll see to her. I've been all through this with my two. I brought some gel with me.' She took the baby from Janet. 'You go on up to Paula. How is she?'

'Not a lot of change since you saw her earlier. She's having such a job to keep anything down and she's lost so much weight. I'm terrified I'm going to hurt her every time I bathe her or change her bed. It's very hard for me not to keep crying. I can't bear to see her like this.'

'I know. But we must try and keep a cheerful face.'

Sue took Janie into the kitchen and Janet went back up to Paula.

'Who's that?' she asked in a faint sad voice.

'Sue. She's brought some soothing gel for Janie's gums.'

There wasn't a reply.

Janet sat on the chair. 'Try to sleep.'

'That's all I seem to do,' Paula said softly.

'It doesn't matter.' Janet looked at Paula and her heart went out to her. Why did it have to be her?

Janet took hold of Paula's hand, as much for her own comfort as Paula's. Then she started to talk. She quietly told her of all the hopes and dreams they could have together. 'When Janie's walking perhaps we can take her to the seaside. She'll like

349

playing on the sand and paddling. Then later on, when she's a bit older we must take a trip to Disneyland. Freda still hasn't got over all the lovely things she saw there. America sounds wonderful.' Janet could hear her own voice droning on. Visits to the park and the seaside were all the things she would have liked to have done with Paula when she was young. She must have fallen asleep for when she opened her eyes Sue was standing next to her holding a cup of tea.

'Janie's sleeping so I thought you might like this.'

Janet wearily took the cup and saucer.

'She looks very peaceful,' whispered Sue, standing over Paula.

They watched the gentle rhythm of Paula's breathing. It seemed that every now and again she stopped and fear clutched at Janet's heart like a vice.

'Why don't you go and lie down for a while?' Sue's soft voice broke the silence.

'I can't leave her.'

'You'll only be in the next room.'

'I know.'

'Please go. I'll sit here.'

Janet felt as if her eyes were hot with fatigue, and she was having trouble keeping them open. 'Only if you're sure. What about Harry and the boys?'

'He's calling my mother later to come and see to the children. So be off with you.'

'You will call me . . . ?'

'Just go.'

*   *   *

Janie's cries broke into Janet's troubled dreams and she suddenly sat bolt upright. It was light. What was wrong? What time was it? She didn't remember getting on the bed. She hadn't even undressed. Quickly she hurried in to Paula. Sue was sitting in the chair giving Janie a bottle. There wasn't any change.

'How long have I been asleep? What's the time?'

'It's six o'clock. She hasn't moved.'

Janet sat in the chair and rubbed her eyes. 'Have you had anything to drink?'

'There's tea in the pot.'

'Thanks, my mouth feels like a sewer.'

Janie let the teat slip from her mouth to give her grandmother a big smile.

Tears clouded Janet's eyes. 'You're such a little darling,' she whispered, taking hold of Janie's tiny hand.

'What time does the nurse get here?'

'About ten. She's really ready for her injection before then. I wish I could give it to her. I hate to see her in pain.'

'They wouldn't let you give someone morphine.'

'No, I know. I always worry that one day she might be called out to another patient or held up in a traffic jam and Paula would have to wait.'

'I don't think that would ever happen. Now go down and get yourself a cup of tea.'

'OK. Are you sure you're all right?'

'Yes. But I'll go home later and get some clean knickers.'

'There's plenty of clean ones here.'

'I know. Before I go I'll give Tina a ring. She'll come and sit with Paula or take Janie off your hands for a while and if you've got any shopping to do I can get it for you.'

'No, we've got plenty.'

'What about bits for Janie?'

'I don't know.'

'Well, have a check and let me know. And I'll take all that washing. It only needs bunging in the machine. Mum will see to it.'

Tears slowly ran down Janet's cheek. 'I don't know what I'd do without all your help.'

'That's what friends are for. Now drink your tea.'

'Thanks, Sue.' Janet gave her a weak smile.

'I'll take Janie back home with me after the nurse has been.'

At ten o'clock Paula was restless. Janet repeatedly looked out of the window for the nurse. Where was she? Why wasn't she here? When Paula cried out Janet hurried to her side and held her close. 'The nurse will be here soon.'

Paula looked at Janet with her deep sunken eyes. 'Please, make this pain go away. Please, Mum.'

Janet let her tears fall. 'If I could I would, darling. I wish it was me and not you.'

'Mummy, I love you.' She was like a small child crying out.

How many times in her life had she called out and Janet hadn't been there to comfort her?

'I love you, Mum. I really do.' Her voice was just above a whisper.

'And I love you.'

Janet felt Paula go limp. She closed her eyes, she couldn't look at her. She knew it was all over. Gently Janet rocked her daughter back and forth, her tears falling on her hair. She wanted to pick her up and run away with her. She wanted to breathe life into her. She wanted to turn the clock back and recapture all those wasted years. She didn't want anyone to come and take her baby away.

*   *   *

The doorbell ringing made Janet open her eyes. She could hear voices and footsteps coming up the stairs.

Sue came and stood in the doorway of the bedroom. 'Jan, the nurse . . .'

Janet looked up at Sue and the nurse. She was still holding Paula tight. They didn't have to be told, they could see it in Janet's sad eyes.

Sue let her tears fall. The nurse very quietly moved into the room and came and sat next to Janet and gently patted her back.

'I can't tell you how sorry I am. She was a lovely girl.'

Janet was still rocking Paula back and forth. 'I didn't want to give her away.'

'Of course you didn't,' said the nurse with a puzzled look. She took hold of Paula's limp hand and tried to find a pulse.

'It was my mother's fault.'

The nurse looked at Sue and slowly shook her head.

'Jan,' whispered Sue. 'She's gone.'

'No, she hasn't.'

The nurse moved away. 'I must phone her doctor.'

Sue and the nurse left Janet to her grief.

*   *   *

For days, to Janet everything seemed to be

dreamlike. People kept coming in and out of the house. Janie, and jobs, were taken out of her hands. She ate, slept and bathed almost mechanically. She was taken to the undertaker and the registrar, unable to take everything in. Whenever the phone rang there was always someone there to answer it. Sometimes she was given Janie to feed. Tina sat and talked to her, then it would be Freda, and all the while Sue was on hand.

Finally, the day she had been dreading was here. Flowers had been arriving all morning. She stood at the window and watched the florist lay the beautiful wreaths on the lawn. The sun was picking out the bright colours of the flowers. It was very quiet; even the ticking of the clock on the mantelpiece was becoming unbearable. Janet watched as a huge heart-shaped wreath of red roses was put down. She knew that must have been from Trevor. Sue had told her she'd put a notice in the paper, mainly to see if Paula's adopted father would get in touch; he hadn't but Trevor must have seen it. Would he be at the funeral? Would he have the nerve?

Janet's hands became sweaty and her mouth went dry as slowly and silently the long black shiny hearse drew up outside her door. In the simple wooden coffin was her daughter. The daughter she had spent twenty-five years of her life trying to find. Now she was being taken away from her for ever.

She had told everyone that she was taking Janie with her to the crematorium. Sue came and took her arm, while Freda was holding Janie.

Janet sat silently in the big black car behind the

hearse, and stared in front of her. Her eyes never left the coffin that held her daughter. The thought that kept returning was this must be a bad dream and she was going to wake up soon.

After the service they wandered outside to admire the flowers.

Sue was standing at Janet's side. 'There's Trevor,' said Sue, nodding towards the far side of the grounds.

Fear gripped Janet. 'What does he want?'

'Shall I go and tell Danny?'

'He can't take Janie away from me, can he?'

Sue shook her head. 'I think Danny has all that sorted.'

'Where is she?' Janet looked round in panic. 'Where's Janie?'

'Don't worry, Tina's got her and I don't think Danny will let anyone come near her. I'll go and have a quiet word with Trevor.'

Janet was trembling as she stood and watched them. They were deep in conversation. Then, without a second glance, Trevor left.

'What did you say to him?' asked Janet when Sue came back to her.

'I told him he'd better go otherwise he could find himself in a lot of trouble. He said to give you his condolences, Paula was a lovely lady and he was very fond of her, and he said her daughter is just as lovely.'

Janet wanted to hit him for coming to share their grief.

'He also said that he won't make any claims on Janie.'

'That's bloody big of him.' Tears filled her eyes.

'Now calm down, Jan.'

'I'll kill anyone who tries to take her. I couldn't go through all that searching again.'

'Nobody is going to take her away.'

'I know full well they won't.'

'Danny has put your mind at rest over that.'

Tina brought Janie to Janet, so that they could look at all the beautiful flowers and read the attached cards together. 'We will have to write and thank all these kind people for your mummy's flowers,' she said to Janie. A movement at her side made her look up.

'Mark.' Once again the tears flowed. 'When? How?'

Freda came and took Janie from her and Mark held Janet close.

'Sue phoned me and I came as soon as I could get a flight. Jan, what can I say?'

She sniffed. 'What, all the way from Canada?'

He nodded. 'Words aren't enough. All you've been through. I'm so sorry, Jan.'

She let herself be held. She desperately wanted comfort and love. 'When have you got to go back?'

'I've only managed to get a week.'

Janet noticed the congregation starting to move. 'Have you got a car?'

'Yes.'

'Are you coming back to the house?'

'I would like to.'

'Can I come back with you?'

Mark looked around. 'Well, if you want to, but I don't think it's the right thing for you to do.'

'I don't care. I don't want to sit in one of those damn great cars ever again.'

'We'd better tell Sue.'

Mark left Janet and spoke to Sue. She could see

356

her nodding her head.

'It's all fixed. Danny is taking care of the undertakers.'

As everybody began to leave Janet touched Mark's arm.

'I'm so glad you're here. You didn't know my Paula. She was a wonderful girl and she would have loved you—if only you hadn't gone.'

'Don't, Jan. Please. I've told you how many times I regretted going off without you. The times I wanted to come back to see you.'

'But you didn't come back to see me, did you?'

'No. Not till my father died and then I realized how short life is.'

Tears filled Janet's eyes. 'Yes, life is bloody short.'

'I told you that I didn't have the courage to look you up. I was frightened of being rejected.'

'So now why this sudden interest?'

'For years I thought you wouldn't want me messing up your life again.'

'So you got married.'

'I knew at the time it wasn't the right thing to do.'

'So why did you?'

'Please, Janet.' He looked around, feeling very embarrassed. 'This isn't the right place or the right time either for this.'

'Does everything always have to be just right for you then?' Janet was beginning to get angry.

'Janet, I love you and want to—'

'Don't.' She put her hand up to stop him. 'I'm not going to Canada.' She straightened her shoulders. 'I've got Janie to think of.'

'Please, Jan. Think about her future and yours.'

357

'I am.'

'You could have a wonderful life with me.'

'What if you run out on me again?'

'I'll never do that.'

'No, Mark, I'm staying here.'

'What are you going to do?'

'Spend the rest of my life looking after my dear granddaughter. Giving her all the love she'll never get from her mother.'

'She would have a wonderful life in Canada.'

They reached the car.

'Is this all you've come here for?'

He shook his head. 'No. I came because I wanted to to. To share your grief, give you a shoulder to lean on.'

'You are twenty-six years too late.'

'I seem to be upsetting you. Perhaps I'd better not come back with you.'

'That's up to you. You're very good at walking out on me when I need a friend.'

'I'm not walking out on you.'

'No, this time I'm walking out on you.' Janet walked over to Danny, who was watching them.

'Can I come in your car?' she asked Danny.

'I thought you were going with Mark.'

'I've changed my mind.'

'Jan, what's he said to you?'

She gave him a warm smile and gently touched his arm. 'It's nothing.'

From the car's window she looked across at Mark. He stood watching as their car slowly moved away. He looked so sad part of her wanted to run to him.

* * *

Back at the house everybody was talking. Janet wandered out into the garden and sat in her favourite secluded spot. Her thoughts were miles away when Freda came and sat next to her.

'Penny for them.'

'I was just thinking, I'm going to get a couple of rose bushes and plant them for Paula.'

'She loved this garden.' Freda took hold of Janet's hand.

'Freda, I'm so unhappy.'

'Of course you are.' Freda put her arm round her and held her, childlike, stroking her hair while Janet cried pitifully.

After a while Freda said, 'You've been through a lot, but you must remember you've got to be strong. You've got Janie to bring up now.'

'I know. Thank God for that.'

'I know it ain't none of my business but we've been friends for years and you can tell me to shut up if you like. But what was all that between Mark and you back there? I thought he was bringing you back here.'

'He was, then suddenly I got cold feet. Freda, he wanted me to go with him, but what if he walked out on me again?'

'Use your loaf. He ain't come here all the bloody way from Canada to walk out on you again.'

'I suppose not. But seeing Janie's father made me feel that all men enjoy making us suffer.'

'Now that one is a right bastard.'

'He was at the crematorium.'

'So Sue said. By the way she said he sent a wreath, but I didn't see it.'

A slight smile lifted Janet's sad face. 'I put it in

359

the bin. I didn't want Paula to see it.'

'You are daft . . . So where's he gone?'

'Who, Janie's father?'

'No, Mark.'

'I don't know.'

'Well, if you ask me I reckon you should have given him a bit of a chance.'

'I don't know. I'm so scared of being hurt again.'

'I don't think he'd do that. He loves you, Jan.'

She looked across the garden. 'I know. Perhaps I was a bit hasty, but I'm all mixed up.' She stood up. 'Well, it's all over now. I've lost my chance this time for good.'

'Do you care?'

'I don't know. I don't really know.'

CHAPTER THIRTY-TWO

As the following morning was fine and bright, Janet, with Janie in her pushchair, went to the hospital to hand in her notice. Until now she had only been on temporary leave.

'I'm really gonner miss working with you, Jan,' said Mary, squatting down to fuss over Janie. 'It's not the same without you here.'

'And I'll miss coming into work every day. But I think I'll have my work cut out looking after this one. After all, I'm not getting any younger.'

Mary smiled. 'You'll never get old. How you going to manage for money?'

'Well, Paula left a will and when the flat's sold . . .' She stopped to blow her nose. 'I'm sorry.'

'That's all right. I understand.'

'Well, I must be off. I wish you luck. Thanks for the card and flowers.'

'That was the least we could do. I only hope the one who takes your place is as nice.'

'Thanks, Mary.' Janet kissed Mary and left. Another chapter in her life had come to a close. What did the future hold for her now?

*   *   *

In many ways Janet was upset that Mark hadn't got in touch with her again before he'd left. At the end of the week she knew her chance of finding any happiness with him had gone. Why had she been so stupid? Their timing was wrong again. She was distraught at losing Paula and wanted to hurt him like she had been, but in the end it was only herself she had hurt.

The weather was very warm and at the weekend Janet had planned to go with Sue to Paula's flat to sort out her clothes.

'I'm not looking forward to it,' said Janet as they opened the front door.

'There isn't any hurry. You don't have to do it just yet.'

'But what if someone wants to buy the flat?'

'I'll show them round. Why don't you leave it for a week or two? We'll just empty the fridge and take her plants. Then perhaps you'll feel more like it another time.'

'I don't think I'll ever feel like it. I feel I'm intruding, going through her personal things.'

'You know, Janet, you don't have to do it. Me and Freda can manage if you can't face it.'

'No, I'll be all right. But I'll leave it till next

week. Perhaps Tina will look after Janie for the day.'

'I'm sure she would.'

Janet was pleased when she phoned Danny and Tina and they invited her for the weekend.

She was looking forward to seeing them that Friday evening and began packing all the bits and bobs she would need.

The traffic was heavy as she drove to Clapham Common but the thought of dangling her toes in their pool was inviting. And she knew Emma would love having Janie around.

She turned on the radio and began to hum softly with the music. She looked in the rear-view mirror at Janie, who very soon was fast asleep. Janet wanted to cry whenever she saw the contented look on her granddaughter's face. She had so much to tell her. If only she could have told her about her mother's childhood, but that wasn't to be. How would she be able to explain to Janie that she gave her mother away? She knew she mustn't dwell on this, that she had to look forward. She had a job to do and that was to give this little girl all the love and happiness she could.

As always they were made very welcome when they arrived at Danny's, and Emma was jumping up and down, begging to be allowed to help bath Janie. Janet could see this was going to be the best weekend she had had for many months.

'You just relax,' said Tina, helping her to unload the car. 'Danny said he wasn't going to be late tonight.'

They were all crowded into the bathroom bathing Janie when Danny called up the stairs to tell them he was home.

'Daddy, Daddy!' yelled Jason, disappearing out of the room. His shouting and the clatter of his feet could be heard despite the thick carpet.

A few moments later Danny popped his head round the door. 'Hello, girls.'

Emma ran to her father, who hugged her and gave her a kiss. He kissed Tina, then Janet. 'She's a little cracker, ain't she?' he said, nodding towards Janie, who was laughing and busy smacking the water.

Janet nodded.

'Look at those rolls of fat,' said Danny.

Janet thought her heart would burst she was so proud to have Janie to look after. Tina handed her a towel and when she lifted Janie out of the bath she began to yell.

'Well, she's certainly got a pair of lungs on her,' said Danny. 'I'll go on down and pour out a drink. D'you two want one?'

'Yes, please,' they said in unison.

'Can I have a word, Tine?'

Tina shrugged her shoulders, gave Janet a funny look and followed him out of the bathroom and down the stairs.

'What is it?' she asked as he went into the dining room.

Tina stood in the doorway and let out a gasp. 'Mark. Mark.' She ran to him and, holding him close, kissed his cheek. 'What are you doing here? You were supposed to go back last week.'

'I phoned the office and asked for another week. I had to do some business over here as well. I called Danny this morning and he said Jan was going to be here for the weekend, and, well, here I am. I hope it's all right?'

363

'It is as far as I'm concerned, but what about Jan?' Tina and Danny knew that Janet had sent Mark away after the funeral.

'I just had to see her again.'

Danny handed Tina a drink. 'I reckon we ought to let Mark take Jan out tonight. We can look after the little 'en.'

'Yes, that's all very well, Danny, but what will Jan say?'

'You talking about me again?' Jan walked in with Janie over her shoulder. She suddenly stopped. 'Mark,' she whispered. 'I thought . . . You were only supposed to be . . .'

'Hello, Jan. Yes, I should have gone back but I got another week. I have to go back on Wednesday.'

Janet's mind was in a turmoil.

'I'll take the little 'en,' said Tina. 'You two go out in the garden and have a talk.'

'I don't think we have anything to say to each other; it's all been said,' said Janet. 'I'll just finish seeing to Janie.'

Tina followed Janet out of the room. 'I'm going to say something now that might put our friendship in jeopardy. I love you, Jan. I think you're a smashing person but I don't want to stand by and watch you throw away the chance of happiness. There, I've said it. Mark really loves you and I think you still love him.'

Janet looked at the ground and shifted her feet.

'You've got the rest of your life so why not share it with him?'

'I don't know.'

'Well, I've had my say. If you want, we'll look after Janie while you and Mark go out for a meal and a long talk.'

'He might not want to.'

'He hasn't stayed over to come and see us. Jan, do you still love him?'

'I don't know.'

'You've never married anyone else.'

'No. I didn't find anyone I wanted to spend my life with. Besides I was too obsessed with finding Paula.'

'Well, that's all over now. I'm sure she would like you to find happiness.'

Janet swallowed hard. 'I'll go out with him tonight for a meal, but that's all.'

Tina took Janie from her. 'I'll see to her while you and Mark go into the garden. Right, young lady, it must be time for your bottle.'

Janet walked up to Mark who was sitting staring at the pool, which was shimmering in the early evening sunlight. She sat beside him.

'I'm pleased to see you, Mark.'

'Are you? Are you really?'

She nodded.

'Jan, shall we try to start again?'

'What d'you mean?'

'It seems whenever we meet we always end up— I don't know—with one of us walking off.'

She smiled. 'That's true.'

'Well, at the risk of you going off again I'm going to say what I feel.'

Janet shifted uncomfortably. Did she really want to hear?

'Jan, I've loved you for years. I know I was wrong not hearing you out all those years ago. I was young and stupid and I suppose, thought I had high morals, but that's all in the past. Now I've found you again I don't want to lose you. Janet, will you marry me?'

Janet sat and stared at him. 'I wasn't expecting you to say that.'

'We're not getting any younger and we haven't got time for any more pussyfooting around, so I thought I'd come here and try my luck once again. Well, what do you say?'

'I don't know.'

'Do you think you could love me?'

She wanted to throw her arms round him. She knew she loved him and she didn't want to lose him again. 'Would that mean me going to Canada?'

He nodded. 'We can always come back and forth. I have to come over to help set up business at this end.'

'I've got Janie to think of.'

'She would love Canada.'

'But would I?'

'Yes, I know you would.'

'But what about my friends? I just can't up and leave them. I might not see them again.'

'Of course you will. As I said, when I come back you can come for a holiday.'

Janet knew she was beginning to weaken but half of her had to keep finding as many obstacles as she could. 'What will your mother say about it? She won't want me interfering.'

'She's going to find a place of her own. In fact, she's looking now. She'll be more than pleased to have you over there, and I've told her all about Paula and Janie. She was very upset about everything that has happened.'

'I don't know.'

'Janet.' Mark's voice was hard. 'I'm not going to

366

plead any more. If you say no this time then I'll walk out of your life for ever. I promise that I'll never see you again.'

Fear clutched at her heart. She didn't want to spend the rest of her days without him.

Mark stood up.

'Where are you going?' She looked up in panic.

'To say goodbye to Danny and Tina. There's no use staying here any longer.'

'Please, sit down.' She pulled at his sleeve.

'Is there any point?'

'Yes. Mark, I do love you. I have done all these years. I've never married because I couldn't find anyone I loved. So if you think we could make a—'

She didn't get a chance to finish the sentence because his lips were on hers, kissing her hungrily and passionately.

'Jan,' he whispered, 'I have got to go back on Wednesday.'

She sat back in alarm. 'I can't go on Wednesday.'

'I know. You let me know when you're ready to come over and perhaps we could get married here.'

'I'd like that.' She began to laugh.

'What's so funny?'

'I think Freda's still got her bridesmaid's frock.'

'No! What, after all these years?'

Janet nodded. 'She didn't like to throw it out just in case. I can still ask her to be my bridesmaid.'

He laughed and held her tight. 'Will she still fit into it?'

'I think it's a bit old-fashioned by now, don't you?' Tears began to run down her cheeks. 'It's a bit like turning the clock back, us getting married, with a small baby to look after.'

Mark swallowed hard. 'I've been such a fool. I

367

missed out on Paula but we've got Janie and I promise you she'll have a wonderful life with plenty of love.'

Janet smiled through her tears. 'Paula would have liked that.'

'We've got a lot of years to make up.'

Janet knew that in the years to come Janie would know all about her mother and who her father was. But in many ways Janet would be pleased to be out of the country! Trevor wouldn't be able to reach them in Canada and as a family they could now legally adopt Janie.

She smiled at Mark and once again she was in his arms and being kissed. She knew her daughter would have been happy with this arrangement.

*   *   *

Tina, with Danny close behind, was watching them through the kitchen window.

'That ain't no goodbye kiss,' said Danny.

Tina, who was holding Janie, said, 'Looks like you and your nanny could be going to Canada.'

Danny put his arm round his wife. 'It's taken them both a bloody long while to come to their senses.'

'I know they're going to be happy together,' said Tina.

'They deserve it.' Danny walked away. He didn't want the children to see his tears.